Praise for Kyell Gold's previous books:

"[*Volle*] and ***Pendant of Fortune*** are arguably the best anthropomorphic novels yet written. The writing is of high quality; literary yet naturalistic, never becoming esoteric or pedantic. The setting is a well-thought-out, detailed anthropomorphic civilization in which species characteristics such as scenting are major plot elements. The homoerotic subplot in ***Volle*** (which ranges from lyrical to unpleasantly brutal) becomes the key to the murder mystery in ***Pendant of Fortune***, where its anthropomorphic nature is especially important. Readers must decide for themselves whether the very strong homoerotic theme is to their tastes; but these novels are too well-written to be simply ignored."

-Fred Patten, *Anthro #7*

"***Volle*** provides an engrossing combination of intrigue and erotica."

-S. Ardrian, *Fearless Reviews*

"If you are looking for a well-written book with beautiful characters that breathe, think and feel, if you are looking for an intelligent, well crafted environment that encompasses spirituality, beauty and emotion, a book with glowing touches of humor, tenderness, sensuality and tears, then ***Volle*** is a beautiful journey you'll want to experience again and again."

-Timothy Albee, the Sofawolf Press catalog website

"***Pendant of Fortune*** is one of the best follow-up novels I've read ... another wonderful example of how anthropomorphic fiction can unquestionably still be literature; Kyell Gold's skill at storytelling and his way with words are both at their best, here, in a story that fans of fantasy, intrigue, romance, or any of the above should not miss."

-K.M. Hirosaki, the Sofawolf Press catalog website

THE PRISONER'S RELEASE
AND OTHER STORIES

by Kyell Gold

THE PRISONER'S RELEASE AND OTHER STORIES

Copyright 2002, 2006 by Kyell Gold

"The Prisoner's Release" was previously published in serial form in *Heat* #1 (2002) and #2 (2003).

Published by Sofawolf Press
St. Paul, Minnesota
http://www.sofawolf.com

ISBN 978-0-9769212-7-1
Printed in the United States of America
First trade paperback edition: January 2007
First POD printing: July 2021

Cover art by Sara Palmer

Interior illustrations on pages 28, 64, 98, 132, 142 by Vince Suzukawa

Interior illustrations on pages 150, 156, 167, 178, 186, 197 by Taurin Fox

Interior illustration on page 206 by Adam Wan

Interior illustrations on pages 240, 254, 282 by Leo Magna

Dedicated to Brer and Alopex:
Tireless publishers, eagle-eyed editors, and good friends.
My thanks, many times over,
for your encouragement and assistance
in bringing these projects to light,
and for your constant friendship,
which no mere dedication can adequately describe nor repay.

Truly, you are a credit to your species.

Contents

Author's Note

When I sat down to write "The Prisoner's Release," I never expected to see it in print, much less in the third of three volumes. The land in which it took place, Argaea, didn't even have a name until after the second volume was published. The story did get published, in *Heat*, and by that time, **Volle** had been written and **Pendant of Fortune** was under way. It was easier to introduce readers to a brand-new author in the pages of a magazine than with a book launch, and "The Prisoner's Release" did well enough to encourage Sofawolf Press to publish **Volle**.

The logical next step would have been to re-publish "The Prisoner's Release," the next story in the chronological sequence. However, that story was too short to make a book of its own, and though I'd always intended to write more stories to package as a set with it, those stories weren't done to my satisfaction, and **Pendant of Fortune** was. We reasoned that most people would have read "The Prisoner's Release," or could find it in back issues of *Heat*, so we published the novel rather than wait for the collection of stories to be finished.

And here, at last, it is. I am glad to see "The Prisoner's Release" in a book, finally. I have been unable to resist the temptation to edit the story one more time, but not extensively. I tightened some language, and made Volle's confession of loyalty to Ferrenis subtler, as I felt that was more in keeping with his training. The original illustrations from the magazine are included here as well. If you haven't yet read the story, I hope you enjoy it.

"Home Again" is the other story about Volle in this volume, a short piece that takes place immediately after "The Prisoner's Release" and sets up some of the other elements in Pendant of Fortune. "Inside the Cage," the first story in this volume, and "For Love or Family," the last, both begin in the Jackal's Staff, the all-male brothel introduced in Volle, and follow characters from that setting through their own adventures.

Together with the two novels, these are the complete writings about Volle to date, but there are years between Volle and "The Prisoner's Release," and more stories to be told. Argaea has many more characters and stories than I could exhaust if I wrote nothing else for the rest of my life—thanks in no small part to the enthusiasm of my readers (especially the community at http://kyellgold.livejournal.com, whose regulars have been immensely helpful), which never lets me escape Argaea for long. I look forward to happy future explorations with all of you, and my deepest thanks for your company on the journey so far.

—Ky, January 2007

INSIDE THE CAGE

Chapter 1

There were things about Sasha that Jonas couldn't understand, even after five years of deepening friendship working side by side at the Jackal's Staff. For example: his constant need to spend all his spare money on the finest clothes and jewelry he could afford. "You'll have nothing left for later," the cougar would protest when the old(er) mouse showed off his latest acquisition. And Sasha would smile that sad smile of his and say "There won't be any later for me, kitten."

Jonas never enjoyed those conversations, and he would walk away from them lashing his tail, annoyed not at Sasha for his obdurate avoidance of the issue, but at himself for forgetting and bringing it up again. He would resolve to have a long and serious talk with Sasha about putting money aside, something he himself was doing assiduously, and then he would forget about it, and the next time Sasha proudly twirled in front of him to show off his new silk wrap, Jonas would be upset at himself for forgetting and would blurt out the same thing again.

Other times, Sasha was a wonderful companion, always ready with a quick joke or a gentle paw, and it wasn't hard to see why he was in such demand. Tally's patrons knew the mouse well and although none of the staff knew what their prices were, they knew that Sasha's were the richest. Despite that, he never flaunted his wealth; even though his purchases were ostentatious, the pleasure he took in them was so childlike and innocent that nobody could be offended.

On the last day he ever saw Sasha, Jonas was entertaining a bear and cursing his luck for being the biggest staff member. The bear was on top of him, most of his weight pressing down on Jonas's back and ribcage, the massive hips thrusting in and out in what was, despite the amount of lubricant Jonas had applied, a somewhat painful experience. The bear was not interested in Jonas's pleasure, so Jonas gritted his teeth, extended his claws into the pillow, and endured the thrusts.

Finally, the bear grunted, pushed so hard Jonas thought he would be squashed into the mattress, and then sighed and settled his weight on the cougar. Jonas tried to work his paws under his chest to give himself a little more room to breathe, and that helped him make it until the bear levered himself up. The sense of relief he felt as the bear's member slid free was the first pleasure he'd had since his client had come in.

"Thanks," the bear grunted, pulling his clothes on.

"You're welcome, my lord," Jonas panted. He didn't know the bear's name, only that he was young enough to be a noble newly arrived at the city. With a bear on the throne, odds were that a bear dressing in nice new clothes was a noble of some sort. Jonas could only hope he wouldn't become a regular.

After the bear had left, Jonas cleaned himself up and went to tell Tally he was done for the night—six clients, busy night, and he was exhausted.

The back room held a wooden board with the numbers of all the rooms on it and several metal hooks beside each number. From some of the hooks, a wooden name tag dangled. Jonas found his next to the "6" and took it down, hanging it at the bottom of the board in the area marked "off."

Next to his tag hung one marked "Pike." Everyone else was either out or working. Jonas looked for Sasha's tag and found it in the "Out" space. The young cougar sighed. He'd been hoping to spend a little time with the mouse tonight, but Sasha often left as soon as he was done, as did most of the non-resident staff members. Jonas, Richy the wolf, and Alicar the bobcat were the only three who made their permanent home at the Jackal's Staff.

He wondered where Pike was, if he was off but not out. The sturdy raccoon was often up for a game of cards, and Jonas would welcome that if he couldn't get a massage from Sasha. Perhaps he'd forgotten to put his tag by his room number. Pike had been known to do that often, but Tally usually caught it.

Tally had an official office where money was kept under lock and key, and where he held meetings that he didn't want people to walk in on, but before Jonas could look there, the white cougar walked in from the buzzing front room, smoothing down a close-fitting white satin dress that shimmered in the torchlight.. He glanced at the board, then at Jonas. "Hi, dear," he said. "Signing off early tonight?"

Even though Tally's white fur was clear of any colored designs, the dyes he used never really washed clean. Close up, the faded patterns showed ghost-like in his fur. Jonas preferred to see Tally at a distance, when he remained pure white.

Jonas smiled at the other cougar and nodded. "I'm worn out. The bear almost killed me."

"All right. You can go in with Van Wyck when Pike's through. Oh, don't give me that look. It'd be easier if you didn't fight it every week."

"Wouldn't it be better to go before I worked?"

"It would," Tally said, "if you didn't start work early purposely to avoid it."

"Fine." Jonas occasionally managed to miss a week, but never when Tally had specifically told him to go.

"Good boy." Tally grinned and patted his rump. "Do you know where Sasha went? He was supposed to be around through the morning."

"No. I was just wondering that."

"If you see him, tell him to find me."

"All right." Jonas watched as Tally moved back out into the main room, tail held high, in his best maitre'd manner. The cougar greeted a guest, asking where he'd been, making Jonas wonder again how Tally could keep all those names straight in his head. Jonas could barely remember the names of the six clients he'd had that night, and he didn't even know all of them.

He touched Sasha's tag again, wondering where the mouse could be. If Jonas and Tally didn't know, then Sasha hadn't told anyone, and that was unusual even for him.

Movement in the adjoining room, where he guessed Van Wyck was, distracted him. Despite Tally's order, he decided to take a couple minutes in his room to unwind. Maybe Richy or someone would wander in and keep Van Wyck busy.

Even though the back room was off limits to customers most of the time, it wasn't until Jonas left it and walked down the hallway to his left that he encountered a door marked "Staff Only." The painting over the door depicted a jackal holding a wooden staff and glaring menacingly out of the door in intentional counterpoint to the much more lewd jackal that hung over the main entrance outside.

Jonas wouldn't have known it was a jackal if not for the name of the establishment. Sasha had recounted a tale from the famous bear explorer Pantithon describing the near-mythical creatures who supposedly lived far to the south of Tephos, but neither Jonas nor Sasha had ever seen one, nor, for that matter, ever met anyone who'd seen one. Both this picture and the sign over the main entrance bore a strong resemblance to a fox, and it was likely that both had been modeled after one.

The Jackal's Staff sprawled in the middle of its block, with additions reaching around behind other buildings and actually on top of one. Its stone and wood construction had been retouched several times, so that it appeared to be several different buildings glued together. Inside, the décor was impeccable, attended to by Tally personally, and you could barely tell when you were passing from the original building into one of the newer additions.

The original building had been what was now the lounge, a large, comfortable room where the patrons could rest and listen to music while waiting for a staff member--they made that joke a lot--to become available, or while checking out the other patrons. Tally employed two young male servants, currently a grey fox and a weasel, to serve drinks and clear the tables. Jonas had performed that job when he first arrived while he was trained for his current work; after him there had been nobody and the clients were allowed to serve themselves. He hadn't met the fox or weasel, and likely never would unless they were being groomed to join him in working the back side--another joke they made a lot.

On the other side of the "Staff Only" door were the staff lounge and the staff's private rooms. The staff lounge was the room in the Jackal's Staff that felt most like home to Jonas. He spent a good deal of his time here on one of the sofas playing cards or dice, chatting with the others, or reading the graffiti left by the many people who'd worked there. Jonas had contributed his own little bit, an uninspired "Jonas was here" over the sofa in one of the corners. Other pieces of graffiti bespoke the hard work that the residents put in ("Sucked a dozen cocks tonight / I can't talk, can only write –Yeffis" or "Entertained a group of four / They had fun and now I'm sore—Wallace").

He could see only a few of the words in the low light of the one lit oil lamp, but his nose told him who was in the room, curled up on the sofa furthest from the lamp. He padded past the empty sofas and unlit lamps to the sleeping figure and touched his shoulder gently, then shook it.

"Mmm. Mmf?" The bobcat blinked and looked up.

"Alicar. You seen Sasha?"

The bobcat shook his head, then sniffed the air. "Can smell'm, though."

"Yeah, I thought he'd been here with you. Sorry to wake you."

"No problem." Alicar yawned, showing his narrow teeth. "Catch you later."

"Yeah." Jonas padded to the back of the room and opened the door. Chances were Sasha was gone now; the corridor he now stood in had eight small rooms off it and ended in the plain door above which some long-gone wag had painted a generic rear end with the tail raised and the tailhole clearly visible—the "staff entrance," Sasha had explained to a perplexed Jonas his first week.

Sasha had probably just forgotten to see Van Wyck in his rush to get home through the streets of Divalia to his family. Jonas yawned, and then snapped his muzzle shut with a snap when he opened the door to his room and found the mouse sitting on the edge of his bed.

"Sasha?"

Sasha was holding his head in his paws and rocking back and forth on the edge of the bed. He was wearing his nicest clothes and several of the gaudy rings he liked to buy, but he didn't look elegant or showy. He looked like a terrified mouse lost in a fashionable person's laundry pile.

"Jonas, I can't," he squeaked. "I can't do it."

"Can't do what?" Jonas's tail lashed as he padded across the small room and sat on the bed.

"I can't go back in there. Not Van Wyck. He'll see, and that'll be it. I can get it fixed, I can get it cured, I just need, I just need some time." Now he turned to Jonas and his dark eyes were large. "You won't tell Tally, will you? Please?"

The fur on Jonas's shoulders prickled. "Get what cured?"

Sasha shook his head and moaned. "I didn't see until it was over, and I was so careful because he was another mouse, and that's the only way you catch things, you know. But I didn't see until it was too late. Oh, Jonas, please say you won't tell Tally. He'd never let me come back."

"You got...?"

Tears were already soaking Sasha's cheeks. He nodded. "I need to see a doctor, for a few days, kitten. But I'll be back. Just tell Tally, tell Tally that it was a family emergency, that I won't be back for a couple weeks, that I'm very sorry."

"Sasha, if you're..." Despite himself, Jonas edged away from Sasha. He knew he couldn't catch a disease from the mouse, especially just by sitting next to him, but his fur was already nearly standing on end and he wanted to run out and wash in the communal bathroom.

"Thank you, kitten." Sasha patted his knee. "You'll see. I'll be back and all better in no time. I promise. I'm really sorry about this. I'll make it up to you." The last few words spilled out in a rush, and at the end of them Sasha squeaked again as though he'd said something wrong. He jumped to his feet, rings clinking together, waved to Jonas, and disappeared through the open door. Jonas heard the staff entrance door clack shut a moment later.

Disease. He knew that he had to watch out for whitemouth, but that was only transmitted through bites. Some of his customers liked to bite, and he'd bled a few times, but Tally had herbs on hand that he claimed would protect against whitemouth. There were other diseases, venereal ones, that one could only get from one's own species or Family. Before he'd been allowed to start working, Jason had been thoroughly educated in all of this by Tally, and had met Kitta, a blind, syphilitic fox who'd worked at the Staff years ago and hadn't been careful. Now he worked in a weaver's shop and his paws were cracked and bleeding because he couldn't see to keep them out of the way of the shuttles.

Jonas had taken the lesson to heart. After his first year, he'd learned to look for signs of disease discreetly, and he'd done so without fail. He couldn't fathom how Sasha had let his guard down, especially with another mouse.

Footsteps sounded in the hallway, and a moment later Pike's masked muzzle came into view. He stepped into the room and gestured back towards the main building. "You better not miss Van Wyck this week. Tally'll kill you."

Jonas nodded, getting up from the bed. The raccoon was also naked, but where Jonas was kept modest by his fur, the organ that had given the raccoon his nickname was on full display. Jonas gestured down and grinned. "You should put that thing away before you hurt someone."

Pike leered up at the taller cougar. "You got somewhere for me to put it?"

"Go take another client."

The raccoon snorted. "I'll be in the lounge."

It sometimes mystified Jonas how Pike could be so relentlessly randy. Some nights (like tonight), if Jonas hadn't come all night, he wanted something quick to get him off. Most nights he just wanted to curl up in bed and sleep. The staff lounge often saw casual sexual activity, sometimes before a staffer went on shift, to relieve any pressure, and sometimes after, if he needed relaxation. They called it training, and occasionally it was that, but more often it was a chance for them to be intimate without pressure or obligation.

Alicar had gone back to sleep on his sofa, but this time Jonas didn't wake him. He walked back to the back room (empty, to his relief), and then into Tally's office.

The smell wasn't the worst of Van Wyck. The herbal, medicinal odor was no worse than the smells on the patrons that Jonas got pressed into his fur every night. And the room wasn't hard on his eyes. It was very bright—Van Wyck kept four oil lamps lit—and the walls were bare, but he didn't mind that. What he hated most was just being in this room, lying on the raised bed against the far wall while the weasel's paws measured and shaped his fur.

The weasel was at his cabinet, washing his paws in a basin and washing some of the silver instruments he kept in a black case. "Hello, Jonas. Please lie down."

Jonas nodded without saying anything and walked over to the bed. He could smell Pike on it as he lay down, and Alicar, and Richy. Everyone else who worked at the Staff, in fact, except Sasha. He wondered how long it had been since Sasha'd been seen.

"How are you feeling, hm?" The weasel was gathering some tools, but still over at his cabinet.

"Fine."

"No coughing? Blurred vision? Running nose, trouble hearing? Muscular cramps?"

"No."

"Any sores, itches, swelling, unexplained pain?"

"No."

"All right. Let's see your fur."

Jonas closed his eyes. Moments later, the weasel's paws were patting every inch of him, trimming the fur here and there, rubbing some herbal-smelling lotion into some of the areas. It was all the cougar could do to keep from flinching as the paws and scissors attacked his ears, his whiskers, his cheek ruffs, his neck…but he gritted his teeth, waiting for it to end.

End it did, but the examination and grooming of his back and arms was not much more relaxing. And then his tail, which he absolutely could not keep from lashing ("this would be easier if you would stay still," Van Wyck complained, as he always did), and then under his tail, where the weasel pushed the fur apart gently and brushed Jonas's tail hole with a cold metal probe. When that examination was complete, the scissors trimmed fur from his sac and the inside of his thighs, and Jonas opened his eyes then to stare at the wall and pretend he were someplace else.

Inside the Cage

"Turn over, please." He paused as long as he thought he could get away with and then rolled onto his back. The paws and scissors trimmed his chest fur, groomed lines into his stomach ("breathe in,...hold it..."), and evened the fur on his sheath. The whole process made him feel like a living toy, an exhibit with no free will of his own. Van Wyck never asked him how he wanted his fur; he groomed it in accordance with Tally's orders, and Jonas never had a choice. He envied Richy's bushy tail fur, Alicar's longer body fur, and Pike's fluffy cheek ruffs, but he was never given the chance to grow his fur, or to dye it like Tally did. His fur was always short and trim, showing off his muscles.

"Almost done." The weasel set the tools down on a small table to the side, and picked up a linen cloth. "Just one more thing. Please try to cooperate."

His small paws rubbed at Jonas's sheath, and Jonas sighed. He tried to think of erotic images, but as usual, his mind refused to cooperate. He imagined Pike sliding into him from behind, but his mind skittered away to recall the crushing weight of the bear on top of him. Finally, he thought of Van Wyck as a client, and his instincts took over, focusing warmth at his sheath and pushing his stiffening member out into the air.

Van Wyck grasped it gently in the cloth and lifted it, examining both sides. "No sores, no pain while working or urinating?"

"No." Jonas stared at the ceiling.

"All right. You can go." Van Wyck gathered his instruments, hopped down from the stool he'd been standing on, and walked over to the cabinet, washing his paws in the basin again.

"Thanks." Jonas got up and padded quickly to the door.

"See you next week," the weasel called after him. He grumbled in reply.

Nobody was in the back room, though Jonas saw by the board that Richy and Ishel, a rabbit, were now off as well. He lingered by the door of the main room, attracted by the scents of desire that filled it. Back in the corridors and the private rooms, the scents were of lust and mating, and Jonas had his fill of those. Desire was more enticing, so he occasionally let himself sample it. He didn't linger long tonight, because there were other things on his mind.

When he walked back into the lounge, it was just as dark as it had been, but Richy and Pike now lay in the light of the single lamp. Richy was bobbing his muzzle up and down in Pike's lap, and Jonas could see the glistening of Pike's member reflect the lamplight when the young wolf slid up. On the opposite side of the room, Alicar's eyes reflected the light, shining greenly in the shadows.

"Hey, Jonas," Pike said. "Richy says he can get us both in his muzzle at once. Wanna call him on it?"

Richy didn't react, but Jonas was sure the wolf had said nothing of the sort. He flicked his tailtip and walked through the room. "Another time."

Behind him, he heard Pike's voice, and then the click of claws on wood. He hurried to his door, but the raccoon caught him before he could go inside.

"What's with you, anyway?"

"Nothing. I just don't feel like being part of a threesome, okay? Been a long night."

The raccoon slid the paw down to his tail, and Jonas angled his hips away. "All right, all right," said Pike. "I'm just trying to be nice, you know. You always disappear with Sasha or else go straight to bed, and I can see you're still all tense from the night and Van Wyck. Thought you might like a little fun to help you relax."

"You thought wrong." But still he hesitated. Of all the people still about, Pike was the oldest and the most likely to know what he wanted. And though he hated to admit it, he *was* still tense and wouldn't mind some release before bed.

"Oh, come on. Out there it's work. Here it's fun, it's for us. And besides," the raccoon purred, "I'm better than any of your clients."

As unlikely as it seemed, the words were arousing him. He felt a heat in his groin and his erection, which had faltered since Van Wyck had summoned it, was gaining life again. Jonas didn't understand why he was responding like that until he glanced down and saw Pike's paw brushing him so softly he only registered the arousal, not the touch. He should pull away, he thought, but his body ignored his mind.

"So?" Pike grinned, showing the tips of his canines in the lamp light from Jonas's room. His paw slid down Jonas's sheath and cupped his balls. "The thought of sitting in ol' Pike's lap sounding better to you?"

Jonas turned, backed up, and sat on the bed. "Just paws," he said, spreading his legs. "I'll do you and you do me."

"Hell, I could get that in the lounge," Pike said, but he stepped forward anyway.

"And close the door."

The raccoon grinned. "You're so cute when you're shy." He eased the door closed with a paw and came to the bed.

To Jonas's surprise, Pike didn't lunge right for his sheath. He put his arms around the cougar and nuzzled his chest, then gave his muzzle a small lick. Jonas returned the caresses automatically, then allowed himself to relax a bit. The foreplay didn't last long, but Jonas enjoyed it, and after Pike's gentle paw had reached down to Jonas's full erection, Jonas didn't mind closing his paw around the raccoon's thick shaft and stroking in return.

He barely noticed when Pike stopped stroking him, as he'd let himself become attuned to Pike's breathing and body language, the way he did with his clients. But as when he was with Sasha, he was able to appreciate the communion more because there was no responsibility. He didn't know Pike as well as he did Sasha, but he'd been working alongside the raccoon for a couple years, and he got a vicarious thrill when Pike shuddered against his paw and came.

"You're pretty good yourself," Pike panted, and kissed Jonas on the nose. He rubbed his paw over Jonas's and then curled it around Jonas's erection, rubbing slickly up and down. The musky scent and the slickness of the paw felt lovely, enticing Jonas to let himself go, and so he did, basking in the sensations. When he came, it felt good, so that for a moment he forgot he was with Pike and not Sasha.

But only for a moment. He panted, resting back on the bed, and didn't object when Pike lay beside him. "See? Wasn't so bad, was it?"

"It was okay." He felt reluctant to concede more than that.

"Aww, cat miss his mousie?" Pike was half-sympathetic, half-teasing. "Enjoy what we can give each other, but don't get attached. Worst thing you can do. Short of catching something."

He lay quiet while the question burned in his mind, revived by Pike's comment. Discretion warred with worry, and worry proved the stronger warrior. "Pike?"

"Mm."

"If we did catch something…there's medicine, right?"

Pike's head snapped up, his whole body tense. "You sick? No, you couldn't be. You just went to see Van Wyck." He relaxed again. "Yeah, there's medicine. Not cheap, though."

Jonas brushed the raccoon's fur lazily. "Really expensive?"

"More than I could afford." Pike yawned and showed every sign of wanting to go to sleep right in Jonas's bed.

Jonas wasn't sure how he felt about that. He was rather sleepy himself, and Pike's eyes were closed. He let his eyelids droop, and it felt good, so he let them fall all the way.

He heard a low sigh beside him. "Sasha."

"What?" His turn to tense now, though he didn't startle as Pike had. But when he opened his eyes, Pike was looking at him.

"Sasha's sick. That's why he skipped early, missed Van Wyck."

"Uh…"

Pike patted his chest. "And he told you not to tell anyone. Sweet." He yawned again. "It happens every now and then. Sad. But best to put him out of your mind. You won't see him again."

"Why not? There's medicine."

"Tally won't let him back in, for one thing. For another, he'd have to sell all his pretty things to pay for it. I don't know if he'd do that."

"Tally doesn't know yet. And Sasha said he'd come back."

Definitely awake now, Pike patted Jonas's paw, swung his legs down, and stretched as he got up.. "People say all kinds of things, kitty. Sometimes they even mean them. Thanks for the paw. Maybe I'll work you up to more later. It could be really good with us." Jonas drew his legs up, thinking about Sasha and not wanting to. Pike patted his knee and grinned. "And I mean *that*."

"Pike? You won't say anything to Tally?"

The raccoon paused, studying Jonas, and then shook his head. "I won't."

When he was gone, Jonas snuffed the oil lamp and lay in bed on his side, staring into the darkness. He could see the walls of his small room in the dim ambient light, but there were black corners where even that light faded and died. He stared at those corners now, praying to Felis and Rodenta that Sasha would be all right, and the repetition of his prayers soon lulled him to sleep.

The dream begins familiarly. Sasha was playing cards with him. They were in a jail in the center of town, naked and vulnerable to the eyes of everyone walking by. Some stayed to watch and some just glanced as they passed. Jonas knew they had committed a crime but couldn't quite remember what.

He couldn't see Sasha's face any more behind the cards he was holding. "You've got to get out of here, kitten," Sasha said.

"I know," Jonas heard himself say. "But they made the bars out of wood."

"You can cut through," Sasha said. Jonas turned to look at the bars, and when he turned back, Sasha was Pike, holding his erection out. "You can cut with this," he leered.

"I have claws." It was as if he were seeing them for the first time. He scored the bars with his claws, and then scored them again, and two of the bars gave way. As he pushed his way through, the crowd suddenly surged against him, pushing him by the shoulders...

"Jonas. Jonas."

He shook awake and looked up. Tally was shaking him by the shoulder. "Get up."

He blinked at the white cougar. "Mmmf. Client?"

"Yes, a wolf."

"Get Richy."

"He doesn't want another wolf. I'll double your tip."

Jonas forced his tired body awake. Double tips was a good deal. He stretched, sniffed himself, and nodded. "All right. Let me clean up." If he got a good tip, he would get some money to Sasha.

"Thanks, dear. Room five." All smiles, Tally kissed his ears before hurrying out.

The water in the washroom was always cold, but it woke Jonas up. He scrubbed his fur clean hastily and then threw on a robe in case the client wanted to undress him.

The corridors were deserted as he padded through them. He heard the muffled sounds of pleasure from one room. Ishel, back at work, he thought. But the sun was rising and the Jackal's Staff was mostly quiet.

The door to room five creaked as it opened, as did most of the doors in the old building. Even though they were laid out identically, Jonas could tell any of them by sight now. Five was one of the largest, windowless, with one discolored board in the paneling of the far right corner. Despite the cleaning to erase the smells, he still remembered every client he'd had in this room every time he walked in.

Tonight, it smelled of young wolf. He was on the bed, sprawled out and naked, energetically rubbing his sheath. *He wants a blow job,* Jonas thought instantly, and sure enough, he was on his knees moments later, taking the wolf's thick shaft into his muzzle. He couldn't say how he knew; Sasha had worked twice as long as he had and still couldn't predict what a customer would want. Jonas saw them as types that reminded him of other types, across species borders. He knew without being told that the wolf had never been here before, had saved up money, or perhaps gotten a gift, for this special occasion, and that his tip would therefore probably be minimal.

But he saved his anger for Tally. It wasn't the wolf's fault, and if he wanted a special time, it was Jonas's job to give it to him. Judging from the spastic twitching of his arms and legs, and the energy he poured into his howl as he came, the wolf had a very good time indeed. Jonas never even had to take off his robe. He got a breathless 'thanks' as he left, and he did get some pleasure out of the wolf's broad, satisfied grin.

Too restless to go back to sleep, he stayed in the staff lounge, absently stroking Alicar's fur. Tally walked in a few minutes later and dropped three coppers into Jonas's paw. "Here. He didn't leave anything, but I promised you something."

Jonas closed his paw around the coins and nodded. Tally'd made at least three silvers, more if he'd charged full price. Sasha said Tally discounted for younger clients so they'd keep coming back. But three coppers was better than nothing. He'd pass on a silver to Sasha—maybe that would help.

Over the years he'd dropped many coppers and silvers into the small lockbox in his room. Sasha periodically changed the coins for him, so that now he had a scattering of coppers, thirteen silvers, and six precious gold Royals. When he dropped the three coppers in tonight, however, he heard them thunk against wood, not metal.

Fur prickling, he opened his chest and retrieved the lockbox key from under his bed. Even though he hadn't touched it in weeks, it wasn't dusty. He sniffed it, but it was metal and wouldn't take a scent that he could smell over his own. Dreading what he might see, he fitted it into the lock and turned it.

The box held a few copper pieces, and nothing more.

He held it upside down and shook it in disbelief as the copper coins rattled into the bottom of the chest. Robbed? Who would come in here? Why was nothing else touched? And nobody knew where his box was, much less the key, except...

Except Sasha.
He sat down heavily on the bed.

Chapter 2

The Jackal's Staff never closed, but between sunrise and noon, most of the staff slept, so "morning" was defined as the few hours before lunch when the staff got together for calisthenics. Tally didn't force attendance, but most of the non-residents showed up anyway. A worker who didn't stay in shape got fewer tips and would be out of a job before long.

After exercises that day, everyone except Jonas and Richy had left to go home or to go on duty. Jonas was ignoring Richy and finishing up his stretches when the wolf came up behind him and put a paw on his shoulder.

"Hey," he said.

Jonas grunted, and kept stretching.

"Listen," Richy said, "you haven't said two words since Sasha left. I know you guys were close, but you need to get over it."

Jonas shrugged off the paw and started walking away. Richy followed him. "It's going to start affecting your work."

"My work?" Jonas turned and glared at the wolf. "My *work*?! This isn't work. This is slavery. This is…" He groped for words. "A trap, a prison. If I could walk out of here and get a good honest living, I would."

Richy had folded his arms defensively and laid his ears back, though he looked more bewildered than angry. "Why don't you, then?"

"Because I'm not trained for anything!" Jonas hissed. "Who's going to take an eighteen-year-old apprentice?"

"I thought you were happy here."

"You thought. You thought. What would you know, anyway? Take your mouth out of Pike's lap and look around once in a while."

Richy flicked his ears. "I do look around. You don't act like this. Not usually."

"Maybe I just never realized before."

"What did you realize?"

Jonas wanted to tell someone, felt the hard lump of Sasha's betrayal in his stomach and wanted to get it out. But Richy, this lap dog of a wolf who crawled up to Pike every night no matter how he got treated by the raccoon, couldn't understand. Nobody could understand, not in this place. He growled and clenched his paws in frustration. "Just…forget it."

"Jonas."

"I said, forget it. Hey, I don't think Pike's left yet. Why don't you see if he wants a quick one before he goes?"

Richy's ears flattened again. "That's not your business," he said.

"It's all of our business. Do you see how he treats you? Do you see how little he cares? Did you see him push you away to come jack me off the other night?"

"He wanted to make you feel better."

"Make me feel better. He wanted to get under my tail, is all."

"Maybe that's what he thought you wanted."

"That's what *he* wanted. There's a difference." He looked at the wolf's muzzle. Richy was a year younger than he was but had been working at the Staff for a year longer. Sometimes he forgot that. "He's already been under your tail, hasn't he? He got what he wanted from you and now he just tolerates you."

"I like to make him happy."

"I'm sure he loves it, too. 'Til he gets bored of you."

Richy lowered his arms and turned, walking the other way out of the room. Jonas called after him, "Hey! Why don't you worry about making *me* happy?"

He'd meant it as a jab, but his voice cracked on the word 'me.' Richy turned and looked at him. "Oh," he said softly, "I don't think I could. I don't think anyone here could." Then he turned, tail still between his legs, and left.

Jonas cursed himself. Then, for lack of anything better to do, he got dressed and walked through the streets of Divalia.

The walk did nothing to improve his mood. The weather was already turning colder, and his ears kept flicking to keep warm no matter how hard he tried to hold them down against the occasional bursts of wind. He'd left his heavy shirt back in the room, and his newly-trimmed fur didn't keep out the cold well—another discomfort that he added to his tally of grievances against his current position. His tail lashed back and forth as his mood grew blacker, and the delightfully warm smells of pastries from pubs and bakeries only served to remind him that he couldn't afford to treat himself now, and maybe not for a while.

The worst part was almost not that Sasha had abandoned and betrayed him; it was that he couldn't tell anyone about it. If he reported the theft, Sasha would be possibly arrested; at the very least, Tally would definitely be told about his condition if he didn't know already. Jonas had been avoiding the other cougar for the last couple days, but knew he would have to face him eventually. He couldn't stay out on the streets forever, as cold as it was and as poor as he now was.

On the previous days he'd gone out, he'd sat in the park, but it was now too cold for that. Again, he cursed Van Wyck as he rubbed his short fur. The warm fires crackling inside public houses beckoned him, but he was reluctant to go in without any money in his pocket, so he searched for a place where he could sit down and get warm without buying food or drink.

Such a place did not seem to exist in Divalia. But as he passed the Cup and Crown and glanced in, he saw a familiar muzzle. He laid a paw

Inside the Cage

on the door handle, unsure whether he could presume on a semi-regular client; a cold gust of wind broke his indecision and sent him inside.

The room, half full, turned to look at him, then glanced away again. Nothing about him held their attention, for which he was grateful. He rubbed his paws together and found an empty spot at the bar.

The patrons ranged from middle-class tradespeople to nobles from the nearby palace. Some pubs catered to a particular House, but the species in the Cup and Crown ran the gamut of all six Houses. Jonas counted one other Felid, two wolves and a coyote, a pair of rabbits, a quartet of goats and another of rats, and even a raucous table of weasels and raccoons arguing amiably just behind him, not to mention Mani, the host.

Mani glanced at him and nodded as he would to any new customer, then did a double-take. Jonas was used to seeing the bear's muzzle contort, but the open-jawed expression of surprise was so comical he almost grinned. Instead, he just nodded back. Mani got his muzzle shut, but not before a couple patrons looked down the bar to see what was so unusual. Jonas stared intently forward, not making eye contact.

"What can I get you?" Mani moved in front of him, smiling now, but Jonas couldn't tell if the smile encouraged familiarity or distance.

"The thing is," Jonas said softly, trying to keep the coyote beside him from hearing, "I can't really pay right now. I was hoping…"

Mani nodded. "What can I get you?" he repeated.

"Something hot."

"Cider?"

"Perfect." Jonas smiled. "Thanks."

"Why don't you have a seat, sir? I'll bring it out to you."

Jonas nodded. The communal space around the fire was crowded with chattering wolves, weasels, hares, and mice. Looking around, he spied a table not too far away that was obviously meant for larger species. He walked over, slid into the bear-sized chair and waited, turning toward the fire to get as much warmth as he could.

When Mani brought the steaming mug to the table, he sat down in the chair across from Jonas and rested his elbows on the table. "I didn't know you knew where I worked."

Jonas shrugged, and sniffed the cider. It smelled delicious. "I didn't. I just happened to see you."

"And you never did before?"

"I never walked around the neighborhood before."

"Oh." Mani settled back. "So you didn't come here looking for me."

Jonas couldn't help but grin at the bear's worry. "Why would I do that?"

"Oh, I don't know. If something were…wrong, maybe."

Disease. Sasha. Jonas's grin faded, and he buried his short muzzle in the mug, inhaling the cider's fumes. "No, nothing like that. Just out for a walk."

Mani looked away, then back. "*Is* something wrong?"

"Everything." Jonas sighed.

"Want to talk about it?" The bear grinned at Jonas's look of surprise. "I know your skills. Listening's one of mine."

"All right." The need to tell someone had surfaced again, stronger now that there was a potential listener across the table, and it took only a second before Jonas gave in to it. He told the story briefly, leaving out only Sasha's name, and concluded with his current state of mind. "I just feel trapped. I can't get out and I can't keep going."

"Why do you suddenly feel trapped now? So your friend turned out to be not so good a friend. What's that change?"

"It's not that. It's...I..." He couldn't verbalize how the betrayal had ruined the only good things about his job. His claws scored the table in his frustration. Mani glanced at them and paused before continuing, in a more soothing tone.

"Can I just say that you're pretty good at what you do?"

Jonas nodded without returning the bear's smile. "Thanks."

"And you're lucky to have a job. Half these guys in here, they won't be in next month. Times are good now, but come the winter, most of the nobles head south, and the farmers head home. Nobody needs to hire help, so they'll be tightening their belts." Jonas nodded. Winter was a slower time for the Staff, too. "But you'll still have a place to live, food on the table, and a job. Your profession and mine, they're about the only ones you can count on day in and day out."

"Could I get a job here?"

"Doing...what you do?" The bear's eyes widened, and his voice dropped to a whisper. "I can't. The police would take the pub."

"No, I mean...serving, or...or...keeping the books."

Mani looked skeptically at him. "You got a head for numbers?"

His father: *can't you even add two numbers together? Why can't you be like Trias? Two years younger and he did all his sums without one mistake! Not one!* "I'm...I've had experience with..."

His tongue stumbled and halted. Mani shook his head. "I got all the help I can use. I could, um, ask around..."

But it was clear the bear's heart wasn't in it. "That's okay." Jonas took a sip of the cider, then a longer drink. The fumes had given his head a pleasant spin.

"Really, think about what I said. You're pretty lucky."

"Yeah. Thanks."

Mani got up, and pointed at the cider. "Don't worry about paying that back. On the house."

"Thanks." He put more sincerity into that one. "See you on Ursiday."

"Yeah." Mani scratched behind his ear and got up, bending over a nearby table to ask if they needed any more ale.

Jonas sat at the table, letting the cider warm his stomach and head, while his thoughts continued to chase each other around and around. He couldn't stand to keep doing what he was doing, but he couldn't do anything else. The cider vanished quickly, the headiness more slowly, but when they were both gone, his dilemma remained.

A raccoon cleared away his mug, and Mani signaled from near the fireplace to ask if he wanted another. Jonas shook his head. He'd imposed enough, and he was content to sit in the bar, absorbing what he could of the fire's warmth, simply being away from the Staff until he had to go back.

Tally was waiting for him when he walked into the back room. Jonas pulled his robe closed and looked at the board.

"My office." Tally stepped into the room without waiting for Jonas to acknowledge him. Jonas sighed, and followed.

"So what happened to Sasha?" Tally's arms were folded, his ears cupped forward. They were dyed light blue today, as were the sides of his cheeks. His paws were hidden in the crooks of his arms, but Jonas was sure they were dyed blue too.

He stared at them and shrugged, avoiding the other cougar's eyes. "Family emergency."

"Come on, Jonas. You're not doing him any favors by covering for him. He skipped out the night Van Wyck was here, so it's not hard to put together what's going on. Either he got hurt or he got sick and he didn't want Van Wyck to know. But I know you two were close and I know you know."

He can't know, Jonas said to himself, but another voice spoke up and said, why not betray Sasha? He betrayed you. It would serve him right. Imagine if he came back and didn't have a job any more. "He got sick," he said abruptly.

"That's what I thought." Tally nodded. "I'll go back and find out what mice were here in the last few weeks and ban them. We don't need that kind of customers. You report any sick ones too, you understand?"

"Sure."

The other cougar softened and walked forward, brushing Jonas on the cheek. "I just don't want anything to happen to you, kit." When Jonas remained silent, Tally dropped his paw. "I've got a client waiting for you. When you're ready in seven, I'll send him over."

"I'll be there in a minute." Jonas was left numb by how quickly his resolve not to betray Sasha had crumbled, but felt the stirrings of righteousness inside him; Sasha should have asked him for help, not taken it from him. The mouse had ruined their friendship, not he. His paws flexed, the claws sliding out and back in, and then he lifted his muzzle and walked through the corridors to room seven, to go to work.

His third client of the night was a familiar one, a lanky fox by the name of Alexan who had been coming to him every week for several months. Aside from his dominance habits, which he shared with many of Jonas's clients, he had a curious quirk: a habit of calling Jonas "your highness" when he was inside him and about to come. Usually, Jonas was too distracted to think about it, and forgot afterwards; after all, people said all kinds of things when their energy was mostly focused away from their muzzles. Once or twice, though, he'd felt a sort of déjà vu, as though he'd met Alexan before somewhere else, but he'd never been able to remember where.

On this night, Alexan was in fine form, growling and thrusting hard, his teeth clamped in Jonas's neck ruff. It was a little uncomfortable, but Jonas was lost in his own thoughts and hardly noticed when Alexan growled "yrrrf rrrnsss, rrrrf!" and shuddered above him, his knot expanding inside Jonas.

Afterwards, Alexan rested his muzzle between Jonas's ears, the only fox Jonas had ever met who was tall enough to do so. He murmured, "Are you okay?"

"What?" Jonas was jolted out of his reverie.

"You seem a bit listless."

"Oh." Jonas swallowed. "I am sorry. If you have any complaints, please see Tally and he'll refund—"

Alexan nosed his ear. "No, no, don't be silly. I'm just a bit worried. You're usually more lively."

"I'm sorry," Jonas repeated. "I have a lot on my mind." He shut his muzzle immediately. It wasn't good practice to talk too much to the customers.

"Oh." Alexan stroked his chest. "Tell me about it."

"It's just been…just been a hard week." Jonas sighed. The paw on his chest felt good. Larger than Sasha's, but its gentle, firm touch reminded him of the mouse. "Friend of mine left."

"Left?"

"Left the Staff."

"Oh, I'm sorry to hear that." Alexan's paw continued to stroke, his claws ruffling through Jonas's chest fur. "I suppose you two were close."

"Yes." Jonas felt himself relaxing. "But I shouldn't let that affect my job."

"Nonsense." The fox nuzzled him. "It makes you seem more real. I like that. You know, you're the best thing about this country."

"Country?"

"Mm. I told you I'm Ferrenian, didn't I?"

"No." Jonas had heard very little about Tephos's eastern neighbor. He knew vaguely that there was some sort of tension between the countries. He considered whether this made a difference to him, and decided it didn't. "What brings you here?"

"I'm a merchant. I come here in the summers to sell and buy fine weapons and other things. But mainly weapons."

"I didn't know they allowed merchants between the countries."

"Oh, yes, you just have to know who to get the right paperwork from. And of course, nobody here asks questions. Still, not the sort of thing you want to advertise. But it feels nice to talk to someone about it."

"I won't tell anyone."

Alexan laughed lightly and kissed him on the ear. "Thank you, sweetie. But I go back in another week anyway. Though I do hope to keep coming back, especially now that I have you to look forward to." His paw brushed up under Jonas's chin.

Jonas automatically said, "I hope you come back too. I'll miss you." Standard talk he'd learned, and learned how to put some heart into, even if Alexan would be gone from his mind like all his clients when the day was over.

"If things keep going well, I'll be able to. There's a fellow here who is making some really nice designs. And I might branch out into books. Ever read any P. Zinsky?" Jonas shook his head. "Ah, you'd like him." Alexan wiggled inside Jonas and tugged, sliding out.

"I'll have to look him up sometime." Jonas clambered off the bed and took a towel from the side, rubbed some scented oil into it, then came back to the bed where Alexan was sitting with his legs spread. Jonas cleaned his sheath and member, making the fox squirm and yelp in delight.

Alexan pulled on his clothes and patted Jonas gently. "Thanks again, Jonas." He flashed a grin. "Wish I could take you with me."

"Me too." Jonas returned the smile, and then caught himself wondering, *What if…*

Alexan was already gone before he could voice the thought. But his mind kept spinning while he went through the motions of cleaning himself up and straightening the room. He tucked the robe under his arm and went back to the back room.

From then on, Jonas nursed his fantasy of escape. He could have asked any of his clients to take him, but there weren't many he liked. Besides, his contract promised compensation to Tally if he didn't stay four more years, and he doubted his father would be willing to pay up, which would leave a sticky situation. Alexan, though—he liked the fox well enough, and the thought of being able to escape the country was thrilling. He could leave all this behind, start over again, maybe end up helping Alexan with his business. He could be good at it, given a proper chance and nobody waiting to outshine him.

Even his weekly appointment with Van Wyck wasn't as bad as usual. He wandered back into the lounge afterwards and kept himself hard, thinking about Alexan and teasing himself as he sat down. Pike and Alicar were chatting on the other side of the room, and Ishel was picking at one of the wall carvings, turning to join in the conversation from time to time.

Pike was describing the new Cantor at the church down the street. "I tell you, if anyone had Ursis behind him, this one does. He's the biggest raccoon I've ever seen. Maybe he's part bear."

Alicar snorted. "That's as likely as me and Jonas having a kid."

Pike glanced at Jonas. "Looks like he's trying to have one himself. Come on, Jonas, give us a show."

Ishel looked over his shoulder at Jonas, and said, "Don't stain the couch, okay?"

Jonas took his paw away and leaned back into the couch, enjoying the fact that he was teasing Pike. "Don't worry, I won't."

"What's on your mind, big kitty?" Pike asked. The raccoon was naked, too, but not aroused, and though his paw brushed his sheath briefly, he made no effort to match Jonas's show.

"Oh, I'm just thinking of the king's announcement that he's going to be lowering the countrywide tax on ale following the rich harvest last year." Jonas licked his lips and grinned at Pike. In fact, Mani had mentioned that on his last visit, which perhaps had accounted for his extra excitement.

Ishel laughed. "Cheaper to get drunk, eh?"

"Actually," Alicar stretched as he spoke, "it's a sop designed to make up for raising the taxes on the farms that produce the grain two years ago, which the king needed to do in order to pay for the armies he's sending to the Reysfields to protect them against the Ferrenians. The Uprising fifty years ago left the king in power but wary about offending the people, so each tax increase since then is met with a drop in taxes. But if you look closely," he yawned, "the drops rarely make up for the increase."

The room fell silent. Alicar looked around. "Oh, come on, it's not that complicated."

"You amaze me," Pike said. "You eat dinner with your father, what, once a week? And you still remember all that?"

"History," Alicar said stiffly, "is the most important teacher."

The raccoon grinned widely. "You haven't had a lesson from Pike."

Alicar flicked his ears and grinned back. "Don't need to. I already know how to be an obnoxious oversexed prat. I just choose not to make use of that knowledge."

"Oooh!" Pike squeaked in a falsetto. "My goodness, one would almost think you hadn't just been cleaning come out of your muzzle."

Alicar stuck his tongue out at Pike. The raccoon grinned. "You missed a spot."

Jonas kept quiet, his tail sliding back and forth across the couch. Glancing around, he wondered where Richy was. The group in the lounge included everyone he knew well except for the wolf, and it felt comfortable and familial. He began to have pangs of doubt about leaving. If he stuck around, he might lose his nerve altogether.

"Goodnight," he said, standing and stretching. "I'll see you all in the morning."

"Night, Jonas," three voices chorused. He waved as he padded back into the hallway and to his room.

Lying on his bed, he took his member in his paw again and thought about making love to Alexan, under the night sky on their way back to Ferrenis, the stars sparkling down on them. He'd never had sex outdoors and thought it must be very romantic.

"Whoever you're thinking about, I can take his place."

Jonas's eyes flew open. Pike was standing in his doorway.

"You don't take a hint, do you?" he snapped.

"Oh, but I do. You were handing them out pretty liberally tonight." The raccoon closed the door behind him and walked to the bed.

Torn between his fantasy and annoyance at Pike, Jonas sat still. The raccoon was showing now, a bit of pink at the tip of his sheath. "Who is it? One of us? No, a client. Someone you just met today?" His paw grasped Jonas's member and slid along it.

"Ohh." The touch felt good. His clients had touched him, but none with that gentleness. He shook his head.

"No, of course not." Pike stroked him softly. "You've been like this for a week. A regular, then, someone you're looking forward to seeing again. Don't you know you shouldn't fall in love with a client? It doesn't matter, I suppose, if it makes you more excited to see him. Makes the experience better for him. I fell in love once, did I ever tell you? Ah, a story for later, then." His paw worked all the time he was talking, while his other paw moved around Jonas. "You're thinking about his touch, his scent, his body against yours." Somehow, Jonas was on his side and his tail lifted, and Pike's paw was under it. "Imagining him back there, wanting him to be part of you like that." Then the words stopped and a soft tongue replaced Pike's paw under his tail.

Jonas moaned. He hadn't come at all tonight, and the tension was returning, building up in him. He lifted a leg and felt the tongue move deeper. Then Pike slid up behind him. "And he wants to be part of you, too," he whispered. "Do you want him?" Jonas felt a pressure under his tail, waiting anxiously for permission.

Dimly, he realized what Pike was doing. He scrambled to convince his logical mind that it was okay: he would be gone tomorrow, and so it didn't matter, and besides, if he let Pike do this, he'd regret leaving that much less. He wasn't sure it made sense, but his logical mind was not really controlling much anyway. He nodded and said softly, "yes."

Pike was good; experienced, of course, but also good, with a natural sense for how his partner was feeling. Jonas knew how big he was, had had his paw around Pike, but good Felis, it felt like a tree trunk being pushed into him. Amazingly, though, apart from an initial discomfort, he was enjoying it. He tried to imagine Alexan, but between the raccoon scent and the pressure (*Felis save me, he must be three times as big as Alexan!*), that was next to impossible, so Jonas just closed his eyes and enjoyed it.

They finished within a few seconds of each other, Pike controlling Jonas expertly with his paw. As their moans and panting mingled and faded into the cool morning air, Jonas felt himself relax, and felt the discomfort start to make itself known in his rear again. Before he could say anything, though, Pike slid out. The relief made him shudder again, and the raccoon, arms still wrapped around him, chuckled. "Feels as good goin' out as goin' in, eh?"

"Yeah." Jonas was already starting to regret saying yes as his logical mind woke up. "What's wrong with us? You'd think we hadn't just spent six hours having sex."

Pike grinned. "Six hours of foreplay, dear. That's all it was. I didn't come until now; did you?"

"No." Jonas was sleepy, too, now, and trying to work out how to get Pike out of his room before he fell asleep.

"I liked this, Jonas. Was nice. You're as good as I thought you'd be."

"Mm."

"I really mean that. This was really special."

"Mm."

"Didn't you feel that?"

Jonas cracked his eyes open. He almost wouldn't mind if Pike stayed with him if he would just shut up. "Better than with Richy?"

Pike was quiet for a moment. "This was different. Wasn't it for you?"

Different from the six hundred previous times I had someone up my tail? "Sure."

Pike rested a paw on his side. "This job can get tough if you can't keep a bit of yourself aside for the people that matter. Make some occasions special. You know?"

"Mm." Jonas had closed his eyes again. "You said...never fall in love."

Pike chuckled. "So I did. Caring about someone, though, that's what our job's all about."

"I care."

"You'll do okay." Pike was stroking his side. "You'll be good. I can tell. You won't let this job wear you down."

"Mm. Won't have to."

"What?"

There was some reason he shouldn't be telling Pike, but he couldn't see that it would hurt. "Gettin' out."

"Oh. With your client?"

"Mm."

Pike was quiet for a long time. Jonas was hovering on the edge of sleep when he thought he heard the raccoon say, "Then this was a very nice goodbye."

Chapter 3

Jonas was so excited when the night started that he almost came all over the belly of his first client, a weasel merchant who had insisted on being on bottom. Picturing the fox beneath him, Jonas felt his groin tighten, and he drew his paw away with an effort.

Every time he got his assignment that night, he opened the door expecting the sharp aroma and russet fur of his savior. Every time, he was disappointed.

After his fourth client, he was given a break. Tally was in the back room for the first time all night, and Jonas took advantage of the opportunity.

"Tally? Was there a fox in tonight asking for me?"

"I lm?" Tally was taking some notes and not paying attention to him, or pretending not to.

"A fox, tall and thin. He usually comes tonight."

The cougar shook his head. "If anyone asked for you, dear, then you've already seen them."

Jonas sighed. Maybe Alexan had spent the night packing and would be late. He couldn't accept that the fox wouldn't come back one last time. He'd said he was leaving in a week and he hadn't said good-bye. He *had* to come back.

"I haven't seen Shurian, either. This was his night, too."

"The night isn't over yet," Tally said absently.

"I guess not."

"Let me get you a drink from the bar," Tally said. He had never offered that to Jonas before. *Must sound pretty pathetic.*

"All right." He sank down into the wooden chair and curled his tail around one of the legs. Alexan would show up, he kept telling himself, but the hollowness of his vision was seeping through his self-assurance. Why would a successful merchant bother with a prostitute? He'd never promised to take Jonas with him, after all; that had all been in Jonas's mind. Maybe he had a wife and family. Or maybe a mate. No, he didn't have a male mate, Jonas was fairly sure of that. It was one of those things he knew. But he knew precious little else, and though he tried to hold on to his dream, he felt the futility of his hope.

Tally brought him a glass of wine, which he downed rather faster than he had intended to. "You feeling better now?" the white cougar asked, taking the glass back. Jonas, his head recovering from the brief spin it had taken, nodded. "All right. Room two."

Once Jonas had nodded his acknowledgment, Tally smiled and patted his cheek. "We all have bad days, dear. It'll pass." And then he was gone, back into the main room.

Jonas sighed, pushed himself up out of the chair, and went out to only the third disaster of his three-year career.

It wasn't as bad as the time he'd come right across the muzzle of the cougar beneath him, nor was it as bad as the time he'd let his teeth press down on the huge member of a noble bear — *that* one would've gotten him fired, or worse, if Tally hadn't intervened, telling the noble how *young* and *new* Jonas was, practically a *virgin*, and how the noble's *enormous* and *impressive* equipment had intimidated the poor young cat. The bear had left with a full refund, grumbling, but hadn't taken any other action (for fear his wife would find out, Tally said), and had even come back a few months later.

This client was another cougar, a soldier or something, one of the ones who came to the Jackal's Staff perhaps once or twice in their lifetime, having heard of its reputation for servicing nobles. Usually it was enough for Jonas to be well-groomed and meet them in an insect-free room. This particular cougar's fantasies went a bit beyond that, which was okay with Jonas (he'd done stranger things) except that part of the cougar's fantasy involved Jonas coming in his mouth.

Usually this wouldn't have been any trouble either. Unfortunately, the combination of the wine and Jonas's mood, together with apprehension about his earlier near-mishap, proved impossible to overcome. Not only did he not come at the proper time, he was not even able to stay fully erect.

The client refused to listen to his apologies, and so Jonas stopped offering them, taking several cuffs across the muzzle as the soldier ranted on about how much he'd saved up, and how this had completely ruined everything, and this place was no better than the seedy Open Hole brothel down the river, just more expensive and pretentious, and on and on while he pulled his clothes on. "Your owner's going to hear about this," the soldier concluded, shaking a fist at Jonas, and then he slammed the door shut behind him.

Jonas sank back onto the bed and curled up, hiding his head in his arms. He didn't pause to examine the thoughts that whirled through his mind, just let them pass by while he waited for Tally.

The door opened and closed. "Done for the night?"

Jonas sat up with an effort and looked at Tally. "I'm sorry."

"It's all straightened out. I'll keep your tips for tonight and you just go to bed and don't worry about it. Take the day off tomorrow. Okay?"

"Thanks." The word sounded hollow, but he wasn't even sure if Tally had heard. The door was closing before he was finished.

Jonas lay back. The bed was more comfortable than his, but he knew the cleaners would be in to freshen up the room before too long. Indeed, once he finally forced himself into the corridor, he passed one of the cleaning mice, keeping to the wall and walking quietly. He ignored it, as he always did, and walked back to the lounge.

Alicar was there, getting dressed and chatting with Pike, who was already dressed. As Jonas entered, Pike's eyes flicked to him and then away. "I guess I'd better get going and get some sleep," he said. "Goodnight, Jonas."

"Night." Jonas waved.

As Pike slipped out, Alicar said, "I thought you were sick."

"No, just thinking about a lot of things." Jonas sighed. "I screwed up with a client tonight."

"Oh, okay, that's probably what he meant, then." Alicar pulled on a shirt.

"Who?"

"Tally. He gave me a couple of your regulars, said you weren't feeling well."

Jonas felt his fur prickle. "Who?"

"A redcoat and a cougar."

"The fox...was he tall? Thin?"

"Yeah, he said to say goodbye to you. I guess he's leaving town or something."

"Shit!" Jonas ran for his room, not bothering to close the door, rummaging through his chest and grabbing clothes from it, throwing on his heaviest pair of pants and his shirt and vest.

Alicar appeared in his doorway. "What's the matter?"

"Pike, damn him. He told. He told Tally, and they fixed it." He grabbed his money, what little there was, and slipped a pendant over his neck, one he hadn't worn in years. It carried his family sigil on it and was his only link back to them. Even though he never expected to see any of them again, he couldn't force himself to leave it behind.

"Don't go dark," Alicar warned. He blocked the door as best he could.

"Get out of my way."

"Listen, don't..."

Jonas pushed the bobcat aside. "I heard you the first time. Tell Tally goodbye." He stalked out and down the corridor.

"Jonas, wait!" Alicar grabbed at his arm and Jonas pushed him aside. A moment later, Jonas could hear him running back down the corridor to get Tally. The cougar didn't care. He pushed the back door open and walked out into the cold early morning.

He didn't know exactly where Pike lived, but he'd heard him talk about the Kingsbridge quarter, and the main road that led there was not crowded at this time of night. Once his eyes adjusted to the dimness, Jonas saw two figures down the road. He ran up the road toward them, eyes fixed on them, hoping they wouldn't notice him.

And they didn't, not until he was close enough to see that the closer of the two had a long ringed tail. Then he saw Pike and the rabbit ahead of him turn and look at him. Pike squeaked; they both started running, but

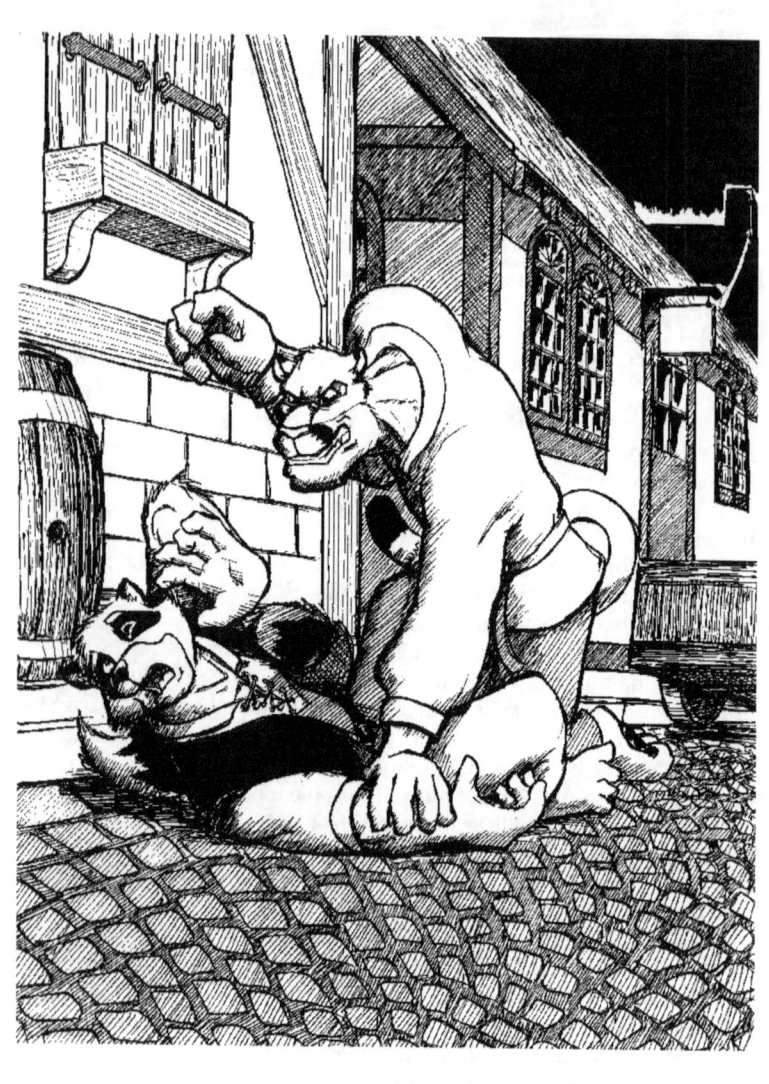

He threw the raccoon to the ground
and landed on top of him.

Inside the Cage

Jonas focused on Pike. The distance between them melted away; if Pike had ducked into a side alley, he might've lost Jonas, but he ran straight down the open street and Jonas caught him easily.

He threw the raccoon to the ground and landed on top of him, cutting off the plea of "Jonas!" with a hard paw to the muzzle, claws out. Pike's nose smacked against the stones of the street and blood welled up in the white fur around his whiskers. His eyes widened until Jonas could see the whites behind them. "Darkness!" he panted.

"Darkness take *you*!" Jonas snarled, and lifted his paw to strike again. Pike flinched, and Jonas's paw glanced off his muzzle, raking through the raccoon's cheek ruff and tearing out some fur.

"Jonas! Please!"

"You told!"

"I was trying to help you!"

"Help me!" Jonas's anguish echoed off the buildings. "Help me stay trapped, imprisoned?"

"Prison? I was trying to stop you from making a mistake."

"What could you know about that?" The blood on Pike's muzzle was black in the dim light. Jonas couldn't stop looking at it. The scent had just reached his nostrils.

"You're still young. You'll believe anyone who asks you to run away with him." Pike coughed. "It never ends well, that sort of thing. Just save your money, kit, you can quit in a few years. You don't have a family to support yet."

"I don't *have* any money!"

In the wake of that cry, as Pike stared at him, footsteps approached at a run. Jonas saw shapes coming down the road and got up, taking a few steps back in a panic before Pike grabbed his arm and pulled him into an alley. Too confused to do anything else, startled at how quickly the raccoon had gotten up, Jonas just followed.

They splashed through puddles that chilled their paws and then huddled against a dark wall, listening to the would-be rescuers shout. "Hey! Call out if you're hurt! We can't find you!" They held silent, a couple feet apart, until the noises of searching died down.

"I'm sorry," Jonas whispered.

"Why don't you have any money?" Pike whispered back.

Jonas hesitated. "Come on," Pike said. "I want to sit in front of a fire. Tell me on the way."

They walked for another half mile, and Jonas told Pike how Sasha had been such a good friend, how he'd discovered the money gone, how Alexan had seemed so tender and had asked Jonas to come with him (he embellished that part), how Jonas couldn't think of anything he wanted to do more than just run away. He even told Pike how devastated he'd felt when the fox hadn't shown up for his appointment, and the raccoon was silent. Jonas hoped he felt guilty.

They stopped outside a small row house. Pike unlocked the door and slipped inside. "Just keep your voice down," he said. "The cubs are sleeping."

"Doesn't your wife mind what you do?" Jonas asked, wondering for the first time.

Pike shrugged. "She died giving birth to Kirish."

"Oh." He didn't know what to say to that. "I'm sorry."

The raccoon busied himself lighting a fire. "Her mother stays with the cubs. I make enough money to keep everyone fed, and to pay our taxes."

Jonas sat down on the rug and watched as the fire caught. Pike tossed some wood onto it and then left the room. He came back wiping water from his muzzle and handed a wooden cup to Jonas. "Here. I don't have anything fancier."

Jonas sipped the water, curling his tail around him. The fire felt good on his wet paws, but he felt uneasy inside when he saw the wetness on Pike's muzzle, remembering the black traces of blood he'd put there. "I'm sorry," he said again. "Are you hurt?"

"It's a little tender." Pike sat beside him. "It really was for your own good, Jonas. You know, that merchant would've just taken you to Ferrenis and then either abandoned you there or abused you 'til you ran away. And then you'd be in a foreign country with nowhere to turn."

"You can't know that," Jonas said, but his dream had faded even further. The darkness was going with it, driven out by Pike's warmth. He felt that all of his other life was a dream, but this was real, and he should hold onto it.

"It happened to one prostitute I knew. He ran off with a client and came back seven months later with...he was hurt. And sick. He died a couple months after that. Tally said it had happened at least five times since he started working at the Staff. Neither of us wanted to see it happen to you."

"Hasn't anyone ever run off and been happy?" Jonas filed away the surprising knowledge that Tally had once been a worker at the Staff. He always thought of the cougar as the manager and couldn't imagine him spreading his legs for anyone or putting that pretty muzzle between someone's legs.

Pike stared into the fire. "Maybe. But it's not often. Not as often as the other way. Think about it, Jonas. If these people wanted commitment, would they keep coming to us?"

"Maybe they just can't meet people," he said.

Pike shrugged and sat quietly, and Jonas sat next to him, basking in the fire's warmth. "Anyway," Pike said after a couple minutes, "your fox didn't come look for you too hard. If he really wanted you to come with him, he'd have asked about you, wouldn't he? He'll be on the road and you'll see him again in the spring. Meanwhile, just try to relax. There are good things about our life, you know."

He covered Jonas's paw with his, and Jonas moved his paw away. Pike withdrew his, and folded his arms in front of him. They didn't speak again until Jonas said, "I think my paws are dry."

"Better get back to the Staff, then," Pike said. "I'll see you for exercises."

"Yeah." They both got to their feet, and stood awkwardly before Jonas pulled Pike into a hug. "I'm sorry again about your muzzle. Really. I was just..." He struggled to find words to describe how that betrayal had felt on top of Sasha's, but Pike touched his lips with a finger.

"I'll tell Tally I don't want to do blow jobs for a couple days. Don't worry, no permanent damage done."

"I didn't know we could do that."

"*You* can't. Age has its privileges." Pike stood on tiptoes and touched noses. "It's not as bad as it feels, kitty. Trust me. Okay?"

"Yeah." Jonas stepped back. "Thanks."

The glow of morning was creeping into the sky, making it easier for him to get his bearings. He found his way back to the main road, and trudged back towards the Jackal's Staff, turning his back on the dawn.

He couldn't escape the feeling that he was returning to jail. Having been given a taste of freedom, would he be able to tolerate his life for much longer? What he really needed was someone he could trust, someone he could devote himself to, and he didn't think he would find that at the Staff. What choice did he have, though? Alexan was gone, and there was nobody else in his life he could trust.

His paws slowed. Alexan hadn't gone yet. The gates would be locked until dawn.

Tally had given him the day off. He wouldn't be expected to come in.

If he were to be stuck at the Staff for years to come, at least he would not have passed up every chance to make a new life for himself. After a glance in the direction of the palace and the Jackal's Staff, he turned and walked purposefully towards the rosy skies over the eastern gate.

Chapter 4

Jonas beat the sun to the eastern gate by a few minutes. He hesitated at the back of the fifteen wagons waiting to leave, mounts asleep in their traces, the owners just stirring. Alexan would be near the rear of the pack if he'd been to the Staff the previous night. As stealthily as he could, Jonas investigated the rear wagons, but none of them held the smell of fox. Heart pounding, he padded through the darkness to the wagons closer to the front, and now that the owners were waking up, he could stroll by and see that only one contained a fox, and he was short and stocky, definitely not Alexan.

Jonas had just walked past the next-to-last wagon when a heavy paw fell on his shoulder. He was not accustomed to looking up at anyone, but he had to raise his muzzle when he turned in order to meet the eyes of a large, muscular wolf guard.

"Looking for something?"

"A friend," Jonas said.

"Right. Clear off."

Jonas twisted away from the guard's hold. "Really, he's supposed to leave today and I lost track of him..." He trailed off, realizing how improbable it sounded.

The wolf stared down at him. "I suppose you wouldn't mind waiting with me and the other guards over at the guard house to see if any of the drivers recognizes you."

"No, not at all."

That surprised the guard. "Really?"

"Sure. I'll help out if there's anything I can do."

"I'm sure you'd like that. No, we're appointed by the King himself and you're not. So there'd be nothing for you to do but stand there all day."

"That's fine." Jonas started to walk towards the guard house.

"Hey." The guard hurried to catch up with him. "Look, you can't just stand at the guard house."

"You told me I could."

"I thought you were a thief!"

"Well, I'm not a thief." Jonas folded his arms. "Will you help me find my friend?"

The wolf looked at the guard house, then back at Jonas, his nose twitching. Jonas suspected that for the first time, the wolf was really taking his measure, and he leaned forward politely to return the scrutiny. The wolf was one of the largest he'd ever seen, and his scent was rough but clean. And also, Jonas noted, not the least bit aroused. He was sure the wolf could sense even the mild appreciation Jonas felt for his sturdy form and soft brown pelt.

"All right." The wolf stepped in front of him and gruffly motioned him forward. "But only this one day."

"That's fine." Jonas nodded and fell in behind the guard.

He watched the guards pull the gates open and check the contents of the wagons cursorily before waving the merchants through. The first fifteen wagons passed, and four more after that, none carrying the fox. He remained in the shade of the guardhouse as the sun rose, and it was just when he was starting to feel the warmth of the day that a small wagon rattled up to the gate with a long, lanky fox at the reins.

"Property?" the badger guard asked as the wolf went around back to sniff at the wagon.

"Wooden weapons, and some leather," the fox said, and then blinked. "Jonas?"

Jonas smiled, stretching, and walked towards the wagon. He put his paws up on the riding board. The wagon was shabbier than he would've thought, and a little smaller, but he only looked at the fox holding the reins. "Hi, Alexan."

"Come to see me off?"

Jonas fidgeted. Here was the part that he had always imagined would go smoothly, and now his tongue felt two sizes too large for his muzzle. "I was hoping, er…I mean, I want to go with you."

The words hung there between them, as the wolf came back and nodded to the badger. The badger waved Alexan through. "Go ahead. Safe passage to you."

Alexan appeared not to have heard. "Back with me? And do what?"

"Well…" Conscious of the stares of the two guards, who were now watching him and listening, Jonas said, "You said you wished I could come with you. So now I can."

The guards turned to look at Alexan. He flicked his ears, and said steadily, "Don't you have responsibilities?"

"I'm giving them up."

In the silence that followed, the wolf said to the badger in a loud whisper, "Five coppers says he takes him."

"You're on," the badger whispered back. Jonas ignored them and just looked up at Alexan's thoughtful muzzle.

Finally, the fox extended a paw down to him. "Come on aboard, then. We'll figure it out."

Jonas was up on the board in a second. He smiled at Alexan and waved down to the guards. "So long. Thanks."

The wolf grinned at him, but the badger looked cross and just waved the wagon through. Jonas saw him reach for his purse as they rumbled by.

Alexan stayed quiet as the wagon clattered down the road, so Jonas didn't break the silence. Houses of wood rather than stone crowded both sides of the road, newer buildings put up quickly and inhabited, by the look of it, by poorer people than lived inside the city walls. Jonas saw naked cubs chasing each other through the narrow spaces between the houses, and once a pair of wolf cubs darted in front of the mounts pulling the wagon. Alexan didn't seem to notice, and his mounts barely snorted, stepping placidly around the scampering forms. The cubs vanished behind a row of hanging linen clothes, carefully patched, and Jonas heard squeals and giggles as a linen shirt was dragged down to fall atop the two cubs.

"Someone's going to get switched for that," he said, looking back as the wagon moved on. The shirt was no longer moving, but it was definitely filthy. A small muzzle peeked out from under it, looking around, and then ducked back under.

"Mmm." Alexan kept staring forward.

Jonas sighed. "I thought you'd be happy to see me. You said you wished I could come with you."

"Did I?" Jonas felt his heart sink, but the fox turned to him a moment later and smiled. "I guess I did. It's just a little surprising, that's all. It'll be good to have your company on the trip back."

Jonas smiled in return. "How long a trip is it?"

"Two weeks or so." He paused and glanced at Jonas's shirt. "Through the mountains it can get kind of cold."

"We'll have to cuddle up together for warmth." Jonas touched the fox's leg tentatively. "No charge, now."

Alexan flicked an ear and grinned, but the grin faded quickly. "Don't you have an apprenticeship or some kind of contract?"

Jonas stared straight ahead at the road. "You don't have to worry about that."

"Who does?" Jonas didn't answer, but Alexan persisted. "I just want to make sure that there's not a policeman waiting for me next spring."

"I said, don't worry about it," Jonas said.

"If you don't tell me, you can just step down right here." Alexan spoke quietly, but his tone was deadly serious.

Jonas laid his ears back. This wasn't at all what he'd envisioned. Pike's warning echoed in his ears, and for a brief moment, he thought he would step down and let Alexan go on his way. But he looked around at the poor housing, envisioned himself in one of the rickety houses, and sat back against the board. "My father got a payment from Tally when he sent me there. If I didn't last seven years, he had to give part of it back. And I wasn't allowed to go to any other establishments. Not that I'd want to."

"How long had you been there?"

"Three years."

"Mmm." The fox stroked his muzzle. "Does your father keep track of you? Is he likely to come after me for money?"

"I haven't talked to him since he sent me there."

"All right." Alexan flicked his ears. "I don't expect there will be a problem with you working in Ferrenis. Contracts don't hold much weight across that border."

"Work? I thought I could just…"

Alexan looked at him. "Just live with me? I'm not that successful yet. I don't know if I can feed us both."

"I thought you said you were doing well."

"I *hope* to be doing well." Alexan patted Jonas. "But I like the idea of having you all to myself. If I can make it work, I will."

Heartened by that, Jonas brought his ears up and smiled. The houses were thinning out, and the countryside ahead of them was mostly farmland. As they crested a small hill, Jonas could see the range of mountains in the distance. "We have to cross that?"

"Aye. The pass should be okay for another few weeks. I'm cutting it a bit close. I had some negotiations to wrap up." He glanced at the cougar. "So why didn't you work last night?"

"I was working." Jonas told Alexan the whole story, adding only a little bit here and there to make the fox feel more sorry for him.

"I didn't know they beat you when a client complained." Alexan looked sideways at Jonas. "You were really thinking about me?"

Jonas nodded. "I was thinking about you all week."

Alexan's tail twitched. "Does it still hurt?"

"Hurt? No, I'm here now…" It took Jonas a second to realize what Alexan meant. "Oh. No, I got used to it. The bruises fade pretty quickly."

"That's good. You're a tough one."

Jonas smiled and leaned back, breathing a little more easily. "I'm just glad to be here. Thanks for letting me come along."

Alexan patted his leg again. "You'll have plenty of time to thank me." He winked, and Jonas smiled, looking up at the sky as they left the last of the city behind them.

They stayed that night in a small inn. Two other wagons, both driven by farmers, had joined them in an informal caravan. After dinner with the farmers and their wives, they retired early to their small room.

Jonas had thought that Alexan's feral intensity in bed might have come from going a week between trysts, but apparently the cause was deeper, because the previous night's activity hadn't mellowed him at all. Once he'd barked and snarled out his climax, though, he panted and licked Jonas's ear. Then, tied to Jonas, he turned with some difficulty, setting the cougar on his back while he knelt between Jonas's legs and proceeded to apply his muzzle. Compared to Pike or Sasha, or even some of Jonas's more experienced clients, he wasn't very good, but Jonas was aroused enough that it didn't take him long to finish.

Alexan looked down at him and licked his muzzle, smiling. "So now you can enjoy it too." He slipped out of Jonas and pulled the cougar into a hug.

"Mmm. I did." Jonas smiled and held the fox against him, and drifted into a warm, happy sleep.

They kept company with the farmers for the next few days. The elder farmer, a raccoon, left the road first, followed the next day by the younger couple. The husband, a rugged-looking rat, had told them he and his wife were settling out on the fringe of civilization, where there was a lot of land. Jonas and Alexan waved as the rats' wagon turned down a narrow lane, leaving them alone on the road.

Several wagons bound for Divalia passed them going the other way, and from the drivers they gathered that the pass was still navigable, but that there were bandits about. Only one wagon had been attacked, but many had seen them.

"I'm glad I've got you with me," Alexan said to Jonas after a bobcat had painted a vivid picture of the bloodthirsty bandit leader he'd spotted. "Even if it is unlikely that he saw him that close."

"There don't seem to be many attacks," Jonas said, and Alexan shook his head.

"I've never been bothered. But I'm still glad to have you with me."

That was the first night they did not have an inn or a farmhouse to sleep in. The mountain loomed ahead of them, snow-covered peaks rising above the dark mounds of the nearer hills, and they stopped just on the eastern side of one of the hills, sheltered from the wind. Alexan brought out some cured meat and they shared it, sitting in the grass on the side of the hill while the mounts grazed, tethered, below them. Jonas had his arm around the fox and his eyes on the stars twinkling above them. The air was chilly, but his fur was warm enough, and Alexan didn't seem to be complaining either.

When they'd finished, they lay back on the grass. Jonas turned towards Alexan, and they kissed under the stars and then made love slowly as the mounts watched through sleepy eyes. Perhaps Alexan was affected by the stars and the romantic moments, or perhaps it was simply that he was unused to having Jonas more than once a week; whatever the reason, he was gentler than usual. He insisted on being on top still, but this time he slid a paw under Jonas, and they came within a minute of each other.

Lying on the grass, panting, Alexan moved his hips and said, "I love this. Being locked inside you, feeling your body under me…"

"Mmm-hm." Jonas's eyes were closed. He couldn't remember when he'd felt this happy. He wound his tail around Alexan's leg and inhaled the scent of the grass and earth in the crisp, cool air. The fox's weight atop him was warm and comfortable, and after a while, the soft sound of his even breathing lulled Jonas to sleep.

They reached the border outpost the next day, two clusters of buildings astride the road at the base of the first mountain. As they came into view, Alexan stopped the wagon. "Get in the back," he ordered Jonas.

"Why?"

"I give them some papers, some money, and they let me across. If they see you, they'll want more money and there might be other complications."

"But…" Jonas saw from the set of Alexan's ears and jaw that he was not going to win this argument. "All right."

He clambered into the back of the wagon and curled up as Alexan threw a blanket and some boxes over him. It felt as though he were being hidden because the fox was ashamed of him, but Jonas drove that thought from his mind. Of course it made sense not to vary a routine, especially when it came to a border he wasn't supposed to be crossing.

When they emerged from the pass the next day, Alexan drew up the team for a moment. Jonas was already staring breathlessly at the vista before them. The slopes of the mountains ran down into a plain whose emerald contours were interwoven with a shining river that ran to a city. It hurt Jonas's eyes to try to see the tiny details of the city, but he could see plainly to the south of it the reddish hills and the large lake, almost a sea, that lay at their feet. Though clouds still hung in the air over them, the plains were bright with sun, and Jonas couldn't wait to get there.

"Officially, we've been in Ferrenis for a day," Alexan said, and pointed a black paw down at the plain. "But that is really Ferrenis."

Jonas tried to follow the road as it wound down towards the sea of trees and fields. "Are there towns on the way to the city?"

"Sure. Right there, by the river—see?"

And there was a small collection of buildings there that he hadn't noticed before. He continued to gaze down at the plain as Alexan started the cart again and the wagon picked up speed. They traveled faster as they descended out of the snow, and with the warming air, Jonas's mood improved.

They reached the first town in Ferrenis the next day. Foothill was a small town, but Alexan seemed happy to reach it. "The edge of the country," he called it. "The Royal Patrol takes care of most bandits from here on."

They saw two patrolmen, a burly wolf and a surly-looking weasel, when they went to get dinner in the local pub. The patrolmen looked up as they walked by and sat up straighter. Jonas thought at first that they knew Alexan, but then realized that they were looking at him. In fact, everyone in the pub was looking at him.

Even after he sat down across from Alexan, he heard murmurs and caught glances in his direction. Alexan didn't seem to notice, or if he did, it didn't surprise him. Jonas finally leaned across the table and whispered, "Did I do something wrong?"

Alexan's ears flicked and he grinned. "No. Why?"

"Everyone's looking at me."

"Are they?" Alexan looked around, and Jonas felt certain now that he'd noticed and was just pretending he hadn't.

"Yes."

Alexan chuckled. "You really don't know why? Don't you know anything about Ferrenis?"

"No. Just that they don't understand the Houses of Gaia and they don't like us."

"Religious differences aside, the ruling family of Ferrenis are cougars. All cougars in this country belong to some sort of nobility."

Jonas didn't see Alexan's amused reaction to his surprise. The fox's growled "your highness" now made sense, and he remembered another fox now who had done something similar; that was where Alexan seemed familiar from. It had been a couple years ago, the fox was some noble at the palace who'd chosen between Jonas and Richy, he recalled. And he'd called him "your highness," then denied it. Jonas filed that thought away for later reflection.

"So they think I'm a noble?"

"My guess is, they're wondering why you're so shabbily dressed."

His clothes weren't any dirtier than anyone else's in the place, but Jonas suddenly felt very self-conscious. "Maybe we should go."

"Why? Let them look." Alexan waved to the rabbit walking by with a tray. "Two ales and two dinners, whatever's hot."

She nodded and walked away. Alone among the people in the bar, she didn't seem interested in Jonas at all.

Jonas didn't quite manage to ignore the scrutiny over the course of the evening; he was so used to being in tune to what people wanted of him that he found himself staring back at the pair of mice, the raccoon, the weasel, wondering what they wanted. By the end of the meal, he'd managed to stop himself from looking back at them, but he still felt their eyes on him, like fleas in his fur.

He told Alexan he wanted to eat in the wagon at the next town, but the fox dragged him into the public-house anyway. By the time they got to Caril, Jonas had been stared at more than in his entire career at the Jackal's Staff. When they reached Alexan's house, he thought, and met his friends, they would get used to him. There, he could feel comfortable.

The house was small but neat, one of ten in a row along a side street not too far inside the western gate. Brick with white wood trim, like all the other houses, it differed from them only in that one of the front windows appeared to have a broken pane. It stood two stories tall, but was narrower than it was high, and the roof was slanted to the back. Despite Alexan's long absence, the house looked to be kept fairly neat, with the exception of the broken window. A grey fox came out of the house when they pulled up, wearing a simple linen dress, a blue apron, and a surprised expression.

"Master Alexan," she said, curtseying as he stepped down, though her eyes remained on Jonas. "Is this good news?"

Alexan grinned at her. "Julianna, this is Jonas."

"Pleased to meet you." Jonas extended a paw, and Julianna took it warily.

"Are you sponsoring Master Alexan? Or are you here to investigate…?" She eyed his clothes as she spoke.

"Neither," Alexan cut in. "Jonas is going to be staying with me."

"Oh," she said, and then nodded, almost winking at Alexan. "I see. Very good, sir. Shall I prepare the spare room?"

Jonas started to say no, but Alexan spoke first. "That will be fine, thank you, Julianna."

"Pleasure to meet you, sir." The grey fox curtsied and walked briskly into the house.

"The spare room?" Alexan was already walking back to the wagon, but Jonas stayed where he was standing.

"Sure. What about it? It's clean."

"No, I mean…"

Alexan was starting to lift a crate out of the back of the wagon. "Will you come give me a paw with this already?"

Jonas didn't say anything more as they moved the crates of weapons into the house, to a storeroom in the back. Several crates were already stacked there, and the smell of wood was strong in Jonas's nostrils. "Why didn't you take these to Tephos?"

"They weren't here when I left." Alexan glanced at the crates. "Some of the merchants I deal with bring things by while I'm away. They know by now that I'm good for it." He hurried out again.

Jonas watched Alexan as they moved crates, trying to figure out the fox. At times he didn't seem to want Jonas around at all—and then he'd given him his coat and smiled that smile. And he had invited Jonas into his house. So maybe it was presumptuous of Jonas to have thought they'd be sharing a room. These things would come in time, he told himself. And it was nice going to bed without a sour aftertaste in his muzzle, or an ache under his tail.

All the same, as he pulled the blankets over him and curled up alone, he missed Sasha, Pike, Richy, Alicar, and even Tally more than ever.

Chapter 5

Jonas had a chance to examine Alexan's merchandise before he got to meet his friends. Alexan had him inventory the stock as he carried it out to take to his local market stall. He had a number of finely carved bows with intricate designs that made Jonas want to trace them over and over with his claws; he had a number of wooden handles without blades that had simpler designs but were made from exotic-smelling woods. They felt smooth and good in Jonas's paw.

Also in his inventory were a number of finely fletched arrows—without tips—and some narrow wooden darts. Then there were shields, all wooden and of various sizes; they took up the most room. A few had beautiful designs around the edges, but most were unfinished in the front.

"The buyer has them painted," Alexan said when Jonas asked him about it. "Just count them, okay?"

He'd come back from the market that day in a bad mood. Normally he liked to talk about the weapons because he was proud of his merchandise, and Jonas had hoped that would distract him from whatever was bothering him. "What's the matter?" he asked, but Alexan ignored him and went on inspecting Jonas's numbers.

"Are they okay?" Jonas asked when the fox put down the paper. Alexan had a strange look in his eye, a worrisome look.

"Come on." He grabbed Jonas's wrist and led him to the bedroom, where he pointed to the bed. "Get undressed."

"What? We haven't even had dinner yet."

"We'll eat later. Get your clothes off." The fox was already unlacing his own trousers, pushing the door closed with his body.

Jonas stared at him for a second, then undressed. Whatever was bothering Alexan, he'd be more relaxed after sex.

He'd barely turned over before the fox was on him, thrusting and biting harder than Jonas had ever known him to. He bore the assault steadfastly, even when the fox's sharp teeth sent lances of pain through his shoulder. "*There*," Alexan growled, "your *majesty*, how do you like *that*," with thrusts and bites punctuating his words.

It was all over soon enough, and Alexan was left locked inside him, panting hard. He licked Jonas on the shoulder and said softly. "You're bleeding."

Jonas wasn't surprised; he'd had to make an effort to keep from crying out at the sharpness of the pain. All he said was, "You were upset."

"Yeah." Alexan started to lick at Jonas's wound. "The king…" He shook his head, then went back to licking.

"He did something?"

"Maybe. See…the reason I can trade in weapons is because the law prohibiting weapons trade between us and Tephos only says that trade in "bronze and steel" is forbidden. Wood and string aren't mentioned. So I'm legally safe, even if really nobody is supposed to be going over there. But the king is considering a provision banning anything that could be used as a weapon. It'd ruin me. It's because of that whole trouble with the assassin a couple years ago. Like that had *anything* to do with weapons!"

"Ow." In his excitement, the fox's claws dug into Jonas's side.

"Sorry." Alexan relaxed. "Not your problem."

"If it's bothering you, then it worries me."

Alexan stroked down Jonas's side and found his sheath. He squeezed it, but Jonas wasn't very aroused. "You don't need to be worried."

"What are you going to do?" Jonas tried to relax and enjoy the stroking.

"I need to find a noble sponsor, someone with the King's ear. If he can sway the king…there are a couple merchants who supply to me who I might be able to get to join me."

Jonas let the stroking wash over him, closing his eyes. "Is there something I could do? Maybe help get in with one of the cougars?"

Alexan laughed without breaking his strokes. "You? You're just a prostitute. Don't worry about it."

He kissed Jonas's ear. Jonas sighed, stopped talking, and focused on his growing arousal. But his climax, when it came, was more a relief than a pleasure.

The next night, Alexan was more relaxed, and Jonas enjoyed himself considerably more. Afterwards, he lay with his arm around Alexan and the fox's paw brushing his stomach's fur, and he felt good enough to give the fox a kiss.

Alexan nuzzled him back and kissed his nose with a smile. "You don't have to go back to your room tonight if you don't want to."

"I'd like to stay."

"Mmm."

Jonas nuzzled his ear. "Will I get to meet some of your friends?"

"Sure." Alexan sounded amused. "Why?"

"Well, it just gets lonely here during the day. Julianna doesn't talk to me much."

"You should spend more time with her, maybe help her out a bit. You're almost done with the inventory, right?"

Jonas nodded. "A couple more days."

"Okay. Well, help out Julianna for a bit, and I'll bring some friends over soon, I promise." Alexan squeezed Jonas's paw. "I do want you to meet them."

That made Jonas smile, made his heart swell, and reassured him that everything was going to be all right.

When Alexan did bring his friends by, three days later, Julianna had made a nice stew for them, and Jonas had helped her clean up the dining room. He wanted to get dressed up, as Alexan had, but the fox didn't have any clothes that would fit him, and of course Jonas had no other clothes. "You'll be fine," Alexan assured him. "They won't be looking at your clothes."

He was wrong, but Jonas tried to ignore the searching stare he got from Mikka, the short grey fox who was the first to arrive. In truth, Jonas was staring just as hard down the foot and a half at the fox, never having seen someone so flamboyant. Even Tally didn't have metal bangles in his ears, gold or silver, though he might have worn the fox's loose purple shirt. It was open at the chest, revealing a fluffy white chest ruff bordered with rust-colored fur that also ran up his throat to his chin. White cotton pants below an arched tail drew Jonas's eye down to the really remarkable part of Mikka's wardrobe: a pair of leather boots decorated with a beaded pattern.

Jonas had heard of footwear, but had never seen anyone wearing any. He wondered whether Mikka's paws were injured; if so, his stare would be considered rude, but Mikka didn't seem to mind. "Like them?" he said. "I can get a pair in your size without a problem. Though you really would want to get more than just that."

"Thanks," Jonas smiled as Alexan looked on, amused. "Aren't you cold?"

Mikka ran a paw through his chest ruff. "Oh, a little, but you know, it's worth the sacrifice."

"Sacrifice?"

"To give the rest of you something to look at." Mikka gave him a slow wink.

"All right, that's enough," Alexan said. Jonas half expected him to be angry, but he was smiling. He led Mikka into the dining room and Jonas followed.

The next guest to arrive was Taypha, a small, portly bear. He too looked over Jonas's clothing, but without the implicit judgment Mikka had applied. Jonas smelled ale on his breath, and thought that ale was probably also responsible for at least two of the stains on his worn vest. His linen shirt was clean, as were his pants, and though they were the same material as Jonas was wearing, both were of better quality and in better shape. "Pleased," was all Taypha said when his meaty paw grasped Jonas's, weakly.

Jonas shook back and smiled, and as a second carriage was just drawing up, he waited to greet it while Alexan took Taypha into the dining room.

A small red fox got out, about Mikka's height. He paid the wagon driver and started up the stairs, and only then did he see Jonas.

His reaction surprised Jonas. Instead of mild surprise, as the others had shown, he did a double take and took a step backwards. Then he peered more closely and came forward, ears back in what Jonas thought was embarrassment at his initial reaction.

Jonas extended a paw. "Hi, I'm Jonas. I'm not a noble."

"Oh. Benton. Pleased to meet you." He looked Jonas up and down. "Alexan didn't say…"

"It's okay, everyone has the same reaction." Jonas smiled. "I think you're the last to arrive, so we can go in."

"It's not that," Benton said, following him inside. "It's…"

"Hi, Benton." Alexan met them at the door. "Come on inside."

Alexan sat at the head of the table, with Mikka and Taypha on his right. Jonas sat on Alexan's left, with Benton on the other side of him. Julianna served the wine to start with and everyone turned towards Alexan.

He raised his glass. "I would like to introduce you all to Jonas, who has come all the way across the mountains to stay with me."

The others raised their glasses and Jonas, caught off guard, didn't know whether to lift his and drink or not. He left his on the table and just smiled as everyone else took a sip. Three glasses came back down almost in unison; Taypha's came down several seconds later and he signaled Julianna for a refill.

"So is this a permanent thing?" Mikka smiled, both paws on the table. "He is a cute one."

Jonas blushed and smiled, taking the opportunity to sip his own glass of wine. "I hope so," Alexan answered, smiling as well. "But it's only been a week. We both have high hopes, don't we?"

"I know I do." Jonas put down the wine and wiped his muzzle.

"So where do you come from?" Taypha asked, slurping his second glass of wine. "What'd you do? I guess you're not a noble."

"No, I'm from Tephos."

"How did you meet?" Mikka, this time looking at Jonas.

"Well…" Jonas paused.

"He worked in a brothel and I was his best customer," Alexan said cheerfully.

Benton looked down at the table; the other guests looked with interest at Jonas. He glanced quickly across all their eyes, feeling as though Alexan had stripped his clothes off in front of them. "A prostitute, really?" Mikka said. "I always wanted to try that. If I hadn't had to take over my father's business…"

"You wouldn't have had the money to gain so much knowledge about brothels," Taypha rumbled.

"And if he'd been working at the Cat's Tongue, I'd have spent a bit more. Speaking of which, if you're looking for work here, I'm sure they have an opening."

He looked around for someone else to chuckle at his joke, but the

Kyell Gold

closest was Alexan, who merely smiled tolerantly. Mikka flicked his ears and made a little throaty noise that Jonas couldn't interpret.

Taypha lowered his goblet, signaling to Julianna again. "That must have been pretty interesting. But I imagine it would get tiring after a while."

Jonas was grateful to the bear for at least the polite pretense of understanding. He ignored Mikka's dainty snort. "There were a lot of good things, but there were a lot of things that I got sick of. I couldn't do any of the things I enjoyed."

"And so you rescued him from sexual slavery. How romantic!" Mikka had turned to Alexan.

"Actually, he came and found me," Alexan said with a smile. "And I couldn't resist."

Jonas smiled. "He was the one I never got tired of." That had more than a little truth to it, and even Benton raised his head to smile then.

"Cheers to you both, then," Taypha said, raising his goblet again and draining it before anyone else had a chance to lift theirs.

"Where's Gaff?" Mikka asked Alexan. "You know Jeni's expecting again, right?"

"Again?" Alexan shook his head. "She's been lucky twice."

Taypha shrugged. "She's healthy enough."

"I hope she'll be all right."

"We all do." Mikka grinned around the table. "After all, none of us is having cubs anytime soon."

Julianna brought their dinners then, and the conversation was soon lost to hearty slurps and chewing noises. The stew she'd made was chicken, spiced with some kind of pepper that Jonas loved. After a week, he was getting over his surprise that the food on this side of the mountains was so similar. The meats and breads were the same, of course, but even the basic spices were very familiar. There were a few that he found exotic, like this pepper, and he liked them all. The wines and ales he'd tried had been different, but the meals he'd had could have come from any pub or house in Tephos.

After dinner, they retired to the living room, where Jonas sat next to Alexan while the fox talked to Mikka, on his other side, about his plan to approach the king. "I'll need some nice clothes, if I can get you to loan them to me."

Mikka jerked his muzzle towards Jonas. "For one night with him, you can *have* them." He was grinning slyly as he said it, and everyone laughed. Alexan didn't say anything further about it, but Jonas remembered what the fox had said about him taking up his work again, and felt a stir of unease.

"Benton, does your master already know about this proposal?"

The small fox nodded. "He is arguing with the woodcraft guild to gain their support. Since most of them don't make weapons, they are

Inside the Cage

divided about what to do."

"Ask him if there's anything I can do to help his cause."

"All right." Benton was sitting on the other side of Mikka, and the grey fox now turned to Alexan.

"Nice clothes," he mused. "The sort you might need to pay a visit to the palace?"

"Just that sort. I'm hoping to get a noble sponsor. I think that's the only way this will work. I have a couple names, but I need to sound them out and see how they feel about this issue."

"Very bold!" Mikka clapped the other fox on the shoulder. "Have you thought about maybe giving away some of your stock to the nobles? I can tell you, that really helps."

"Give away? Don't they have enough to afford anything?"

"Some maybe less than you think." The grey fox winked. "But regardless, if you couch it as a gift, they don't have a choice about whether to buy it..."

Jonas listened to the conversation for a little while before noticing that Taypha wasn't paying close attention. The bear sat patiently tapping his claws on the couch, and although he affected nonchalance, Jonas sensed that he felt bored, and maybe a little bit left out. He shifted a bit to his right, closer to the bear, and smiled when Taypha looked up.

"You're not in the merchant business?" he said, quietly enough that he didn't intrude on the other conversation.

Taypha shook his head. "I'm in the city guard." He shrugged. "Not very exciting."

"I'm sure there are exciting times." Jonas smiled.

Taypha shrugged again. "I guess."

"What would you rather be doing?"

"Drinking." The bear had brought his glass out into the living room, but was nursing this drink. He gave Jonas an abashed grin. "No, it's okay. It just seems like these fellows here get to see more things."

"Than a guard?" Jonas was genuinely surprised. "I bet you see all sorts of things they've never seen."

"Not pleasant things. Drunk people, criminals..."

Jonas laughed suddenly, so that everyone in the room looked at him. He waved the foxes away and waited until they'd resumed their conversation before turning back to Taypha. "Sorry, you just reminded me of something. We had this one customer...this otter. He used to come in roaring drunk and demand to be serviced, but usually he couldn't... you know, manage to..."

Taypha nodded, a smile creeping across his muzzle. Jonas continued. "Anyway, he'd start cursing really loudly and then usually he'd fall off the bed, stagger around for a while, and fall asleep. Once he surprised the guy who'd taken him," it had been poor Alicar, who didn't know what to expect, "and staggered into the hallway naked. He shut the door behind him and nearly got out into the main room before we caught him."

Taypha was laughing quietly now. "The funny thing was, he would come back the next day, pay handsomely, apologize, and say he couldn't remember anything but he was sure he'd had a great time. So once we got to know him, we used to fight over who got to take him. He was the easiest client I ever had."

"Well, I never met a drunk that interesting. Though there was this one raccoon who climbed up to the rafters of the inn and peed on everyone below him." He grimaced. "That was funnier when it was over."

Jonas giggled behind a paw, picturing the scene. Taypha leaned back and smiled, then tilted his head. "Who was your most difficult customer? Heh. I was about to say 'hardest,' but that's a different story, isn't it?"

Jonas was spared having to reply by Alexan, who leaned over and put an arm across him, mock-growling at the bear. "Hey, no flirting with my cougar."

"I'll snap you in half, stick-fox," Taypha said mildly, grinning.

"You'll have to get past him first." Alexan squeezed Jonas's upper arm. "Look at these muscles."

"I have been," Mikka murmured from behind him.

Alexan went on. "Anyway, you're so drunk you probably can't tell which of the three foxes you're seeing is me."

"One, two, three," Taypha pointed at Alexan three times, and everyone laughed. "Don't worry, Red, I couldn't possibly compete with you."

Alexan shook a finger at him. "That's right."

Jonas put an arm around Alexan and smiled. "And I wouldn't let him."

The fox resisted the touch for a moment, and then leaned against Jonas. His earlier conversation apparently over, he glanced around the room. "Your boyfriend couldn't make it, Benton?"

Benton shook his head. "Working late again. He's in charge of a whole regiment," he said proudly to Jonas.

"Glad you could get away, at least."

Benton smiled. "Your dinners are always fun."

Jonas thought he heard Mikka murmur, "You don't know the half of it," but halfway through whatever it was Mikka said, Alexan was telling Jonas that Benton's boyfriend was also a cougar.

"Oh? He's not a noble either?"

"He is, yes," Benton nodded. "He's from a small barony out east. So he has an honored position in the guard."

"Oh." Jonas sat back on the couch. It would have been nice to find other non-noble cougars employed somewhere.

"Speaking of which, I should probably get back to him." Benton stood up. "Thank you for the hospitality and the interesting ideas, and welcome back, Alexan."

"I should go too." Taypha put his glass down and stood up. "Got to be up early tomorrow."

Mikka was showing no signs of leaving. Alexan glanced at him and then patted Jonas on the shoulder. "Can you see our other guests out?"

"Sure." Jonas stood and waited while the bear and fox paid their respects briefly to Alexan, then followed them out the front door.

"Got to walk up to the main street there to catch a cab." Taypha gestured and started walking down the small street they were on. Benton and Jonas followed behind.

"So you're going to be staying with Alexan," Benton said. "That's nice. I'm glad he's got someone. And another fox-cougar couple, too. Mostly the gay cougars pair up among themselves. And the straight couples, you know, always same species." He flicked his ears. "That's how we do it in our country. I don't know about over the mountains."

Jonas smiled. "It's the same there too. I'd like to meet your cougar someday."

"I'm sure you will. He just works a lot in the evening."

"How long have you known each other?"

"Known? Years. We've only been together for a couple years though." Benton's tail swished.

"It sounds like there's a story there."

"Maybe for another time." Benton grinned. They'd reached the main street, and Taypha was already looking down the street to an approaching cab and signaling it. The goat driving pulled the cab over to the side.

"Benton, you want to share? I think you're on my way."

"Sure." The fox extended a paw to Jonas. "Nice to meet you, Jonas. Hope to see you again soon."

"Same here." Jonas clasped the fox's small paw in his own, then turned and grasped Taypha's paw as well.

"Good to meet you."

"Likewise." Taypha didn't seem to be showing the effects of his drinks, but then again, he weighed as much as the three foxes put together, so maybe he had a higher tolerance for it.

They climbed into the cab and rattled away down the mostly-empty street. Another cab came up from the opposite direction driven by a bear; he slowed in front of Jonas, then sped up again when the cougar waved him on.

Jonas took his time walking back down the street, while the few people who were out hurried past him, not even looking up to see the clouds part around the moon. He admired the sight all the way back to the house, thinking that it had been a promising night. He'd enjoyed meeting Alexan's friends. True, he wasn't really a friend to any of them yet, but he felt that would come in time. None of them seemed off-put by his profession, and if Mikka was more interested than Jonas was comfortable with, the interest seemed harmless.

The house was empty when he returned; at least, all but Alexan's room was, and that was locked. He rattled the door handle once, then retreated without pushing his nose to the door to sniff who might be inside. Alexan must have seen Mikka off and then gone to bed, he thought, but even though he tried hard to convince himself that that was the case, he knew that Mikka hadn't gone far, and Alexan hadn't gone to sleep.

Chapter 6

If Mikka had stayed the night, he left without Jonas noticing. Alexan was cheerful the next day, and Jonas didn't ask him why his door had been locked. He would just have to be a better mate, he told himself. And he couldn't expect Alexan to just give up any relationships he'd had. After all, he'd imposed himself on the fox's life. And maybe nothing had happened. All the same, he let Julianna clean the fox's bedroom that day, fearful of the scents he might pick up on the sheets.

They sat down to dinner that night and Alexan looked very pleased, relaxed, and content. He always did, after sex. But Jonas listened to the echo of Pike's words and smiled, determined that he would not be one of the former prostitutes who fled relationships. Alexan was providing him with a roof, and food. If he were patient, and showed Alexan how much he trusted him, the fox would return the sentiments, he was sure.

After dinner, they sat together in the living room and sipped wine. "Did you have a good time last night?' Alexan asked.

Jonas nodded. "I like your friends. Are those your closest friends?"

"Some are. I've known Mikka forever. Benton only for a year or so. But those are my gay friends. I thought you'd be more comfortable with them. We'll have Gaff and his wife over next week."

"All right." Jonas relaxed and lapped at his half-glass of wine. "How did your planning go?"

"Very well. I think we have a good chance of success. It will take a couple months, I'd say, but certainly before I would be leaving next year."

"Good."

After a pause, Alexan said, "But there's something else I wanted to ask you about."

"Hm?"

"Do you think you could handle the cleaning by yourself?"

Jonas tilted his muzzle. "Why? Is Julianna leaving?"

"Could you?"

"I guess so."

"Okay." Alexan took a drink. "It's just more expensive than I'd thought providing food for us both, and this plan is going to take money too. If we could do without her, that would help me out a lot."

"All right." Jonas sighed and brushed the fox's ear. "If it'll help you."

"It will. Thanks, Jonas." Alexan smiled and kissed him.

Jonas still felt uneasy about it, but Alexan kept kissing him, and he had little choice but to kiss back. And then their clothes somehow ended up on the floor, and as Alexan was fitting Jonas's erection into his muzzle,

Jonas knocked over his glass of wine. *I'll have to clean that up*, he thought, but the thought faded away into pleasure at the caresses of the fox's tongue. Alexan took him all the way in and finished him nicely, licking as Jonas thrashed in pleasure under him. And then it was Jonas's turn to swallow the fox, and he tried not to imagine that he could taste Mikka's scent on the long member as it slid over his tongue. He held Alexan as the fox gasped and thrust into him, and then his muzzle was full of distinctive musk and he didn't have to worry about other scents.

They curled up together in the bed Julianna had made for the last time that day, and Jonas thought it wouldn't be all that bad.

And for a while, it wasn't. Alexan got angry twice at mistakes Jonas made in cleaning, but after that Jonas learned well and did a better job. After all, mates could have fights, but the important thing was to learn from them. Jonas knew that, and so he did his best to learn.

They visited Gaff and his wife for dinner, partly because Jonas didn't feel he would be up to cooking a dinner, and partly because Alexan didn't want to pay to host another dinner so soon. Gaff proved to be charming and witty, and his wife was pleasant as well. Jonas met the older of their two cubs, a precocious young vixen who was hushed by her parents for commenting that Jonas's clothes were dirty.

Mikka and Taypha returned frequently, but Mikka did not stay the night again. Benton returned only once in the month following the first dinner, again without his mate. Jonas didn't have much of a chance to talk to him except for a brief conversation when Benton was showing off a wooden knife hilt he was working on.

They went to Gaiaday services in a small chapel nearby that did very generic services and allowed each member of the congregation a moment of silence to say prayers to their own god. Alexan found the passage in the book for Cougar, but Jonas was unused to such a specific god and intoned the prayers he knew by heart for Felis. The services were similar enough that he felt he was still heard.

Otherwise, Alexan didn't include Jonas in many of his plans during the day. Only once did Jonas get to see the small booth he rented in the market, and then the excitement of the market overwhelmed his reaction to Alexan's booth and wares, most of which he'd already seen. The fox was petulant after that, and no matter how much Jonas apologized, Alexan never invited him back to the market.

Jonas did manage to surprise Alexan one night when he met him with a fully cooked fowl and a nice, smooth honey mead. Taypha had brought them by at Jonas's request and he'd given Jonas a little bit of cooking help and advice. The bird was a little dry, but not bad, and the mead was wonderful. Alexan didn't even realize until Jonas told him that it had been exactly one month since their arrival in Caril.

"An anniversary?" Alexan sounded amused.

"I thought it was worth a little extra." Jonas sniffed the fowl. "Taypha

Inside the Cage

helped me with the cooking. I've never done a whole bird before."

"Your cooking's getting better," Alexan said, chewing. "I really don't miss Julianna."

"I do," Jonas said. "Just 'cause I'm doing all the work now."

Alexan laughed, and when dinner was over, they moved immediately to the bedroom. It was good; Alexan remembered to slide his paw underneath for Jonas, and they came almost at the same time. And afterwards, Alexan hugged him affectionately and said, "I'm glad you came with me."

The next week, Alexan came home with Mikka, unannounced. Alexan was wearing a beautiful white silk shirt with ruffles cut into it, and blue and turquoise patterned pants that Jonas didn't recognize. Both he and Mikka were in high spirits. The grey fox actually greeted Jonas with a hug, the first time he'd done so, and Jonas hugged back tentatively. "I hope we have enough food."

"I'm sure you'll make do," Alexan smiled as he and Mikka sat down. "I've been telling him about your cooking."

Flattered, but still flustered, Jonas retreated to the kitchen and hurriedly cut an extra piece of bread. He apportioned the meat three ways in his mind and stroked his whiskers. The portions would be a little small, but would do. But there were only two carrots. He decided he would do without.

"I don't really like vegetables," he explained to Mikka when he put the plates down.

Mikka touched the carrots and smiled. "Well, I appreciate them. I'm sure this is delicious. Where's the sauce?"

"He tends to burn the sauces," Alexan said.

"Only twice!" Alexan had been angry the first time, but tolerant the second, either as a result of his mood that day or of just being used to it. The fact that he was joking about it was a good sign, Jonas thought.

After dinner, Alexan opened a new bottle of wine, one of the nicer ones from his collection. Jonas accepted the proffered glass with a little surprise, and sipped from it while Alexan and Mikka took longer drinks of theirs. They made small talk for a few minutes, and then Mikka excused himself to use the outhouse.

As soon as he'd left, Alexan put down his glass and leaned towards Jonas. "I need your help again," he said.

"Of course." Jonas set down his glass as well. "What's wrong?"

"I borrowed those clothes from Mikka." Jonas nodded. "Only...I couldn't just borrow them. Because I'm a fox, see, and my scent gets into the fabric...you know. So he said I had to buy them from him. But I don't have enough money for that. So I asked if there was another way I could pay for them."

"Oh." Jonas fought to quell the slight nausea in his stomach.

Alexan nodded. "It would really help me out. It's only one night..."

"All right."

"…every two weeks."

"What? For how long?"

"Just a few months."

'So, six times?"

"More like ten."

Jonas sighed. "You already told him I'd do it?"

Alexan shrugged. "I didn't think it would be that big a deal. I mean, you used to do it all the time anyway."

"Yeah, but that was…" *Another me, a long time ago.* He looked into the fox's eyes and thought, well, it wasn't that long ago. And he did warn me that I might have to work. And really, he never said that we wouldn't be sleeping with other people. I just thought (*hoped*) it.

And deep down inside, wasn't there a part of him that was just a little bit curious, that missed the variety of all his clients? Less than he would have thought, surprisingly.

"All right," he said. Mates helped each other out, he reminded himself, but a little voice that sounded like Pike asked in the back of his head, *don't they also care enough to ask first?*

The fox smiled, giving Jonas another uncomfortable twinge because he thought it didn't look like a smile of relief, but rather a smile of satisfaction. Of course, he was just being suspicious because he was upset. He put it out of his mind.

When Mikka returned, Alexan got up immediately. "I'm a little tired," he said, but Jonas didn't miss the flick of the ear he gave to Mikka. "I think I'll turn in, if it's not too rude of me."

"That's okay. We can use the other room if you want," Mikka said.

"Whatever you like." Alexan turned and touched Jonas's nose with his own, and then bowed. "Good night, Mikka. Do visit again soon."

"I will," the grey fox purred. "Sleep well, my friend."

And then Alexan was gone, and Jonas was left in the uncomfortable silence of the living room. "I think I'd prefer the spare room, if you don't mind," Mikka said, and got up, tail swishing. For a moment, Jonas considered not following him, but he couldn't see any other course of action open to him. He got up and walked into the room that he'd grown to consider his, and closed the door behind him.

Mikka had his shirt off almost before Jonas had the door closed, and dropped it beside him on the floor. "Now, let's see what's under those clothes," he said, running his paw through his own chest ruff.

Jonas undid his own shirt and slipped it off. He moved a paw to his pants and then stopped, trying not to notice Mikka's rapt attention. The whole scene felt almost surreal to him, as though he'd just dreamt the last month and he'd never left the Jackal's Staff. Maybe, he thought as he undid the lacings on his pants, Mikka was a new customer, and Jonas had been dreaming about him with Alexan in the dream. Perhaps he would wake up in his bed, and he could walk out in the morning and tell Pike about his dream. But then he'd be sad that he wasn't free. Wouldn't he?

"Ooh," Mikka breathed, stepping close to Jonas. "Pretty." He cupped Jonas's sac and weighed it, then stroked a paw up his sheath. "You think I'm pretty too?"

"Oh, yes." Jonas fell into the old patterns easily. It helped that Mikka was really rather striking.

"Want to see more?"

"Very much." He found the fake eager smile somewhere back in his memory and pulled it to his muzzle. The arousal was harder to fake, and slower to arrive, but once he set his mind down a certain path, he grew harder against Mikka's paw.

"Ask me."

This was not an unfamiliar game to him. "Please, show me more."

"Do you really want it?"

"I really do." He licked his lips for effect.

Mikka seemed pleased by that. He grinned and turned around, arching his tail, and wiggled his pants lower. Jonas whistled appreciatively. "I like that." Some clients liked to be touched at this point, some didn't. Jonas felt that Mikka wanted him to wait for permission before touching, so he held back.

The grey fox wiggled more, showing off his rump, and stepped out of his pants to turn around. He was already fully aroused, cupping himself in his paws. "May I?" Jonas said, stretching a paw forward.

Mikka nodded eagerly, and from there on it was all routine. He slid his paw up the fox's long, thin member, up and down, and Mikka returned the favor with a small, firm grip. Jonas was careful not to go too quickly, gauging the fox's arousal level and changing his strokes to match. His paw was slightly sticky from the dripping shaft when Mikka pulled away from him with a gasp and turned around, dropping to all fours.

"Get on top," he panted, "and don't be afraid to get me all sticky."

The fox proved easy to slip into for such a small body. He'd obviously had a lot of experience. Jonas shut off those thoughts before they could lead back to the other fox in the house, and just thrust in and out, making sure to apply his paw below the fox's quivering belly, not stroking too hard, because he thought Mikka would come pretty soon anyway.

He was right. Barely thirty seconds later, the trembling fox erupted all over his paw. The body beneath him tensed as throaty gasps of pleasure rose to his ears. With practiced ease, Jonas mimicked the gasps and started to thrust harder himself, as if gripped in the throes of similar passion. Mikka wouldn't be able to tell until maybe later.

"Ohhh," the fox moaned under him, wiggling free. He panted and rolled to one side, lying on his back, his tongue lolling out as he grinned up at Jonas. "I wonder if Alexan wants any more clothes. I'll have to ask."

"Mm-hmm." Jonas grinned back and allowed Mikka to caress him a couple more times before stepping carefully off the bed and retrieving his pants.

"Aww," Mikka said as Jonas pulled them on, and for a moment Jonas was afraid the grey fox would have more demands. But he remained quiet as Jonas dressed, and only when the cougar was done did he slide off the bed and do the same.

"Thank you," he said, standing on tiptoe and reaching up with his muzzle. Jonas lowered his and accepted the kiss. "I'll see you at least in a couple weeks. Maybe sooner. Just for dinner," he laughed, petting Jonas's chest.

"Oh, okay."

"Unless Alexan buys more clothes." Mikka winked and swished his tail as he left. "I know the way out, thanks, dear."

And then he was finally gone. Jonas sat on the edge of the bed and wondered why, with his past, he felt so guilty. Alexan had pushed him into this, and they had no arrangement, so there was no question of betrayal. Not on his part, anyway. He wanted more than anything to go curl up with Alexan, but not the Alexan in the other room; he wanted the Alexan who'd come to see him at the Jackal's Staff, who'd been so kind to him, and so understanding, who'd promised him a release from that life. He'd wanted that release, and had thought that a single mate would provide it, but how could he reconcile that with what he'd just done? He would have to find a way.

The sheets were sticky, so he pulled them off the bed and curled up on the bare bedding, trying to imagine somewhere he could wish to be.

Inside the Cage

Chapter 7

"I don't want to do that any more," he told Alexan the next morning.

The fox looked at him with some surprise. "All right. I won't make any more deals after this one without asking you."

"I don't want to do the rest of this one." He folded his arms, trying to disguise his nervousness.

Alexan sat back and studied him. "Oh. I see. Was Mikka that bad?"

"No, it's me. I left that behind. I don't want to do it any more."

The fox stroked his whiskers and nodded. "Well, all right. I'll come to some other arrangement with Mikka."

"Really?" Jonas lowered his arms.

"Sure, if that's what you want."

Jonas sat down at the table. "Well…thanks. I really appreciate it."

Alexan tapped a claw on the tabletop. "It means I'll have to find some other way to pay him, of course. I won't be able to afford to feed us both, so you'll have to find some kind of work."

Jonas's tail sagged. "I…I don't know what I could do."

"You'll have to do something. I can't afford to be trying to improve both of our lives and feed and clothe us if you're not willing to help me."

Alexan had never bought him clothes, but Jonas was feeling too panicked to bring that up. *Abused you 'til you ran away*, he could hear Pike saying. He wanted to run, but he wasn't really being abused. Alexan was giving him a choice, after all. Besides, if he ran, where would he run to? And what could he do other than be a prostitute?

He lowered his muzzle. "All right."

Alexan was gracious in victory. He patted Jonas's arm. "I don't like it either. I'd rather have you all to myself. Someday, when this plan comes together, I will." Jonas looked up to see his bright smile.

Every day, Alexan went to his market stall in the morning, and in the afternoon he courted his noble sponsor. He was affectionate when he came home, and Jonas was usually able to coax him out of a bad mood on the few days when things didn't go right. Mikka's next "payment" came and went without much incident, leaving Jonas still feeling dirty, but at least accepting his role and looking forward to the end of the term.

Then Alexan brought home Phineas, a nervous-looking rabbit who kept fidgeting from foot to foot and looking over his shoulder. Alexan explained to Jonas that Phineas dealt in jewelry and had agreed to be a partner in his small enterprise. But the jewelry Alexan needed to borrow was fantastically expensive. Phineas would agree to loan it to him provided he signed over his house as collateral to the loan, but the price of the loan itself also had to be settled...

And Tarrit, the otter who had access to another noble who might prove strategic to his cause...

Jonas complained again, after Tarrit, but Alexan met his complaints with anger. "Do you know how much money this is costing me?" he growled. "Do you know how hard it is to find a merchant who'll take anything but the money I don't have? I'm risking all of this to make a better life for us."

"I know. It's just..." Jonas wanted to say, I don't want you to see me as a prostitute. I want you to see me as a mate. But how can you when you just keep whoring me out to pay for things? But he knew that was unfair. Alexan was a shrewd merchant who was using every resource he had to attain what was a very difficult goal.

"Just what?"

"Nothing. I'm sorry." And he didn't complain again. It helped that the people Alexan brought home were mostly well-to-do and kept themselves fairly clean. And none of them had violent tastes. Mostly they seemed to want to pretend that he was a noble, usually the king or the prince.

The snows fell, the festival of Gaia came and went, and Jonas felt his life falling back into familiar patterns. He had fewer clients than he'd had at the Staff, by far, but then again, he often reflected, at least at the Staff he'd been paid. He resumed his exercise routine, which he'd let slide, and found himself grooming his fur, keeping it short—doing all the things Van Wyck used to do. It disturbed him when he thought about it, so he stopped thinking about it.

He tried to bury his frustrations and worries in his home, but the few good nights were barely enough to keep his spirits up. The evenings with Alexan's friends were a welcome distraction, and though they treated him well (*better than Alexan*), he still felt hesitant about presuming on his nascent friendships with them. They all had their own lives, after all, and better things to worry about than a lonely cougar. So he cleaned obsessively, and searched out delicacies in the marketplace more for the satisfaction of cooking with them than out of any hope of making Alexan happy.

Stubbornly, though, he did cling to hope—that this was just a passing phase, that when Alexan's scheme had succeeded he would pay off the deals, get rid of Jonas's "clients," and that they would stay together happily. He hoped that there wouldn't be any more days when Alexan stalked around the house glowering at everything, and that all of the coldness he felt was just because of the weather.

Jonas stepped outside one day and found that the chill in the air had broken. Playful breezes tossed scents from throughout the city to him, borne further than usual on the humid air of spring. A fox cub ran down the street laughing, his tail streaming out behind him, and his exuberance broke through Jonas's numbness and brought a smile to his lips.

Inside the Cage

Whether it was the weather or not, Alexan's mood lightened from that day on. He returned home with a spring in his step that night, greeting Jonas with a kiss and the news that his noble had been spending the day talking to the king. He gave Jonas a necklace that night, a small pendant with a golden cougar's head on it. "I borrowed this from Phineas," he said. "I want you to have it."

"Oh," Jonas said, and his eyes filled with tears. He hugged Alexan tightly and kissed him. "I love it. Thank you so much."

"You deserve the best," Alexan said.

They kissed again, and made love, and long after Alexan was asleep, Jonas held the pendant and turned it this way and that, watching it catch the moonlight in its curves, holding its weight in his paw, feeling the smoothness of the gold against his pads. When he woke in the morning, Alexan was gone, but the pendant had been carefully placed on the night table and it glinted in the morning sun as he opened his eyes. He took his old family pendant and left it on the table that morning, wearing the gold one instead.

Alexan remained in good spirits for the next few days, until the day of his noble sponsor's appointment with the king. The noble had promised to espouse his cause, he told Jonas, and the king was inclined to listen to him. There was a meeting of the merchant guild leaders scheduled in a week, and the king was expected to announce his decision there; having the noble's audience so soon before the expected announcement was considered good.

The night of the audience, Alexan brought Mikka, Phineas, and Benton home. He'd stocked wine and mead in preparation for the occasion, and they had obviously already been celebrating. Phineas tripped twice on the way in, and Mikka's laugh was more high-pitched and frequent than usual. Jonas tried to join in the celebration, but felt more comfortable sitting near Benton, who was also quiet and apparently sober.

Dinner was a quick, informal affair, and they were soon sprawled out all over the living room talking about their noble sponsor and congratulating Alexan on his success. Jonas could see why Benton would be happy, but he didn't understand why Mikka and Phineas stood to benefit until Mikka made a remark about his clothes getting wider distribution, and he realized that Alexan must have promised to distribute their goods in Ferrenis in addition to his other payments.

Phineas fell asleep in the middle of one conversation, and after shaking him awake, Mikka said, "I'm tired too. Come on, Phineas, I'll take you home."

"A'right," the rabbit mumbled.

"Oh, stay a while," Alexan said. "At least you, Benton. You're not d-drunk."

Benton eased back into his chair. Alexan accompanied Mikka and Phineas to the door, entreating them to stay over Mikka's quiet refusals.

"Your mate's still working late?" Jonas asked Benton.

Benton nodded. "He's trying to help us afford a better apartment."

"Can't he get help from his family?"

The fox shook his head. "He doesn't want to ask them." He sighed. "It's complicated. But it's all right."

Jonas could see that it was, even if Benton's smile was a bit hesitant. He smiled back. "I'm glad to hear that. I still hope I can get to meet him."

"Me too." Benton's tail wagged, which Jonas thought was just adorable.

Alexan came back into the room, and a glance at him made Jonas uneasy. The tilt of his ears and the set of his muzzle were familiar—not bad, not yet, but not far off. Before Jonas could say anything, Alexan waved a paw at him. "Getting all comfy? Why not show Benton some real hospitality?"

"Oh, I'm fine," Benton said brightly.

"Jonas has a lot of ta-alent. I'm sure he could think of something."

Benton looked puzzled now. "I don't understand."

"Oh." Alexan sat on the couch and fumbled at the lacings of his pants. "Jonas, come over here and show him."

"I..." Jonas looked at Alexan, hoping the fox could still stop.

"Why not?" Alexan smiled and let his sheath and rising erection out into the air.

Benton was still looking down at the floor, but as Jonas glanced at him, he got up. "Maybe I should get going. It's kind of late."

"Oh, sit down, Benton," Alexan said lazily, grinning widely now. "Don't be a prude."

Benton paused and then reluctantly sat down, tail curled around his lap. Jonas almost encouraged him to leave, but Alexan had leaned over and pulled his head around. "Come on, kitty," he said, smiling. "It's a happy occasion."

Jonas abandoned his pleading eyes and lowered his head. Alexan, unlike some clients Jonas had known, did not have the ability to perform well while intoxicated. Jonas's tongue badly needed a rest by the time the fox's seed splashed across it.

"Now do Benton," Alexan said. "We don't want to leave him out."

"I don't..." Benton started.

Alexan cut him off. "Come on, Benton. You're used to c-cougars. Jonas wants to d-do it. Don't turn him down."

Jonas looked at the smaller red fox and saw his reluctance in his eyes and ears. He stood up. "Actually, I think I'll go to bed. I don't feel so good."

"You've got time," Alexan said, no longer sounding drunk.

"I really don't feel so good." Jonas glanced at Benton and gave him the briefest of encouraging smiles, and then walked into the spare room.

The water jug by the bedside table was empty, and there was nothing else in the room to wash the taste out of his muzzle with. He sat down on the bed and closed his eyes, drawing his knees up to his chest and curling his tail around himself.

He deliberately tried not to listen to the noises outside. Focused inward, he didn't even hear Alexan come into the room until the fox spoke.

"What the hell was that?"

Jonas raised his head. "What?"

"You embarrassed me. In front of my friends and business partners."

"I said I don't feel good."

"I know what you said. You felt good enough to do me. How do you think that made Benton feel?"

Jonas couldn't think of any response to that. Hadn't Alexan noticed, hadn't he seen? Jonas thought Benton couldn't have broadcast his feelings any louder if he'd shouted "I feel extremely uncomfortable with all this!"

Interpreting his silence as guilty assent, Alexan continued. "He left right away. He works for one of my most important contacts!"

"You don't…"

"Quiet." Alexan slapped his muzzle, hard, and Jonas recoiled, eyes wide. "I don't understand how you can suck anyone who pays you a few silver pieces for years, but suddenly you get all squeamish when it really matters. You think this is bad? If you cost me a relationship with Master Talid, just wait and see. You'll be doing this full time again."

Shocked, and more than a little afraid, Jonas watched Alexan leave the room and close the door behind him.

In the dark hours of that night, Jonas imagined asking Benton to help him get away and establish himself, because Benton was the only person he'd met in Caril who didn't view him as a prostitute (apart from Taypha, but the prospect of Jonas joining the guard was ludicrous). But each time the idea surfaced, he dismissed it as ridiculous. Benton had his own life and his own boyfriend, and Jonas didn't fit in anywhere that he could see. The problem, the thing that he couldn't get past, was that he didn't fit in with Alexan either. He no longer really believed they could have a life together.

The next morning, he lay curled up in bed as the light streamed in through the windows. Normally, he would get up to make breakfast, but the events of the night before had left him listless. He watched dully as the light grew brighter and higher, and if Alexan hadn't come in around mid-morning, Jonas might have spent the whole day in bed.

He cringed when he heard the door open and caught the fox's scent, but Alexan's voice was cheerful. "Hey, sleepyhead. Come on, I made some oatmeal and it's getting cold."

Bemused, Jonas rolled out of the bed and stretched, then walked into the dining room. Sure enough, two bowls of oatmeal sat steaming on the table. He sniffed, irrationally worried that one might be poisoned or something, but they smelled fine. Alexan had even added honey.

"Go on, sit down. It won't get any warmer!" Jonas jumped at the touch as Alexan patted his back, then sat down. He wanted to say something about the previous night, but if Alexan had forgiven him then he didn't want to bring up the matter again. Maybe, he thought suddenly, he doesn't actually remember. Maybe he was drunk and that's why he got so angry. It wasn't really him.

As the day wore on, he became more and more convinced that that was the case. Alexan talked about what a great party it had been, and how excited he was that things were finally coming together, and the ugliness that the dinner had degenerated into never entered the conversation.

Jonas spent the next few days convincing himself that that night had been an aberration, and that he'd overreacted by thinking of leaving the fox. Alexan was unfailingly sweet to him for the remainder of the week, and at the end of the week, in services, Jonas prayed to Cougar to keep the fox in a good mood. Did Cougar have any influence over his brother Fox? He hoped so. He didn't know what else to do.

The following day was Feliday, and the king's meeting with the merchant guild was scheduled to happen at midday. Actually, an increasingly nervous Alexan told Jonas, the king would meet with his ministers in the morning, and then would accompany the minister of Trade to the meeting, but the minister of Trade would do most of the talking. His noble sponsor was going to try to be in attendance but had not been able to secure an invitation. He would hear of the decision from one of the ministers, but Benton would hear from his master before then. News would trickle down to him somehow.

He expected Benton first, or perhaps Phineas or Mikka, when Jonas heard the knock and hurried to answer the door, Alexan behind him. When they saw Taypha, Alexan's ears flicked up and he smiled. "Come to wait for the news?"

Taypha shook his head. "I've got the news," he said, and Jonas could read what it was in the slant of his ears and the flatness of his voice.

"Well, come in, come in!" Alexan ushered the bear into the living room. Jonas closed the front door and sagged against it. All for nothing. What would they do now? Alexan's business was worthless, his contracts with Mikka and Phineas probably worthless as well. He had a clientele in Tephos, but they knew him as a weapons dealer, and Jonas suspected the fox didn't have the inclination to build up a new trade.

Taypha came back to the door a moment later. He put a paw on Jonas's shoulder. "I'm sorry," was all he said. Jonas nodded and let him out.

He started to walk back to see how Alexan was doing, but the fox brushed past him and headed for the door as well. "Alexan, are you..." Jonas didn't even get to finish his sentence before the fox was out the door and down the stairs, his bushy tail waving furiously behind him.

Should he go after him? Jonas decided against it. Better to let him work out his anger and then come home. He closed the door softly and went to the kitchen to see what he could find for dinner.

There were some leftovers from the celebratory party, which he'd been saving for tonight. Now, they seemed full of hubris, and he felt that neither he nor Alexan would have the stomach for them. The only other thing he had was some old fowl from two nights ago and a loaf of fresh bread. If he had any money, he could go to the market and get some vegetables, at least, but Alexan hadn't left him any money.

He was just throwing some wood into the stove to start preparing the chicken when he heard a faint knock at the front door. Maybe Alexan had sent someone home with food, he thought, and then he realized that it was more likely to be Benton, not knowing that they already knew the news. It sounded like Benton's knock.

The short red fox was indeed standing on the stoop when Jonas opened the door, his ears back, staring down at the ground. He looked up and saw Jonas, and his muzzle worked for a couple seconds without producing any sound.

"It's okay," Jonas said. "We heard." Then, because he wanted some company, he asked, "Would you like to come in?"

"How did you hear? I came here as soon as I heard."

Jonas stepped back, and after a moment's hesitation, Benton followed him into the house. "Taypha came by. I don't know how he knew."

"Oh." Benton fidgeted. "Master Talid wasn't happy. He dismissed the new apprentice. Says he won't have enough work to keep us all busy."

"Does he blame Alexan?"

"Oh no! He knows Alexan did the best he could. He said the king told the guild that it was a very difficult decision, and that he weighed the different sides very carefully. He even almost apologized to Alexan's sponsor, I guess."

"I wonder what the other side was," Jonas mused.

"Master Talid said that the king preferred to err on the side of caution. The assassination," he said that word in a whisper, "still hurts him to think about, and he said that the one thing he would never forgive himself for would be if a Tephossian assassin succeeded in his mission using a Ferrenian weapon."

"I guess I can see that." Jonas sighed. "Alexan isn't happy."

"No, I don't imagine. What's he going to do? Where is he?"

"I don't know. He ran out." Jonas looked toward the kitchen. "Benton, could you do me a favor? I want to make a nice dinner, but I don't have any vegetables or fresh meat, or any money. Can you pick up a couple things for me? I promise I'll pay you back."

The fox smiled. "Sure." He patted Jonas on the arm. "I hope you can help Alexan get over this." But as he said that, his ears flicked partway back, and Jonas knew he was remembering his last visit.

"I'll try my best." The cougar returned Benton's smile. "I appreciate your help."

Watching the fox's bushy tail as he walked away, so much calmer than Alexan's, Jonas realized that he hadn't been overreacting, that night after Benton's last visit. He knew that things would not get better with Alexan. He sat alone in the living room, thinking, and the decision was not hard to make.

Benton returned before Alexan did, with a bag of vegetables and a freshly killed fowl. "You'll have to pluck it yourself," he said apologetically.

"That's fine. That's great." Jonas took the bag with a smile. "Thank you so much."

Benton's tail wagged and his ears perked up. "Take care of Alexan."

"Listen, Benton..." Now that the moment had come, his resolution wavered. He shored it up. "I might need to find some work, and...and a place to live."

The fox's ears flattened. "To live?"

Here was the hard part. Did he tell Benton everything? The fox had seen Alexan the other night. He settled for generalizing. "I'm just...I don't know if he'll be able to afford to keep me here. I know it'll hurt him, but I can't stay."

Benton chewed his lip. "I don't know if there's anything I can do."

"Just keep your ears open. Please."

"A-all right. You know, you could stay with us for a couple days if you really need to..."

Now he felt guilty; obviously he'd made Benton feel bad so that the fox was offering something he didn't really want to. "No, I don't need to. Just...if you hear anything..."

"I'll let you know. I promise." Benton clasped his paw before leaving.

Jonas occupied himself with plucking the fowl, normally a job he detested. Today he was happy for his paws to have something to do so he wouldn't be occupied with worrying about what Alexan was doing or what his future would be like, or about what he'd just done. He was afraid of leaving, but he was more afraid of staying, and however Alexan felt about his departure, the fox would have to deal with it. Jonas wanted badly for it to work out, and he still hoped that maybe it would, but he would have to prove that he could do something other than prostitution.

But even though he kept telling himself he wanted it to work out, a part of him told himself that he was running away, betraying Alexan. For that reason, maybe, he put extra work into the meal, attending the stove more faithfully than he usually did and roasting the vegetables with some of the spices left over from former meals.

The first warning Jonas had of Alexan's return was the slamming

Inside the Cage

of the front door. He heard the fox's claws click on the wood floor and called, "Give me fifteen more minutes for dinner."

Alexan appeared at the doorway to the kitchen. He held what looked like a golden circlet in one paw; it took a second glance before Jonas realized it was a wooden crown, painted gold. "Later," he said roughly.

Immediately wary, Jonas backed towards the stove. "Just a few minutes."

Alexan jerked his head back into the house. "Now."

Jonas glanced to the stove, then back at the fox. He nodded. "All right."

He followed Alexan into the fox's bedroom. Alexan kicked the door closed and held out the circlet. "Put this on," he growled. "Take everything else off."

"Alexan…"

The fox shook the circlet at him. "Do it. I need this."

Jonas breathed hard. Didn't he owe Alexan this one last time? One last time for now, he amended. Please, Felis, let it be quick.

He took the circlet and settled it on his head. As quickly as he could, he removed the rest of his clothes and got up onto the bed. Alexan muttered behind him, "Do that to me, will you? Your Highness, you'll pay for this, yes you will." He didn't have to turn around to know that the fox was aroused; he could smell it and a moment later he felt it as Alexan pushed up behind him and into him, hard.

He winced and tried to take it, but he was starting to feel sick. Each thrust burned and Alexan was trying to force his already swollen knot in. And then the fox's teeth met in his shoulder, and he yowled.

"Shut up!" Alexan half-panted, half-growled, and his claws dug into Jonas's chest.

Jonas rolled over, unable to take any more, and pushed the fox away. Alexan was already breathing hard, and his eyes were wild as he stumbled back. He still wore his shirt and his pants were half down. He lunged back at Jonas, and Jonas scrabbled wildly, getting a foot pulled back and planted in Alexan's stomach.

"Don't," he gasped.

Alexan swiped at his face. "Get back on your knees." His breath was coming in ragged gasps.

Reacting to the swipe, Jonas kicked and then kicked again when Alexan came back at him. The fox stumbled back and slammed hard into the wall. He took a step forward and then collapsed back against the wall, wheezing. Slowly, he dropped to the floor, his back against the wall. He put a paw to his chest, muzzle gaping open.

Jonas sat up and backed away on the bed, watching with wide eyes. "Alexan."

"You…" Alexan's gaze was fixed on him, his ears flat back against his head. "You…"

His paws hovered, helpless.

Inside the Cage

Jonas watched as the fox fell forward, clutching his chest with one paw while the other supported him. "Alexan?" He crawled cautiously to the edge of the bed and only clambered off it when the fox fell to the floor.

The fox's eyes were not angry now. They were scared and pleading. "Can't…breathe…"

Jonas's paws traveled over the fox's chest, but he didn't know what to do. His paws hovered, helpless, as Alexan struggled to pull air into his lungs. He knew he should go for help, but he couldn't bring himself to leave the fox. Jonas held him for five more agonizing minutes, until the light went out of his amber eyes and his slender frame stopped struggling.

Terrified, Jonas let the body drop to the floor. He moaned, shaking his head and trying to pull his eyes away, but he couldn't make himself move. This must be another dream, he told himself, and any minute now I'll wake up. The room's eerie silence reinforced that feeling, until it was broken by a low whimper that it took him a moment to realize he was making.

Alexan's body stared vacantly at his paws. Jonas backed away from the body and then grabbed his clothes and fled the room. He dressed as quickly as he could and then he ran.

Chapter 8

The tears finally came when he realized he was lost. The houses around him were unfamiliar and no familiar smells came his way. He stumbled around corners and past startled-looking people, and only when a cub called out, "Is that the king?" did he realize that he was still wearing the fake crown. He threw it into the gutter and ran away from it.

A plan formed in his mind as he wandered blindly through Caril, and he turned towards the reddish light of the sunset. When he came to the wall, he followed it until he came to the gate. Three wagons stood in the small area there, and he approached them cautiously, listening to the people inside talk.

In the third wagon, a pair of rabbits was talking in low voices. He listened to them and his spirits rose when he heard one of them say "With Herbivora's help, we'll be there in a week." Herbivora. Not Rabbit.

He coughed and said, "Excuse me." The talking inside stopped. One of the rabbits poked his head out and looked warily at Jonas.

"Yes?"

"Please take me with you," Jonas said. "Back to...back across the mountains. I was brought here against my will to be a prostitute, and I need to go back."

The rabbit considered. "You have money?"

His spirits sank. "No."

Dark eyes flicked down to his neck, to where the golden chain disappeared into his shirt. "Let's see that pendant."

His paw covered the small bulge in his shirt where the golden cougar head rested. "No."

"Well..."

"Wait! I have information...that the King will pay you well for." He dropped his voice to a whisper. The idea had come to him suddenly.

"What's that?" The rabbit's eyes narrowed.

"There's a noble in the palace who's a Ferrenian spy."

"Lots of nobles in the palace."

"I'll tell you his name when we get there." Jonas didn't know the name, but he could find out from Richy. The thought of seeing the young wolf lifted his spirits unexpectedly.

"What's his species?"

"I'll tell you when we get to the mountains."

"He doesn't have any information," a lighter voice inside said.

"He's a fox," Jonas said quickly.

"Red or grey?" came the voice from inside, but the rabbit watching him raised his paw.

Inside the Cage

"Enough," he said. "All right. Be back here at daybreak and we'll take you."

"Thank you." Jonas stepped back as the canvas at the back of the wagon dropped again and was fastened in place.

He found a sheltered store entrance where the slight wind couldn't reach him, and huddled in it to try to sleep the night. Worried about the rabbit's interest in his pendant, and fearful that someone else might come by, he took it off and slipped it into a pocket before resting his head against the chilly wooden door and closing his eyes. The wood was cold, hard, and unyielding, like iron...

The cage was made of iron, but he knew he could break it and get away from the jeering crowd if he could just find the right tool. He was alone and the cage was bare, but on his head was a golden crown. He pulled it off and looked at it, and then it was snatched away by a rabbit in the crowd, who put it on himself. 'Look, I'm King Cougar,' he said to great laughter.

'Give it back!' Jonas reached through the bars, clawing to reach the crown. His paw caught a fox that he knew, it was the noble who had called him "Your Highness" back at the Jackal's Staff, just as Alexan had done. "Give it back or I'll kill him!"

He watched, horrified, as his dream-self said those words and held the struggling fox against the cage. The crowd laughed at him and he felt his arms crushing the fox, felt him struggling to breathe, and then felt him go limp.

The crowd grew silent. He let the fox slide to the ground.

The cage door swung silently open.

But the fox's body lay across the threshold, and now it was Alexan's blank eyes who stared up at him, and Jonas couldn't cross those eyes because as soon as he put a paw near them, he knew they would reach for him and drag him down, and then when the dead body started pulling itself toward him anyway, and put a cold paw around his ankle, that was when he started to scream.

"Easy, easy," a voice said roughly, and it was a familiar voice, but Jonas in his half-awake state thought it was Alexan's, and he moaned wildly, trying to scoot over on the bed. Only he wasn't on a bed, he was on a cold stone slab and the paw wrapped around him was not slender and black, it was large and brown.

"Taypha?"

The bear looked at him, and only then did Jonas notice that he was in uniform, and flanked by two other guards. "You okay?"

The sun was up. He twisted his head around to see the gate standing open, all three wagons gone. "I killed him," he said.

"Hush." Taypha put a paw to his muzzle. "Don't say anything yet."

He got stiffly to his feet, stooping at the shrill complaint of his muscles. His back was stiff and his legs cramped, but he managed to follow Taypha at a good pace.

"Benton came to see me," the bear said. "He went back and found Alexan...we've been out looking for you all night." When Jonas didn't say anything, Taypha continued. "You shouldn't have run. Are you okay?"

Jonas nodded. He felt a growing relief that he would not have to endure the trip over the mountain again, that he would not have to worry about how the rest of his life would go. He was headed for jail, and that was fine. After all, he had killed Alexan, unintentionally or not.

The guard station was a small building, but solidly built in reddish stone. The doorways and front windows were made of a matching reddish wood that looked more faded and worn than the stone itself. Above the doorway, a sign read "Divalia City Guards, Fourth Division." Jonas walked placidly up the stairs and let Taypha lead him into a small room with one barred window, high up.

"Shackles?" the wolf guard who followed them in said. He swung a key ring from one grey-furred paw.

Taypha shook his head. "He won't cause trouble. I'll vouch for him."

"All right." The wolf left, and Taypha knelt beside Jonas.

"Jonas, I'm going to come back with the head of the guard unit. He's Benton's mate. I brought you here because of that. Just...don't say anything that will get you in trouble, okay?"

Jonas nodded without really listening. He looked up at the window after Taypha had left, at the bright sunlight outside, and felt a pang of regret. If he'd never left Tephos, he would be miserable, perhaps, but certainly better off, and Alexan would still be alive. How much suffering had his foolish decision cost? All because he thought he deserved better, because he thought that he could be a good mate. Well, here he was, getting what he deserved. He sat down and looked away from the window.

It was probably an hour before a well-muscled cougar in a more gaudy uniform stepped through the door and closed it behind him. From his seat on the floor, Jonas looked up. The captain was striking, his uniform neatly pressed, and he walked with a noble assurance. His scent was clean and imposing, and beneath it Jonas could detect Benton's scent as well. The reminder of the small fox heartened him until he remembered Benton's hesitation when he'd asked for help the previous day.

The cougar squatted down beside him and gave him an encouraging smile. Jonas felt the small comfort of relaxation that came from meeting another of his species, and returned the smile.

"Hi, Jonas. My name's Jherik. Why don't you tell me what happened?"

Jonas started haltingly, but got the whole story out. "I must have... kicking him must have broken his chest. I didn't know what to do." He didn't tell Jherik about his prayer to Felis to help him, nor about his intention to leave Alexan as soon as he could. Those things sharpened the edges of his guilt, even buried in his mind; he didn't think he could stand to have them voiced aloud. He also didn't tell Jherik that Alexan had brought home a crown for him to wear, for fear of sullying Alexan's memory.

"I don't know if there's anything you could have done," Jherik said.

Jonas raised his eyes to the other cougar's. "What's going to happen to me?"

Jherik sighed. "I don't know. He was a respected merchant. You might be able to make a case for self-defense, but I have to admit I'm not convinced."

Jonas nodded. He wasn't either.

Jherik left him in the cell after bringing him a small meal. To his surprise, Jonas found that he was hungry, and he wolfed down the bread and cheese. When it was gone, he settled back against the wall. His paw came to rest on a pocket of his pants, and he felt a small bulge beneath. Reaching in, he drew out the golden pendant Alexan had given him.

It still looked beautiful, even in the half-light of the cell. He ran his paw over it again, and remembered the fox's face when he'd handed it to Jonas, and the tears started again. He clutched the pendant, rocking back and forth, and when he'd cried himself out, he curled up in the corner and held the pendant against his cheek.

They brought him another meal late that night, but no news, and when the light faded, he slept.

His sleep was untroubled by dreams, but when he woke, he had a moment of disorientation when he thought that he was back in Alexan's bedroom and the dead fox was just in the other shadowy corner. He thought he could see the glassy eyes staring back at him.

A guard outside pounded on the door. "What's going on?"

Jonas shook his head. "What?"

"You yelled. What's going on?"

"I did?" He closed his eyes. "I'm sorry. It was nothing."

"Hmph. Keep quiet, then." He heard the guard walk away. Jonas stood up, stretching his legs, and thought he might as well do his exercises, since he had the time and space. The workout let him clear his mind, and so he went longer than he usually would, until he nearly collapsed from exhaustion. Then he pulled his knees up to his chest and rested his muzzle on them, and tried not to think about the wagon of rabbits heading west, or of how long it might be until someone came to get him, or about whether he would rather be executed for murder or released onto the streets of Caril.

Around midday, by Jonas's estimation from the shadows on the floor, the door opened again and Jherik beckoned to him. "Come on," he said.

Jonas stood on unsteady legs and followed him out the door. They passed several guards and a pair of prisoners before arriving at a small office.

"Can you write your name?" Jonas nodded. "Can you read? Good. I wrote up this report this morning. This says that we took you into custody and have investigated the case and found you innocent of any crime. Alexan's death was an accident."

Jonas shook his head. "I don't understand."

"We're letting you go," Jherik said patiently.

"I know, but...what changed between yesterday and today?"

Jherik leaned back. "I went back to my commanding officer with our report and your account of what happened. He said, and I agreed, that if we could find someone to vouch for your character, and there was no family member to press charges, we could let you go. We contacted Alexan's only surviving relative, and he wasn't interested in pressing charges. And then, this morning, your character was vouched for."

"By whom?" Jonas could barely get the words out. Someone had stood up for him? Said enough good things about him that Jherik was ready to let him go? Then he caught the lingering scent of fox in the air, and he knew even before Jherik answered.

"Benton. He said he'd known Alexan for a while and had gotten to know you well enough that he was sure you wouldn't do anything intentionally to harm him. He said you were planning to leave him, and my commander pointed out that while that might mean you were planning to kill him, you probably wouldn't have said anything in that case. You didn't tell me about that part."

"No." Jonas shook his head.

"Why not?"

There was a chair just in front of him, and he stepped forward to sit in it. "He'd brought me here, been so kind to me, and I felt so ashamed about leaving him. I thought...there was no point in saying it now that he was dead."

"You've no reason to be ashamed, from what Benton said. I only met him a few times, but from what I heard, Alexan didn't sound like a very nice character. No disrespect intended, of course."

"There were sides to him that nobody saw. When he wasn't trying to impress his friends, or worry about his success..." Jonas trailed off, aware of the weight of the gold pendant in his pocket. He wasn't sure whether he'd be allowed to keep it if he told Jherik about it.

The other cougar shrugged. "I suppose you knew him. Anyway, this is where I sign, and this is your signature affirming that I've explained the report to you." He scratched a signature on the bottom of the document and then tapped a blank section of the parchment as he slid it over to Jonas. Jonas took the quill and wrote a neat "Jonas" in the space Jherik had indicated.

Jherik examined the signature. "No family name?"

Jonas hesitated, then shook his head. Jherik shrugged. "Okay. Benton's outside. He wanted to wait for you."

"All right." Jonas wasn't quite sure what to do. "Are you joining us?"

"Nah. Too much work." Jherik grinned and patted him on the shoulder. "Go ahead. You're free to go."

"Thank you."

Inside the Cage

He felt curiously light as he walked out of the guard house, past the guards in uniforms who barely gave him a glance, past the prisoners and supplicants out into the daylight. The day was warm and the small fox on the front stoop stood with a smile when he saw Jonas walk towards him.

"Hi." Benton's tail was wagging.

"Hi, Benton. Thank you. I guess you helped get me out."

Benton smiled. "You deserved to be free. I know you wouldn't hurt Alexan intentionally. I just told Jherik that."

"Why?"

"What?" Benton looked puzzled.

"Why did you vouch for me? You barely know me. For all you know, I could've murdered ...him."

"Shh." Benton waved paws as a goat turned upon hearing the word "murdered." "I did it because I know you didn't. I mean, I know you're a good person and you deserve to have someone stand up for you. I didn't know if anyone else would."

"And Jherik believed you because you're his mate?"

Benton's ears tilted. "He believed me because he knows me and knows that I'm a pretty good judge of people."

"I don't know if I am a good person." Jonas looked down at the fox. "I was going to leave Alexan. And..." He didn't even know the name of the other fox, the one whose secret he'd sold, the one who'd collapsed in his arms in the dream.

Benton took his elbow and guided him down the street. "I saw the way Alexan treated you, showing you off like a piece of jewelry. I guess he had the right to, but you had the right to leave, too."

"He loved me," Jonas insisted.

"Maybe. I've seen love that looked awful strange." Benton let go of Jonas's arm, and the cougar paused for a moment before he continued walking.

"What do you get out of this?" he asked as he followed the fox. "You changed your mind about me living with you?"

"What?" Benton laughed. "One cougar is plenty for me, thank you. No, I just thought you needed help and it didn't look like anyone else was going to give it. Mikka...he and Alexan used to be close. I haven't seen him in a while, though. Taypha didn't know what to think. Phineas just wanted to get his paws on the house."

Jonas thought he heard a faint growl in that last sentence. He followed Benton into a pub, still trying to understand what the fox had done. During most of the lunch, he wondered whether Benton's motives could really be that simple, and at the end of the lunch, he was forced to admit that he could not see any other reason for what Benton had done than the one the fox himself had presented.

That disturbed him, mostly because he was forced to look back on his own life and realize that he had never done anything like that. His kindnesses to Alexan had been out of fear he might be put out onto the street. And then, as if the fox could read his thoughts, Benton said shyly, "I never thanked you. For the other night."

"What other night?"

"When Alexan made you...you know. And I didn't want to."

"Oh. You're welcome. I just knew you wouldn't enjoy it much." He smiled. "Or at all."

"I hope you didn't get in too much trouble for it."

Jonas touched his cheek. "No. Not too much."

"Good." Benton drank the remainder of his ale and looked thoughtfully at the cougar. "So what will you do now?"

"I don't know. Did you have a chance to look around?"

Benton shook his head. "I'm sorry. I asked Jherik about the guard, but he said there'd be complications, since you're a cougar and everyone would expect you to be a noble, and it might undermine the authority of the others."

"I can't fight anyway."

"What can you do?"

"Only..."

Benton lowered his ears and looked down. Then he smiled, peering up. "Well, there are a lot of people who pay for that. You might be able to make a good living at it. Oh, but you don't want to."

"I probably could." Jonas sighed. "But I'll have to think about it."

"You can stay with us for a couple nights if you need to."

He shook his head. "Thank you, but no. I already owe you enough."

"Just one night. We have a space where you could sleep. Until you decide what to do."

Jonas didn't want to accept, but he was too tired and confused to resist the allure of a safe place to sleep. "All right."

Benton and Jherik lived in a small apartment building with three other couples. They had their own stove, in the front room, and a separate bedroom. Benton unrolled a blanket from the closet and placed it by the stove. "I know it's not that chilly any more, but the nights can get cold here."

"Thanks." Jonas looked around the small space, and especially at several crossbows hung on the walls. "You did these?"

Benton nodded, and spoke up as Jonas leaned in for a closer look. "These are the ones that weren't balanced right or were mechanically flawed. Master Talid let me take them to practice designs on. Here, this one took me forever but Master Talid said he was very proud of it. I did it again on a good crossbow and he sold it for five gold pieces to a noble."

Jonas saw an intricate mesh of swirling lines. When he moved one way, he thought he saw a pattern, but when he reached forward to touch it, his fingers moved along a different path. Shifting his head to the other side, he saw still another false pattern, but his fingers found the true way even when his eyes were confused. "It's beautiful," he said.

"Thank you." Benton's tail was wagging again. Jonas envied him his enthusiasm about his work. He wished he too could make something lasting that people could admire. He didn't let the feeling flare into jealousy; Benton was not showing off weapons to shame him or show him up, and he still felt tremendously grateful to the little fox.

When Jonas stepped back from the weapons, Benton said, "I need to get back to the shop. Will you be okay here?"

Jonas nodded, confused again. Not only had Benton gone out of his way to rescue him; now he was trusting him alone in their house? "I'll be fine. I won't touch anything."

"We don't have much food, but that pub is just down the street."

"That's okay." Jonas smiled thinly. "I don't have any money."

"Didn't Alexan leave you anything? We'll have to go over there and see if we can get you some money later. I'll ask Jherik about it."

"You don't have to—" Jonas began, but Benton waved him quiet.

"Don't worry about it. Just think about what you want to do and if we can help you out, we will."

"Okay," he said softly. "Thanks."

When Benton left, Jonas paced around the apartment. No door separated the bedroom from the main room, but he still hesitated to step inside. It was rich with fox and cougar scent and the musk of intimacy, and it reminded Jonas strongly of Alexan's bedroom. He stood for a moment, feeling the low ache of regret, and then turned away.

The apartment on the whole looked prosperous, if a little on the untidy side, but he certainly couldn't fault them for that. He could, however, help. Forgetting his promise not to touch anything, he started organizing clothes and dusting the wall hangings in the outer room. At first, he placed the clothes in the doorway to the bedroom, but as the living room grew cleaner, he pushed the clothes into the bedroom, and then he felt guilty about that and went into the bedroom to organize them. He worried for a moment about invading their privacy, but having started to clean, he felt compelled to see it through. He found their wardrobe and hung up the clothes, and while he was in there, straightened and dusted until he coughed.

The thought crossed his mind that he could do this for a living, as he returned to the small table in the living room and sat down, but he was sure he wasn't very good at it, even if the apartment did look markedly better, and he was equally sure he wouldn't enjoy it. Looking out the window, he tried to absorb all that had happened to him in the last two days, and where he would go in the future. Possibilities flitted through his mind like shadows, none solid enough for him to grasp except for the long shadow of his former job.

He felt lonely again, wishing he could talk to someone like Benton, or

Richy, or Pike. His eye fell on an inkpot and a heap of discarded parchment sitting in a small cabinet beside the table. There was a small stack of clean parchment as well, but the discarded pile had the beginnings of writing on it. He recognized Jherik's handwriting and saw that they were mostly reports he'd begun writing and then discarded when he made some error. One of the pieces had only a couple words on it and then a large splotch. The obverse was quite clear and usable, if a little rough. Almost before he realized what he was doing, Jonas had taken it down and dipped a quill in the inkpot, and started to write.

Dear Pike, he wrote,

You were right. There. I haven't wanted to admit it, but you were right. I wish things could have turned out differently, but I find myself alone and friendless

He thought for a moment, then crossed out "friendless."

without prospects in a foreign country. I probably should have listened to you, but I was so desperate to get away that I did what I felt I had to. I would like to return to the Jackal's Staff, but I don't think I have the means at the moment, and I am sure Tally would not welcome me back anyway. So I will simply write to let you know that I am alive and healthy, and that I miss you and the others.

He put the quill down and looked out the window. When he'd started the letter, he thought he would just help clear his head by pretending to talk to Pike. But as the letter took shape, he felt more and more that he wanted the raccoon to see it. Pike had cared about him, and even if he'd betrayed him to Tally, he'd done it with good intentions and he'd been honest about it.

It was a while later before he concluded the letter.

If you should care to write back, please do it in care of Jherik at the City Guards, Fourth Division, Divalia.

All my love,

Jonas

He folded it and wrote "Pike, Jackal's Staff, Divalia" on the outside, then slipped the letter into his pants pocket. Maybe Jherik or Benton could find someone to take a message to Tephos.

Benton brought dinner with him when he returned home: a loaf of bread, some cheese, and a slab of fowl. He set aside a portion for Jherik ("he'll be home later") and then insisted on giving Jonas nearly two thirds of what remained.

"I talked to Master Talid," he said between mouthfuls, "and he said I can take tomorrow morning to go with you to Alexan's house and claim any money he might have left behind. I don't know if he had any family. They might already be there, if he did, but chances are there'll be something left. You probably know where he kept things better than they did."

Jonas nodded. "Jherik said he had some relatives but they didn't sound interested in him. So it's just 'finders keepers'?"

Benton shrugged. "Basically. For people with a lot of property there's laws, but Jherik says they're hard to enforce. In his case probably the big fight will be over his house. I don't think you'd have a chance of getting that, so you might as well take what you can."

"All right." Jonas thought about some of Alexan's things that he might want. He was sure that very little of the fox's clothing would fit him, but money and some of the other possessions would certainly be helpful.

Jherik came home late, and after eating his share of the dinner and telling them about his day on the job, he announced that he was tired and needed to sleep. "You can stay up and talk," he said, but Benton shook his head.

"I'm tired too," he said with a smile that told Jonas that he wasn't being entirely truthful. The cougar smiled at the affectionate gesture as the two of them bid him good night.

They had placed his blanket so that when he was lying on it, he couldn't see into the bedroom, but he could hear perfectly well. They kept their voices low, but he caught snatches of the conversation.

"...wish you'd asked me." Jherik's voice rose a bit. Benton murmured something back to him, and the cougar sighed. "I don't mind, but we don't have that much room."

Jonas didn't hear Benton's response, if he made one, but Jherik's voice rose and got sharper. "I'm not going to go through this argument again. I don't need their help. I wish you'd stop suggesting we run to my family for money."

Now Benton's voice was rising. "It's not running for help. They've offered. You're just too stubborn to accept."

"Maybe I want to make my own way."

"Everyone gets help from their family. It's nothing to be ashamed of."

"Really? When was the last time your father sent you money?"

There was a silence, and the next voice Jonas heard was Jherik's again. "I'm sorry. I shouldn't have..."

Jonas rolled over and tried to shut out the private conversation. He felt like an intruder again, and while he'd originally hoped to stay another night or two, now he felt he would have to get out the next day. He sighed and raised his eyes to the window, where he could see the silvery glow of the moon. *Felis,* he prayed, *show me what path to follow.*

Halfway through his silent recital of the "Our Mother," he heard a breathless squeak from the bedroom. His ears flicked back to listen, and he grinned. Apparently Jherik and Benton had already made up. A stirring in his sheath urged him to take a look, against his better judgment. He finished the prayer and then gave in, cautiously rolling over to the bedroom door and cracking one eye to peer inside.

He needn't have bothered with the pretense of sleep. Neither the cougar nor the fox were looking in his direction, and both were absorbed in each other. He'd thought from the pants and moans that they were nearing the finish, but there turned out to be a good deal of action left. Jonas didn't watch for very long, but he was struck by the difference between watching Benton and Jherik, and between watching the other workers at the Jackal's Staff. The fox and cougar were certainly passionate and affectionate, but their technique was imperfect and occasionally awkward. Jonas found himself wanting to tell them, "No, don't switch paws…don't lick quite that fast…" Watching Richy with Pike, for example, the technique had been very good, but now he wondered whether he'd imagined any affection on Richy's part. The interaction had been more like grooming than intimacy.

His body was responding to the sight. He rolled over and pressed his erection into the blanket, flexing his claws into the fabric and keeping his panting as soft as he could. Celibacy did not appear to agree with him, but he didn't feel that pleasuring himself would be appropriate on someone else's floor. He waited until the noises from the bedroom peaked and then subsided into warm murmurs, and then lay on his back and closed his eyes.

When he opened them again, light was streaming in through the window and Jherik was just opening the door to leave. Jonas watched him go and lay back and closed his eyes again. He felt calmer in the morning, and as he contemplated his future, he realized that his options were not very numerous. He kept coming up against the fact that he was only trained in one area. Remembering the previous night, he couldn't deny his interest in sex, but he still felt reluctant to look around for a brothel to work in. He knew that the Jackal's Staff was one of the most high-class places in Divalia, and he'd been lucky to get a position there. Even if he could find an equivalent place in Caril, though, the prospect of working in that same position didn't appeal to him.

His other option was that he could do the work on his own. He knew vaguely that there were independent prostitutes in Divalia, so there must be in Caril. He would need a nice place, of course, someplace he could invite clients to, and he would need some nice clothes. He knew where to get the clothes, and hopefully Mikka would know where to look for a good place, and if he could get money from Alexan's house, that would get him started.

By the time Benton came out into the living room, Jonas had formulated his plan. He was surprised that the idea of returning to prostitution didn't bother him as much when he thought about doing it on his own. With no Tally and Van Wyck, nobody ordering him when or how much to do, with the freedom to just focus on the client, he thought he could endure it, and maybe even enjoy it.

Benton paid for the cab to Alexan's place, and on the way over, Jonas hesitantly told the fox his idea. Benton approved, but didn't know enough to be any help. He didn't frequent any brothels in Caril, and he didn't know anyone who did, so he didn't know where to tell Jonas to go or who to talk to. He offered to ask around, a polite gesture that Jonas knew was nothing more. He thanked the fox anyway.

Disembarking from the cab, the first glimpse they had of Alexan's house was not promising. Jonas felt his fur prickle with memories of the fox's death flooding back to him. He heard Benton's sharp indrawn breath, and then he noticed that the door was slightly ajar.

They walked up the stairs in silence and eased the door open, and Jonas saw immediately that he was not going to get any help for his new start. The floor was littered with broken pieces of pottery and piles of cloth, and the part of the living room he could see was empty of furniture. Dazed, he wandered into the spare room and saw that it had been stripped bare; his bed and nightstand were gone, and his family pendant with them. The rest of the house was no better. Even the stove was gone from the kitchen; marks on the floor and a broken window (with damaged frame) showed where it had gone. The food, of course, had been cleared out, and when he returned to the living room, he saw Benton in the doorway of Alexan's bedroom shaking his head, and knew it wasn't worth even going in.

"Did Alexan have a…a secret hiding place? For money, or something?" Benton's voice was soft.

Jonas shrugged. "I didn't know of any."

Benton sighed. "I'm sorry. I guess someone saw them take the body out and just forced their way in. Jherik says that happens sometimes. I just didn't think it would be so soon."

Jonas nodded, already walking quickly to the front door. He felt uncomfortable in the house to begin with, and seeing it stripped and ravaged was even more unsettling. He also hadn't realized how much he'd been counting on getting some of Alexan's money until it had been taken from him. The feeling reminded him of the sickness in the bottom of his stomach when he'd found his chest empty and his savings gone, only here there was no Sasha to blame, just himself and shadowy unknown figures. He worked his paws as he stepped out of the doorway, claws sliding in and out as he tried to calm down.

The quiet in the familiar street outside soothed him and stopped his tail from twitching. After a moment, he sat on the front stairs and breathed slowly in the cool morning air. His paws rested on his knees; his claws remained sheathed.

Benton closed the door and sat on the stair just above him. "I'm sorry," he said.

Jonas sighed. "It's so strange. Two…three days ago, everything looked so good. I thought maybe if his plan worked, things would get better."

"You weren't happy," Benton said softly.

It felt like a betrayal of Alexan's memory, but Jonas slowly shook his head. "But it's not his fault. I mean, not all of it. He could be so sweet sometimes, he was just worried about losing his business. And I forced myself on him, and that gave him one more thing to worry about. If I'd only been..." He wrenched his thoughts away from that last encounter, feeling himself dangerously close to tears.

Benton let him sit in silence, only placing a paw on his shoulder. Jonas found comfort in the gesture, as he relaxed and tried to calm his breathing and his tail, which had started to lash again. He watched the narrow street, each of the houses he'd come to know on his way to and from Alexan's place. The house across the street whose door had been recently replaced was the most familiar to him. He knew the peculiar patterns of its walls and the flaws in both windows that faced the street, and he knew the family of badgers that lived there. The other houses had their place, too; he knew their quirks and some of the residents, but as he thought about them now, his feeling of comfort was tarnished by wondering which of them had broken in and taken Alexan's things. *Which one of you has his carpets, his glassware, his clothes?* he thought. He glanced two houses down, where he knew a family of foxes lived, and for a brief moment he thought about going there to demand that they return whatever they'd taken. With a guilty thrill, he remembered the satisfaction of hitting Pike across the muzzle, but the memory faded to a dull ache as he remembered the raccoon's friendship even afterwards. His claws had extended to prick his knees; he forced them back in again, pulling his gaze back from the house to stare at the cracked stone of the step in front of him.

Benton coughed, and when Jonas turned, the fox was studying the position of the sun. "We should start to head back," he said softly, and Jonas nodded. But when they reached the main street, Benton trudged along the cobblestones, not even looking for a cab. Jonas started to hail one, and the fox pulled his arm down. "I don't have enough money for one," he said, ears down. "I thought...I thought we'd use some of Alexan's money to get back."

"Oh." Jonas fell in behind Benton. "I'm sorry."

"Not your fault." After more silence, Benton said, "If you need to stay with us again tonight..."

"No." After what he'd heard, he was determined not to cause more problems for them. "I'll go to Mikka. He might be able to help me out."

"I'm sure he'd be glad to have you staying with him, at least," Benton said.

Jonas felt his fur prickle, but he didn't say anything. No matter what help he asked from Mikka, he was sure sex would be part of his price. Benton's tail flagged briefly. "I'm sorry," the fox said. "I shouldn't judge. Anyway, you used to do that professionally, so I'm sure you're good at it and worth whatever he'd pay."

When Jonas still didn't reply, Benton went on. "There's nothing wrong

Inside the Cage

with it. It's a noble occupation, and certainly not one everyone can do. I just hope you get paid well."

Jonas sighed. "I can always just go join a brothel somewhere."

Benton looked at him. "Does it matter whether you do it on your own or in a house?"

"I didn't think so, but maybe it does. You know, if it's me, then I'm making the decisions. I worked in a brothel for a while and I hated it."

"Was it just that someone else was telling you what to do? I mean...I thought...that was part of the job."

"It is, but when I'm with a client..." He searched for the words. "They can ask for something specific, but I can tell what they want and I can figure out how to make them happy. So I'm making the decisions. But people telling me how short to keep my fur, or how many clients to see... I just hate that."

"You hate your fur being cut, but not having sex with some stranger?"

Jonas bristled, then relaxed as he saw the fox's grin. "I thought I hated all of it. And I think if I really had a choice, I would find something else to do. But my other choice seems to be to starve."

Benton folded his ears back, and his grin wavered. "Well...from what I saw that one night, you are pretty good. And I know that, uh, that's not easy."

Jonas wasn't sure how much he wanted to talk about that night. "It would've been harder if he'd been more drunk."

"Oh, when Jherik's even a little drunk, he can't focus long enough to do anything."

Jonas put a paw on the fox's shoulder. "Let me tell you a little trick..."

He felt like Sasha for a moment, telling Benton the trick Sasha had taught him for dealing with drunk clients. The fox grinned when Benton was done. "I'll have to remember that one. I'm sure I can dig up a cheesecloth somewhere."

"A linen napkin will do, if you can't." Jonas smiled at Benton's perked ears and smile. It was nice to know that there was more than one way he could make people happy.

For nearly an hour, they walked through the winding streets of Caril. Benton knew exactly where he was going, and Jonas followed, noticing the stares of the people passing them on the street more than where they were going. When he'd begun to run errands for Alexan to the small local markets, he'd gotten the same stares until the people were used to him. A cougar in this part of town was unusual enough; one dressed like a... well, like a peasant...that was nearly alarming. He tried to avoid looking at them, because as soon as they met his eyes, they would look away quickly, either ashamed of their own stares or embarrassed for him. But he felt their eyes on his back after he passed.

He'd never been to the Great Market, but when the sounds and smells reached him all at once, he knew what they were approaching. The palace, ever-visible above the rooftops, had been drawing closer, and though they were still probably an hour's walk from it, they were closer than Jonas had ever been. Just ahead, as they turned a corner, the noise and scents rose into sharp relief as a raucous jumble of stalls and wares came into view. Here, finally, the attention on Jonas diminished; people were hurrying to or from the market, and he supposed that cougars weren't as unusual here.

"Come on," Benton said, "and stay close. Mikka's shop is near Master Talid's, off the High Market."

"Is this the Low Market?" Jonas asked, but got no reply, as Benton dove into the crowd.

It was all Jonas could do to follow the fox's red pelt and scent through the bustle of people. He didn't dare glance to either side to see the goods for sale, though he did catch glimpses of colorful clay pots, thickly woven and patterned rugs, birds in cages, birds on racks, hundreds of different wooden crafts, and many things that caught fleetingly at the edge of his vision without registering a form or a name. Benton dodged expertly through the crowds, and Jonas had to use his height and strength to force a path behind the fox, thanking Felis that there weren't more red pelts in the throng.

On the other side of the market, Benton pointed up to a collection of stalls on a small rise. "That's the High Market," he said. "The nobles all shop there. Master Talid and Mikka both sell mostly to the High Market, so their workshops are down over this way." He pointed down a street. "Master Talid's store is there. I still have enough time to walk you to Mikka's. It's only half a mile away."

They walked around the High Market and down a narrow street. In this part of town, Jonas felt, the stares from passersby were not because he was a cougar, but because he was an ill-dressed one. His clothes, still the ones he'd fled Tephos in, were ragged and dustier than they'd ever been, and his feet were filthy from the walk along the streets. He did his best to ignore the looks.

Benton led Jonas up to a low building, clean and neat, with a smoothly polished door. "Mikka should be here. He goes up to the market in the mornings, like Master Talid, and then comes back to supervise work in the afternoons."

A young weasel opened to Benton's knock and peered out, his eyes widening a bit as he saw Jonas. He addressed Benton, but his glances kept flicking back up to the cougar. "May I help you?"

"Is Mikka—Master White—in the shop?"

The weasel nodded. "Are you representing a noble?"

"He knows us." Benton nodded at Jonas. "This is a friend of his."

"Oh. Come in, then."

Inside the Cage

"I'll get back to the shop." Benton clasped Jonas's paw and smiled. "Good luck. Please come by and let us know how you're doing."

"I will. Thanks for everything." He pulled the fox into a hug. "I promise I'll repay you some day."

"Oh, don't worry." Benton returned the hug and then stepped back, giving a cheerful wave. "Just stay happy."

Happy? Jonas thought. That wasn't even on his horizon. He was just hoping to stay alive.

Chapter 9

Mikka was brushing his paws together when Jonas stepped inside. Small pieces of thread and something that glittered drifted to the floor in his wake, and some remained on his paws as he walked up to Jonas. His ears canted back and his eyes were sympathetic. "You poor thing. Did you walk all the way here? Come in back, we have some water you can wash up with."

Jonas was staring around the shop, at the richly colored and decorated garments that were carefully hung in rows on the walls, from racks attached to the ceiling, from standing racks on the door, and even on the back of the door that Mikka gently closed before leading Jonas to the back of the shop, past a counter upon which several shirts were folded, and through a small door into the back.

The young weasel who'd answered the door was climbing up to a shelf that contained small bins. He turned as Jonas and Mikka entered, as did the two apprentices who were carefully sewing at a workbench. One was a rabbit, the other a mouse; both were male, slender, and attractive. A separate table with a partially-finished scarf on it appeared to be where Mikka had been working, as it was scattered with sparkling flakes, and a second separate table was not in use.

"Jarga, Kerial, Millick, this is Jonas. Jonas..." Mikka waved vaguely in the direction of the three youngsters. "Jarga, Kerial, Millick."

Jonas waved and then followed the disappearing fox tail through the door at the back of the back room.

He emerged into a small courtyard, open to the air. The only other visible exit was a small wooden door in the back wall. The strong scent from that direction indicated that an outhouse lay behind it, probably a common one shared by many residents of the street. Several small juniper bushes grew beside the door, obviously meant to mask the smell, and they did a good job, but not a complete one. Otherwise, the courtyard was very pleasant, neat and well-kept, and decorated with touches of paint and a line of drying clothes that looked almost artistic.

Mikka pointed to a tub with a few buckets beside it. "Rather cold, I'm afraid, but it's clean. If you need it heated up, place it in there..." he gestured to a metal plate in the back wall that was hinged to drop down. "The stove's lit. It takes about half an hour to warm up the water."

"No, that's okay. I can handle the cold. I'll just rinse the dust off."

"Good. I'll find you something nicer to wear."

"I..." The fox had turned to go back into the store and now turned at Jonas's hesitant word.

"What's the matter?"

Inside the Cage

"I can't pay you for clothes," Jonas said.

Mikka shrugged and smiled. "We'll work out some arrangement." He walked back into the store and left Jonas to think about that.

The water was not unbearably cold, and Jonas was happy to get the accumulated dust and dirt out of his fur. He washed until he started to shiver, and then got out and shook himself as dry as he could. He was smoothing down his fur with his paws when he noticed that Mikka had returned.

"Been keeping up your exercises, I see." The fox grinned, making no effort to avoid looking at Jonas's naked body.

"I do what I can." He was torn between trying to act embarrassed and acting nonchalant, and decided it was less trouble to act nonchalant.

"Is that one of Phineas's pendants?"

Jonas touched the gold cougar and nodded. Mikka set a pile of clothes down on a bench and tossed a large towel to Jonas. "It's nice. Here, dry off and then put these on."

"Thanks." Jonas caught the towel and rubbed it through his fur.

Mikka sat on the bench next to the clothes. "Alexan must have given it to you. He does have a sweet side, doesn't he? Well. First of all, tell me why you finally ran away."

Jonas froze. It hadn't even occurred to him that Mikka wouldn't know yet. The fox went on when he didn't answer immediately. "If you don't want to talk about it yet, I can understand that. I thought it might happen before long. Alexan hasn't found the one person who can take him, and I didn't think you'd be the one either. Though I did think you'd be able to take him for a bit longer. I guess he got upset when his plan failed, right?"

"Yes." It would be easier just to not say anything now. What if Mikka thought he was responsible for Alexan's death and threw him out into the street, naked? Literally. Jonas clutched the towel to him. At that chilly moment, it seemed eminently possible. He would tell Mikka later, when he was clothed and more prepared. Or at least warmer.

"Well, all right. If you want to stay here, you'll have to work. You are cute, but you're not that cute. Only I am that cute, and I already keep myself employed full time." Jonas sensed that Mikka wanted a chuckle or a laugh in response, but his throat was still tight and all he managed was a kind of squeak. "I already have enough apprentices in the shop." He tapped his muzzle.

"I…" His voice came out a hoarse croak, so he cleared his throat. "I had an idea for a business." If he hesitated, he wouldn't be able to say it, so he charged ahead. "I could go back to prostitution. But on my own. I'd just need some help getting set up. Getting a place, and I suppose I'd need some clothes." He dropped the towel and eyed the clothes on the bench.

"I can help you with the clothes and we can track down some places for you." The fox smiled. "You can pay me back in the usual way. I'd gotten the impression that you didn't want to go back to that full time, though."

Jonas sorted through the clothes on the bench. Mikka had chosen a light purple shirt, with ruffles down the arms, a pair of simple white underclothes, and some light trousers, very unlike the linen Jonas was used to. The fabrics were smoother than he'd ever worn, except once at an official function his father had taken him to, and, he thought with a pang, they looked like something Sasha would have liked. He pulled on the underthings, the trousers, and finally the shirt. They fit perfectly, though the airiness of the trousers left his legs cold. "I don't," he said, "but what choice do I have?"

"There's always work," Mikka said gently. "But it is a noble profession, you know. Unsavory sometimes, I'm sure, but necessary, and it can be very rewarding. Besides, I would hate to see your talents wasted."

"You haven't," Jonas said, surprised at how bitter he sounded.

Mikka set his ears back in surprise, then brought them slowly up. "Ah. Alexan told me his payment scheme was your idea, but it wasn't, was it?"

"No."

"I see." Mikka looked away. "Well. That's rather awkward. A credit to your professionalism, though."

"About the clothes." Jonas fingered them. "I'll find some way…"

"No, no, keep them. They're not my best anyway. And now I feel guilty."

"No. I want to pay for them."

Mikka smiled. "You can do chores around the shop if you want."

Jonas thought about that, imagining himself fumbling around the clothing store, and winced. "I already know what you like."

Mikka's tail gave a twitch, and his smile receded. "Are you sure?"

"*I'm* telling you this time." As much as the thought of sex with Mikka stirred up bad memories, the thought of the amount of hard labor he would have to do for the equivalent payment was daunting. At least he was practiced at sex, and at dealing with what it made him feel.

"Listen," Mikka said, his muzzle and ears set back seriously. "I flirt, I joke, but I don't want to pressure you. I'm sure Alexan did that and you've had enough of it. I used to date him, remember?" he said at Jonas's expression.

Jonas nodded. "I know. Thanks."

"Come on inside, and let's talk about your business. I can take the work I'm doing into the front so the apprentices don't have to hear."

Jonas walked inside, past the busy apprentices, revising his opinion of Mikka. The mouse glanced up at him and then back down hurriedly when Jonas met his gaze. The others ignored him, or pretended to.

Mikka closed the door as Jonas entered the front room. "They're good helpers, but they do gossip," he said. "I had to stop bringing my 'friends' here because of that. At least, during the day."

Jonas managed a grin, and Mikka hoisted himself onto the counter, curling his tail around behind him. His muzzle was closer to level with Jonas's now. "Oh, I'm just kidding." He grinned back at Jonas. "So you want to start a business. Have you thought about where your customers will come from? With your talents, you could be very successful, but if nobody knows about you, then nobody will pay you."

The fox was waiting for him to jump into the conversation, Jonas could see, and after a moment he figured out why. His father had brought him along on some business meetings at a very young age, hoping he'd show some interest in the business, or the numbers. Or anything. Jonas remembered one thing his father had told him, that the most important things said in business deals were not spoken aloud. He'd never really gotten the hang of the numbers, but he had been able to read people fairly well, a skill which he carried over into his other line of work. Here, Mikka's body language was telling him that the fox didn't want to be the one to make the first offer. "I'd need someone to help me get some customers. Would you be able to help? I'd pay you."

"I believe I could." Mikka examined his claws. "I would want a quarter of whatever they pay you."

His father had sometimes paid commissions or "finder's fees" for people who brought him business. "Just the ones you send me?"

"Just the ones I send you."

Jonas curled his paw back and forth over the smooth floor. He examined Mikka's posture, noting a little tension, and wondered how far he could negotiate. "Copper for silver." That was ten percent, one copper for every silver spent. He'd heard his father use the term years ago.

Mikka looked up at him now, appraisingly, and Jonas met his gaze. "Two coppers," the fox said.

"One and a half."

"Two."

Jonas grinned suddenly. "Two, plus the clothes."

Mikka's ears flicked back and forward quickly in surprise, and then he laughed. "Am I that disgusting?" Jonas raised his eyebrows, afraid he'd hurt the fox's feelings, but Mikka was still smiling as he riposted. "All right, two plus the clothes, but you give me a discount if I want to pay for a session. Say, half price?"

"And I don't pay your commission on those sessions."

Mikka laughed again. "I should hire you to do my negotiations. All right, deal." He held out a paw and extended his muzzle.

Pleased with himself, Jonas took the fox's paw and brushed his whiskers against the fox's on either side of his muzzle. He had the feeling that he'd passed some sort of initiation or test, and that gave him a boost of confidence he hadn't felt in a long time.

"All right. Do you think we need to draw up an agreement? Can you read and write? Oh, of course you can. I found this in your pocket." He pulled out Jonas's letter to Pike. "Sorry, I'd forgotten about it. Did you want to send it to Ferrenis?"

Jonas had forgotten about it too. "I...I don't really know how."

"There are ways to get it there."

Mikka was waving the letter back and forth. "Yes, all right. Just...I'll pay you back later."

The fox grinned. "No charge for this one." He hopped down off the counter. "So do you want to draw up an agreement?"

Jonas nodded. "If you don't mind."

"Of course not. I still have a lot of work to do today, so maybe you could do the writing. I've got paper and ink in that drawer and I'm sure there are quills around somewhere. Just write down what we talked about and leave four places for signatures." Mikka padded to the back room.

"All right. I'll just..." Jonas trailed off as he heard the click of the back door. He reached for the drawer, then hesitated and took a moment to look more carefully around the room.

He could have jumped from the counter to the front window; the room wasn't large. But every inch of every wall was covered by clothing, some of familiar fabrics, others he could only guess at. There seemed to be no rhyme nor reason to the arrangement, as beaded shirts hung next to fine silken pants like the kind Jonas was wearing. Near the door, a wooden stand with five hooks held two flat bags full of clothes, and in one corner was a pile of empty bags. The wood floor was clean and smooth, and the scent of the shop was a pleasant mix of fabric and dye, under which ran Mikka's fox scent, like a brand.

Obviously the fox was successful. Jonas hadn't thought there were this many fine clothes in all the city, but since Mikka was clearly not the only tailor, this must be just a fraction. He shook his head and applied himself to the task of writing out the agreement.

He was halfway done—he kept stopping and starting, trying to find the right words—when the door creaked open and a well-dressed bobcat walked in. He wore a red shirt with a beaded pattern that looked familiar to Jonas; glancing to one side, Jonas saw that a similar blue shirt hung on Mikka's wall. He also sported a jaunty red cap with a feather in it, which bobbed as he strode up to the counter, but his expression didn't match the light frivolity of his clothes.

"Where's Mikka?" he snarled.

"Uh...in back."

The bobcat's paws came up. "Easy," he said. "I'm not mad at you. I don't blame you for taking a deal, sir. I just thought we had an agreement. Mikka!" he roared unexpectedly, and Jonas flattened his ears. "Sorry!" The bobcat held up his paws again.

Jonas shook his head, puzzled. Mikka opened the door and padded in. "Xaric," he said. "Your merchandise is there by the door, but you're early."

"I thought we had a deal, Mikka. What's this?" Xaric pointed at Jonas.

"Oh. He's not a noble, he's a friend."

"Really." The bobcat crossed his arms. "He's a cougar in your shop wearing your clothes, but he's not a noble and you're not selling directly to him."

"I'm not a noble," Jonas said.

Xaric's scowl didn't fade. "Then what's that agreement you're writing out?"

"It's a private business matter." Mikka turned the parchment over.

"You're selling him clothes directly."

Mikka started to say something, but Jonas put his paw down on the paper and looked down into the bobcat's eyes. "I'm a prostitute," he growled.

The bobcat stared back, then he threw back his head and roared with laughter. "A cougar prostitute! Oh, Mikka, you do know where to find them. All right, all right, I'm not mad any more. Go ahead, tell me what's really going on." Still chuckling, he looked back and forth between them.

The grey fox watched Jonas with a half-smile. "It's true," he said. "Jonas is trying to go into business for himself. I'm just helping him out."

"You're joking. No, I guess not. You know, it was only a matter of time with you. You going to support him all by yourself?"

"I'm going to help him find customers."

"There aren't that many gay merchants or tradesfolk, but I daresay you know them all. What?"

Mikka had tilted his muzzle and was smiling at Xaric. "Oh, I don't think they'd have to be gay."

"He is male, isn't he?"

"Very much so. But wouldn't you like to get a blow job from a noble?"

Xaric blinked and looked at Jonas. Jonas smiled back and then licked his lips for effect. By telling himself that he wanted to bring in the bobcat as a customer, he overcame a good deal of the unease he normally felt while talking in public about his trade. He had always been good at showing off at the Jackal's Staff; he just had to find that mindset again.

The bobcat wrenched his eyes away and back to Mikka. "But he's not a noble."

"You didn't know that, and didn't believe me when I told you," the fox purred. "It wouldn't be so hard for you to pretend, would it?"

Xaric looked back at Jonas. "Aye," he said. "The times I've had to abase myself…I'd pay money for that!"

Mikka grinned, showing teeth. "I'll hold you to that." He patted Jonas's paw. "And he's so good you'll come back."

"We'll see about that. I do have a lovely wife."

"Mmm, but is she adept at all the pleasures you enjoy?"

Xaric growled. "Our business relationship does not give you leave to pry into my private affairs. I have a lovely wife who has given me two fine kits." But his eyes were reluctant to leave Jonas.

"My apologies." Mikka bowed. "I overstepped my bounds."

"It's all right." Xaric waved a paw. "Just leave my wife out of this."

"Of course. Your clothes are by the door. Will there be anything else?"

The bobcat hesitated, then shook his head. "No. No."

"I'll be sure to let you know where Jonas sets up his business," Mikka called as Xaric walked back to the clothes rack. The bobcat acknowledged him with a wave, took his clothes, and left.

"Thinking about it so much he didn't even bother to say good-bye." Mikka rubbed his paws together and patted Jonas on the back. "We're going to make a *lot* of money."

Chapter 10

Mikka slept in a bed above the workshop, and that night he invited Jonas to stay in the bed while he slept on the floor. Wary of the arrangement, Jonas offered to sleep in the workshop, but Mikka pointed out that the fire was out and it would be a very chilly night. Normally, Jonas wouldn't worry about the chill, but he'd spent the last two nights in the cold, and he eventually gave in to the promise of a warm stove to curl up near.

Despite the clean beddings, the room still smelled strongly of fox. Jonas waved off Mikka's apologies with a smile. The bed was a little small, but no smaller than his bed at Alexan's had been, and by now Jonas was used to his feet hanging over the edge.

Mikka had made a bed of blankets for himself on the floor, and sat there with his back against the wall while Jonas got comfortable. They'd both removed their clothes; at first, Jonas had stopped at the pants, until he realized that the fabric might be damaged if he slept in them. And then he felt silly in his underthings while Mikka was naked, telling himself that they'd seen each other many times already. Now, safe under the blanket, he curled his tail over his legs comfortably and leaned on his side, facing the fox and the stove. The warmth made his whiskers twitch and his eyelids heavy.

"I don't have time to go with you tomorrow," the fox said, "but I'll give you directions to three landlords I know. One of them will probably rent you a room to do business in."

"I have to tell them what I'm doing?"

"Uh-huh. If you don't, you could be kicked out when they find out. And they will find out."

"Oh."

"They'll probably want a cut. Don't give them any more than a copper per silver. If you can make it a fixed amount per month, something like one gold will be a good price, I think. They'll probably want a couple gold a month in rent, but you should be okay."

Jonas had the feeling that Mikka was talking about an awful lot of money, but when he tried to figure out how much would be left for him in a month, he got lost in the figures, so he just said, "Mmm."

After a period of silence, Jonas slid into a half-dream of Mikka presenting him with a shirt woven of gold. He thought it would be heavy, but it turned out to be as light as silk. "Jonas," Mikka said.

"Hmm?" The vision of the shirt faded slowly.

"What do you want? From this, I mean."

Jonas opened his eyes. The fox's were shining back at him. "To start a business."

"I know, but...why?"

"Because I can't do anything else."

"All right, but...there must be something you want, really *want*. Like...when I started making clothes, I wanted my clothes to be worn by the king. I still hope that someday I'll see him wearing a shirt that I made, with my own paws. That would be the best day of my life." He sighed, and Jonas didn't need light to see the broad smile. "Is there anything like that for you?"

"I suppose," Jonas said doubtfully, "it'd be nice to have the king as a customer."

Mikka laughed, a full belly laugh that trailed off into a series of chuckles. "If that happens, I insist you give him the shirt I gave you. Then come right here and tell me *all* about it. And that will be the second best day of my life."

Jonas grinned. "Okay."

"But that's not really what I meant."

"I know." Jonas sighed. "I don't know what I want. I just want to stay alive and have some sort of control over my life."

"Well, that's a start. Do you want a mate?"

"No." Not any more.

"Sorry. I know it's soon. But you can still want that, even if Alexan wasn't the right one."

"No." He didn't deserve a mate, or even friends like Benton and Mikka. He thought about the people he'd betrayed and squeezed his eyes shut. His tail arched up against the blanket, then settled down again.

The room stayed silent. He could hear Mikka's breathing, and the regular sound in the warmth and darkness eased the tension of remembering his past. "Maybe," he said into the dark, eyes still shut, "I just want to be the sort of person who could have a mate."

"Why couldn't you?" Mikka said softly.

Jonas thought about how to answer that question without confessing his failures. Sasha danced in front of him, and Alexan, and Pike, and the fox whose name he didn't know. *Because I can't be trusted*, he thought, but he couldn't make his mouth say the words. *Because I'm better off on my own. Because I don't want anyone to have that power over me.* The ruminations faded away into the blackness of sleep.

He woke into darkness some time later. The short bed and the smell of fox confused him for the span of several heartbeats into thinking that he was back at Alexan's, and the soft breathing he heard was the red fox's. They must have brought him back to life, he thought nonsensically, and as he came more awake, he remembered where he was and who was in the room with him.

He was lying on his stomach, his erection pressed into the bedding. He shifted a bit, purring at the sensations, and wondered what kind of dream he'd been having. Slowly, he eased onto his side and slid a paw down his belly, brushing his length. He shouldn't do more, he knew, not with Mikka right there; if the fox didn't wake, he'd certainly smell it in the morning. But his paw kept moving. He could curl up and take himself in the muzzle, he decided.

He peered down at the floor to make sure Mikka was asleep, and saw that the grey fox had lost part of his blanket during the night. Like Jonas, the fox was fully erect, though he was lying on his back, so Jonas could see his sheath and the long taut length protruding from it very clearly. Lust and indecision seized him. "Mikka," he whispered. If the fox were asleep, and stayed asleep, Jonas could proceed with his original plan.

Mikka didn't move. Jonas watched him while his mind raced through fantasies of sneaking over and taking the sleeping fox's member into his muzzle. He dismissed those and bent his body around, sliding his erection between his lips. He closed his eyes as he licked with his tongue, body shivering in response, and he let out a low, inadvertent moan.

A rustling from the floor answered him. Slowly, he slid his muzzle back and turned. Mikka was now lying on his side, facing away from Jonas.

"Mikka?" Jonas whispered again.

"I'm not looking," came the soft response.

When Jonas thought about it, the decision wasn't all that hard, really. He was aroused, and lonely, and there was a familiar partner three feet away. Still, it took him nearly a full minute to get up the nerve to whisper back, "I'm not in business yet."

The grey fox turned over, his eyes gleaming in the darkness. Jonas could see the duller gleam of his member's skin against the white of his belly's fur. Jonas slid back, making room on the bed.

"Are you sure?" Mikka whispered.

Jonas nodded, then said, "Yes," not sure if the fox could see him in the darkness. But Mikka apparently could see very well, because he was moving to the bed before Jonas got the word out.

They squeezed together on the small bed. Jonas hadn't expected Mikka to evoke any memories of Alexan (*and how his eyes had looked when…*), but he had a short burst of panic as the fox slid into the bed, remembering his dream. Fortunately, the only memories the grey fox brought to his mind were of the times Jonas had serviced him. He put his arms around Mikka, a gesture he'd never really felt confident doing in the past; nor did he now, but his arms moved almost automatically when the fox pressed against him. He expected Mikka to tell him what to do next, but Mikka's arms slid around him and the fox snuggled closer without a word.

Jonas felt the fox's erection press into his stomach, and he rubbed gently back and forth against it. Mikka shivered, his thighs rubbing against Jonas's erection in return. The sensations were pleasant, but not intense, and Mikka seemed as content as Jonas to go on rubbing for some time, their paws sliding gently through each other's fur.

Kyell Gold

Finally, Jonas nuzzled the fox's ear and said, "What do you want me to do?"

Mikka rubbed his muzzle into Jonas's chest and murmured, "Save that for the paying customers. Let's do what you want for a change."

Jonas thought about that while his paws searched out Mikka's tail. He wasn't sure what he wanted, except to finish, and his instincts pushed him to make sure Mikka was happy. And he knew very well what would make Mikka happy.

With one paw, he probed under the fox's tail. "I'd like to be in there again," he breathed into the fox's ear.

Mikka let out a low moan and pressed against him. "Okay," he panted. "You talked me into it."

Jonas smiled, nuzzling the fox's ear and sliding his paw around a little more. He enjoyed the way his touch made the fox squirm against him, so he kept playing until Mikka gasped and whimpered, and rolled over with some effort, pressing his rump against Jonas's erection. Jonas pulled Mikka against his chest and mouthed his ear, stroking the fox's fur down his chest and stomach. Mikka wriggled against him, rubbing his paws down the insides of Jonas's legs and trying to wag his tail against the cougar's belly.

He'd often been in this situation with some of his clients, when they approached him submissively, and once he'd gotten over the fact that it was the more aggressive Mikka beside him, he felt much more at ease. He switched arms, working the lower arm out from under the fox and groping around the bed. The strongest scent in the room was fox, but beneath it he could smell the linens, the straw of the bedding, and the scent of an oil which he knew he was going to need in about a minute. And if he knew Mikka at all, he knew the fox would have it within arm's reach of the bed.

Indeed, his paw found a small pot after several seconds of groping. He brought it up to the bed and balanced it carefully in front of Mikka's belly, wedging his arm back under the fox. With one paw, he stroked the fox's member, enjoying the way it slid through his slick paw pads. Mikka was enjoying it too, if his reactions were any indication. In fact, Jonas stopped when the fox's panting and his body's tremors started to roughen. "Don't finish without me," he murmured in Mikka's ear, and the fox made a small whimper in reply. His shaft was hard and dripping more than just oil as Jonas removed his paw, giving the already-thick knot a squeeze that made Mikka shiver again.

"Just a second," he murmured, and Mikka turned to lie on his back.

"Let me?" The fox didn't wait for an answer, but dipped his paw in the pot and then slid it over Jonas's length.

"Ohh…okay." Jonas panted as the delicate paw moved up and down his member, far more than was necessary to get it slickened with oil. Mikka might not be an expert, but he certainly knew how to use his paws,

Inside the Cage

with firm strokes and teasing touches of his blunt claws. A detached part of Jonas's mind reflected on how useful it was to have claws made dull from an inability to retract them; had he tried what Mikka was doing, he would certainly draw blood. And even though his body was trembling with arousal, that part of his mind kept analyzing what Mikka was doing, figuring out the shortcomings, and appreciating the expertise.

There were few enough shortcomings, he had to admit. Mikka was lifting his shaft away from his body, using both paws to stroke the length and concentrating on the tip, and paying attention to when Jonas moaned or squirmed particularly hard. He came back to those places, and nibbled at Jonas's chest fur and around his stomach, tickling pleasantly. Jonas shivered, listening to the analytical part of his mind tell him that pretty soon he'd better remove Mikka's paw unless he wanted to get his stomach sticky.

Mikka grinned when he did, white teeth showing against his grey fur, and turned around without being told. Jonas dabbed some of the oil under the fox's tail, pressing it up into the warm opening there and working his finger around. He would've teased Mikka longer, but he found that he badly wanted to get in there himself, and so he did, sliding in easily all the way up as he pulled the fox's body against his.

"Oh!" Mikka squeaked. Jonas reached around to stroke the fox's member but found that Mikka was already taking care of that, stroking with quick whimpers, so Jonas just thrust in and out, closing his eyes and burying his nose in the fox's warm fur.

"Oh. Jonas. Oh. Ohhh." Mikka was writhing now, bucking back against him, pulling Jonas along, and the cougar was pounding his hips hard into the fox now, feeling the muscles of the fox's rear tighten and release, tighten and release, stroking his erection with each thrust, and when Mikka cried out in a series of staccato barks and Jonas felt and smelled the fox's climax, it did not take him much longer. Mikka had barely started to relax when Jonas growled, thrust against him hard, pulling the slight body into him, and shuddered as he came.

"Oh." He pushed his head into the thick neck ruff, panting.

"Mmm. You never came like that before."

"Mmm."

A feather touch of claws brushed the back of his paw, and his arm. "I liked that. No, stay in." Jonas had started to pull out, but Mikka pressed his rump back into Jonas's hips. "I like it in."

"Okay." His lust sated, Jonas was now very sleepy and fast returning to a state of confusion. He didn't know what to say to Mikka now. After all their previous encounters, the fox had gotten dressed and left. Memories of Alexan surfaced again, but this time Jonas found them oddly comforting, a barrier to his doubts and nightmares. They softened the night and carried him into a blessedly dreamless sleep.

He woke with a sudden start, not sure why. The smell of sex had faded slightly, but he still had the uncomfortable feeling of having dozed off in one of the Jackal's Staff rooms. Turning over, he saw Mikka sitting by the stove, wearing a black shirt and dark blue pants, his ears back and his eyes soft. If Jonas hadn't been able to tell that Mikka was mourning Alexan's death from the black shirt (and initially, in the disoriented just-awake state, he couldn't), he could not mistake the shine of tears in the dark brown eyes.

"Why didn't you tell me, dear?" Mikka dabbed a handkerchief at his eyes.

"I was afraid you'd be angry."

"Angry?" Mikka barked a laugh that had little humor behind it. "With you or with him?"

"Who?"

"Alexan." Mikka sighed. "He never did take care of himself. Always reaching for the precipice and not really watching where his feet were. He could be so sweet and then he would just forget. I hoped you could take his rough periods and smooth them out, but maybe that was too tall a task for anyone to handle. I'm sorry, dear." He placed a paw on Jonas's arm. "I don't mean to make you feel bad. There's nothing you could have done."

"Who told you?"

"Benton. He stopped by this morning to see how you were doing. He asked how I was handling it. I said, 'Quite well, judging from his response.'" He chuckled softly and then had to dab at his eyes again. "That confused him."

"I'm sorry I didn't tell you."

"I understand. At least, I think I do. The family is burying him today, if you want to go."

"No." He knew he should, but he couldn't bear to face the family members he'd never met, and he knew the funeral would only bring up bad memories again.

Mikka looked surprised, and then disappointed. "All right. I'll give you the landlords' addresses again so you can go round to them today. Do come back tonight, though. I feel like I want to talk about him a little more. Nobody else really knew him like we did."

Talk more about Alexan? Jonas couldn't imagine anything he'd want to do less. He was still trying to adjust from the heated lovemaking of the night before to this somber and tearful remembrance. In a way, he was grateful for it, because it completely circumvented the potential awkwardness of the morning. It worried him too, though, because although he knew how to handle sex, death and mourning he had only a passing acquaintance with.

He nodded anyway, and Mikka smiled at him. "Go ahead and get dressed. You can wash in back again if you want to, but cover yourself. The boys are downstairs."

Inside the Cage

"Thanks."

"I'll see you tonight, kitten." Mikka climbed down the stairs.

Jonas sniffed himself and decided to wash. The cold water woke him up further; he scrubbed his fur, shook, and dried off quickly. The silk clothes didn't protect him from the wind, but at least the workshop was warm.

Mikka had given him three names and approximate directions to find them. All were close by, ostensibly so Jonas wouldn't get lost, but Jonas suspected ulterior motives on the grey fox's part. The previous night had been nice, but looking back on it, Jonas wasn't at all sure that it was something he wanted to repeat. How long would it be before Mikka started asking him for other favors too? Did he really care for him, or did he just think he was something pretty, like his shirts and pants, that he wanted to have around? In either case, could Jonas be sure he wouldn't betray him somehow? He didn't love the fox, but he was beginning to like him, and he didn't want to see him hurt.

So he started with the furthest of the three landlords, working in reverse order from the instructions Mikka had forced him to repeat twice. The first (or last) of the three owned a building on River View Drive, which had probably been aptly named before the proliferation of buildings on its east side. But Jonas could smell the river, standing on the front stoop, and it was a pleasant smell. The Jackal's Staff had been close enough to the river that the smell had been a constant background, but so ingrained into the surroundings that Jonas hadn't even realized he'd missed it until now.

A well-dressed wolf in white shirt and red vest opened the door, adjusting the spectacles on his muzzle to peer at Jonas. "Yes?"

Jonas bowed and extended a paw. "My name is Jonas. Mikka sent me to ask about renting a room from you."

"Renting?" The wolf looked him up and down. "What's happened to your family?"

"I'm not a noble." Jonas wondered if he should just open conversations with that.

The wolf's ear's flicked. "I've got no rooms, son. Give Mikka my regards." He closed the door before Jonas could answer.

Backtracking towards Mikka's shop, Jonas walked in circles three times before he found the second address. The river smell was just noticeable here when the wind was right, but the street was not a large promenade; rather, it was part of a small square that was set back from Denning Street. Mikka had told him to look for Chrillich Square off Denning Street, but there was no sign on the square and so Jonas had walked past it twice before realizing that there were no other squares in the neighborhood.

He found the number 5 affixed to a two-story brick building with bright blue wood trim. The shutters were blue as well, but a darker blue, and so was the wooden porch he walked up on to approach the door. Jonas knocked, and then sat on the bench, looking at the well-swept floor and the bright shine on the windows.

He didn't hear the door open, but he saw the black-and-white flash as a skunk's muzzle appeared in the doorway. It found him immediately and a female voice said, "Yes?"

Jonas stood quickly. "Mikka told me to come see you about a room."

She scanned him up and down, and he prepared his ritual denial, but she just gave a small 'hmph' and nodded. "C'mon in."

He followed her into a tidy room and shut the door behind himself. The skunk's bosoms nearly bounced out of her linen blouse as she spun her ponderous weight around to face him, brushing aside the mop of black and white fur between her ears so she could see him clearly. Her eyes were black, but caught the light and danced with it, so that even when she was looking at him sternly, as she was now, there was a playful air about her.

The distinctive smell didn't bother Jonas much; it reminded him of Alexan's, only stronger and less vulpine. Several jasmine plants blooming by the window helped make the odor tolerable, and the skunk obviously kept a clean house. The small room he had entered held two chairs and a large stuffed sofa, and a clean rug with a simple pattern in the center of the floor.

"My name's Hazel," the skunk said. "What's yours?"

"I'm Jonas."

"Good. Now we got that outta the way. The room is three gold a month. You keep it clean, you don't have guests without askin' me, and I don't come in the room 'less you say so. You got an outhouse, and my boy will carry hot water up to you every morning. I do laundry once a week. You give me yours, I do it. You don't, I don't. I don't come lookin' for it, is what I mean. Gaiadays the house has dinner. You can come or not. You want me to cook for you other nights, it's another five silver a month. " She cocked her head at him. "Still interested?"

Jonas smiled. "I'd need to talk about the guest thing. What if I had customers, rather than guests?"

"Friend of Mikka, it doesn't surprise me you sellin' something. What's your line?"

"What?"

"What do you sell?" she asked patiently.

"Oh. Well...me."

Now she folded her arms and he thought he detected a smile in the black fur of her muzzle. "You going to be whoring outta my house, boy?"

Her manner put him at ease in a way that, he was surprised to find, reminded him of Tally's. "Yes, ma'am." He managed his best grin.

"And what is my incentive for letting this activity go on?"

"A portion of every customer's payment." She didn't react, so he said, "Or I could pay more monthly rent."

"Hmm." She brought one large paw up to stroke her muzzle. "Let me see the goods."

"What?"

"I need to make a business decision. Got to have all the information." She sat down on the sofa and waved downwards with her paw. "Take your trousers off, boy."

Jonas moved a paw hesitantly to the fastenings of his pants. "Go on," Hazel said. "I promise I won't touch."

How could it hurt? Even if she were just doing it out of interest, he didn't really care. And he liked her, and he was sure the playful gleam in her eyes was friendly. He undid the knots and let his trousers fall to the floor.

"Mmm." Her gaze lingered on his sheath. "Nice. You know how to use that, I guess."

"Four years working for a house." Technically, three plus half a year "working" for Alexan.

"Oh, so you've experience. You do boys, right?"

"Males, mostly, yes."

"Not much market for women, but there is some."

"Really?" The Staff had technically been open to both sexes, but Jonas in all his years had only seen one female customer.

"Oh, sure. Trust me." She laughed, but it was a warm, inclusive laugh, and Jonas grinned along with her. "Okay, boy, pull your pants up and let's talk numbers. I seen enough."

She motioned him to a chair beside a small table, and after fastening his pants, he sat down. "You gonna be charging what, four, five silver a customer?"

Jonas hadn't thought about it. The Staff charged five, but that was a large house. He'd supposed he would start with one silver and increase as his reputation grew. "You think I could make five?"

"With some folks. The cougar thing, that's worth a lot. Better to start out expensive than try to increase your price later."

"Maybe four."

"Okay. I want one of the four. I'm sure Mikka's takin' some too, but probably no more than one. That leaves you two per, which is good money."

Jonas tried to do the figures in his head, but he couldn't get them to work out. "I was thinking more like one copper per silver."

"Well, that's not quite the same, is it?" She peered at him shrewdly. "How about two coppers per silver?"

He wanted to suggest something in between, but although he remembered his father talking about half-coins, he didn't know how that worked. If he suggested one and a half, would she laugh at him? All he

"I need to make a business decision."

Inside the Cage

could come up with was, "Mikka said I shouldn't give more than one."

"Oh, did he? Well, I'll take one for now, then, and I'll have a talk with that fox."

Immensely relieved, Jonas smiled. "Okay."

"Well," Hazel said, "looks like we're in business." She got up and walked over to a small cabinet, where she poured two small glasses of an amber-colored liquid. "Let's celebrate, then I'll show you the room."

The rich smell of the port filled the room before she turned around, even over her scent. She grinned as she handed him the glass. "I can't stand reg'lar wine. Too bitter."

Jonas chuckled and touched his glass to hers. She said, "To a long relationship." He repeated the phrase, and drank with her. The port was sweet, went down smoothly, and lingered on his lips afterwards.

"Good, eh? Tapha gets it for me. He's got the room below yours. Won't tell me where he gets it 'cause he knows then I'd go get it for myself." She laughed. "Come on up and look at the room."

The apartment was very similar to Jherik and Benton's rooms. Now that he thought about it, Jonas realized the building itself was very similar. The only furnishings in the apartment were a small table and chair in the outer room, and a bed in the inner room. Hazel waved at the bed. "I don't know if that'll suit. I can see about getting a nicer one, but it might take a while."

"Please do," Jonas said, "but that one is fine for now."

"You can bring in whatever else you want. I got some friends, let you have some stuff a bit on the cheap."

"Thanks."

"Think nothin' of it. Just helpin' my investment." She laughed again. Jonas put aside the odd feeling that this was his new home, and joined in.

He returned to Mikka's late that afternoon, having taken some time to explore his new neighborhood. He was pleased in general; the people seemed friendly, or at least not hostile, and the streets were clean and smelled good. He would be close to the market and about fifteen minutes from Mikka's shop.

When he told Mikka about his agreement with Hazel, the fox nodded. "I figured she'd be the one. She's sharp and saw a good opportunity in you."

"I like her," Jonas said, and Mikka smiled.

"That too. Come on. Let's eat. Kerial is a pretty good cook, you'll see."

Jonas had to agree that the dinner was good, but Mikka started talking about Alexan before he'd taken two bites, and the mood didn't help the taste of the meal. Mikka and Alexan had met at the market two years before Alexan's parents had died, and at first the attraction had been purely physical. Jonas squirmed through a rather lurid description of their first night together that he was sure was improved over what the reality had been, especially when Mikka told him it had been his first time.

They'd dated for a couple years, across Alexan's trips to Tephos, but soon after his father died, Mikka said, "I just couldn't be with him like that any more. He felt like the world owed him something, and so I think it was harder for him to appreciate the things he had."

"Like you?" Jonas felt a stab of empathy.

"Like me." Mikka's eyes and warm smile reflected Jonas's feelings.

"I know what you mean. I think he always expected his plan to work. You know, to get the noble's support."

"What happened…I mean, how did he react?"

Jonas looked down at the table, trying to compose his thoughts. Mikka touched his paw. "I'm sorry, kitten. If you'd rather not…"

"No, it's okay. You deserve to know." Jonas told the story quickly, but honestly, watching Mikka's ears fold back as he got to the part where Alexan made him wear the crown and forced himself on Jonas. "I didn't mean for anything bad to happen," Jonas said. "I just wanted him to stop."

Mikka nodded. "I know," he said, and then rolled up the sleeve of his shirt. He held up his forearm so Jonas could see the neat white line running from the top of the forearm to the white fur underneath. Only an inch of white cut through the grey, but Jonas could see when he looked closer that the scar ran two more inches through the white fur.

"Alexan did that one night when we'd both had a lot to drink and I wasn't feeling so good. I tried to fend him off and he bit me. Afterwards, he was so sorry and fussed over me so much that I just said, well, we'd been drunk and it was a one-time thing. But I think it was always there, under the surface. I thought you might be able to handle it, because you're bigger and stronger than he is."

Jonas took another drink of the mead Mikka had laid out. "I wish it hadn't been that way. I wish the king had changed his mind."

Mikka sighed and shook his head. "It wouldn't have changed anything. You see? Something would always have come up."

"If you think that," Jonas said slowly, "how can you be sorry?"

Mikka took a drink and folded his ears back. "Because he walked all the way here to see me when he couldn't afford a cab. Because he brought back a beautiful curio from Tephos and it was exactly what I loved. Because I wish there hadn't been that dark side to him. You see?"

Jonas pulled the gold cougar pendant out. "He gave me this a…a week ago." Had it really been only a week?

Mikka peered at the pendant, and then whistled. "Phineas was looking for this. There was a big argument between him and the family at the funeral. They were disputing his claim to the house, and he said that as that item hadn't turned up, his claim was legal. Then they accused him of keeping it for himself so he could have the house. I thought it was the one I'd seen you with, but I didn't say anything."

"I don't want to return it." Jonas closed his paw over it and stuffed it back down his shirt.

"Nor should you. His brother didn't care a fig for him while he was alive."

"I didn't even know he had a brother."

"Dixan. He apprenticed himself to a lawyer when he was fourteen. Over his parents' objections, I might add. He has a wife and a couple cubs, and I believe he's a junior lawyer himself now." Mikka waved a paw. "Fox teaches us to respect our family. He turned his back on his. Darkness take him."

In the awkward silence that ensued, Jonas finished his mead. He held up a paw when Mikka offered to refill his mug. "I should be getting to sleep. Hazel said she doesn't stay up too late, and I don't have a key yet."

"Oh." The grey fox's ears flicked back. "I thought...you might stay here again tonight."

"I'm sorry. I've, uh, got a lot to do tomorrow." And if he stayed one more night, would that turn into another night, and a week, and a month?

Mikka took another swallow from his mug. His ears had flattened slightly. "Well. Thanks for staying up with me."

"I'll see you again soon," Jonas said, trying to lighten the blow. "I'll be opening for business the day after tomorrow, I hope."

Mikka nodded. "I already have a couple clients for you. I'll send them along."

"Thanks. Maybe I could come over for dinner sometime too."

"I'd like that." But the fox didn't look like he meant that, and Jonas, aware that he had managed to hurt Mikka while looking out for himself, left as quickly as he could.

Chapter 11

His first client was a marten by the name of Jeffis, who had a nervous habit of looking around as though he were being followed. When he saw Jonas, his eyes widened and he had his head halfway down in a bow before he remembered where he was. After that, he agreed to the price of four silvers quickly, and told Jonas that what he wanted was to get up inside him and stay there through as many climaxes as he could manage. Jonas had done that before for weasels at the Staff, and while it wasn't his favorite activity, it was fairly easy. Weasels didn't require much in the way of activity from their bottoms. In fact, all Jeffis asked him to do was leave his clothes (mostly) on, which Jonas took as a sign that his "noble" guise was working well. He moaned in all the right places, complimented the marten's endowment, and got two extra silvers for his trouble.

After he'd washed up (a process which took nearly as long as the marten himself had), Hazel told him he had another customer waiting. This time, it was Xaric, come to fulfill his fantasy. He bucked and thrust into Jonas's muzzle, gasped and shuddered as he came, and left looking very satisfied. He didn't leave a tip, but he did say he would be back.

At the end of the day, he put the ten silver into a lock box Hazel had chosen for him. As an afterthought, he added the gold pendant. Sleeping with it was uncomfortable, and he didn't see any reason to do so now that he had another place to put it. He set it down carefully in one corner, and then just sat and looked at the sum total of all his fortune in the world.

The silver coins glinted under his paw. He moved them around, reflecting on the course his life had taken. Truthfully, he hadn't minded servicing his clients, and seeing all that silver in the box (even knowing some portion of it had to go to Hazel and Mikka) made him feel better. All he really wished was that he had Sasha's paw, or even Pike's, to help him pleasure himself that night.

His next customer didn't come until three days later. He spent most of that time berating himself for trusting Mikka and starting this business, and the remainder worrying about what he would do when the end of the month came and he couldn't pay Hazel. Hazel told him not to worry about it. "They'll come, boy. You didn't expect to be busy right away, did you?" Jonas mumbled that he had, and Hazel laughed and patted him on the back. "Mikka believes in you, and so do I," she said, and Jonas didn't realize until later that she must have gone to talk to Mikka about him.

He had one customer the next day, and Xaric came back the day after for another blow job, and when he was done, Jonas asked him to tell his friends if he thought they would appreciate his service. "Hrrf," Xaric panted. "I already have."

Inside the Cage

That cheered Jonas a good deal. For his first week in business, he'd had four customers and made probably half his rent. That Galaday, he went to services with Hazel at a cathedral near the palace. "This is where the nobles go," she told him. "Just not at the same time."

"Like where I come from," he nodded, though the cathedral itself was very different. It was broad and low, stained glass dotting each of the wall sections. Unlike the Great Cathedral in Divalia, which was split into six sections, this cathedral was one large room, and the Cantor (whatever the Ferrenian equivalent was) was a cougar whose deep voice made Jonas shiver. He led them through the services, which Jonas now knew well enough to follow along on his own (his first time with Alexan, he'd started to sing the verses for all the families until Alexan had nudged him hard in the ribs). Afterwards, Hazel asked what he'd thought.

"It was impressive," he said.

"I go there every once in a while," she said. "Usually just the one closer by, but I thought you'd like to see it. It's somethin', ain't it?"

"Sure is," Jonas said. He wondered how many people had been to both the Great Cathedral in Divalia and the cathedral of Caril. Not many, he thought with a small amount of satisfaction.

He was in good spirits until he got back to his rooms and found Mikka waiting there. The grey fox greeted Hazel, then headed upstairs without waiting for Jonas.

"Looks like you got another customer," Hazel said.

"Yeah." Jonas braced himself and marched up the stairs.

Mikka was already taking his clothes off. "How's business?"

"Good so far. Thanks for sending customers over."

"It's my business too," the fox said, stripping down to his fur.

Jonas closed the door to his rooms. "Look, Mikka…"

"Your money's on the table. You know what I want." The fox climbed on the bed and crouched on all fours, lifting his tail.

For a moment, Jonas was about to try to continue to apologize, but he wasn't sure it would do any good. He could see that Mikka was closed to him, and he would have to wait until the fox opened up. He stripped his clothes off and climbed onto the bed behind Mikka.

Afterwards, Mikka seemed to open up a little while he was getting dressed. "How many of my referrals came to see you?"

"Three, I think. Xaric twice."

"And you're charging four silver?" Jonas nodded. "That makes three silver and two copper you owe me."

"Take it from the box," Jonas said. He didn't want to admit he had no way of knowing if Mikka was correct or not.

Mikka reached in and pulled the coins out. "And Hazel gets one and six. Do you want to do that now or wait until the end of the month?"

"I think she said end of the month."

"All right." Mikka rested his paw on the door handle. "Jonas…"

"Yes?"

"Would you like to come to dinner tomorrow night?"

"Sure." Jonas smiled. "Are you coming to dinner tonight?"

"Here? I hadn't planned on it."

"Would you?"

Mikka hesitated, then nodded. "I'll ask Hazel."

"It'll be nice to see you again."

"It's good to see you, too. Good luck, Jonas."

Mikka did come to dinner, and even seemed to enjoy himself. Jonas realized that it would be tricky to remain friends with Mikka while simultaneously keeping him as a client and business partner and not letting himself get trapped into a more confining relationship. It would be easier, he reflected, to just drop all pretense of friendship.

But he didn't want to do that. As wary as he was of letting the fox get too close, he also realized that he felt comfortable around Mikka, that their shared experiences gave them a bond that he'd last experienced with Pike and Sasha. When they were saying their good-byes at the door, and Mikka thanked Jonas for inviting him, Jonas smiled and said, "Thanks for being there," and he meant it.

He saw Mikka twice more over that month, once for business, once for dinner, and he would've spent more time thinking about how to handle his relationship with the fox if he hadn't been busy worrying about money and working out the details of his job. "I never realized how much Tally had to manage," he said to Hazel one day after he'd had three clients waiting at the same time in her lounge.

"I don' mind," she said. "Two of them bought cakes to take home."

Jonas grinned, but still asked her to help him draft a schedule, and he began making appointments to avoid conflicts—on days when he had any customers at all. It seemed as though he would have two or three days in a row with no customers, and on those days he grew more and more convinced that he would never succeed, that in a month he would be unable to pay his rent and would have to leave. He watched the sun set, thinking of his friends in Ferrenis and wondering if he could possibly walk there.

The drought would end with a flood, and leave him exhausted on his bed at the end of the day, wondering how three clients could tire him out when only a year ago he'd been serving six and still had energy left at the end of the day. It was a happy, or at least content, kind of wondering, as he had silver in the box and the sunset on those days brought relief rather than anxiety.

At the end of his first month, he had enough to pay his rent, his commissions to Hazel and Mikka, and still have a box lined with silver. The fact that he'd survived his first month and had three regular clients now (not counting Mikka) eased his mind. He knew that however much they liked him, if he stopped making money, he would be back out on the street. When the droughts came, as they still did, he pushed his worries back and allowed himself to enjoy the freedom from work, helping Hazel with chores around the house or strolling around the neighborhood.

The following Gaiaday was bright and sunny, the first promise that the heat of summer was coming. Jonas had purchased a new outfit, a simpler one than the fancy clothes Mikka had sold him (which he now thought of as his work clothes). He wore it to the cathedral for the day of Sacrifice, a joyful festival with a somber sermon describing Gaia's giving of her body to her children so that they might thrive and multiply. The service, twice as long as a regular one, seemed familiar to Jonas, though he wasn't sure whether it was gaudier and larger because he was in a different Church, or just in a gaudier and larger one.

Hazel held an party at her house afterwards, which Jonas attended for the first hour, before his busy afternoon. She had piled her tables and counters with small cakes and bowls of fruit-laced wine and mead, and the small room was crowded with people. An "Indulgence" party, she called it, but she was too busy with preparations for Jonas to ask her what that meant.

Jonas talked for a short time with one of Hazel's daughters, then drifted away and found himself standing near Mikka as the fox was picking a raisin-covered cake from the table. They'd said 'hello' when Mikka arrived, then drifted apart, and this was the first time Jonas had seen him alone since then. He watched the fox's ears for a moment, unsure of what to say to him in this social situation. Mikka didn't seem to be avoiding him, but neither had he sought Jonas's company. Jonas recalled that Mani hadn't been eager to be seen with him in public, but at least Mikka wasn't running away. He smiled at the fox as he turned.

"Hi, Jonas." Mikka returned the smile and sipped the glass of wine he'd filled.

"Hi. So, what's an Indulgence party?" Jonas asked, taking a black-currant cake and nibbling on it.

Mikka waved a paw around the room. "This."

"Mmm." He chewed and swallowed. "I know, but what does it mean?"

"We're celebrating Gaia's sacrifice by taking advantage of what's been given us. Sundown tonight we observe the Priva."

"Priva?" This was definitely new to him.

Mikka looked up at him. "You never heard of Priva? When you give up something for a month? Mostly people give up on baked and cooked food, eat raw vegetables and only cook meat very simply. No sauces."

"Oh." He licked the pieces of cake from around his teeth. "So this party is to eat the good stuff while we can."

"If you observe strictly." The fox shrugged. "I've always thought that Gaia sacrificed herself to leave us this earth and the good things in it, and to deprive yourself of them for a month is rude. But it does get difficult to get more than just lettuce and roast fowl for the next month."

"Not so bad." He'd subsisted on worse, and it was only for a month.

"Don't worry about my visits, though." Mikka smiled at Jonas as he said that, and then walked across the room to talk to a weasel who was trying to catch his attention, leaving the cougar confused.

Jonas found out what Mikka meant in short order. Apparently, many of his clients believed it was permissible to eat cakes and flavored meats if you gave up something else you enjoyed. His business dropped off precipitously over the next few weeks, with Mikka alone accounting for over a quarter of his earnings. By the last week of the month, he had barely made half his takings from the previous month even before he gave Hazel and Mikka their shares.

Two days before his rent was due, he watched the sun go down from his window, staring at the stacks of silver on his table. The lock box lay empty in front of him. He had two stacks of ten silver coins and one stack of two. Some of that money would have to go to Mikka, some to Hazel. And he would not have enough left over for his rent. He cursed himself for buying clothes, for buying his meals at the pub and paying to have them sent over (he'd stopped that last week and was now paying slightly less for Hazel to cook for him), and for his general inability to predict that once things had gotten good, they might not always stay that way.

Where would he go when he couldn't pay the rent? He was back to where he started. He would have to leave in the middle of the night, take what silver he had left, leave Hazel and Mikka without their money and rent, and hope he had enough to make it back to Tephos. Or he could just live on the streets. Twenty-two silver would keep him alive for half a year, perhaps. Maybe he could join a brothel.

He turned quickly from the window at a heavy creak on the stairs. The scent floating up to the landing was unmistakable. Terrified that she'd heard his thoughts or had guessed his intentions, he scooped the silver back into the lock box and closed it just as Hazel's black and white muzzle appeared around the corner of the landing.

"Oh, son, you don't need to worry 'bout ol' Hazel. I ain't after your money." She grinned at him. "'Sides, I kept a spare key to that box when I gave it to you."

He wasn't sure whether or not she was kidding, but he smiled. "No, I was just, um, counting…"

"Been a slow month, I know."

"Yeah."

"So I thought, since you ain't busy, and I'm all done with cookin' tonight, maybe I could get a first-hand closeup look at what's goin' on in my house these last two months." She grinned at him and dropped four silver on the table.

He stared at her.

"That how you greet all your clients?" She clucked. "It's a wonder any

Inside the Cage

of 'em ever come back. You want the money?"

"Uh, if you're...I mean, if you want..."

She tapped his nose with a black fingertip that reminded him fleetingly of Alexan's, with a sharper odor. "I may be your landlord, but I'm still female. I got needs too. And you're handsomer than any of the boys who come a'courtin' lately."

"Sure, okay." Still bewildered, he got up and extended a paw. "Would you step inside with me?"

She smiled and took his paw. "Now you're talkin'."

Jonas hadn't had a female customer in a long time. Males he knew: he could smell and see in the way they carried themselves what kind of thing they liked, and rarely did he make a mistake. Fortunately, Hazel was not one to leave her desires to his interpretation. By the end of a half hour, she was panting, a blissful, lazy smile on her muzzle as she straddled him.

"Good?" he asked when her eyes opened.

"I can see why you get paid so much."

"I didn't really do anything. But I'm glad you enjoyed it."

"Mmm." She leaned over to nuzzle his ear, and then slid off him. He reached back and handed her a towel, seeing her searching for one, and she smiled as she wiped herself. "Well, I think you're worth keeping around."

The comment rekindled his worry about paying his rent and killed any arousal he had left. He got dressed silently and followed her out into his foyer. "Listen, Hazel," he began, "about the rent this month..."

"Don't you worry your head about it." She paused on the landing of the stair. "We'll take care of it. You'll be okay."

And he was, miraculously. When Mikka came over and went through his money and his records with Hazel, they left him with three whole silvers in his box. He thanked them, suspecting that they were short-changing themselves to allow him to stay, and after dinner, went upstairs to his room.

He had discovered in his floor a small hole that looked down into Hazel's rooms. From the placement of it and the fact that it was hidden by the rug the previous tenant had left behind, he suspected that the tenant had used it to spy on Hazel's private moments. Jonas had no desire to do so, but he was curious to hear what she and Mikka were talking about. He made sure his lamps were extinguished and then carefully lifted the rug, angling his ear towards the opening.

"...know what you've been yelping about all those times," Hazel was saying.

"Oh, you took a turn?" Mikka's voice was quieter and amused.

"Sure did, hon. I figured if I'm going to be short this month I might as well get a little ride out of it."

"And?"

"Good ride. I haven't come like that in years."

"I thought you gave up males."

"I gave up sharing my property with them, not sleeping with 'em." She laughed. "Ain't gonna make a habit of it though. Wouldn't want to get hooked."

"I'm not hooked," Mikka said, and then he said something else that Jonas didn't catch.

"Hoo!" Hazel laughed again. "You been investing more than you been thinking you have." Mikka muttered something else, and Hazel said, "Ain't nothin' to worry about. He's a sweet kid and he won't hurt you."

"I know he's sweet, dear," Mikka said. "I just don't want to confuse business with pleasure."

"You can afford to."

"This month, sure."

"Won't have to very much longer, if I read things right."

"Hope not. I'll have to spread the word a little more."

Jonas set the rug down quietly and crawled into the other room, where he slept on a mat on the floor on days when the bedroom still smelled too strong for him to sleep. He was a little troubled at the thought that Mikka might still be infatuated with him, but he felt he was handling things as best he could. And he felt guilty about Hazel saying he was sweet—if only they knew he'd been spying on them. But he had liked listening in on the conversation; they talked more freely when he wasn't around. Spreading the word about him, for example. They hadn't said anything about that to him, just that he shouldn't worry about getting more clients.

And a couple days later, Hazel didn't seem to suspect anything when he asked her how he could let more people know about his services. She asked if he'd had any ideas, and he said (as if he hadn't been thinking about it for the last couple days) he wondered if going to a couple of the local pubs and getting to know the barkeeps there would help. And when she said she thought it would, he felt warm and proud of himself.

So he started going back to the pubs, this time making an effort to talk to the bartenders and let them know what he did. One of the bartenders didn't seem to care much, but the other was interested and friendly, and Jonas ended up spending the majority of his time in the Green Dragon pub as a result.

He also spent more time listening to Mikka and Hazel through the hole in the floor. They didn't always talk about him, but he enjoyed listening anyway. He and his brother had held their ears against the door of their room when their parents were talking some nights, and Jonas had enjoyed listening in then as much as he did now, even if his parents were just arguing about money. Once, they had eavesdropped on their parents making love, and though his brother had fled back to his bed when it was apparent what was happening, Jonas has listened, fascinated, to every growl and pant.

That wouldn't happen with Mikka and Hazel, he was pretty sure, but he still liked to listen to them talk, and sometimes he picked up tips like the one he had that first night. The month following Priva was still bad, but the Green Dragon bartender sent a couple clients his way, and one of them became a regular too, and the next month he only had a few days with no clients.

His biggest surprise of those first few months came when a familiar-smelling female bobcat stepped up into his foyer. He was surprised, but his experience with Hazel gave him enough confidence to wave her into the bedroom. She just shook her head and smiled, and when she said "I'm Delena, Xaric's mate," he realized why he recognized her scent.

"I, uh," he stuttered, not sure what to say, though she obviously wasn't angry at him.

She held up a paw. "I just came here to say thank you." When he didn't say anything, she patted his paw. Her pads were soft on his fur. "Xaric's a little high-strung, but since he's been coming here, he's been much more relaxed. And he hasn't tried to put that thing in my mouth for two months. It's delightful, really."

Jonas grinned, still a bit nervous. "He told you he comes here?"

"Gaia, no!" She laughed. "But we have servants, and I noticed that some of our money has not been going to the local pub. I thought he might have a mistress, but it didn't take me long to figure out the truth. This is definitely preferable, trust me."

"Well…I'm glad to be of help."

"Is there anything I could do for you?" She smiled. "Make him bathe before his appointments?"

Jonas laughed, and then an idea occurred to him. "Well, if you have any other friends who would like their husbands to have a distraction, I could use the business."

Her smile broadened, and she held her paw out to him. "Done."

"Thank *you*, in that case." He took her paw gently and brought it to his nose, taking in her scent politely. She bowed, and left him feeling curiously happy.

Chapter 12

Business was good, finally, with enough regular clients to pay his rent and several one-time clients from referrals each month. With his extra income, he bought a nicer bed (moving the old one to the foyer for sleeping) and a trip to the local surgeon. His fur was long and getting shaggy from the winter, and although it stirred memories of Van Wyck, he realized he needed to get it trimmed. The surgeon was a raccoon with very gentle paws who did excellent work, and Jonas went back to him every month after that. He still hated being groomed, but he took great pleasure in instructing Doctor Hewill where to trim and where not to trim. And it was surely no coincidence that his tips went up the month after his first trim; more than one of his clients mentioned it.

Jonas settled into a routine more easily than he would like to have thought possible. He mostly saw his clients, occasionally the other lodgers, and Hazel and Mikka. He enjoyed the dinner conversation he was included in, and the guilty pleasure of eavesdropping afterwards, sitting in the dark with the rug held in one paw, ear cocked to the stream of dim light that filtered up from the lower floor.

Summer was at its peak, and Hazel had opened all the windows in the house and spent most of her time on the porch, as much because it was cooler there as because, she told Jonas, "in this heat you can smell me comin' a mile away." Jonas didn't put on a shirt for weeks at a time, and many of his clients arrived nearly naked themselves. Skirts coming down to mid-thigh were fashionable for both sexes, but some thicker-furred species like wolves wore even less when they could get away with it. Mikka complained that this time of year was hardest on him, and he could barely afford to keep himself and his apprentices housed. While Jonas was eavesdropping one night, he heard Mikka make reference to some competitor who seemed to be trying to make things difficult for him. It was odd, he thought, that Mikka wouldn't discuss that when Jonas was around, but maybe he was just private about his business. Hazel's response was odd, too. She said he would "get tired of it" soon enough, which didn't make sense to Jonas.

Jonas was reflecting on this and, for the fortieth time, the fact that it got much hotter in Caril than it had in Divalia, when he heard steps and claw-clicks on the stair and sat up to greet his client. To his surprise, the scent that greeted him was as familiar as the muzzle that rounded the corner a moment later.

"Benton!"

The fox gave Jonas a warm hug, tail wagging. "Hi there, Jonas! Sorry I haven't come by before. I kept meaning to, but I always thought you might be busy, and then things have been busy at the shop and I just haven't really had time."

"That's okay." Jonas matched the fox's wide grin. "It's great to see you. What have you been doing?"

Benton was carrying a folded piece of parchment, as there was obviously no place for him to put it in his skirt. Without his shirt, he looked thinner than when Jonas had seen him last, though that might've just been Jonas's memory playing tricks on him. "I've mostly been working. But that's not why I came by. You got a letter." He handed the parchment to Jonas.

"A letter?" Jonas took the parchment and read the outside, and when he saw the handwriting, he forgot for a moment that Benton was in the room watching him, that he was in a stuffy, hot building in a different country from where he'd grown up. "Pike," he whispered, and broke the seal on the letter.

"You want me to go while you read it?"

"No, no, that's okay. I want to talk with you some more."

"I'll wait downstairs, then." Benton smiled and padded down quietly.

Jonas sat down on the sleeping bed and unfolded the letter carefully.

Dearest Jonas,

I can't tell you how delighted I am to hear from you. We were all worried when you left, myself most of all. We asked the guard whether you'd been hurt, but they had no reports. Tally said you'd run away, but I didn't think you would. I guess he was right. And you are right to think that he would not take you back. But that's nothing personally against you. He doesn't take anyone back once they're gone.

I'm dying to hear about your adventure! How did you travel to Tephos? And with whom? And is there anything I can do to help you? I hope that sending this letter to the guards doesn't mean you are in prison.

Do write back as soon as you can.

Love, Pike

He read the letter several times over. He wanted badly to reach out and hug the raccoon , but in lieu of that he vowed to write back as soon as he could.

After storing the parchment in his money box, he took Benton out to the Green Dragon for lunch and a drink. "So that letter was from someone you knew back home?" Benton asked when they were seated.

"A friend I used to work with."

"Did you have many friends there?"

"A few."

Benton looked down at his ale and sipped it. "I guess not too many, or you wouldn't have run away."

"It wasn't really my friends. It was my life. My friends couldn't help with that."

Benton thought about that for a second and then said, "Don't you have the same life here, now?"

"Not really." He took a drink and then, since Benton still looked curious, said, "I'm my own boss now. That seems to make a lot of difference."

"Oh. Okay." Their food arrived and Benton took a big bite. "Thanks for lunch," he mumbled around his food. "Sorry I haven't come by more often. I really did mean to."

"It's all right." Jonas smiled at the fox's lowered ears. "I'm glad you came by now. If you want, you and Jherik could come to dinner sometime."

"I'll see if he wants to. I'd like to."

They ate quietly, and as Jonas was finishing his stew, he said, "How's Master Talid's weapons business?"

"Busy. I haven't had a chance to relax in months. The orders for customized weapons are coming in more than ever. I think all the nobles are worried about tensions with Tephos." His ears flicked down as he said the name of the country. "Sorry."

"Why?"

"Well, because you…"

"Oh." Jonas waved a paw. "I don't care for politics either way."

"But still, all this talk of war…don't you worry about your friends, your family?'

"I try not to." But now that Benton had mentioned it, he did start to worry about Pike, about Richy. How would they fare if there were a war and they were conscripted?

"Which side would you fight on?"

"I…never thought about it. I guess I would have to fight for Ferrenis."

"Against all your old friends?"

Jonas sighed. "Should I fight against all my new friends?"

Benton's ears drooped. "I guess not."

"Let's hope it doesn't come to that."

"Yeah." The fox nodded. "If it did, you know, Jherik might be able to help you get out of fighting. He has some connections. Or I might be able to get you a job with Master Talid. Weapons-makers are protected from conscription. But I don't really know if I'd be able to."

Jonas gave the fox a small smile. "Like I said. I'll keep hoping I don't have to worry about it."

"I hope you won't too." They finished the meal in silence.

As they were draining the last of their ales and preparing to leave, Benton looked at Jonas's chest and said suddenly, "Say, has Dixan come bothering you?"

"Who?" The name was vaguely familiar, but Jonas couldn't quite place it.

"Alexan's brother, I guess. He came by Master Talid's a couple days ago to talk to me. Wanted to know something about a pendant—maybe that one you're wearing. Don't worry, I didn't tell him anything. I was just wondering if he bothered you at all. I don't know where he got my name from. Probably Phineas."

"Oh. No, he hasn't come bothering me yet." Though it sounded to Jonas as if it were only a matter of time. He stopped himself from pressing a paw to the gold pendant around his neck.

"Okay. Cause I didn't tell him about you."

"I appreciate that." Jonas said the words distantly, hearing Mikka talk again. "Listen, did...Dixan? Did he say anything about Mikka?"

"Um..." Benton chewed his lip. "He didn't say anything directly. But he didn't seem to believe me."

The fox looked worried. Jonas leaned over the table. "What else did he say?"

"Nothing." Jonas tilted his muzzle, frowning, and Benton lowered his ears. "He said a couple things as he was leaving. I think he was just frustrated."

"What did he say?"

Benton hesitated again, but talked before Jonas could prod him. "One of the other apprentices heard him talking to Master Talid on the way out. Something about keeping an eye on me and that I might bring him more trouble than I was worth. But listen, he was in a really bad mood and I didn't help when I couldn't tell him anything."

Jonas nodded. "Maybe."

Benton glanced out the window and stood up quickly. "Oh, Fox, I'm gonna be late back. Listen, Jonas, thanks for the lunch. I really appreciate it. Let's do it again sometime?"

"Absolutely. Soon." Jonas smiled and clasped Benton's paw. "Thanks."

He knew he should get back himself; he had an appointment later that afternoon. But he kept hearing the worry in Mikka's voice when he talked about someone making things difficult for him. *He's cost me a couple sales already*, he'd said. *But it's nothing I can't handle.* It wasn't a competitor, Jonas knew now. It was Dixan, pursuing Mikka for the pendant that would get him his brother's house back, now going after Benton, too. Maybe he had just been frustrated, like Benton said. But Jonas remembered Alexan's single-mindedness, and he didn't think so. Thinking back to their conversation, Jonas didn't think Benton thought so, either.

When the rabbit came around to ask if that was all, Jonas ordered another ale. He drank it slowly, and he thought about Benton and Mikka. He wondered how much trouble they could be in, and he thought a good deal about a fox who might be primarily made up of Alexan's worst traits.

The following day, he got up earlier than normal and took a walk to Benton's shop. His work hours usually kept him from enjoying the cool summer mornings, the way the brisk breeze ruffled the fur on his chest and occasionally snuck up under his skirt. Today, it was his preoccupation with Dixan that kept him from enjoying these simple pleasures; his paw played with the golden pendant in his skirt pocket all the way to the shop as his mind grappled with the problem.

Of course, they didn't allow him into the shop itself. Benton came out a minute later, ears askew with curiosity when he saw Jonas.

"Hi, Benton. Listen, I need to ask you something important."

The fox gave him a wary look. "Okay."

"When that Dixan talked to you, he told you where to go if you found out anything, right? He gave you his office address?"

After a pause, Benton said, "Ye-es."

"Can you give me that address?"

"Look, Jonas, there's no point in you getting mixed up in the middle of this. Dixan has no idea where you are and he doesn't have to."

"I'm not going to tell him where I am," Jonas said patiently. "I just want to talk to him."

"Please don't, Jonas. It'll just make things worse."

"I don't want you getting into trouble on my account. I just want to tell him to leave my friends alone."

"O-okay."

Jonas waited patiently. "So?"

"Maybe we should go see Mikka."

"Benton, I just want to know where to go. I'm going to go tell him to stop worrying about the pendant."

Benton sighed. "All right." He gave Jonas an address. "Just go up towards the palace and don't cross the river, turn right along it. You'll see a rose marble building at a busy corner. It's the one just before that, on the riverside."

"Okay. Thanks." He reached out and squeezed Benton's shoulder. "Don't worry about me. I'll be all right."

Benton didn't look convinced, but Jonas couldn't think of what else to tell him. He left the fox and walked back out into the sunlight, shading his eyes as he followed Benton's directions towards the river. The day was already getting warmer and the streets more crowded. Around lunchtime, he knew, the crowds would hit their peak, but that didn't worry him. In this part of town, where his clients mostly came from, nobles were not unfamiliar. Dressed in Mikka's finery, he barely merited a second glance from most of the wolves, raccoons, bobcats, and other non-cougars he passed.

Wooden buildings gave way to stone, adorned with ornate reliefs and plaques proclaiming the name of the king they had been built under. At the river, he looked across for the first time into the Palace Quarter,

Inside the Cage

where the minor nobles lived. All the grey and white buildings sported elaborate towers and decorations, the most ostentatious being a two-story high sculpture of some cougar noble holding a long sword in front of him. Jonas leaned on the railing and looked across the river at them, then down at the river itself. A steady stream of barges floated down the river, while two lone ships headed upstream and a flurry of small craft darted between them. To his right, a thick stone bridge spanned the river, with pillars on either side topped by bronze statues of eagles.

Just on his side of the bridge, he saw the rose-marble building Benton had described, looking across at the lofty splendor of the aristocrats. A small bronze plaque on the building next to it bore the name "Dixan of Paravul, Esq." Jonas touched the words briefly. He'd never known Alexan's family name.

Inside, a female weasel greeted him from behind a high small wooden desk, her muzzle slightly below his eye level. A portrait of a fox dressed in elegant formal wear hung on the wall; Jonas looked at it only long enough to note the resemblance to Alexan. The soft pile carpeting of the room felt soothing to his paws, but he felt anything but relaxed as he walked up to the weasel's desk.

He asked to see Dixan, and she told him that he would have to wait, that Mister Dixan was engaged in important business and would not be free for another hour.

"It's very important," Jonas said, leaning over the desk.

"I'm very sorry, but his time is otherwise occupied right now."

"All right," Jonas said, turning. "Just tell him that I'll be back in an hour and that I know where that pendant he's looking for is."

"I will tell him, sir."

He wandered along the river until he found a small bakery. With a small roll of spiced bread and a square of cheese from the shop next door, he made a small lunch and leaned on the balustrade, looking across the water. He wanted to walk around the other side, but there were guards on the bridge and he wasn't sure if he needed papers in order to go across.

The people on the far side were mostly cougars, dressed finely (though, he noted, not much more finely than he was). He was sure they were eating better than bread and cheese, though his bread was very fresh and the cheese soft and sharp, just to his taste. All in all, he thought, there wasn't much to indicate that the cougars over there had it much better than he did over on his side.

When he returned to Dixan's building, a lanky fox was leaning against the weasel's desk, and Jonas caught his breath; for a moment, he'd thought it was Alexan. But the fox's head turned when he came in, and the smile had a nasty edge to it that even Alexan had never had.

"Well, well. Right under my nose this whole time and I'd no idea. And now you've come to see me. How priceless."

"What?"

"I knew Alexan had found himself a whore somewhere who'd gone back to the street after he died, and I knew he'd had a cougar staying with him. I just never put together that they were the same person. I thought he was putting up some hard-luck noble's son, trying to get in good with a noble, maybe sharing the whore with him. And it was you all along. What are you, some wastrel from the provinces run away from home?"

Jonas felt his temper fray and struggled to keep it under control. "Listen," he said, "I just came to deliver a message."

"Errand boy and whore. A cat of many talents," Dixan said. "Go ahead, whore. I'm all ears."

Jonas felt his claws extending and willed them back in. He took the pendant out of his pocket and dangled it in front of Dixan. "I heard you were looking for this. So I just wanted to tell you to stop."

The fox's eyes narrowed when he saw the pendant. "So you had it. You've no right to keep it, whore."

"Your brother gave it to me," Jonas said through gritted teeth. "That's all the right I need."

"It's mine by right," Dixan said. "And I can make the court see it that way too."

Jonas paused for a moment, unsure. "You're welcome to try," he said finally, and stuffed the pendant back into his pocket.

Dixan's manner changed again; his features relaxed and an oily smile replaced the sneer on his muzzle. "Listen," he said, "it's not worth my trouble or yours. I'll give you the pendant's weight in gold. You can sell it and get yourself another outfit maybe."

"Don't waste your time." The anger was being replaced by disgust. Jonas turned to leave.

"Ten gold."

"Forget it."

"You're making a mistake." Dixan said it quietly. Jonas almost turned around, then. The fox's resolve and confidence alone felt like weapons he couldn't match. Giving in would end all the trouble, after all. His paw closed around the pendant, and he remembered again Alexan's smile when he'd given the gift, the family pendant he'd lost. Why should he give this up and tell the fox that his bullying tactics had worked? He forced himself to open the door and walk through it without another word.

He hardly saw any of the town on the way back. Dixan's last words echoed in his head, and he couldn't banish the feeling that maybe he had made a mistake. Going to confront the fox had seemed that morning like the only course of action he had, but would it have hurt to lie low and help out his friends as he could? He was tempted to throw the pendant in the river, just out of spite, but the meeting had deepened his attachment to it, if anything. It represented the sweet Alexan that he preferred to remember, the one who was nothing like the creature in the office with the fancy carpet and the portrait and the weasel who looked down on everyone.

By the time he reached his home, he was so lost in thought that he didn't even notice Hazel sitting on the porch until she called out to him.

"Come sit here a minute, Jonas, and you tell me what's wrong. I never seen a tail droop so low."

Paw on the door handle, he paused and started to shake his head, but he was starting to worry, really worry about Dixan, and telling Hazel what he'd intended to be a noble secret felt far preferable to stewing in his own worry. Besides, if Dixan intended to make trouble for him, she would probably be involved.

He sat next to her and she put a large arm across his shoulders, pushing him down a bit so she could be comfortable. He didn't talk immediately and she didn't ask him to. Finally, he said, "I went to see Dixan."

She exhaled and squeezed his shoulder. "Why would you do a fool thing like that?"

"I heard," you and Mikka talking, he'd been about to say, and then realized he wasn't quite ready to confess that, "that he was looking for me. I mean, for the pendant."

"Where did you hear that from?"

"Benton."

"That fox who was here yesterday?" He nodded. "I shoulda stuffed his fluffy tail into his muzzle. Why would he tell you, when Mikka's been doin' all he can to keep that lawyer away from you?"

"He has?"

Hazel nodded. "Well, spilt milk. What did you say?"

"I showed him the pendant and told him to give up looking for it."

"I don't imagine that went over well."

Jonas shrugged. "He offered me gold and then said I was making a mistake."

"That all?"

"Yeah." Jonas sighed. "But it was a mistake, wasn't it? I mean, I should've just stayed out of it."

He said it more because he wanted her to agree than because he believed it, and he was surprised when she said, "I don't know 'bout that, Jonas. Why did you go see him?"

"Because...I wanted him to leave Mikka and Benton alone."

She laughed. "I think you made sure of that. Listen, kitten, you acted from the heart, an' that's good. Maybe it wasn't the smartest thing to do, but it wasn't your brain telling you to do it anyhow. Now it's done, your brain's kickin' in with all the things you shoulda thought about before, but sometimes you need to just go and do, and that's what you did."

"But I made more trouble for myself and everyone else."

"Don't you worry 'bout that. We know what kind of trouble he thinks he can stir up. I'll make sure all your licenses are in order and you'd best check all your new customers pretty carefully for a while."

"New customers?"

"I wouldn't put it past him to send someone over and leave somethin' valuable here, then claim you robbed him. Old trick, but a good one." She grinned. "Used it m'self, once upon a while."

"I'll be careful."

"I know you will." She pulled her arm back. "Now let me get a letter and if you're not too busy you can take it to Mikka. He'd best hear it from you anyway."

"All right." Jonas started to get up with her, but she pushed him down. "Just set right there and I'll be back soon."

"Yes'm." He grinned at her and leaned back in the seat, a little surprised at how much better he felt already. Hazel certainly didn't seem worried, and that made him relax. Maybe he'd been working himself up about nothing. He closed his eyes and let the heat of the day warm him, enjoying the occasional breeze that ruffled his fur.

His reverie was interrupted by the brush of parchment against the fur of his arm, and the scent of skunk. He opened his eyes to a black and white arm and Hazel's smile. "Here." She pushed the paper at him again. "Just give that to Mikka. You can read it after he does. It's just telling him not to worry like I know he's gonna."

"Okay." Jonas took the paper and stood up. "I'll be back for Felter's appointment."

"I'll let him know if he comes early." She grinned. "Don't you go worryin' neither. This is gonna be okay."

"Thanks, Hazel." Jonas gave her a warm smile. He was tempted to brush her muzzle or hug her, but they hadn't touched much since she'd taken advantage of his services; at least, he hadn't touched her.

Mikka, on the other paw, he brushed muzzles with regularly, and the grey fox was smiling when he came out of the back of his shop to see Jonas. They nuzzled and Mikka said, "What brings you here?"

Jonas glanced at the back room, but the apprentices were not in evidence. He handed Mikka the note. The fox wrinkled his nose. "From Hazel?" Jonas nodded. Mikka opened the note carefully and read it, and his ears lowered as he did.

"Okay," he said, setting the note on the counter. "I'm calm, and I'm confident that all your business papers are in order. I have them upstairs. Now why am I remaining calm?"

It had been easier to tell Hazel. Jonas fidgeted and then said, "Benton came by, and he mentioned Dixan…"

"Oh, no."

"I just wanted to tell him to leave you guys alone."

"You didn't go see him?"

"I thought if I showed him the pendant that he'd know not to bother you."

Inside the Cage

"Jonas, dear…that's a really sweet thought…"

He pointed to the note. "Remember what Hazel said."

Mikka looked down at the note and then grinned. "Okay. I'm staying calm."

"Hazel said not to worry. She said all the papers are in order and there's nothing he can do to us."

Mikka patted the counter beside him. Jonas sat up on it. "Hazel may be a bit optimistic," the grey fox said, putting a paw on Jonas's knee. "There's plenty of trouble a lawyer could dream up. But panicking now won't help." He beckoned for Jonas to lean forward, and stood on tiptoe to kiss the cougar on the nose. "It was a *very* sweet thing, dear."

Jonas managed a half-smile through his confusion. "Oh, you're welcome," he said. He hadn't really thought of it as something he was doing for Mikka and Benton, just that it was, well, some trouble he'd caused that needed to be made right. And, he supposed, the fact that it was hurting his friends led him to pursue it with greater passion than he might normally have had. That aside, he didn't want Mikka to mistake this for more than it was. Their relationship had stabilized at a level that Jonas was comfortable with, and he no longer feared that he would be kicked out into the street if he hit a bad patch of business, but now he worried that Mikka was just waiting for a sign from him to pursue something further again.

Fortunately, the fox didn't seem inclined to follow up the kiss. "I'll make sure all your licenses are in order. I filed them away upstairs. Maybe you should take them and keep them with you, just in case there's an inspection or something."

"All right." Jonas prepared to hop off the counter, but Mikka waved him down. "I'll get them. You just wait there."

Mikka came back a moment later with a small packet of papers. He spread them out on the counter and looked up at Jonas. "Just so you understand, okay? I am listed as the business owner because I paid the fees on it. I listed this place as the main business address, because if things didn't work out with Hazel, you could move. And here you're listed as the employee, and remember signing this here? So you're all legal, and he can't touch you, at least there." He grinned at Jonas. "I guess if he paid, he could touch you somewhere else."

Jonas shuddered. "Not funny."

"Sorry, dear." Mikka patted his knee. "You'll be okay with these?"

"Sure. I can read."

"I know." Mikka smiled. "I trust you. Go on back. And tell Hazel I'm calm."

"I will."

"And Jonas…" Jonas turned as he hopped down from the counter. Mikka smiled at him. "Thanks. Really. I know it must have been hard for you to do."

"Oh, it was…" He shuffled, unsure what he wanted to say.

"It was sweet, dear." Mikka smiled. The fox took one of his paws and squeezed it. "And we appreciate it. That's all."

"O-kay." Jonas fidgeted, and finally squeezed back. Mikka let go, and Jonas smiled at the fox. "You're welcome." He left quickly, but as he glanced back through the window of the shop, he saw Mikka's pointed muzzle and dark eyes watching him with perked ears and a slight tilt to his head, a look that Jonas could only interpret as curiosity. The fox smiled when he saw Jonas's gaze, but didn't turn away. Jonas raised a paw, and went on his way.

Chapter 13

Trouble was not long in coming. The next day, as Jonas was finishing up with one of his newer clients, he heard conversation below and Hazel's voice saying, "I'm telling you, he'll be right down. He's with a client."

The wolf on his bed gasped and came, and Jonas hurried the cleaning up process as much as he felt comfortable doing. His client was still relaxing, pulling his clothes on leisurely, when Jonas heard footsteps on the stairs. The wolf heard them too, and gave Jonas a sharp glance. "You should schedule your customers better."

"They aren't customers," Jonas said just as the two guards appeared at the head of the stairs. He drew the curtain across the bedroom door and stepped out into the foyer to greet them.

Reminding himself that they were just agents, not the cause of his annoyance, he said, "I'm with a customer."

"This will be quick." The stag looked bored. His younger partner, a bear, looked around with flattened ears that Jonas interpreted as mild disgust. "We just need to make sure your license is in order."

"It's right here." He unlocked his money box and handed the paper to the stag. "What's this all about?"

The stag examined the papers very carefully. After a moment, his partner said, "Royal directive. Lots of unlicensed prostitutes working in the city and it's bad for health reasons."

"You got a surgeon's certification?" The stag looked up from the papers.

"No. I didn't know they did that. My doctor is Hewill, over on Marsh Street. You know him?"

"We know him. We'll be checking."

They didn't seem inclined to leave, even when they'd handed back the papers. The bear, keeping the same look of disgust, nevertheless was sniffing the air so strongly that Jonas could see dust motes swirling around his nose in the sunbeam. The stag kept looking at the curtain and trying to see around it. He lifted a hand to it, and to forestall him, Jonas said, "Anything else?"

The stag dropped his hand, looked at the curtain one more time, and then shrugged. "No. Come on, Jars."

They tromped down the stairs and out. Jonas waited until he heard the door close, and then drew the curtain back. The wolf was sitting on the edge of the bed.

"I'm really very sorry about that."

His customer smiled and held out a gold. "I feel better knowing you're licensed and inspected. Can I see you again next week?"

"Of course." Jonas took the coin and bowed. "Thank you."

He followed the wolf downstairs and saw him out. When he told Hazel what had happened, she laughed. "If that's the best that fox can do, then I'm not worried."

"It's annoying."

"Yeah, but he can't do it forever."

Jonas sighed, walking back upstairs. "Let's hope not."

He was in the Green Dragon the next day chewing on the bread and reflecting that it was not as fresh as usual when he heard a small sniff behind him and caught the scent of a mouse. He knew the scent vaguely; she was someone he'd seen often in the bar, with a variety of different males, but he'd never paid her much attention.

When he turned, he was surprised to see that she was waiting behind his table—waiting for him. The fur under her eyes was damp and crusty, and she was wringing her paws as she stood there. Her tail was curled tightly around her legs. She sniffled again when she saw him, and said, "H-hello, sir."

"Hi." Jonas turned his body, giving her a more thorough look. The only mouse he'd known well was Sasha, and although there wasn't a physical resemblance, there was something in her demeanor that reminded him of his friend. "Is there something you want?"

"No. Yes. Please, I—" She broke off and looked at the floor.

Jonas slid over in his booth. "Why don't you sit down?" He was still brooding over yesterday's episode, but it occurred to him that maybe her troubles were a little worse than his.

"Oh. Oh, thank you." But she stood motionless.

Jonas patted the seat. "Really. Sit down."

She shuffled forward and then lifted herself up onto the bench. "Thank you," she said again in a whisper.

He saw the way she was eyeing his bread, and said, "I'm done with that. You can have the rest if you want."

"Sir, I couldn't—"

"Take it, really." He cut off her protests.

"I..." But then she grabbed the bread and attacked it.

Jonas watched her finish it in under a minute, and couldn't help grinning. "Want more? I can order some."

"Oh, no, sir, no." She started to slide off the bench, and then stopped. "It's only that...you see, I'm...well, we're..." She looked at the bartender. Jonas followed her gaze and saw that the old boar was watching them both. The mouse dropped her voice to a whisper. "He said we're in the same line of work."

"Oh?" But it made sense as soon as she said it. That was what she and Sasha—and he—had in common.

"Yes, sir. But I'm not...I don't have a license. I used to work here, and he'd let me, but the guards came yesterday and..." She sniffled again, and

Inside the Cage

wiped her muzzle. "My little kit and I, sir, we don't have anywhere to go. I don't know what else I can do. And Elgyn said, he thought you were successful and maybe you could help us."

Jonas glanced at the bartender again and then looked at the mouse. "I don't really know any of the...houses in this area..."

"Oh, sir, we can't go to a house, not with my boy. They won't take us. I had to leave one when he was born."

"That doesn't seem..." He paused. "The father was a client?"

She nodded, head down.

"I see."

"Please, I just want to know if I can go somewhere the guards have already checked, or beyond their reach. I don't know the city. I thought if you were successful, you must have been other places that maybe might want me..."

Jonas tapped the table, claws extended. He couldn't think of anything to tell her, but he couldn't ignore the nagging feeling that he was responsible for her situation. It was possible that the sudden interest in unlicensed prostitutes was not related to his visit to Dixan. Not likely, though.

She started to edge her way off the bench, glancing nervously at his claws. "If you don't know of anywhere..."

"Wait." He retracted his claws. "Follow me."

It was crazy, he told himself all the way home. His license didn't cover anyone but him; he'd seen that on the paper. And where would she sleep? Could she bring in enough money to support herself in a more expensive place? He turned these questions over and over in his mind on the way back, and in the end he knew it didn't matter. He couldn't find it in himself to turn her out onto the street. He saw immediately when he introduced her to Hazel that the skunk felt the same.

"What's your name, child?" she asked the mouse, a question Jonas was shocked at himself for having neglected.

"Selia," she said in a voice barely above a whisper. "Thank you, ma'am."

"Well, Selia, you go bring your son here, and tell your friend at the bar to send your clients here in about a week. You hear?"

Selia's eyes grew so wide that Jonas thought they might drop out of her head. "R-really, ma'am?"

"Really. And stop that 'ma'am' nonsense. I'm Hazel. Understand?"

"Yes, ma'am. Thank you, ma'am!" Selia turned to Jonas. "And thank you, sir!"

"You're welcome," Jonas said, but the mouse was already out the door. He watched her go and turned to Hazel with a grin. "I didn't know you wanted to run a brothel."

Hazel poked his shoulder. "I saw the same thing you did: a poor young thing in trouble. And just like you, I helped her." She shrugged.

"You're good business. I'll take a chance on repeating good business."

"You going to try her out, like you did me?"

Hazel grinned at him. "Jealous? Don't worry, if she's been on her own for a year and survived, she can't be bad."

"I'm not jealous." He flicked his tail, hesitated, then decided to tease her. "Just seems like you've got a thing for tall, handsome cougars."

She stared at him, and for a brief moment he thought *I've gone too far, I've presumed on our acquaintance.* Then she threw back her head and laughed, and he relaxed. "A skinny boy like you? I like my men with more meat on their bones. Though you do have plenty of meat on one bone..."

Once he would have been embarrassed by such a comment, and he still felt his fur prickle slightly. But he just smiled back at her and said, "That's what keeps them coming back."

Selia settled in quickly. Mikka wasn't thrilled about taking on another "employee," but he allowed Jonas and Hazel to talk him into altering the license. Jonas had enough spare money to pay for the change and for Doctor Hewill's inspection, and Selia promised to pay a share of her money equal to Jonas's. Mikka's last resistance was broken down when Selia's son toddled over to him and rested his head on the fox's knee.

Jonas had half-thought that Selia might have made up her son for sympathy, but he was real and a definite charmer. Hazel took to him immediately, and once he got used to the smell, he took to her as well, following her around everywhere and playing with her black-and-white mop of a tail. His name was Selish, and he was not yet talking, but he was clearly aware of what was going on around him and would have things to say once he learned how. His bright dark eyes followed them everywhere, and he clapped happily whenever they played with him. He had just started to walk upright in the last month, Selia told them, and she'd had to move all her things to higher shelves.

"I've raised three of my own," Hazel said, "and what they didn't break can't be broke." She was delighted to keep the kit in her quarters, away from Jonas's clients, and for the first week Selia stayed there too. They arranged that she and Selish would stay in Jonas's work-bed while he slept out in the foyer as he usually did. Selia obviously preferred the privacy of the inner room, though she never said so out loud, and she said over and over again that she didn't mind the smells on the bed. Selish had his own wicker cradle, which went downstairs during the day and back upstairs at night.

When Selia had been with them a week, Mikka came back with the approved license change. "It was difficult," he said with a glance at Jonas, "because I think someone is just trying to make trouble. I had to spend another ten silver bribing the officials to get the signatures notarized."

"Thank you so much, sir," Selia said, clutching the paper and staring at it. Jonas thought she must be overjoyed to see her name on it, as she couldn't tear her eyes from it.

"I'll go get your money," Jonas said.

"Oh, you don't have to..." Mikka began, but Jonas ignored him.

"I want to come too!" Selia scampered after him, still clutching the paper. When they got upstairs, Jonas opened his money box to get the silver out, and Selia laid the paper on the table and looked at it.

"You're pretty excited," Jonas said.

Selia nodded, then looked up at him and back down at the paper. "Could you...show me which mark is my name? Is it that one?" She pointed to her name. "I remember the snake at the beginning."

"Yes." Jonas smiled. "That's your name. S-E-L-I-A." He traced each letter as he said it.

Selia didn't respond, just drew in a breath and shook her head. "It's too wonderful."

For a moment, Jonas thought this was what Sasha might've looked like when he was younger. Selia's eyes were bright and she was smiling the sort of smile that she normally reserved for Selish. He felt protective, and so he tried to pass on something Sasha had said. "It's not a pretty business."

"Oh, I know that, sir. I mean, Jonas. But a week ago, when the guards came, I was so scared. I thought my kit and I would die on the street, I really did. And I don't hold much for church, but I prayed to Mouse that whole morning. I just wanted Selish to be healthy. And Mouse answered! I think I should start going to church again."

"We go every Gaiaday," Jonas said. "There's a small church down the block and a big cathedral where the nobles go."

"I'll go with you then," Selia said. "If I may..."

"Of course."

She spied his paper records as he was closing the money box. "I suppose if we'll be doing business together, we should keep our records together." But her tone was doubtful.

"Okay." Jonas was wondering how he would keep track of someone else's income when he could barely keep track of his own. "Who keeps yours? Elgyn?"

"I do."

"You? But you can't..." He glanced at the license she hadn't been able to read.

She padded back into the bedroom and came out with a small book. "Just here." She seemed almost ashamed to show it to him.

"Oh, it can't be worse than mine." He took it from her and flipped through it, looking at the rows of neat little vertical marks. The left hand side seemed to be simple tallies; on the right were marks he found less comprehensible.

"See, this is the number of customers, broken up by each week. And on this side is a running total of my money. It's not very much." Her voice dropped to a whisper.

Jonas shook his head. "How does this tell you how much money you have?"

Her nimble little fingers scurried across the page. "This column is coppers and this one is silvers, and here is the amount I had to give to Elgyn, and here's my rent and the amount I paid for food, and for the nanny to watch Selish while I was working..." She noticed his expression and her ears drooped. "I didn't have any training, sir. It's the best I could do."

Jonas laughed and closed the book and handed it to her. "And with all my upbringing in a merchant family, I couldn't do that, or anything close to it. Would you keep the books for both of us?"

"Oh, sir, Jonas, I..."

"Please? I'm...I'm hopeless at it, I really am. Mikka and Hazel could be taking twice what they're owed. Or half. I'd have no idea."

"But you can read!"

"And not much more. Tell you what. If you keep the books, I'll teach you to read."

"Oh!" Her paw flew to her muzzle. "I couldn't..."

"You'd like to, though."

She nodded, slowly, and Jonas smiled. "Really, it's no trouble."

"If you're sure, sir."

"Jonas," he said firmly. "I'm sure."

She took to it quickly, spending all that night with him while he read his records to her, helping her complete his records from memory when the written records weren't complete. She scratched some notes in her book, asked him about his rent and about the agreements he'd made with Mikka and Hazel, and somehow, after two nights, she was able to tell him how much money he had in his box, to within ten coppers.

"That could just be some tips you forgot, or lunches at the pub," she said, but she was clearly pleased to have gotten so close.

"That's amazing."

"It's easy, really." She smiled.

"Not to me." He marveled that she could be possessed of such a hidden talent and think so little of it.

She took her first client in the new location the following day. Jonas didn't ask her specifically about it, but it seemed to go well. He and Hazel sat down to manage the schedule so that they had no overlapping clients, and as the final step towards making Selia a part of their household, Jonas took her to see Doctor Hewill.

The raccoon examined them both, and spent a good deal of time grooming Selia. When they were finished, Jonas asked if he could have a voucher of good health.

"Oh, yes," Hewill said. "The guards did come by. I thought you had one, but I guess I was wrong." He brought out a piece of paper and scrawled his name on it, then wrote a short statement about Jonas's health. "For the mouse, too?"

"Please."

He brought out another paper and wrote the same thing with Selia's name, then signed and dated them both. "There you go. She's a good one, by the way. Fairly young and in good health. You've got a good house there."

"We don't really have a house," Jonas said, but as he said it he wondered. Wasn't Mikka financing them, Hazel running the house, and he and Selia now providing the service? But there was no "madam," like Tally, to tell him who to sleep with and when to get up. And when he came to the doctor, he decided how to be groomed.

"Well, post that in your room, then, where people can see it. If the guards were asking, chances are someone else will be."

Hewill's words were prophetic. The certification hadn't been posted for two days before Jonas noticed one of his clients examining it. He happened to be downstairs talking to Hazel when the red fox walked in. Cherko was one of Jonas's favorite new clients, a cheery fox who reminded him of the good times with Alexan, but not too much, as he was closer to Benton's size. Normally, he greeted Jonas with a wave and Hazel with a bow, but today he looked preoccupied. He spotted the paper where Jonas had put it on the wall by the stairs, and spent a moment reading it.

"That's a relief." His ears had come up and his tail perked up considerably.

"What's that?" Jonas glanced at the paper, and Hazel drifted over to listen.

"Oh, I was going to ask you about some rumor I heard. Xaric came by to mention that he heard you had some disease or another. I said that was silly, and how could you get it from a muzzle anyway, but he was still worried."

"Where'd he hear it?" Hazel had her arms folded, and looked formidable enough that Cherko took a step back.

"Hey, I don't know," he said. "I can ask him though."

"Don't bully him, Hazel." Jonas stepped slightly in front of the fox.

"I tell you who it is," Hazel said. "It's that lawyer Dixan."

Out of the corner of his eye, Jonas saw Cherko's ears perk. "Dixan? I've met him. Why would he do that?"

"Because he picked up some sores on his dick and he's tryin' to blame poor Jonas here. But he ain't never been a client here and I tell you what, we wouldn't let his filthy muzzle through that door if he paid us in gold."

Jonas blinked and grinned, and saw that Cherko was relaxing as well. The fox met Jonas's grin. "I'll tell a couple people about that. Stuck-up twat, it'd serve him right whether or not it's true."

"It's as true as that other rumor you heard." Having vented, Hazel was lapsing back into her typical good humor.

"All right." Cherko patted Jonas's tail. "Come on, I have to get back to the shop before too long."

Jonas followed the fox upstairs, shaking his head at Hazel. She gave him a wink and a thumbs-up, and then walked back to take care of Selish.

Over the next month, Jonas lost only one client permanently. After a short time, even Xaric eventually came back, and by the end of the month, the supposed rumors about his health had died down. The rumors about Dixan, by contrast, seemed to have taken hold, partly because he didn't have anywhere to post a certification of health, and partly because many people seemed to want to believe it. Jonas even heard a song that someone had made up—

> *Even lawyers get the pox*
> *Just like our old friend the fox*
> *Laid a vixen with a pock*
> *Now he can't stand in the dock*
> *Slid into a filthy place*
> *Now he can't present his case*

It went on for several couplets along the same vein, and although Hazel denied responsibility, she seemed to know all of the couplets and needed little encouragement to sing them. Jonas asked her not to sing in the house, as the disease theme was a little unnerving for his clients, but he couldn't stop her from going down to the pub every night and regaling the patrons there with verse after verse.

Chapter 14

The heat of summer had faded, and in the nearby park the leaves were just beginning their descent from green to yellow. Since Jonas's visit to Dixan, the neighborhood had become slightly less secure, at least for Hazel and the residents of her house. Coming home late from the pub, the streets seemed to be more alive with shadows than Jonas was accustomed to, and at least twice there had been a definite scratching at the windows. He wasn't worried for himself, but he did worry that Selia and Selish might be harmed. He asked Benton if Jherik could put in a word to step up patrols in the area, and Benton said he would ask, but it was far outside of Jherik's purview.

Jonas was not the only one who noticed the increase in prowlers. One of the other tenants of the building told Hazel that he would be moving out before winter. Jonas suspected that his and Selia's activities were a large part of the reason, but the weasel said only that he was more nervous in the neighborhood and was going to live with his mother. When he left, Selia took over his room. Jonas didn't know what arrangement she made with Hazel for the rent, but whatever it was, it was satisfactory to them both.

Some nights, Jonas stayed awake, hoping to catch a burglar trying to break in, but all he accomplished was to make himself tired the next day. He settled for locking the money box carefully every night and sleeping with the key under his pillow. Hazel bought an additional lock for him that bolted the box to the wall, and with that in place, he felt that the pendant was safe from any incursion.

The summer had been wet, but the fall brought dry winds from the south and pleasant temperatures. On one particularly pleasant Gaiaday, Jonas walked through the park to the market after services, bought a small lunch, and took it to eat with Mikka.

He felt very comfortable with Mikka these days, looking forward to their weekly sessions now. He knew enough of what Mikka liked that he played a sort of game with himself to see how excited he could get the grey fox, and how much of a smile he'd get afterwards. For his part, Mikka had started reciprocating more, so that Jonas had moved his appointments to the end of the day, allowing him to enjoy himself and letting them relax for a bit before dinner. Mikka continued to respect the boundaries Jonas put on their relationship, and as a result, Jonas found it easier to relax around the fox, not worrying that he was skirting around the edge of a trap every time they talked.

With the end of summer, Mikka's business was picking up and he was less available for lunches, but he still made time for Jonas. He showed off some of the new designs he was working on, and, one day, gave Jonas a new shirt from his previous year's designs.

"I don't have the money on me," Jonas said, but Mikka waved a paw.

"I got orders from the Duke of Westerland and the Duke of Vandara. One step closer to the king." He grinned. "I could sell that shirt, maybe, but I'm more excited about the new ones I'm making. And besides, you know..." He paused, looked at Jonas's expression, and said, "You're making me a lot of money."

"Things are going pretty well." Jonas leaned back and looked up at the clear blue sky, then down at the shirt Mikka had given him. He liked the light blue and the sheen of the fabric. It seemed to shimmer in the sunlight. "You know, I don't mind what I'm doing. I look at Selia and I think I've got it pretty good. I make people happy, I do it on my own time and under my own orders. That's not such a bad life."

"Not so bad," Mikka agreed. "There aren't many who could make that claim."

"And...and I have good friends, too."

Mikka smiled at him but didn't say anything. After a drink, Jonas continued. "I was just thinking about it because I got another letter from Pike already."

"More people going back and forth this time of year."

Jonas nodded. "I just thought, you know, I had a good group of friends there, but we were all in the same profession. Like a train of mounts pulling a wagon. I always wanted more and none of them ever seemed to."

"Even Pike?"

"I don't know. I was always wary of him because he chased the guys, so I didn't really talk to him until right before I left."

"He must have made quite an impression if he's the only one you're writing back to."

Jonas nodded. "I wish I'd talked to him more."

Mikka smiled. "Keep writing. I'm sure he appreciates it."

"I will. I like it too. There are a couple things I wanted to ask him."

"Like what?"

"Er...about the business."

"Oh." Mikka grinned and looked up at the sun. "I should get going, I guess. Thanks for lunch."

"You're welcome. Thanks for joining me. Will we see you at dinner?"

"Not tonight, I'm afraid. I've been up late all week working on designs. I think I'm just going to sleep."

Mikka waved as he walked away. Jonas noticed a thin raccoon getting up as the fox walked by him and thought he might be a customer, but even though the raccoon was looking right at him, Mikka walked past him with no sign of recognition and the raccoon just left the park behind

Inside the Cage

him. It was unusual enough to notice, and later, Jonas would be glad that he had.

Jonas had only two customers that day—Gaiaday was usually slow for him—and Selia only had one, so they helped Hazel prepare the dinner. As it happened, it was only the three of them and Selish; Hazel's other tenant had stopped coming to the dinners soon after Selia moved in, whether out of discomfort at the presence of another prostitute or annoyance at the mouse kit's discovery that he could throw food right across the room, they didn't know. Privately, Jonas and Selia speculated that he would be moving out either right before or right after the winter, but they thought Hazel wouldn't have much difficulty finding another tenant.

The sun had set, and Jonas and Hazel were relaxing, letting the heavy meal digest as Selia was cleaning off the walls and floor, a task she would not allow Hazel to help her with. Their conversation was interrupted by a loud knocking at the door.

Hazel looked at Jonas and Selia curiously, and got up to answer it. "Who'd be callin' this time of night?"

"Maybe Mikka came after all," Jonas said.

"He wouldn't knock," Hazel said. The knocking sounded again as she walked across the room. "Hold on, hold on, I'm comin'!"

"Mikka!" They could hear the shout even through the closed door.

"He's not here," Hazel said, opening it. "What's the matter?"

Behind her, in the doorway, Jonas could see a small weasel hopping from paw to paw. "Fire! In his shop!"

"Oh, Gaia." Hazel's paw flew to her muzzle.

"What?" Jonas ran onto the porch. He was about to follow the weasel when he saw a flash of movement out of the corner of his eye. He called to the weasel, "Hold on!" and padded quietly to the side of the house. He placed a paw on the corner and looked around, into the shadowy gap between Hazel's house and the next one.

There was nothing in the alley. He relaxed, and then, just as he was stepping back, saw a dark shadow halfway up the side of the house. Clinging to the wall just below his window, a slender raccoon hung motionless. "Hey!" Jonas yelled.

When Jonas saw the shine of the setting sun in the raccoon's eyes, he realized the thief must have been keeping them closed. He was a thin creature who might have been the same one Jonas had seen in the park. His scent held more than raccoon; in fact, Jonas could barely smell the raccoon at all. What he could smell was pitch. And smoke.

"Hey!" he yelled again.

The raccoon glanced at him, then leaped across the narrow gap to the adjacent house, grabbing onto a narrow shelf. He swung around and landed on the porch roof, and Jonas only heard two footsteps before he was gone.

He ran out into the street and scanned the porch roofs, but the raccoon

He couldn't tell whether Mikka was alive or not.

Inside the Cage

was already gone. Hazel grabbed his arm. "Come on," she said. The weasel was standing in the main street, gesturing furiously to them.

"Tell Selia to stay in my room with Selish and watch the money-box," he said. "There's a thief outside. I think he might've started the fire." The vision of the raccoon leaving the park that afternoon, following Mikka, was foremost in his mind as he sprinted into the street after the weasel. That plus the fire, plus a raccoon smelling of smoke climbing towards his window—it couldn't help but be connected. If it were, it didn't take a genius to figure out who was behind it. He would deal with Dixan later, after the fire.

He smelled it before he saw it, the acrid reek of smoke being pulled into his lungs as he ran. Two blocks later, the crowd of people around the shop forced him to slow as he pushed his way through them. The weasel darted through ahead of him. "Anyone in there? Anyone in there?" he said as he shoved through, but nobody could answer.

Finally, as he got to the front and could see the flames licking up the side of Mikka's workshop, a rabbit said, "I don't think anyone's in there. They're all closed up. Mikka's always gone for dinner on Gaiaday anyway."

"Not tonight." Jonas looked around and didn't see Mikka anywhere. He held a flap of his shirt over his muzzle to protect himself from the smoke, and ran up to the house. A few cries of "stop!" "he's crazy" came from behind him, but nobody tried to stop him, or help him.

Flames licked around the edges of the door. Jonas aimed for the center and kicked hard. The wood shuddered but held. He eyed the glass window, but worried that he'd cut himself if he shattered it. He kicked the door again, and felt it give; one more time, and it groaned, then fell inward in a shower of sparks.

Holding the cloth against his muzzle, he stepped inside and ran for the stairs. They looked to have escaped the worst of the fire so far. All the fabric in the room was burning, and even through his shirt, Jonas felt the tickle in his nose and lungs, and almost sneezed. He leapt up the stairs and opened the door at the top.

Smoke billowed out, the heat was painful on his eyes and ears. It took him a moment to see the grey fox stretched out on his bed. *Please, let him still be alive.* He closed his eyes and stepped forward, sliding his arms under Mikka to lift him, then ran for the stairs and down. He bumped the fox's foot a couple times, but he didn't stop; he couldn't hold the cloth over his muzzle now, and his lungs were starting to sear from the smoke. He couldn't tell whether Mikka was alive or not.

When he burst through the door, the cool air felt so good that he stopped, sank to his knees, and panted. It was only when he looked up through blurry eyes and saw the watery shapes of the rabbit and others holding back that he realized he was still closer to the fire than he should be. He staggered to his feet and lurched forwards. The rush of adrenalin had left him, and his legs shook suddenly. He felt exhausted.

Arms surrounded him, then, taking Mikka gently from his arms and wiping his fur. He collapsed again, taking in huge shuddering breaths of the cool evening air. When his throat allowed him to speak, he rasped, "Is he alive?"

Nobody answered. He asked the question again, searching the muzzles around him. "Is he alive?"

A female goat patted his shoulder. "I'll go look."

"That was very brave," another female voice said. He smelled fox and leaned in that direction, and was met by soft paws that held him up. "Do you want to lie down?" the voice said again.

"My throat hurts," he said, coughing.

"Someone's gone for the surgeon," the fox told him.

"Mikka needs it more." It was important to make them understand that.

"Shh, it's okay. Don't hurt your throat." The fox patted his ears and smoothed them back.

A moment later, the female goat was back. "They think he's alive."
Think?

"There's the surgeon," someone else called. "This way, this way!"

"Go to Mikka first," Jonas said, swallowing against the fire in his throat.

"He is. Shh." The fox smoothed his ears again.

He tried opening his eyes, and blinked away enough water to see around him. The arms holding him belonged to a petite red fox. The goat, seeing his eyes open, was holding up a cloth to wipe them. He allowed her to, just as he heard a crash amidst the roar behind him. Someone said, "There goes the window."

Black and white loomed behind the goat. "What happened?" Hazel said. "Was there a fox inside?"

"Over there," the vixen said just as Jonas waved.

"I'll be right back," Hazel said, bending down to Jonas. "You just relax."

He sighed and closed his eyes, and tried to ignore the pain in his throat and lungs.

The smell of skunk returned some minutes later. "He's okay," she said. "They're taking him to my place. Can you walk?"

Jonas nodded. He got to his feet with the help of the fox and Hazel, and wiped his eyes again. "I can make it." He found if he whispered, it didn't hurt his throat as much.

"Don't talk." Doctor Hewill was there at his side. "Let your throat rest."

He started to say "okay," then just nodded. With gestures, he made them understand that he wanted to see Mikka, and they slowed until the three people carrying the fox caught up with them. Ash drifted down from the fox's fur onto the blanket they were using to carry him. Someone had draped a shirt over his midsection, for modesty. Jonas looked at the unconscious fox's muzzle.

Hewill followed his gaze. "I think he'll be all right. He'll need rest for a while and he might have breathing problems. Depends how much smoke got into him. But he'll survive. Thanks to you."

By the time they reached the house, two guards had joined them and were asking questions of some of the people in their group. The rabbit who'd first talked to Jonas had smelled the fire, but hadn't seen anything suspicious. When Jonas heard the guards asking questions, he waved Hazel over from where she was serving cakes to the people who'd come into the house.

"Oh," she said when she saw the guards, "Jonas here surprised a thief breaking into the house. He said the thief set the fire."

"Can you describe the thief?" the stag guard asked.

Jonas nodded. "Raccoon," he rasped. "Thin. Smelled...smoke." He mimed the raccoon's height.

"Okay." The stag took a note. "And why d'you think there's a connection to the clothes shop?"

"Lunch," he said, and coughed. "Saw him...following Mikka."

"Why didn't you do something then?"

Jonas shrugged, and Hazel said, "No reason to do anything then, was there?" Jonas shook his head.

"All right. Anything else?"

Jonas and Hazel exchanged looks, and Jonas could see that Hazel wanted to accuse Dixan of this. He did too, more than anything, but they had no proof. She shook her head minutely, and he nodded agreement. "That's all," Hazel said.

The other guard, a bobcat, piped up. "What was he after here?"

"Jonas has a lot of money upstairs. Any of his clients could have known that." Hazel put a thick paw on Jonas's shoulder.

"Clients?"

"I'll tell you later," the stag said to the bobcat, but there was no scorn in his voice. "I think that's all we can do. We'll keep an eye out."

"Thanks," Jonas rasped, and Hazel clamped a paw around his muzzle.

"Quiet. No more talking! You want to ruin your voice forever?"

"Mm-mmm." He shook his head and smiled at her.

"Okay. Get to bed then."

Mikka was to stay in Selia's chambers, at her insistence. She had stayed behind to look after Selish, but still apologized over and over again for not coming to help, and nothing would satisfy her but giving up her bed to the convalescent. She and Jonas spent the next day setting up his apartment to return to their previous arrangement, while Mikka rested in Hazel's main room.

At an hour after sunrise, Mikka woke up. Jonas was sitting with him, as Hazel had been up most of the night. Jonas was just preparing to drip some water into his muzzle, as the doctor had instructed them to do, when the fox's amber eyes opened and looked up at his.

"Wh--?" Mikka tried to form a question, but the words came out as a guttural croak.

"Shh." Jonas touched a paw to the fox's lips and offered him the cup of water. While Mikka was drinking, Jonas walked quickly to get Hazel.

He couldn't stay through the whole story. Mikka didn't remember anything, so Hazel told him as much as she knew, which unfortunately included glowing accounts of Jonas's heroism. Jonas stepped into the other room to take a drink—he'd been ordered to drink plenty of water as well—but he could still hear Hazel going on about how brave he'd been. He sighed and let the cool water run down his throat. How could he tell Mikka that he hadn't been thinking, hadn't been particularly brave at all? That his action didn't mean anything except that he didn't want any more lives on his conscience?

And, more importantly, was that all it meant?

He sighed. Hazel was making it sound like he was one of those heroes from the old stories, rescuing the poor helpless maiden from the clutches of the evil wizards. Thing was, in those stories, the hero always married the maiden. He looked out the window and brooded over how to dispel that expectation, if Mikka showed any signs of holding it.

Hazel called him into the back room again. He gulped more water and then padded back in.

"I need to go finish the baking and the chores," she said. "I'll postpone your appointments. You'll stay back here?"

He nodded. Mikka wasn't looking at him. He sat down next to the fox as Hazel left the room, and didn't say anything.

Mikka turned, saw him, and looked like he was forcing a smile. He reached out and squeezed Jonas's paw, then closed his eyes and sighed.

If Jonas had expected adulation, clearly he was not going to get it. For a moment, he resented the fox's detachment. Hadn't he risked his life? Wasn't that worth more than a forced smile? It took him a moment to realize that Mikka had just been told that his shop—his designs, his clothes, all his personal possessions; in fact, his whole life—had been destroyed. Jonas felt deeply ashamed of his selfishness.

"Sorry," he croaked.

Mikka opened his eyes and managed another smile. He put a finger to his lips, and nodded.

But Jonas couldn't stop thinking about it, wondering what Mikka would do next, what he *could* do next. He remembered that feeling of not knowing that he'd had not so long ago, and how Mikka had helped him out.

"I'll help," he whispered, and took the fox's paw.

Mikka opened his eyes, smiled, and squeezed back.

That made two things he had to do, Jonas reflected later that day, while Selia was sitting with Mikka. He had to help Mikka get back on his feet, and he had to put a stop to the lawyer's threat.

He wished he had any idea of how to do either of those.

He thought about that all day and evening, and all through dinner. His throat gave him a convenient excuse to remain quiet, so he half-listened to the others' conversation. And every so often, he looked at Mikka, who had gotten up in the afternoon and spent the entire meal staring down at his plate.

The next day, Jonas resumed taking clients, and sat with Mikka when he could. The grey fox was quiet most of the time, remaining in his bed and only getting up to eat. Hazel and Jonas talked quietly about him that night.

"We have to do something to help him," Jonas said.

"You're right," Hazel said. "A few months ago, I wouldn' have said so."

"Why?"

She shrugged. "We drifted apart. He came to my parties, but no more'n that. Didn't come to more than one dinner a year. 'Til you moved in."

"We're just friends," he said automatically, then flicked his ears at the look on Hazel's muzzle. "What?"

She pointed at him. "You pulled him outta that burnin' building. You saved his life. Ain't no gettin' around that."

"I would've done that for any of my friends. I'd do it for you. If I could lift you."

"Don't change the subject. You're responsible for him."

"Responsible?" For a tense moment he thought she was going to bring up Dixan, rubbing salt in his guilt.

"For his life. That's what Cougar would tell you."

"Oh." He shifted in his seat. Adding responsibility didn't make his guilt any less. "Maybe he can stay here. Take Tapha's apartment when he leaves."

Hazel nodded. "He's sure welcome to, but how will he pay rent?"

"Well…he'll start working on designs again. Won't he?"

"He lost all his tools, all his materials," Hazel said. "An' he sure don't look like he wants to start working again."

"Give him a couple days."

"Maybe." She shrugged. "He's takin' it pretty hard."

"So what can we do for him?"

"We gotta be good friends," she gave him just a hint of a smile as she emphasized the word, "show him that he's still got breath in him. Take him to services, maybe that'll help." She looked as doubtful as Jonas felt at the idea of Mikka being inspired by religion.

"That doesn't sound like very much."

"May not sound like it," Hazel said, "but love can be pretty powerful."

Jonas felt his fur prickle. "I—"

"Oh, hush," Hazel interrupted. "Friends can love each other too. I love that fox just like I love you and that mouse and her kit."

"All right." Jonas grinned.

"'Sides, that's about all we can do for Mikka. Can't get his store back."

Jonas shook his head, and went off to sleep. He didn't sleep right away, though. Replaying the conversation in his head, he thought about his problem, and Mikka's, and slowly nurtured an idea that would, if it worked, allow him to do a little more for Mikka than just be his friend. He was determined not to make things worse by rushing into it this time.

Chapter 15

After two days of thinking and going over his plan, Jonas had an idea of what he wanted to do, but he held off, half hoping that Mikka would regain his spirits. Every day when he looked in on the grey fox, Mikka was lying in bed, sometimes looking out the window, sometimes up at the ceiling, sometimes at nothing at all. With every day, guilt squeezed Jonas's heart a little more tightly; after all, all this trouble was because of him. Hazel was right, no matter what she'd meant: he was responsible.

On the Feliday eight days after the fire, he decided he could not afford to wait any longer. Feliday would be an auspicious day for him, he hoped. He took his pendant out of the money box, weighed it in one paw, and then slipped it into his pocket.

Hazel was cooking some kind of cake, but had lost some of her usual bounce, as they all had since the fire, especially with Mikka's cheerless convalescence.

"Heading out?" she asked as Jonas passed the kitchen.

"Just a short walk."

"Stop by the market and get some flour, would you? Save me a trip."

"Sure." He waved and walked out into the street.

The walk to the river went very quickly; Jonas barely saw the people passing him or the stores just opening. He found Dixan's secretary inside the office, arranging things on her desk. When she saw him, her muzzle curled into a smile and her eyes narrowed, a marked difference from the respect she'd shown on his first visit. Cutting off her "Good morning," he took the pendant from his pocket, put both paws on her desk, and brought his muzzle very close to hers.

"Tell Dixan that I will be out on the middle of that bridge for the next half hour. If he wants his precious pendant to end up in his paws and not at the bottom of the river, he's got half an hour to get fifty gold together and meet me there. If I see guards or thieves, or feel threatened, the pendant goes into the river. Got it?" He dangled the pendant in front of her for emphasis.

She had recoiled from him, and now blinked, staying silent. He felt a bit of satisfaction at having rattled her, but that was all the dark he allowed himself. She was eying the pendant and he knew she was thinking she could snatch it. He gathered it into his paw and watched her gaze return to him. "Got it?" he repeated.

"Yes, sir," she said. "But if you'll just wait, I'm sure—"

"I'll be on the bridge." He pocketed the pendant and raised a paw. "Good day. I don't expect to see you again."

Nobody ran after him. He walked quickly out to the middle of the bridge, only there allowing himself to relax. He rested his elbows on the stone balustrade and took the pendant out again. The smooth lines of the cougar head caught the sunlight as the pendant spun. In his mind, Jonas saw Alexan giving him the pendant again, and felt a twinge in his heart. But the months since then had distanced the memory, and the sacrifice was worth the peace of mind his friends would get.

He glanced left and right every few seconds, half expecting guards to run up the street, but when Dixan appeared, the tall fox was walking alone. Jonas listened for the jingle of coins and didn't hear it, but as Dixan came closer, he saw that the fox was holding a purse in his paws.

"You obviously have no idea how the world works," the fox said, approaching him.

"You can stay right there," Jonas responded mildly when Dixan was two feet away.

The fox stopped. He set the purse on the railing. "Twenty-five gold," he said softly. "It's all I could raise."

"Pity," Jonas said, and reached out over the water. "Alexan's house has to be worth a hundred gold, easily."

"It's not that easy!" Dixan was snarling now, eyes fixed on the pendant. "You think I just sit on a mountain of gold? This is all I have."

"How much did you pay the raccoon?"

Dixan looked at Jonas now, studying him. "I don't know what you're talking about."

"My friend's life is ruined. Burned to the ground."

"How unfortunate."

"What would be unfortunate," Jonas said, controlling the urge to smack the fox in the head, "would be if this pendant were to drop. You lose, we lose, nobody's happy."

"That would be unfortunate," Dixan said. "And there would be further consequences, you can bet on that."

Jonas shook his head. "When someone has nothing left to lose—like my friend—he can become very reckless. How do you think he would feel if he learned I gave you the pendant and only got twenty-five gold in return? If any of us were to lose any further parts of our lives, I think we would care much less for our own safety. Desperation, Dixan." This was the cornerstone of his argument, and he had spent hours crafting it.

The fox's ears flicked at the sound of his name, but he calmed down. "Regardless of whether your friend feels that twenty-five gold is adequate compensation for his *accident*, or whether you feel generous enough to give it all to him, it is all I have. I'm counseling you to take it."

Jonas stared back at the narrow golden eyes. "I would have counseled you not to employ filthy thieves to get this back."

"Then give me another day to raise the money."

Jonas looked up at the sun and yawned. "And raise the guard as well? You have about fifteen minutes left, I would estimate."

The fox glared at him, picked up his purse, and walked away.

Twenty-five gold was a lot of money. But it wasn't enough. Jonas knew the smart thing to do would have been to take the money, but he also knew Dixan, and he knew the lawyer wouldn't bring his final offer first thing. The fox's body language spoke of arrogance, and only after their conversation, Jonas thought, had he really understood that Jonas was perfectly willing to drop the pendant into the river.

He expected to see guards now, though it would've made no sense for the fox to send them. Once Jonas dropped the pendant, as he would if he saw guards coming towards him, he would have nothing on him that Dixan could claim he'd stolen, nor any grounds for being arrested. They could likely send otters to search the river, but the pendant was heavy, the riverbed was muddy, and they might never find it. He trusted the fox was smart enough to work that out in five minutes, even though it had taken Jonas the better part of a day.

The sun kept climbing, and Jonas guessed that five minutes were left in Dixan's half hour when he saw the fox at the end of the bridge, running towards him. This time, as the fox approached, he heard clinking.

"Forty-three," Dixan huffed as he stopped in front of Jonas. "And I had to borrow two from my secretary. That's what you've reduced me to. Are you happy now?"

Jonas gauged the fox's mood. He held the pendant over the water. "I wonder if it'll float."

"This is all I have!" A passing cougar, dressed splendidly in a red velvet suit with a feathered hat, stopped at the fox's shout. He glanced at Jonas and then back at Dixan, and waited.

Jonas spared him a glance before focusing on the fox. "I don't believe you."

Dixan looked at the pendant, then back at Jonas. "I'm telling the truth!"

"Two minutes."

"Listen..." Dixan's ears flattened. "All right. All right. Here's three more. That's all, that's really all."

Jonas looked at the three coins the fox had produced from his waistcoat pocket. "Well, how can I believe you now?" He did, but he wanted Dixan to worry just a little more.

"I didn't count this before because this is the rent on my office. I was hoping not to have to use it."

Another ten seconds. Jonas finally brought the pendant back from over the railing. "All right," he said. "That's good enough. Just hand it to me."

"Give me the pendant first."

"I don't trust you any more than you trust me."

The cougar interposed. "Perhaps I can help? Am I correct in understanding that a transaction is being negotiated?" When they

"I wonder if it'll float."

Inside the Cage

nodded, he continued. "I can hold both items and make the exchange."

Warily, they looked at each other, and then handed the pendant and the purse to the cougar. "And the three extra," Jonas said. Dixan glowered and tipped the three gold into the purse.

"This pendant's probably not worth more than twenty," the cougar observed as he passed it to Dixan.

The fox clutched it. "It has great...sentimental value. It was my brother's." He shot Jonas a venomous look.

The cougar raised an eyebrow and looked at Jonas. "His brother gave it to me," Jonas said.

"Before you killed him."

"He died in an accident." Jonas felt his claws extend, and forced himself to sheathe them.

"A very convenient one." Dixan was regaining confidence now, acting the lawyer in front of this cougar.

"But still an accident," Jonas insisted. "And that pendant is worth his house to you."

The cougar looked at Dixan now. "Is that true?"

Dixan remained quiet. The cougar nodded, and handed the purse to Jonas. "All right. I'm glad to have been able to help you two." He bowed, and walked away without waiting for them to return the bow. Dixan gave Jonas a contemptuous look before heading back to his office.

Jonas hefted the purse and glanced into it, then tied it tight. "Whew," he said to the water, and stayed on the bridge for a long time, watching the boats go by, before he trusted his legs to take him home.

Chapter 16

He took the purse directly into Selia's old room where Mikka was lying, and closed the door. The fox's head turned at the sound of the door closing, and he sat up when he saw Jonas and what he was holding. Jonas walked over and sat next to him.

"Hi."

Mikka smiled wanly. "Hi."

"Listen. I feel like the fire and everything...it's my fault, really. If I hadn't held on to the pendant, Dixan wouldn't have come after you guys. And if I hadn't gone to see him, he wouldn't have known..." He sighed. "Anyway. I know there's no way you can get all that back, but I want you to have this. It's all I can do." He set the purse on the nightstand.

Mikka's ears flicked up at the clink. "Jonas, you don't need to..." He sniffed the purse. "You got this from him? You gave him the pendant."

"It was the only way to keep him from bothering us any more. I did get more than he wanted to pay."

Mikka reached for the purse, then drew his paw back. "It's yours, just as the pendant was."

"I'm giving it to you. Like Alexan gave the pendant to me."

Mikka shook his head. "The decision to keep the pendant was yours."

"I know, and that's what—"

"The decision to stand by you was mine. I knew Dixan might come after me, and I chose to take that risk. That's what it means to be..." He lowered his muzzle.

Jonas tried not to think about what the fox had been about to say. He took a breath. "I want you to take it. I owe it to you."

"You want to be rid of me, right? Not owe me anything?"

"No!" But it was uncomfortably close to the truth. He didn't want to get rid of Mikka, but he didn't want to be in debt.

"You've paid for the clothes, Jonas, a long time ago. You don't have to see me every week any more."

"I didn't mean that."

Mikka shrugged. "Maybe it's better that way, dear."

"No, I..." He took a breath. "I don't want a mate. It's not that I don't want you, it's that I don't want that at all." He couldn't look at Mikka. The words just kept coming. "I thought I did with Alexan, but you know how that went. I'm just happier being independent and I feel like I bring bad luck. Like the fire. Only now I can make up for it."

Mikka was quiet for so long that Jonas had to look up. The fox had an odd, quirky smile on his muzzle. "Sweetheart," he said softly, "whatever

Inside the Cage

made you think I wanted to be your mate?"

Jonas tilted his muzzle. "Well, you...I mean, you kept..." He gestured vaguely upstairs. "And, I mean, you said..."

The fox patted his paw. "You make a living selling your body, and you can't understand why a lonely old fox would want to spend as much time with it as possible? But I do like you, dear. I like you a lot."

"So...?"

"That doesn't mean I want to be attached to you. Except...let me tell you what I think you want, and what I want, and maybe you'll see things differently." He settled back. "I think you want to have a family. You've talked enough about your old friends at your workplace, and I've seen how you get along with Hazel and Selia here. You're happy with them. This is your family." He sighed. "And I suppose that's all I want, really. I have my little family at my shop, but journeymen come and go, and the apprentices are like cubs. Apart from the fact that you are so sweet, I like coming here and being with you because I get to talk to Hazel, and have dinner with you, and I feel like for just a little while, I'm part of your family."

"Oh."

Mikka patted him again. "Part of why I've been so sad this week is that I don't know what I'm going to do next. I don't want to leave, but I can't keep imposing on you. I have to go to my sister's place in the West End and ask her if I can stay there. And then I probably won't see any of you for a while."

"You don't have to..."

"So I won't need your money. My sister will take care of me for a while, and if I can re-create some of my designs, maybe I'll get some buyers again."

"You don't have to go. Take the money. Get started again."

"It's not that easy."

"Then stay with us."

"I'd be a burden."

"Not if you take the money."

"Then I'm just taking your money." Mikka chuckled, without real humor.

"I'm giving it to you!" He felt a twinge in his throat as he cried out the words.

"It's not that easy."

"Only because you're making it hard!" Jonas shook his head. "Do you think I would have worked so hard to make sure that we didn't become mates if I didn't feel anything for you?"

The words surprised him as they came out, and Mikka's ears perked up slowly. "I know you do, sweet thing."

"Then stay. Not as my mate, but as part of our family." He grinned. "You know, I need someone around to explain to me what I'm feeling."

Mikka laughed at that, wincing as he did. He put a paw to his throat. "Well, I don't know how much longer Hazel will put me up here."

Hazel's voice came through the door. "You think I'm gonna let you leave?!"

They both laughed then, and Jonas went to let Hazel in. She swept over to Mikka's bed and stared down at the fox, paws on her hips. "You little furry ball of self-pity. Talkin' about how families stick up for each other an' then sayin' you'd be a 'burden'?"

"Do families listen at doors too?" Mikka grinned slyly up.

"They do if there's foolishness goin' on inside. Now you listen. When Tapha leaves, which he probably will soon, you can have his room. 'Til then..."

"He can stay with me," Jonas said. He grinned back as they both stared at him. "Some of my clothes are starting to wear. I could use someone who knows how to mend them."

"I can do that. But are you sure?"

Jonas nodded. "I've been rather stupid. I don't want a mate, but you know, I don't want you to go, either."

Hazel shook her head. "Never met a man who could say the word 'love.' Don't know how you boys manage without a woman around."

"Fortunately," Mikka said, "we don't have to. Even when we think we're having a private conversation."

Hazel flicked her tail. "It's my house, and you best not think anything you do in here is private, boy. Anyway, I just came up to tell Jonas that his first appointment is here."

"You've been listening the whole time," Mikka said.

"Yes," she was unruffled, "but I only came up to tell Jonas that."

"Tell him to go up to the room," Jonas said. "I'll be there in a minute."

"All right, all right. Though I think he," she nodded towards Mikka, "usually takes longer'n a minute." She winked, and left.

Mikka smiled after her, then beckoned Jonas to lean down. When the cougar did, the fox reached up with a small paw and pulled Jonas's muzzle to his.

They kissed, softly at first, then with more passion, and Jonas slid his arms around the fox's shoulders. Mikka was the one who pulled back, brushing his paw down Jonas's neck. "Go on to your appointment," he said.

"You missed yours yesterday."

"I'll make it up later." He grinned. "If I stick around..."

"If?" Jonas showed his claws.

Mikka pretended to cower. "All right, I'll stay." He touched his throat and got up. "I think I'll go get some water from Hazel."

"Okay." Jonas reached out and hugged him again. "I'll see you later."

"Yes, you will," Mikka said. "You most certainly will."

The cage is made of stone, cold and hard. He can see through the stone columns to the world outside, when he cares to look, but there is nobody out there he recognizes or cares to talk to. Their taunts fade in and out, easily ignored. Mikka lies naked next to him, sharing his bed, and Hazel and Selia are in the next bed over, he knows. The door of the cage is shut, but he is the one who closed it, more afraid of what is out there than he is of being inside. This time, that fear is distant, like the murmuring of the river below the bridge, and as the fox's scent makes its way from his sleeping nose into his dream, he sighs and moves his paw through soft grey fur in both places, and for the first time, his dream inside the cage is not a nightmare.

THE PRISONER'S RELEASE

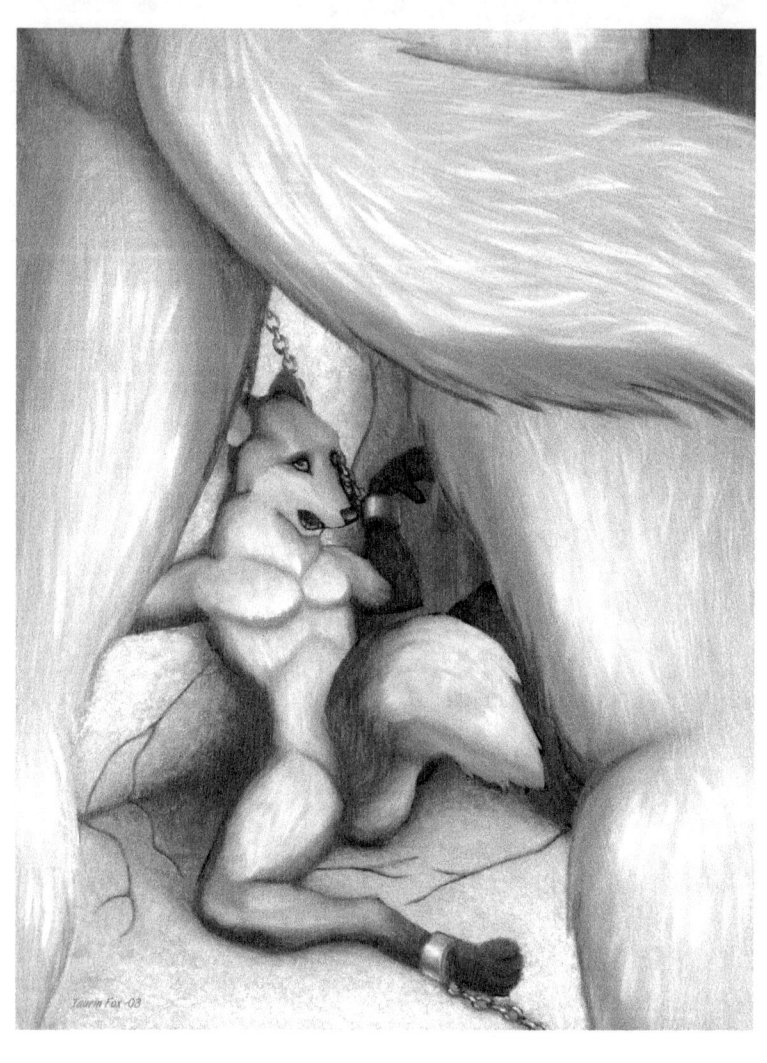

This can't be real, he told himself

The Prisoner's Release

Chapter 1

Volle raised his head at the creak of the door. Something was different, and in prison, something different could be very good, or very bad.

The grizzled skunk guard he'd called "Limp Stripes" after the kink in his tail had been the only creature he'd seen for the past month, ever since the rat (whose name he knew: Dereath Talison, junior Minister of Defense) had given up interrogating him. Dereath's interrogations, though sometimes very painful, had provided something for him to brace his will against. The last of the physical injuries had healed; Volle wondered whether Dereath was just waiting for that to begin another round, or if boredom was his new tactic. The regular appearances of the mute skunk had been his only diversion.

Today, the guard who stepped into the windowless cell wasn't Limp Stripes. He was a young white wolf, white all over except for a little streak of black down his left hip that Volle could see clearly because he wasn't wearing a shirt.

He wasn't wearing a shirt.

And he was gorgeous.

Volle stared at the clean lines of his abdomen, nice and tight under his short white fur, up the well-defined chest, and over to the arms that showed muscle even when hanging relaxed at his side. He looked at the streak of black fur, where it disappeared into the olive-drab guard pants, and at the strong legs that filled out those pants nicely.

This can't be real, he told himself. This is a fantasy I'm having. I'm delirious. Next thing this creature will say is that he's here to rescue me.

A glance at the shapely muzzle did nothing to dispel that fantasy. The wolf's expression was carefully neutral. He'd done nothing since closing the cell door behind him except stare back at Volle. Now he slowly lowered his paws to his pants, and started to unfasten them.

Oh, Fox, thank you for this wonderful dream.

The wolf's snarl finally dispelled Volle's fantasy. "That's right, you fox filth. You should've talked under the lash. Now you get to be my plaything."

So that was how it was. Volle watched the pants slide to the ground and stared at the thick white sheath. He could smell the wolf's arousal now, and he thought he could even see a red tip emerging from the top of the sheath. Below the sheath, a full white sac swung around gently as the wolf worked his pants off. His legs were just as perfect as the rest of him: well-muscled and trim. He didn't have more than a couple ounces of fat anywhere on him.

Watching Volle, the wolf moved a paw to his sheath and started to stroke it. "Yeah, stare at it, fox. I'm gonna …stick this in every hole you have, and when I get tired of those, maybe I'll make some new ones." The words rang hollow; more like a speech he'd memorized than a genuine threat. He was obviously working himself up to it, Volle noted, trying not to get too involved in watching the wolf masturbate. If he'd been here on his own to rape a prisoner, he'd have been fully erect and bursting out of his trousers.

That image made Volle's own sheath stir. He wouldn't have thought it possible, but apparently there were some forces powerful enough to overcome the oppressive cold, dark, and filth of the cell. He shifted to conceal it and watched the wolf's member extend and harden. This is a move by Dereath, he told himself. Counter it. But he couldn't distance himself completely, and even as he thought, he found himself getting hard. Well…maybe that would be useful.

The wolf hadn't noticed. He was staring at Volle's muzzle and licking his lips—an obviously forced gesture that almost made the fox chuckle. His eyes were distanced enough that Volle was sure he was fantasizing about someone else. Probably a young bitch he knew. Certainly not a filthy, emaciated fox in shackles, even if he were into bondage.

Finally, the wolf dropped his paw. He let Volle have a look between his legs, then stepped forward with a menacing grin. "Ready or not, here I come."

Volle let his muzzle hang open. "Oh, put that in here, big boy." His voice was rusty from disuse, but he thought that added a certain something.

The wolf stopped. He looked uncertainly at Volle, registering for the first time that the fox was aroused too.

"Come on, please. I bet I can fit it all in. It's pretty big, but I like that."

"You don't understand, fox. I'm going to put this wherever I want. I'm raping you."

Volle hid a grin. "Oh, okay." His paws were shackled to a single chain that was fixed into the wall, so without much difficulty, he turned over and got onto his paws and knees. His muscles protested, but he forced them through the motions. He lifted his tail as far as he could, which was just enough to give the idea. "I like it there, too."

The wolf didn't say anything, but Volle could hear him breathing. He heard two more steps, and then felt a strong paw on his tail, lifting it up. He was sure his bare, soiled rear was not a very appealing sight or smell. Turning his head, he gave the wolf an encouraging smile. "Go ahead," he said. "It's your duty, after all."

He was pleased to see that the wolf's erection had slid back significantly into his sheath. The wolf looked at him and held his tail for another moment, then threw it down with a curse and stalked back to the door.

Volle turned back over and watched him pull his pants on, admiring the nicely shaped rear and the white fluffy tail. The wolf kept his back to him and left the cell without a backwards glance. Volle heard the familiar click of the key in the lock, and then all was quiet.

He sagged back against the wall. Was this a one-time ploy or a first salvo? It was a good shot, whichever it was. Dereath, obviously, was behind it, but Volle didn't want to give the rat too much power in his mind, so he imagined a cadre of faceless tormentors who knew just what he was attracted to, and exploited it expertly. Unbidden, visions of the perfect white body with the one distinguishing black streak came back to him, standing in front of him aroused. His sheath, which had lost its arousal, swelled again and he felt his member pushing to get out. He tried to keep it down—the bastards had shackled his arms and legs so he couldn't give himself release—but he couldn't get the image out of his head. In his mind, the wolf was smiling, walking towards him with a sway in his step so that his lovely long shaft swung from side to side enticingly. Volle could see the soft white sac, the sheath above it stretched to its limit, and the red slick length protruding from it, as though they were all inches from his muzzle. His tongue flicked out; he panted, moaned, and realized he was uncomfortably hard.

The vision in his mind smiled, standing astride him, and lowered that rump onto his erection. He could feel the warmth, the tight embrace, but it did no more than increase his frustration. With a cry, he rolled over and pressed into the cold stone floor, rubbing back and forth. It eased some of his tension, but it also hurt, and he realized quickly that he would never come to climax that way. Panting, he lay there, listening to the trickle of water running through his cell, and then forced himself to turn back over and look around.

From the far left hand corner of the cell, he could see another set of shackles on the right hand side, empty and rusted. His movement was extremely limited, but he could reach the narrow channel running down the middle of the cell where his drinking water flowed; further down, that was also his toilet. In the center of the ceiling was a small black hole from which he fancied he could feel a breeze sometimes (when the door was open), and beneath that, suspended from a chain, was a small torch whose smoke disappeared up into the blackness. In the center of the far wall, the only door to the cell stood, closed and locked.

Apart from him and the shackles, the only other thing in the room was the plate they'd put his food on. It was formless glop that always tasted like stale bread mixed with dirty water, and he had to lick it off the plate because they wouldn't give him any utensils. Not after the incident with his first guard, a careless rat whom Volle had named Slacker.

He'd only had the two guards; he was not a normal prisoner and Dereath undoubtedly wanted to limit association with him. In fact, the lack of any other contact made Volle wonder whether anyone but Dereath knew he was in here. He hoped he'd see the wolf again. Besides being attractive, he was young and easier to manipulate than Limp Stripes, who did his job with mechanical precision, or Slacker, who just didn't care. Streak, that would be a good name for the wolf, with his undressing and that cute black streak down his hip. His sheath throbbed with the thought of the wolf, and he sighed. The best thing he could do was to go to sleep, and hope that a dream would bring him the release he couldn't give himself.

It didn't, of course. His sleep was black and dreamless, as it had been for the several months or so he'd been in prison. And in the morning, Limp Stripes was back with his early meal, taking the empty plate and setting down the full one without a word. He replaced the torch, as he did every morning (Volle didn't know if it was really morning outside; morning was when he got a new torch), and then left.

Volle ate the small portion of food, which tasted faintly of bean paste today—a treat—and tested the shackles with a series of arm and leg exercises. He had tried to do them every day, though his strength was definitely declining; the last time he'd been out of the shackles had been the last time Dereath had tried to question him. This day, for variety, he practiced turning over on all fours, in case the wolf did come back.

When he was too tired to keep moving, with the shackles still holding fast, he thought about his companions. At some point, he must have realized that they'd given up on him, but he couldn't remember when he'd made that transition. Not when he'd missed the first meeting after his capture, but when he'd missed the second, they must have known that something was amiss. He missed them all: Tella the fiery weasel, as bold a fighter as there was; Sherr the porcupine, their master tactician; Reese the hare, Volle's friend and former roommate, now under cover as a merchant in Divalia; and Seir the mouse, Volle's favorite, who took care of all of them. Seir could become almost invisible when she wanted to, sneaking around markets or an enemy camp, but even if she could become truly invisible, she couldn't help Volle now.

Rescue was no longer a realistic hope, if it ever had been. These prisons dated from the days of King Bucher, and Volle always cringed to think that Bucher had been a fox like himself. Hundreds of workers had died excavating the prisons, and hundreds of Bucher's enemies had died inside the completed prisons afterwards. They were not exactly escape-proof, but they were daunting enough that a prisoner couldn't hope for any help from outside. Even if that help were—but Volle stopped himself from even thinking the name. His contact within the palace would have helped him by now if he'd been able. He had tried to wipe the name from his mind, so that even under torture he wouldn't be tempted to cry it out.

He'd sworn he would take the name to his grave, and now he wondered how far he was from that end. The ploy with Streak smacked of desperation, and if they'd realized that nothing would work, they had nothing to gain by keeping him alive. Well, then, he would die an unsung hero. Or at least an unsung patriot—he wouldn't be a hero unless he got the information he had back to his people.

Dispirited but resolute, he looked around the cell again and sniffed the air. The cells were not cleaned out—ever—leaving the scents of each prisoner's unfortunate predecessors to demoralize him. Volle had been in this cell for two months now, and could no longer smell the bear and stag that had been the most recent occupants. There was nothing but his own rank scent to his nostrils, and he wondered how long it would linger when he was gone.

Limp Stripes was back again with the evening meal, and Volle saw nobody else for the next day. But after the evening meal that day, as he was holding his tail trying to brush the matted fur with his claws, the door opened again, and Streak walked in.

He was scowling, and wasted no time on preliminaries. He stripped his pants off, but before Volle could open his muzzle, he shook a finger at him. "Not a word, fox, or I'll…smash your muzzle into the wall." The threat came with some hesitation, and nowhere near the force it needed to be effective. Volle noted that, like last time, Streak wasn't fully erect, but he strode toward the fox anyway. With a rough push, he flipped Volle onto his stomach.

The shackles clattered as Volle nearly fell, but retained his balance. He felt a paw yank his tail upward, and he pushed his rump in the air. Streak hesitated, and Volle took a chance. "Please," he moaned. "It's been so long."

"Shut up, I said." But the wolf didn't move.

"It's been months since I got laid, and you're so sexy," Volle went on. "Come on, stud. Do me." He thrust his rump backwards and panted.

The paw tightened around his tail, and for a moment he felt the wolf's fur brush his rump. The touch was somewhat arousing, but he managed to keep from thrusting back any more. No need to overdo it.

"Dammit!" the wolf yelled, letting go and standing up.

Volle heard Streak pace back towards the door. He turned over cautiously, watching the wolf get into his pants. This time, Streak turned and met his eye as he pulled his pants up over his rump, and Volle thought he saw confusion there. But it was dark, and he could have been mistaken.

Streak's scent, though, lingered in the cell, and Volle inhaled it greedily; young and earnest, with, yes, a bit of predator, but also confusion and innocence. It reminded Volle of his own scent as a younger fox, and it reminded him of another young soldier he'd known, years ago, who had died for his beliefs. He held it to himself as he drifted into another night, a reminder that he was not alone.

The next time Streak visited him, he opened the door, closed it, and then sat with his back against it, facing Volle. He wore a loose shirt this time, the same color as his pants, and made no move to unbutton it or the pants. He stared at the fox until Volle broke the silence.

"Don't I get a show today?"

Streak shook his head slowly.

"Pity. Aren't I a good audience?"

The wolf's scowl deepened.

"Well, why are you here, then?"

Streak looked away from him, idly glancing around the cell.

"Can I offer you a drink?" Volle gestured at the trickle of water coming down the wall beside him. "I don't want to be a bad host."

This time he was sure he caught the flicker of a smile at the corner of the white wolf's muzzle.

"Oh, come on," he said. "You told your boss that the rape went well, that I was demoralized, that you could get some information out of me. So they keep sending you back for more. Well, you'll never get information if you don't talk to me."

Streak was staring at him. "H-how did you know…"

"Don't I get a show today?"

The Prisoner's Release

"I'm not stupid. You obviously weren't all fired up to do it, and now you're just killing time so it looks like you're in here abusing me. You wouldn't have come back if you were doing this on your own. So your boss must have sent you back in, ergo he thinks it's going well, ergo you didn't tell him otherwise."

The wolf thought that over for a moment, then looked up at Volle. "What's 'ergo' mean?"

Volle smiled. "Therefore."

"Well, you're a traitor, ergo I don't have anything to talk to you about." Streak fixed his gaze pointedly on the other set of shackles.

Volle leaned back against the wall. "First of all, I'm a patriot. And second, I'm dead anyway, so what does it matter?"

"If you'd just cooperate, then you wouldn't be dead. They would move you to a nicer cell, maybe even let you go."

Volle barked a surprised laugh that ended up being a racking cough. "I thought you were a little young to be on prison duty. First tour, isn't it? What, you have an uncle with the King's ear, didn't want his nephew hacked to bits on the battlefield?" When Streak didn't answer, he went on, "Or maybe you have a patron, someone who didn't want his little sex toy all chewed up."

"Shut up!" The wolf leapt up, but stopped himself before taking a step forward. "I'm nobody's toy." He sat down again and glared.

"Well, someone pulled strings to get you on prison duty this young."

"Why do you keep saying that?" Above the snarl, Volle could see confusion in his eyes again.

"I've seen prison guards. They're all veterans who've been through battles. Prison duty is easy. It's a reward. Not only are you young, you're also hopelessly naïve about what goes on here."

Streak shook his head. "I was chosen for duty by Minister Fardew himself. Top of my squad unit in drills."

"Drills." Volle coughed another laugh. "And your first duty was to rape a prisoner?"

The wolf's white ears flickered uncertainly. "He said the other guards refused to do it. He said they wanted someone younger and energetic, more..."

Volle watched his muzzle drop as he trailed off, and smiled despite himself at the guard's self-consciousness. In a pub, it would be adorable. "More virile?" Streak didn't say anything. "Well, you are that. No question."

He drew out the last couple words, and Streak glanced at him. "Why did you say I'm naïve?"

"Because you think I have a chance of getting out of here alive."

"They said—"

"They're playing on your sympathies. The only thing keeping me alive is that I'm not cooperating."

"No. Maybe that's how they do things in your kingdom, but here we keep our promises."

Volle looked at the earnest muzzle and didn't have the strength to argue any more. "You're probably right." He turned to the wall.

Streak got up, dusted off his clothes, and walked out.

Volle watched the door after the wolf left. He lay down on the cold floor, trying to sleep, but he kept asking himself how long Dereath was going to keep him alive. By now the rat knew he wouldn't respond to pain, and his gambit with Streak was failing; what else would he try? He was pretty well versed in most interrogation techniques, but he didn't know everything. The chains of his shackles lay on the stone beside him, and he wondered, not for the first time, if he could wrap them around his neck and strangle himself. The thought circled his head and then he drove it out. Not yet.

Chapter 2

"What do you do when you're not pretending to rape me?"

Streak grinned—a definite grin, this time. "Guard duty on the top floors. I only come down here for special duty."

"Tough duty." Volle shook his head.

"Only the best can do it."

Volle chuckled softly. "What do the other guards think of that?"

Streak paused for a moment, then shrugged. "We don't talk much. They're all older. Like you said." He tilted his muzzle. "How old are you?"

Volle instinctively went defensive. "What does it matter?"

"I was just curious." He looked away, as he always did when he didn't know what else to say.

The quiet in the cell bothered Volle less when he was alone. When Streak was here, he felt that the quiet was a waste of an opportunity, or a waste of something. After a month of Limp Stripes' infuriating silence, Volle couldn't stay quiet for long. "How old do you think I am?"

Streak measured him with his eyes and then shrugged. "I'd say about a hundred from how you look now. Probably forty?"

"You're not out of your teens, are you?"

"I turned twenty two months ago." Streak settled back, smiling smugly. "So you're not right about everything."

"You joined pretty late. Aren't most male cubs conscripted at sixteen?"

"Usually. I got an exemption. My father died and I had to run the farm."

"Sorry to hear that. How did it happen?"

Streak shifted his gaze again. "Fits. He got bit by something and then it started a couple weeks later. We had to tie him up by the end of it."

"I'm sorry," Volle said again. "How old were you?"

"Eight."

"You were running the farm when you were eight?"

"My mom helped. It was just the two of us."

"That's pretty impressive." Volle watched the wolf get up to leave, and couldn't resist asking one more thing. "Who's running the farm now?"

"Jasper. Mom's new mate." The tone and the droop of his tail said more than those four words did. He stepped through the door.

"Hey!" Volle called, and then coughed from the strain on his throat.

Streak poked his head around the door. "What?"

"Twenty-six." The wolf didn't move, wreathed in shadow from the dying torch. "I'm twenty-six."

He couldn't read Streak's expression as the wolf slowly withdrew and closed the door.

A farm-wolf, eh? That explained the physique, and the naivete. Volle thought again, if only we'd met somewhere else. In a pub, in a bath, in the army...his eyes drifted shut, and in the darkness he saw the naked wolf again, reclining in a bath. He saw himself stepping into the bath next to the wolf, clean and well-groomed. Their paws reached out, touched each other's chest, then moved lower...

He stifled a moan. His shaft was fully exposed again, straining against his sheath, and the frustration was like a coiled spring inside him. He growled and tried to bend his head forward to lick himself, but the shackles prevented even that. Panting, he flipped over and pressed his erection into the cold floor. That discouraged it, though he couldn't help rubbing it against the stone, gasping in relief even as he winced at the abrasions.

Was this the game? Sexual frustration? Tie him up so he couldn't pleasure himself, then torment him with a gorgeous wolf, physically perfect, cute and seductive, until he begged for release? That would be perfectly Dereath's style, given their history. He clenched his teeth and swore that he wouldn't let that happen. *I should've just let him take me, the first time,* he thought. But he knew even as he thought it that he couldn't have done that. It would have given the rat power over him.

But oh, he wanted it so badly.

Chapter 3

Streak had questions ready the next time. "Aren't you a little young to be a spy?"

"What did they tell you about me?" Volle was wary, as usual. Streak's visits were erratic, and as they were not on his own schedule, they must be on someone else's. He was trying to determine the pattern between them. This one was the very next day, the first time he'd visited two days in a row.

"That you are a traitor who was captured stealing valuable plans of troop movements. That you're in the employ of the Ferrenians."

"I might have looked at the plans, but I'm not a traitor."

"What was so important about the troop movements that you risked your life for them?"

Volle studied him, and then chose his words carefully. "Do you know about the Pax Valleris?" Streak shook his head. "It's an agreement Tephos and Ferrenis entered into some fifty-odd years ago. It divides the Reysfields plains evenly between them. I heard rumors in the palace that the king was planning to break the Pax and I didn't think that was right. So I went to see if the plans were true. They were. I was chased from the office and captured. The plans were gone and they blamed me."

"Did you take them?"

Volle shrugged. "Go ask your bosses."

"We wouldn't break a peace. Not without a good reason."

"Like a poor harvest in the Reysfields?"

Streak's eyes glinted in the torchlight. "Like the Ferrenians moving first."

"You can check that too, if you like. Maybe they've done something in the last month. But last I heard, they were just fortifying defenses around the plains. Neither side is allowed to have armies on the plains, and neither side has violated that agreement."

"I will check it." Streak stared stubbornly at Volle. "What information do they want from you?"

Volle shrugged. "I don't know."

"Now I know you're lying. They must have asked you."

The conversation was treading too close to dangerous waters for Volle's liking. "Are those your new orders? Get information from the fox with kindness?"

Streak recoiled, but he didn't look away this time. "No," he mumbled. "I was...just curious. I don't know what could be that important to them. Or to you."

"I love my country and my King," Volle said, "and my life is worth nothing to me if it would be better spent in their defense. Don't you feel the same?"

"I...I suppose so..."

"Let's hope you never have to test it."

There was a lengthy pause, then Streak said, "No, I want to test it. I mean, that's why I'm a soldier."

"Aren't you a soldier because they made you one?"

"No." He shook his head. "I could've stayed on the farm, or taken a trade in town. I was past the age of conscription."

"Why didn't you stay on the farm?"

Now, he did look away. "My mom was okay without me. And you know, I'm too old to be living at home."

"Is that what he told you?" Volle spoke gently.

Streak nodded. He looked down at the ground.

"I don't think much of your stepfather, then," Volle said, with more feeling than he had thought himself capable of.

The wolf just flicked an ear, and said, "I'd better go."

Volle watched him go, watched the door close, and settled back against the wall. Poor kid, he thought, and set to grooming his tail again.

It was five long days before Streak appeared again. Volle had gotten fidgety by the third day, and on the fifth was almost tempted to ask Limp Stripes if something had happened to the young wolf. He bit his tongue just in time. That's what Dereath wanted him to do: get attached, pine away for him.

His body wasn't helping him much, either. It seemed every time he closed his eyes, he could see that white shape, highlighted by the flickering torch. The curve of his chest, the bulge in his arms and legs, and the large white ridge of fur between his legs, with the thick red shaft standing proudly above it. Volle envisioned all kinds of positions, most starting with the wolf just wrapping his strong arms around him and pressing that firm body against his. The dreams went on from there, and though he tried to avoid moaning his frustration, sometimes it was just too much. It was worst after he'd eaten, when he didn't have hunger pangs to distract his lust. Amazing that with his cramped, weak arms, his matted and dirty fur, and his imminent death, he could still be so aroused by a dream. He wondered whether at some point the basic urges of life were all that would be left to him.

On the fifth day, after he'd eaten the evening meal, the images returned unbidden to him and he was almost trembling with suppressed desire. He clenched his fists, then pulled all his chains to their fullest extent and let out a loud scream of frustration, then fell back to the floor, panting.

"What's going on here?" He hadn't heard the door open, but Streak was standing over him, a halo of weak torchlight around him. His expression was hidden in shadows, but his tail was twitching as though he were worried.

"Oh. Nothing. Sorry." Volle looked up at the wolf, and saw the slight shift of the muzzle as it examined his prostrate form, from his flattened ears down his gaunt, heaving chest, down to his tense and painfully obvious erection. "Uh…" He tried to swing his bedraggled tail around to cover himself, with only partial success.

"It's okay." Streak sounded amused. He walked back to the door and sat down. "Thinking of your mate?"

"Don't have one." Volle regretted the admission as soon as he said it, but then decided it couldn't hurt.

"So what do prisoners fantasize about?"

"I missed you." He'd wanted to sound coy, but there was too much raw emotion in his voice for that.

Streak's ears snapped up. "What, Gerrold isn't enough company for you?" He tried to keep his tone light, with more success than Volle'd had, but the fox thought he could detect some emotion there, too.

"Is that his name? I call him Limp Stripes."

Streak laughed, for the first time Volle had heard. It was a clean, happy sound, and brought a smile to Volle's muzzle. "Why do you call him that?"

"His tail has a kink in it. I think. Plus, I've never seen him get excited or interested in anything."

"I don't think I have either. Limp Stripes. I'll remember that." He inclined his head. "What do you call me?"

"What's your name?" Volle countered.

"What do you call me?" the wolf repeated, and Volle could swear his tail wagged slightly.

Volle hesitated. "Well, it was a tough choice between Gorgeous and Cute Butt."

Streak's ears flicked. "So? Which is it?"

"I don't think I want to tell you." Volle felt suddenly embarrassed.

"Aw, come on." Streak walked over to him and knelt beside him. He pulled Volle's tail away and brushed his erection with a paw. "I'll—"

He didn't get any further. The touch was electrifying; Volle jerked away from it, panting, and stared at Streak with wide eyes. "That's how you're going to get me? Tease it out of me with sex?"

The wolf had retreated and now crouched two paces away. "No! I didn't mean…I mean, I forgot. I'm sorry, really!"

Still panting, Volle relaxed slightly. He couldn't say anything, torn between his vigilance and his fantasies, which were now so close that he wondered if he were dreaming. Then Streak spoke again, and he was sure he was.

"Listen, I'll prove I didn't mean anything. Just…settle down, okay?" He inched closer, holding his paws out placatingly. Volle tried to stay calm, but his nerves were frayed and he didn't know if he could stand it. Streak was only an arm's length from him, and he couldn't back up any more; the stone wall pressed against his back. The wolf's scent was strong, filling his nostrils and adding to his confusion. He barely heard Streak say, "I'm not asking for anything, okay? I'll just do this and leave."

Volle understood a moment before he felt the warm paw close around him. He shut his eyes and moaned. Oh God, it was better than he'd dreamed. He tried to force himself to relax, but his body was tensing despite him, and the wolf had barely moved his paw up and down twice. He was going slowly, and Volle's hips, acting without his consent, pushed into his paw, forcing the rhythm faster. Sensations coursed through him that he'd almost forgotten, electric currents pushing at his muscles and lifting his fur. His head pressed back against the wall as his breathing came faster, and he strained at the shackles as he finally reached the climax he'd been dreaming about.

It seemed to go on forever, and he lay immersed in it, floating in the waves of ecstasy. As they subsided, he slumped back against the stone floor, and he felt the warm paw unwrap itself from his spent erection. Dimly, he was aware of the opening and closing of the door, but nothing else aside from the strong scent of his musk penetrated his senses before he fell fast asleep.

The musky scent lingered into the next day, when Limp Stripes came in to drop off the morning meal and change the torch. The skunk's nose might have wrinkled, or maybe he imagined it. He didn't care. He was relieved, relaxed, and felt better than he had in weeks. It wasn't just the release of more than a month of sexual frustration. He was looking forward to seeing the wolf again, actively now, rather than thinking about his situation or his companions. That was what they wanted, he knew, but he didn't care.

Streak occupied his mind on and off for the next five days, during which he waited patiently every evening. His fantasies recurred, but without the intense frustration he'd felt earlier. He had the memory of that night to hold him over, and when he replayed it in his head, he felt the response in his sheath. His erection was not one of urgent need, however, but of a warm diffuse pleasure.

When the wolf did reappear, Volle sat up and smiled. Streak closed the door and walked across the cell, sitting down next to him. "I'm sorry," he said softly. "They didn't send me back until tonight. I asked, but they wouldn't let me."

"It's okay." Volle smiled, enjoying the young wolf's scent and proximity.

"Looks like you didn't miss me quite as much." Streak gave him a warm smile.

"Oh, I missed you. It's just not showing as much."

"Really?"

Volle nodded. "I wish...I wish we'd met somewhere else." He voiced the thought hesitantly. It sounded awkward, not as he'd been thinking it in his head, but he couldn't stop now. "We might have been friends. Maybe more." The last part slipped out before he could stop it, and he fumbled to recover. "I mean, if you're interested. I don't know if you like males, or have a mate, or what…"

Streak shook his head. "No mate." He hesitated, and then touched Volle's paw. "And…I do. But, no offense, you kind of look like shit."

Volle grinned. "I feel like shit. But I clean up nice."

"I bet." He paused, ears flicking, and then went on. "Hey. You know something?"

Volle shook his head. "What?"

"I…I missed you, too." He said it bashfully, in a low voice. "I kept wishing I could come down and talk to you. Nobody else cares. They ignore me, or they call me 'pretty boy' when they think I can't hear."

"Well, you know, I'm pretty much a captive audience."

Streak laughed softly. "I guess so. But I wish…I wish we'd met somewhere else, too."

Volle smiled, flicking his ears. "Do they still think you're raping me?"

"I guess so. De—my boss just asks how the session went and if you're any closer to giving out information and I say," here he put on a rough voice, "yeah, I can break that fox, just give me time."

Volle's rough laugh turned into a cough. Streak tilted his muzzle. "Are you sick?"

"Oh, nothing a couple months relaxing in the sun wouldn't cure." He coughed again.

The wolf was quiet for a moment. "I could see about getting you transferred…or getting out once in a while."

"No. Don't put yourself in danger for me." Volle edged a little closer to Streak. "Tell me about your farm."

"We had four fields, all corn. There were two plows, and my mother and I both used them. We had three horses, one that we got to replace Jenny. She was my favorite, but she was pretty old. The other two were foals from Gerta, our old mare who died about six, seven years ago. We named them Gerry and Geena, and the one we got to replace Jenny was a pretty mare named Tanya. Gerry and Tanya were good plow horses, but Geena hated being hitched up. She liked to be ridden, though, especially if you let her gallop…"

Volle closed his eyes and let the words wash over him. He felt he was standing on the porch of the farm, looking out at the cornfields, watching Streak ride by on a beautiful bay mare. He felt the sun on his fur and the wind through his tail, and he smiled.

"…I loved going to market because of all the things that were there. My dad used to buy me maple candy there, but after he died, I didn't want it anymore. Last year we made enough from our corn to replace one of the plows."

He was beaming proudly when Volle opened his eyes. "That's impressive," Volle said, though he didn't really know whether it was or not.

Streak nodded, his tail wagging behind him. "Anyway. I'd better go. See you soon."

"I'll miss you," Volle said impulsively as the wolf got up.

"Me too." Streak smiled warmly, and walked out the door.

So there it was. He was falling into their trap. He couldn't help it, and he didn't care. At some point, when he didn't expect it, there would be a new face at the door, or maybe Limp Stripes would be the one, and he would be told that for the simple price of a piece of paper, or a name, he could see the white wolf again. If he held out, someone would bring him cloth with Streak's scent, to remind him what he was missing.

It would be painful, but he was sure he could hold out. Sure, he'd had plenty of good friends, plenty of lovers, but he'd learned (*the hard way*) to keep himself unattached. That was partly what made him a good spy. But *you've never been this lonely before*, part of his mind cautioned. *Never been confronted by this situation. It doesn't matter that you know exactly what he's doing. The rat knows how people work and he know how* you *work, and you're working exactly the way he wants.*

"I can hold out," he insisted, and then realized he was talking out loud.

And what if you can't? What then?

Chapter 4

Streak held one paw behind his back as he entered the cell three days later. "What do you have there?" Volle asked as the wolf walked toward him.

Streak knelt down just across the channel in the floor and his ears flicked. He was grinning. "Close your eyes."

"Oh, I can smell it…" Volle closed his eyes anyway, and opened his muzzle. A few small cubes landed on his tongue, soft and thick. Meat! Chicken pieces, with some kind of sauce on them. He chewed ecstatically, letting the rich taste fill his head before swallowing. "Mmm. Oh."

"There's more." Streak was holding a pawful of chicken pieces. He placed them in Volle's muzzle a few at a time, smiling as the fox gobbled them down. "They really don't feed you much, do they?"

"Mmm. Just enough to keep me alive. All the same tasteless crap. This is so good."

"Close your eyes."

"It's not, really."

"To me it is." He looked longingly at the wolf's empty paw, then stretched his shackles to lean over and lick the sauce from it. Streak twitched, but kept his paw steady until Volle had licked it clean.

As the fox raised his muzzle, Streak raised his paw to brush its underside gently. Volle looked at him and gave his paw another lick. "Thank you."

"There's more." Streak winked, reaching into his shirt pocket.

"More?" Volle stared in disbelief as the wolf's paw emerged with a thick slab of cake wrapped in a cloth napkin. He felt saliva pooling in his muzzle at the rich smell.

"Here, take a bit at a time..." Streak fed him the cake, piece by piece, and when he was done Volle licked his paw again.

"Thank you. Again. You didn't have to."

"I know. I wanted to. I can smell what they feed you. At least this is something nice I can do."

"You're too nice." The heaviness in Volle's stomach from the rich food was turning to unease, but he tried to ignore it.

"I like seeing you enjoy it."

"Glad to oblige. Were you...always this nice?" The turmoil in his stomach was getting worse. He just hoped he could keep it down until Streak left.

The wolf's ears flicked again, and he smiled that bashful smile. "I try to be. My mom always said to treat others as you'd want to be treated."

"You do...a good job." He was fighting a losing battle.

"Are you okay?" Streak leaned forward.

"Yes. No. Oh, I'm so-sorry." Volle gulped and then lurched toward the wolf, hanging his muzzle down into the channel as the meal came raging back up. His body shuddered and coughed, and when it was over he lay there, the sour taste still in his muzzle, his ears flat in embarrassment.

"Oh, Canis, I'm sorry. All that rich food." The wolf's paw was stroking his head, as grimy and matted as the fur was.

Volle lapped some water from the wall, spit it out, and rolled back over with a little effort. "Not your fault. I probably ate too fast." He gave a wan smile.

"Here." Streak took the cloth napkin and wetted it in the water, then gently wiped off Volle's muzzle. The fox held perfectly still while the napkin brushed the vomit from his muzzle and worked around his head, cleaning the fur between his eyes, along his cheek ruffs, and up his soft ears. Streak had to rewet the cloth several times, and when he was done it was filthy; even in the torchlight Volle could see that. But Streak stuffed it in his pocket without looking at it, his eyes fixed on Volle's muzzle.

"You do clean up nice," he said softly. Volle looked back at him without saying anything, looking into the clear eyes that were blue even in the dim torchlight. They came closer, slowly, until Streak's nose was touching his own. Then, gently, their muzzles parted and met in a soft kiss.

Volle closed his eyes and sighed. He kept his tongue in his muzzle because he still had some of the sour taste on it, but he could feel the light flicker of Streak's tongue against his lips. The wolf's scent at this distance filled his nostrils and made him forget the queasiness in his stomach.

Too soon, it was over, and Streak was sitting up. "I guess I should go." But he didn't get up, or move to the door.

Volle nodded. "I guess so."

They held each other's eyes for the space of several heartbeats, and then Streak got to his feet slowly and fluidly. "Bye."

"See you soon," Volle said.

Streak nodded, and then was gone.

Volle dreamt that night that Streak returned, naked and holding a glittering sword. He held it over the shackled fox and said, "I can cut you free, but you must renounce your country. Promise you won't give them the plans you stole. I'll take you away with me and keep you safe."

In his dream, Volle couldn't take his eyes off the sword. He could see its edge, sharp and menacing. "I can't," he breathed.

Streak's eyes pleaded with him. "It's the only way we can be together."

Yes, his body screamed, but he couldn't make his muzzle form the words. "I can't give up my country."

"If you die here, they still won't have your information. Why should you die?"

He could see his friends beyond the cell, mute and staring at him. Beyond them, the country he loved spread out: the red mountains behind the rolling plains, the sparkling expanse of Kell Lake, and the shining towers of the palace. "We'll know," they seemed to be saying.

He moaned and turned away. "I can't."

Streak's blue eyes closed. Without a word, he raised the sword and swung it viciously downward.

Volle woke with a start. The torch had gone out and the cell was pitch black. His heart was pounding in his chest and his wrists were sore where the shackles held them. He flipped over, pressing his muzzle between his arms and waiting for his panic to subside. What would he do, if Streak came back and gave him that ultimatum? It would never happen, of course, but wasn't that what he was being asked to do?

No, it wasn't. He was simply being asked to betray his country and his friends. There was no chance he would have a life with Streak. He was going to die in this cell, or possibly in an execution chamber somewhere.

When Streak visited him the next evening, the dream was still lingering in his head, but he managed to force a smile. Streak returned it, and sat down across the channel in the floor, looking up at Volle.

"What's this all leading to?" He said it quietly, but the intensity of his gaze betrayed the emotion behind it.

"You're being used to make me betray my friends," Volle said dully. "They sent you here to make me fall in love with you so they could use you as leverage on me."

"They wouldn't…" Streak began, and then stopped, thinking.

"They would. They are." Volle looked away, at the stone wall on his other side. He traced the familiar pattern of cracks with his eyes. "Sometime soon, you'll be told that this duty is over. Depending on what I do, maybe you'll get to see me one more time. Maybe you'll get to see me when they kill me. Maybe not at all. But then it'll be over. You're better off forgetting me."

"I asked to be transferred," Streak said, and Volle turned to look at him. "After that first time. I'd been living alone in the guard barracks for two weeks, and I didn't think I could be the horrible thing they wanted me to be to you. But they wouldn't transfer me. And it's been over a month now, and you're the only person who's said more than two sentences to me in that time." He drew in a sharp breath. "And you seem so much better than the other guards. They just care about their pay, and what pretty things they stuck their cocks into last time down at the pub. You care about your country. You care so much that you went through being whipped and tortured, and you didn't tell. That's honorable. You don't deserve this.

"Maybe I would be better off forgetting you. But I don't think I can."

Volle's eyes misted over. He fought to control his emotions. "It's really the best thing…" he began, but Streak closed his muzzle with a paw.

"Oh, shut up," he said, and leaned over, pressing his muzzle to the fox's in a deep, warm kiss.

Volle arched his entire body into the kiss, his ears coming forward as his eyes closed in pleasure. Streak's tongue was cool and slick against his, and he pulled it into his muzzle as though his life depended on it. He felt the warm caress of the wolf's breath against his muzzle, the soft touch of his fur, and the hard points of his teeth as they slid against his own. The kiss was full of passion, hunger, and longing, and Volle returned it in kind.

He didn't want it to end, but of course it did. Slowly, gently, Streak pulled his muzzle back. Volle lay back and opened his eyes. "Wow."

Streak bit his lip, and rested a paw on Volle's chest, tracing the line of one of his ribs. "I know I shouldn't. But I can't let go. I keep thinking if I can find some way to get you out of here—"

"Don't think like that," Volle said sharply, though his fur was tingling at the touch. "If you have hope then I might have hope, and I don't want hope. That's what they want me to have."

"I think you're being paranoid," Streak said. "They can't know what's going on here. For all they know, I've been torturing you."

"I think they know, somehow. You're too…too beautiful. I thought when I first saw you that you were too perfect to be a coincidence. I've always had a bit of a thing for wolves, and you're just…" He sighed, and smiled. "Sorry. I wasn't expecting you to be as sweet inside as you looked outside. I don't know if they were either. But they (*he*) could easily have found out (*knows*) that I like wolves. I wasn't exactly discreet about my liaisons during my time in the palace."

"I bet you could have had any male or female you wanted."

Volle smiled. "Now you're just saying that to be polite."

Streak smiled back and lowered his muzzle, ears flicking. "So…what do we do now?"

"Now?" Volle flicked his ears and let his smile widen. "Well, I have an idea…"

Streak watched, amused, as the fox flipped over and lapped several gulps of water from the wall. When he turned back over, the wolf grinned. "What?"

"I don't want to think about the future any more. And there's something I've been wanting to do since that first day."

"Oh?" Streak's eyes flicked to Volle's sheath, which was showing signs of life. The wolf grinned. "What's that?"

"Mmm. Maybe you could kneel up here and let me see that equipment of yours up close." Volle tried to sound more bashful than eager, but he couldn't stop his tail from smacking the stone floor as it wagged.

The wolf smiled and stood up, unfastening his pants and sliding them down to the ground. He cupped his paw around his groin for a moment, self-consciously, then dropped it to his side, leaving his sheath exposed with his shirt hanging down on either side.

Volle followed the plump white ridge of fur, already showing some red at its tip, as Streak stepped over him and slowly knelt astride him. The fox craned his head forward until his nose was just brushing the soft white fur, panting with the effort until the wolf's paws slid behind his head to support him. Slowly, he drew his tongue up the warm length of fur, and was gratified to see how quickly it swelled and pushed the wolf's shaft further out.

Above him, he heard a gasp, and he felt the warm rumble of pleasure in the wolf's chest. He started the next lick lower, giving the dangling sac a curl of his tongue before sliding up the thick sheath again. He stopped just below the top, though his eyes were drawn to the length above it. On the next lick, he didn't stop, letting his tongue travel all the way to the tip and stopping there.

Streak breathed harder, and Volle wagged his tail as best he could. His sheath was hard and full too, lying on his belly, and the wolf's tail was tickling the skin of his member as it wagged back and forth. He licked again, and though he'd done this with many other males, was struck by how happy he was to be making this white wolf shiver. Streak had become important to him, and so this act was more than just the hedonistic enjoyment of a male in his muzzle, or a return obligation; it was an expression of his feelings. He was prevented from using his paws to caress the wolf, and this was all he could do.

He licked again and again, and at some point Streak's hips shifted and Volle found himself staring down the glistening length of the wolf's erection. He smiled and slid his muzzle around it, feeling its warmth on his tongue and its familiar hardness against his teeth. He held it for a moment, marveling again at how the feeling could be so new when he'd done this a hundred times.

The wolf's paws guided his head with the impatience of passion, and Volle could taste the wolf's need in the thick musk on his tongue. He slid obligingly back and forth, and the wolf's hips met him and pulled back with him. The musk grew stronger, the wolf's movements quickened and became more erratic, and Volle found himself tensing with excitement. Streak was moaning now, and Volle's erection shivered in sympathy as he felt the thick length in his muzzle drip musk onto his tongue. They were moving together now, as easily as if they'd been together for years, and Volle couldn't say how he knew the moment was coming, but he did.

He braced himself just before Streak let out a breathless squeak, pushing Volle's head into his hips. His knot pushed past the fox's lips, his whole length trembling, spurting musky warmth on Volle's tongue. He swallowed around the thick spasming member as the lovely white wolf above him bent forward, entirely focused on his climax.

It was over entirely too soon. Volle swallowed again, though he was trying to savor the rich musky taste of Streak. Slowly, the wolf sat back, letting his dripping erection slide out of the fox's muzzle. Volle looked up and gave the wolf a warm smile.

"I liked that a lot."

"*You* liked it? Oh, gods, fox." Streak leaned over and let his paws slide down so he was holding Volle's chest. "I've been with a couple, but…never like that."

Volle licked his lips and nuzzled the wolf. "Mmm. I'm glad you liked it." He sighed happily.

Streak held him for a long moment, and then slid off to lie between Volle and the wall. He let an arm rest on Volle's chest, and rested his head on the fox's shoulder. "I liked it, yes. And now I don't want to go."

"You'll always have to." Volle sighed. He nuzzled Streak again.

"You're right, though. I will. But not just yet." He slid his paw down Volle's stomach and smiled. "I think I have some unfinished business."

"You really don't have to." The protest was weak.

"You can't stop me." Streak grinned, eyes half-closed as his paw closed around Volle's erection.

Volle shivered, and closed his eyes as the wolf started to stroke. "Wouldn't dream of it."

Again, he was amazed at the freshness of it. Even compared to the last time the wolf had masturbated him, this felt subtly different, even considering that it hadn't been two months since his last release. Streak's muzzle lay next to his, his soft breaths passing across Volle's matted fur. His taste lingered in Volle's muzzle. His body was warm and close, and his paw's strokes seemed each to be lovingly planned and executed.

It took longer this time, but not much. Volle felt the climax building a long ways off and panted more quickly as it grew. He felt Streak's body respond and felt as though the wolf could feel what he was feeling. And when it came, he felt the warmth between their bodies feed into it, holding him and Streak together in a trembling moment of bliss before he fell over the edge, moaning loudly as his seed spurted out over Streak's paw.

He almost fell back into the wolf's arms, still shivering. "Mmm," Streak said into his ear. "*I enjoyed that.*"

"Oh…" was all Volle could manage. He felt himself drifting off into sleep, his weakened body's reserves used up by the night's activities.

Streak held him, and as he drifted off he heard the wolf say, "I think I can stay just a bit longer."

He woke to inky darkness, alone, but his back was still warm. He heard the rustle of cloth on fur near him, and turned his head, the wolf's smell strong in the cell. "Streak?" he whispered.

The noise stopped, and after a moment there was a soft chuckle. "Is that what you call me?"

Volle flicked his ears back in embarrassment. "Um. Yeah."

"Why 'Streak'?"

"Are you leaving?"

His whiskers and ears told him the wolf had moved. "In a minute. Don't change the subject." His voice came from lower down, closer to Volle's muzzle.

"Oh, well, you have this cute black streak on your hip…and the first thing you did was take your clothes off."

"My clothes? What does that have to do with it?"

"You never streaked as a kid?"

"Don't know what that is."

"It just means stripping and running out in public. You know, naked." Volle chuckled. "It was a big thing at our school for about a year. I did it twice."

"You city boys." Streak sounded amused. "Well, I think it's cute."

Volle didn't know why Streak assumed he was from the city. He had grown up in the city, but the background story he'd told at the palace was that he'd grown up on a farm. He was too tired and happy to maintain the lie now, so he let it go. After a pause, he said, "What do you call me?"

"Just 'fox.'"

"You don't know any other foxes?"

"Not right now. Listen, I don't know how long I was asleep. I should get out of here before Gerrold comes in."

"Yeah. Hurry. I'll see you again soon."

"Count on it." The wolf's muzzle moved tentatively towards his; they found each other quickly and shared a brief kiss. He saw Streak's silhouette in the door's frame as it opened. The wolf turned and looked at him, then closed the door, leaving him in darkness once again.

He lay awake for what might have been one hour or three, thinking about Streak, and about his situation. He tried to concentrate on the pleasant memories, but the thought of what he'd do if they took the wolf away from him kept intruding. They didn't have much time left, he was sure of that. Maybe one or two more visits, and that would be it.

The door opened, and the skunk shuffled in with a plate of food. He set it down next to Volle, and in the dim light from the door, Volle thought he saw the skunk's nose wrinkle at the musky scents in the cell.

"So," he said impulsively, "what's the name of that white wolf who comes in here sometimes? I'd like to report him. He's been very abusive."

The skunk stopped and stared at him, then shook his head and turned away without a word. He picked the torch out of the ceiling bracket but didn't replace it with a new one.

"Hey! Where's my light? You can't just leave me here in—" The door slammed shut. Of course Limp Stripes could leave him in the dark.

This was different. And it didn't look to be good.

Chapter 5

He ate the food slowly, sat against the wall, and waited.

In the darkness, he had no way of telling how much time had passed. He slept fitfully, lapped at the water when he was thirsty, and listened to the rumbling in his stomach. He hadn't felt really full in months, but the meals usually appeared at the right time to take the edge off his hunger.

No longer. He licked the plate clean, and kept licking it even after the smell of food was gone from it. He had slept five, seven, ten times, but he didn't know for how long. The ache in his stomach grew more and more acute, faded away, and returned with a vengeance. His sleep grew more restless, spotted with uneasy dreams.

Dereath was weakening him, he realized, starving him to batter down his resistance. He'd done it before. So this would be the end. Between physical weakness, and emotional, would he would give away his secrets?

He sat up, pulled one paw below his neck, and rested his head on the chain. With some difficulty, he lifted his paw around the other side of his head and then down, so the chain made a loop around his neck. The clinking of the links echoed around the cell. He lowered his body and felt the tension increase in the chain.

Could he do this? He lay down further and heard his breath start to wheeze as the chain tightened. The urge to sit up flooded through him, but his body was weak enough that he could fight it. He panicked as his breathing became more labored, and scrabbled briefly at the chain before pulling his paw away again. Spots appeared in front of his eyes and his body thrashed around, finally jerking forward.

The chain loosened, and he gulped down deep lungfuls of air, half sobbing as he did so. He felt dizzy; spots still danced in front of his eyes. Frantically, he tried to lift his arm over his head again as he felt consciousness slipping from him, but the darkness stole in before he could tell whether he'd succeeded.

"Fox! Oh gods, wake up!" He was being shaken. A grey shape with white edges was hovering over him.

"Stop...shaking..." He panted through a haze of dizziness.

"Are you okay?" The smell, the voice—he recognized Streak now.

He put a paw to his throat. "I...think so." Something was different. He held up his paw and looked at it. The shackles were gone. "What..."

Streak was unlocking the shackles on his legs. "I've got to get you out of here."

Volle paused to digest that. He moved his arms around experimentally. They felt oddly detached. "Why?"

"They're going to kill you. Starve you to death. How long has it been since they brought food? Three days? Four? Five?"

"Don't know. Since you came." Volle's head was clearing, slowly, but now he was becoming aware of the gnawing emptiness in his stomach and the weakness in his limbs. "How did...?"

"I stole the key." Streak picked up something from the floor and shook it out. "Here, put these on." Volle stared at the pants, and Streak sighed. "You poor...okay, here." He slid them over Volle's feet.

"Okay, okay." The fabric rubbed his fur the wrong way, and the sensation pulled him at least partly into awareness. Volle pulled them up and fastened them. They were extremely loose on him, and felt odd after so long without clothes. "Where did you get all this?"

"This is my spare uniform. It'll be loose but it'll fit. I can't carry you naked through the prison." He handed Volle the shirt.

With some difficulty, Volle slid it on. His fingers fumbled as he fastened it around the front, and at the lowest button, his muscles protested. He hadn't stretched his arms that far in months.

"All set?" Streak's ears were back and he looked grim. He set his arms beneath Volle and lifted. Volle felt the muscles in his arms tighten. "You're so light."

Volle put a paw on the wolf's chest. "I think I can walk."

"Later." Streak smiled, a tight nervous smile, and kissed his nose quickly. "When we get to the top."

He pulled the fox to his chest and stood up. Volle tried putting his arms around Streak's neck, but the tension was too uncomfortable and he dropped them to his own chest. The wolf turned and walked toward the open door and the light beyond, and as he turned Volle to walk through it, the fox caught a glimpse of his empty shackles, lying beside the gutter in the floor, water glistening on the wall beyond. Then they were through the door, and out.

He remembered the hallways, dead grey stone with torch sconces placed regularly. Compared to the blackness he'd lived in for the past few days, the light was almost blinding. Volle squinted as Streak hurried through the corridors.

"Do you know anyone in the palace who can hide you? I don't know anyone in the city and you're not strong enough to get out yet."

The name he'd made himself forget floated tantalizingly out of reach. He knew he couldn't go there anyway, though. But Helfer would be okay. Hef would help him. "Yes. West wing, second floor."

"I can get you there."

They hadn't met any other guards, and Volle thought this was strange, but perhaps he was the only prisoner down here. "Where are the other guards?"

"Other wings. You were pretty isolated. There's a back stair we can use. Then you'll have to walk to the palace from there. It's the middle of the night, though. We should be okay."

Volle nodded. Streak was walking quickly but not running, and the motion was pleasant, almost lulling the fox back to sleep. He forced himself to stay awake as they passed scores of open cells, walked up a dimly lit staircase, and passed slowly through a more open series of cells, with windows in the doors.

"Oops." Streak muttered it under his breath as he stopped and turned quickly, and Volle caught a whiff of rat scent. Then it was gone; the wolf marched down another hallway and to a staircase. At the top, behind a closed door, he set Volle down gently.

"We have to walk from here. I'll support you. If anyone stops us, you're my drunk friend, I'm walking you back to the barracks."

"They're not in this direction." He was surprised that the map of the city remained so strong in his head.

"It's the best I could come up with. It'll explain away part of the smell, too."

Volle nodded. "Okay." He stood gingerly, and his knees buckled almost immediately. He grabbed at Streak for support. The wolf had his arms around him in an instant, holding him upright. Volle looked into the warm blue eyes.

"Thank you," he said softly. He nuzzled Streak and braced himself on the wolf's powerful frame.

Streak looked embarrassed. His ears flicked and he nuzzled only briefly before looking away. "Let's get going before it gets light."

He pushed the door open, and Volle staggered at the cold, fresh air. The scents were clear and sharp, the air not musty with memories and pain. As he stepped out, he glanced up and stopped dead, transfixed by the glittering patterns of stars in the sky. The cold air seared his lungs, but he drank it in gratefully.

"Come on," Streak started to say, but trailed off when he saw the glistening in Volle's eyes. "Hey, it's okay."

Volle swallowed. "I really...forgot how beautiful they are." He lowered his gaze to Streak's white muzzle, looking at the blue eyes shining in the starlight. Slowly he lifted his muzzle, and the wolf hesitated, then met it, tightening his hold around Volle.

Volle closed his eyes and let himself be washed away on the sensations: the cold air ruffling his fur, the tight press of Streak's muscles against him, and the warm lupine muzzle locked with his. Their tongues caressed, and then separated.

"We should go," Streak said again, but Volle just looked at him with a slight smile. "What?"

"I never knew...how beautiful *you* are."

Streak swallowed, and Volle saw him fight back tears of his own. "Fox..."

"I know, I know. Let's go." Volle turned, reluctantly, and stepped

"Keep your head down," Streak hissed nervously.

The Prisoner's Release

forward onto the road. His legs were still unsteady, and he needed every ounce of the wolf's support.

The palace's turrets rose about half a mile away, dull grey stone that reflected only a little of the starlight. Only the very tops, gold-leafed, shone at all. The road leading there from the prison was narrow and winding, and Volle kept looking back and forth at the dark houses and shops on either side.

"Keep your head down," Streak hissed nervously, and Volle tried to act drunk.

It took them forever to make it the half-mile. Volle had to stop and rest at one point, so he sat on a house's front stoop while Streak paced nervously. Twice they heard someone coming and tensed, but the passerby gave them barely a second glance. Finally, they came to a stop at a metal gate.

"You gonna be okay?" Streak braced Volle against the wall, and Volle nodded. He flexed his legs gingerly. They were sore and still unsteady, but he thought he could go a little further.

"What, did you steal all the keys?" he asked as the wolf fitted a key to the keyhole in the gate.

Streak didn't answer immediately, as he pushed the gate open. He put his arm around Volle and guided him in. "The guards have a master set," he said, closing the gate behind them. "I just picked the ones I thought would be useful." He jingled his pocket and flashed a brief grin, but he didn't seem to be any less nervous now that they were in the palace.

They had walked into one of the gardens, but Volle had to spot the elaborate flowery design before he knew which one it was. The garden seemed eerie in the starlight, deserted except for the two of them, the flowers' colors all muted and their scents faded for the night. It should be romantic, Volle thought, a nighttime garden, but the silence and the chill disturbed him.

"It's this way, I think." Streak was guiding him down one path.

"I remember. Down here and around that corner there's a door that usually isn't locked." The shortcuts were coming back to him, weak as he was. "Then there's a stair to the right. We can cut through the servants' quarters to the west wing."

"Okay." They walked quickly down the path. Volle felt the crunch of the gravel under his paws, and it brought back other memories. He pushed them aside and concentrated on taking steps.

The door was just as he'd remembered it, decorated with the king's crest in carved wood, not painted like the fancier doors in the main garden and out front. They pulled it open and stepped into the warm air and ancient smells of the palace.

Volle had barely had time to see the staircase when he heard footsteps coming down it. His eyes met Streak's, and then the wolf pushed the door open, looking panicked.

Volle shook his head quickly, then collapsed to his knees with his head out the door. He made retching noises, and tried to shake appropriately.

"Bad night?" he heard behind him.

"A bit too much," Streak said. Volle hoped the other didn't hear the waver in his voice. "Just letting him get it out of his system."

"Okay. Try to keep it down. And clean it up when you're done." The footsteps receded.

Volle braced himself against the door and levered himself upwards. Streak was at his side immediately, helping pull him upward. "You think fast."

"Have to." He gave the wolf a small grin. "Let's go."

They made it up the stairs and through the servants' quarters without incident. On the other side, Volle looked up and down the opulent corridor and headed immediately to the right. He found an ornate door and nodded to Streak, who pushed it open gently. It opened onto a small foyer, with a padded bench and a small side door that Volle knew led to the valet's room. He guided Streak past it and to the larger door on the other side of the foyer, which was made of polished wood, carved with Helfer's family crest, and brushed with gold leaf.

Streak moved to open the door, but Volle stopped him. He raised a paw and knocked. After a few seconds, Streak knocked, louder. They waited, and after a short time they heard shuffling footsteps inside. The door cracked open.

"Do you know what time it is? What is it?" Volle recognized the weasel's voice, which lost some of its sharp irritation when he spotted the guard's uniform. He hadn't seen Volle yet.

"Hi, Hef," Volle said.

The door opened slightly wider, and Volle saw the ruddy fur of his friend's muzzle. His black eyes widened.

"What the—Volle? What are you doing here?"

"Need to stay here for a bit."

"By the gods, you look awful. And smell worse." The weasel hesitated. "I've been hearing things…"

Volle managed a weak smile. "What are they saying about me?"

"That you were taken ill and had to go back to Vinton. That you're a spy, and a traitor. That you ran back to Ferrenis. That was just Dereath, of course."

"Oh, that."

" 'Oh, that'? Volle, if that's true…"

"I haven't been to Ferrenis. I've been in prison." At that, the weasel's ears shot up. "Relax, Hef. You're in no danger."

"I am now! Prison? You've been in prison? You've…escaped, haven't you? What if someone finds you here?"

"That seems a lot more likely the longer we stand out here in your foyer."

The weasel didn't move. Finally, he said, "Oh, all right. Come on in."

Streak helped Volle into the rooms, and Helfer shut the door quickly behind them.

Helfer's parlor, elaborately decorated with yellow velvet curtains and small tapestries lining the walls, showed signs of what the weasel had been up to the previous night. The curtains were closed over the elaborate double window, the door to the large wine cabinet hung partly open, and the loveseat had been moved to sit in front of the now-cold fireplace. On the floor to one side, a half-empty bottle of wine and two empty glasses stood forgotten, and Volle saw more than one article of clothing nearby them, almost forming a trail to the curtained doorway that led further into the apartment.

He often wondered why Helfer bothered to keep a desk in this room at all. Alone of all the furnishings, the desk showed no signs of recent use, and its simple wooden style didn't seem to fit in with the reddish-orange patterned loveseat, or the matching chairs and various small rugs that lay scattered over the floor.

Helfer looked Volle up and down as they stepped in, and now there was concern in his eyes. "You really do look awful. What in the name of Weasel happened to you?"

"He needs food," Streak said. "They starved him for the last three days."

"Mm." Helfer turned to Streak and gave him an appraising look. "At least your tastes haven't changed much. He looks as good as you look terrible."

Streak's ears flicked back. He started to say something, and Helfer raised a small paw. "I know. I'll get food sent up right away. And please, Volle, put something on besides that horrid uniform. It really doesn't suit you."

"Later," the fox coughed. "I was hoping to use your private bath."

"Yes, yes, of course. Phew." The weasel waved a paw in front of his nose. "Worse than the time you drank too much and fell into the gutter."

"Which time?" Volle cracked a small grin.

Helfer flashed a quick grin back, then bit his lip worriedly. "Stay here. Sit down." He gestured towards a richly upholstered chair, and then slipped out the front door.

Streak helped Volle over to the chair, and the fox collapsed into it. "You feeling okay?" Streak asked, bending over him.

"Apart from the hole in my stomach, the dizziness, and the feeling that I couldn't walk another step, I feel great." Volle looked up. "I owe you a lot."

The wolf nuzzled him, and looked away bashfully. "Not so much. I mean, I only did what I had to."

Helfer slipped back in. "He's going to get some food from the kitchens."

"Caresh?"

"Yes. Not even a question. Volle, what is going on?"

"Excuse me," Streak said, "I need to get back and put these keys back before Gerrold comes on duty."

Volle lifted a paw and Streak took it, holding it tightly. "Thank you again," the fox said, and lifted his muzzle.

Streak met it in a soft, quick kiss. "Bye, fox—Volle. I'll be back when I get off duty today. Be careful when you eat. Remember what happened last time."

Volle smiled at the use of his name, and at the wolf's concern. "I will. Be careful."

Streak let his paw go slowly, and walked to the door. Helfer was still standing there, watching them. As Streak approached, he opened the door a crack.

Streak extended a paw. "Pleasure to meet you, sir."

"Far as I'm concerned, you were never here." Helfer shook his paw with a smile, and shut the door behind him after he slipped out. He turned, looked at Volle, then padded over to the chair opposite him and sat down. "Volle?"

Volle gave him a measured look. "Thank you for all your help, Hef. This would be a very nice time of year to visit your Vellenland estate, wouldn't it?"

"Is it that bad?"

"It could be. I don't know yet, but it might. I'll probably be okay. But it would certainly be safer for you not to be here."

The weasel tapped his paw against the floor. "If you say so, I'm not inclined to argue. But Volle, are you really…" He stopped, tilted his muzzle and smiled. "No, don't bother answering. You know I never like to get mixed up in anything serious at the palace."

"I know." Volle smiled, and couldn't keep his eyes from drifting shut. He hadn't had time to make up a plausible explanation for why he'd been arrested, but he trusted himself to be able to later. "It's not true, Hef. Dereath caught me in what he thought was a compromising position. They've been interrogating me…some plans disappeared."

"Compromising position, eh? Probably not the kind I'm thinking of. No, no—I told you not to bother. So who's the wolf? He seems quite devoted."

"He saved my life." Volle opened his eyes again. "We were set up to fall in love, though."

"Why should that make a difference?" Helfer grinned at him. "Does it matter how it came about?"

"It was engineered by Dereath."

Helfer's nose wrinkled. "He kept asking if I'd ever seen you passing messages or doing anything suspicious. I said the only messages I'd seen you passing were to the cute guys down at the Jackal's Staff. He's not changed a bit. But still, your wolf is innocent, right? So does it matter if a rat pushed you together?"

"I guess not." Volle rested his muzzle on his paws. "But this rescue all seems a bit too convenient."

Helfer looked pensive, but before he could reply, there was a rustle from behind the curtain and it was drawn aside. A small brown rabbit poked his head around the curtain. "Lord Ikling? Oh, I'm sorry." He looked at Volle and then back at Helfer.

The weasel smiled. "It's okay, Georgie. Go back to bed; I'll be there in a moment. Wait!" The rabbit had pulled back, and now his head reappeared. Volle saw a bit of his naked hip around the edge of the curtain. "How would you like to be my guest up at my estate in Vellenland?"

The rabbit's eyes widened. "Really?"

"Yes, really. Go ahead and pack, and we'll leave at first light."

Georgie disappeared without another word. Volle watched him go and then smiled at Helfer. "I see your tastes haven't changed either."

Helfer grinned and shrugged. "He's a fantastic lay. He can almost keep up with me. I keep telling you about rabbits."

Volle closed his eyes again. "I'm not going to argue with you, Hef. I'm too weak."

"How long were you in prison? All this time?"

"All this time. They really didn't tell anyone?"

Helfer shook his head. "I couldn't believe you'd just left. Your rooms were left intact, nothing packed. Caresh heard you were running away. The other lords think there was an emergency with Ilyana. But we never heard anything about prison."

There was a discreet knock at the door. Volle opened his eyes in time to see Helfer glance at him on his way to the door. "That'll be Caresh," he said softly, but asked at the door to be sure.

Volle couldn't hear the reply, but obviously it was the valet, because Helfer opened the door. Caresh was a fox, about half a foot shorter than Volle and stocky, but always perfectly groomed. Even woken in the middle of the night, he had somehow managed to arrange his fur meticulously, and the jacket and pants he was wearing looked freshly pressed. He set down a tray on the sideboard with four platters and a small loaf of bread on it.

Helfer shut the door. "Caresh, nobody is to know that Lord Vinton is here."

"Of course, sir." The valet said it as though Helfer had asked for nothing more than a glass of water. He cleared off the small table, moved it over to Volle's left hand side, and put the tray down on it.

"I do apologize for the quality of the food, sir. The kitchen is closed and I was forced to find what I could without the help of the staff."

"I think that's best," Volle said. His muzzle was already watering at the smells coming from the tray.

Caresh lifted the covers from each platter. "Two quails left over from tonight's supper. I believe the sauce is a honey-citrus glaze. Potatoes cooked in the southern Vellenland style with onions and shallots. Beef cubes with gravy. Miss Taffen's celebrated soft rice cake with cinnamon topping. I am sorry, sir, but they were very popular. This was the only one left."

Helfer patted Volle on the shoulder. "I'll leave you to it. Oh, and Volle? Do get out of that outfit. Help yourself to anything in my wardrobe."

Volle nodded, and smiled. "I remember, Hef. Thanks."

Helfer was almost to the curtain when Volle said, "Hef." The weasel turned around.

"I'll stay out of sight when you leave. And I won't be here when you get back. So...good bye, and good luck. Thank you for being a friend."

Helfer walked back over to him and leaned over, giving him a hug. "You too, Volle," he said quietly. "Whatever you're doing, stay safe."

"Can't promise that." Volle grinned weakly. "But I'll try. And maybe someday I will be able to return this very great favor."

Helfer waved a paw. "Don't be silly. Six years of friendship is more than enough. Just keep yourself out of politics from now on. If I've told you once, I've told you a hundred times, it's dull at best and dangerous at worst."

"I'll remember that, Hef. If I get out of here, I'll take your words to heart."

Helfer smiled. "See that you do." He disappeared behind the curtain.

"Will that be all, sir?" Caresh asked.

The platters had given Volle an idea. He lifted the rice cake delicately from the platter it was on and set it on the edge of the potato platter, then handed the empty platter to the valet. "Actually, Caresh, if you would be so kind, there is one small errand I would like you to run. And when that is done, I would be very much obliged if you could draw me a water bath."

"Yes, sir."

When Caresh had left, Volle attacked the platters hungrily. He tried to moderate his eating, but both quails and half the potatoes were gone almost before he knew it. The ache in his belly reduced to a grumble, he slowed down and wiped the juices from his muzzle. He'd barely tasted the quail as he bolted it down, but he took more time with the potatoes and bread. Nothing was warm, and the bread was slightly stale, but he thought it was the best meal he'd ever eaten in the palace.

When he'd eaten most of it, he picked up the rice cake and attempted to stand. After a moment steadying his legs, he made it to the desk, chewing slowly on the rice cake. Helfer had a cherry-wood writing chair that was nicely carved, and comfortable enough. Volle sat down in it gratefully, and began searching through the desk.

He found pen and paper easily, but had to search for the ink, and finally located it in a small side drawer. Still chewing on the rice cake (which was delicious), he sat down and began to compose two short letters.

Caresh returned while he was writing. He placed the covered platter on the sideboard beside the desk, and waited for Volle to turn around.

"Everything go smoothly, Caresh?"

"Indeed, sir. May I draw your bath now?"

"In a moment." Volle finished one of the notes and folded it over itself twice. "Do you know what happened to my old valet, Welcis?"

"I believe, sir, that Welcis easily found employment with Lord Castor's staff. He was not implicated in your unfortunate predicament."

"I'm very glad to hear that. Would you be so good as to convey this note to him? Not today, but when you return from Vellenland."

"Very good, sir."

"Thank you, Caresh. You are a credit both to your species and to your profession."

"One does one's best, sir. May I draw your bath now?"

"Please."

Caresh disappeared behind the curtain, and Volle heard him fire up the small stove. It would take about twenty minutes to get the water bath ready, he estimated, which was plenty of time. He finished the second note, and then made his way over to the window and opened one side. For a moment he just stood there, letting the cold air wash over his muzzle, then he leaned carefully out the window.

It was not yet light outside, but there was considerable activity. He looked down onto the street, checking carefully for palace guards in either direction, then hailed a young mouse who was running by.

"Ho! Mouse!"

The mouse looked up. "Sir?"

"Can you read?"

"No, sir."

Volle waved the second note. "Would you like to earn a silver piece for ten minutes' work?"

"Yes, sir!"

"Take this to the house at…" He gave the mouse an address. "You know where that is?"

"Yes, sir."

"Give it to the person who answers the door. Once they read it, they'll give you a silver piece. Can I count on you?"

"Indeed, sir!" The mouse moved closer to the window and held out his paws.

Volle folded the note over and dropped it from the window. The mouse caught it agilely and waved to Volle, then sprinted away down the street.

Smiling, the fox closed the window. He made it back to the desk and took the papers Caresh had brought back. After checking to make sure they were the right ones, he slipped them into an empty drawer of Helfer's desk. That done, he sat lost in thought until Caresh came to take him to the bath.

He had to lean on the valet to make it through the sitting room behind the curtain. It was a sitting room in name only; Helfer called it his "laying room," or cruder names, if he'd been drinking. The doorway at the far side of the room led to the bedroom, where he slept, and like the doorway back to the parlor, it was filled only with a curtain. Helfer didn't like doors much. The two small doors in the left hand wall, which led to his bathroom and wardrobe, were the only ones in the whole suite.

One entire corner of this room was covered with a thick, plush, Vellenland rug. The other far corner was piled high with cushions. On the near wall, long couches spread against the wall, both large enough for two (or three, Volle happened to know). Against the right hand wall were two chests, both of finely crafted teak wood.

He rested his head on the side of the bath.

The Prisoner's Release

Volle smiled at the familiar room. Only Helfer could get away with something like this. He didn't have time to linger there, though. The bathroom door was open and the scented steam was calling, and Caresh was bringing him there step by steady step.

The bathroom was filled with curling wisps of steam rising from the large circular stone bath in its center. The stove sat off to one side, filling the room with warmth, but Volle couldn't take his eyes off the bath. Caresh brought him right up to the edge of the tub, and he lifted his muzzle to smell the scent in the bathwater. Jasmine, he thought.

"That smells wonderful." Volle put one paw into the water. "Oh. Canis bless you."

"Thank you, sir." The valet stood by as Volle took off the uniform and sank slowly into the water. "Will that be all?"

"Mmm." Volle's eyes were closed already as the meal and the warmth worked their effect on his starved body. He rested his head on the side of the bath. "Caresh, when that white wolf comes back, let him in, please?"

Caresh coughed softly. "Sir, are you anticipating his return before our departure?"

"Oh. No. Well, don't let him in, then, I guess." Volle fought to stay awake, but he barely finished his sentence. He didn't hear Caresh leave, or even hear if the valet made a reply.

When he woke, the water was lukewarm and murky. He could still smell the scent of the bathwater, but it was mingled now with the dirt and grime from the cell. Fortunately, Helfer had soap, so Volle spent a good fifteen minutes making the water even murkier as he scrubbed every inch of his body.

His arms were still sore, and unused to stretching down below his chest. He scrubbed the white fur there, then slowly moved down his abdomen. The water helped his muscles adjust, though he was doubly sore when he tried to pull his legs back and stretch his arms down to wash them. His paws were a fright. He didn't think he'd ever get all the dirt out of them. And his poor tail—would it ever be as soft as it had been? He sighed, working another handful of soap through it.

Lastly, he scrubbed under his tail, and then his sheath. He closed his eyes as he did. It had been so long since he'd been able to touch himself. His fingers caressed his sac and rubbed slowly up his sheath's fur, and he didn't stop when he felt a swelling inside. Might as well clean that too, he thought with a grin. His fingers kept rubbing and squeezing in slow, rhythmic strokes, and he felt himself harden and slide out of his sheath.

He forced himself to wait until it was fully extended. Then he took a handful of soap and gently rubbed up along his length. The sensation made him shiver in pleasure. He repeated it, enjoying the freedom of movement as much as the stroke itself. When he felt his arousal getting more intense, he stopped, with a little effort. No need to waste his energy here when he had Streak returning tonight.

Standing up was still a bit too unsteady for his liking, though his legs were getting stronger. He settled for kneeling in the bath as the water drained out, agitating it to keep the dirt from settling on his fur. There was still a film of grime on him when the tub was empty, but Caresh had left a bucket of warm water for just that purpose on the tub's edge.

His arms were strong enough to handle the bucket as long as he stretched them back over his head. He poured the water over himself, keeping his eyes shut, and then replaced the bucket. Helfer had a pile of soft towels stacked beside the bath; he grabbed the topmost one and got as much of the water out of his fur as he could. He considered Helfer's grooming powder, but decided against it. It had a nice soft scent, but it was expensive, and he didn't want to use it up.

He poked his head out of the bathroom door. A quick sniff of the air told him that Helfer and his bunny had been through the sitting room and had left already. He held the towel around himself and peeked into the bedroom to be sure. Indeed, Helfer's large feather bed was sitting empty, neatly made with the velvet coverlet on top.

Good. One more thing, then. His legs were getting steadier as he walked around the apartment, and he managed to make it to the desk without holding on to anything. He took out the papers Caresh had brought back the previous night (morning?) and returned to the sitting room.

In the wardrobe, he chose an outfit of short yellow robes over a white shirt. Good traveling clothes. Suitably attired, he concealed the papers, and then walked back into the sitting room to wait for Streak.

The Prisoner's Release

Chapter 6

The knock at the door came in late afternoon. He had been nibbling at the potatoes as he got hungry again, and reading one of the few books Helfer kept in the parlor. At the knock, he stood up, pleased to find that his legs were supporting his weight quite well. Nose to the air, he approached the door. The wolf's scent was there, and nobody else's. With a smile, he opened the door.

Streak returned his smile. "Hi."

"Quick, come in." Volle stepped back, and closed the door after the wolf. He put his arms around the muscular chest and gave Streak a warm kiss. Streak returned the kiss with some passion, but cut it short.

"Is something wrong?"

Streak shook his head. "No. I mean, yes. I was nervous all day today. I thought someone would find out. But when Gerrold raised the alarm, they just sent people out searching. Didn't even ask me to do that."

"Well, that's good." Volle smiled and walked slowly across the parlor, Streak following at his side.

"Say, you look good. And smell good. And you're walking!"

Volle spread his arms, showing off his balance. "I feel a lot better."

"I'm so glad to hear that. Listen, Volle, is there anything you need to do? Anyone you need to contact? Cause I can probably get someone to come here without arousing suspicion."

"In a bit." Volle drew the curtain aside. "I thought we'd take advantage of some quality time here, since Helfer enjoys luxuries that we probably won't see again for a while." He gave the wolf a coy smile.

Streak gaped at the sitting room, a bit taken aback. "It would be good to get the business over with fir-irst!" The last word became a squeak, as Volle slid his paw into the wolf's pants and found his sheath. He cupped it warmly, rubbing with his fingers, and even slid one claw into the sheath's opening, teasing Streak's tip just inside.

"Mm-hmm," Volle said, guiding the wolf to the plush rug. "I plan to take care of business." He grinned and unfastened Streak's pants with his free paw. The other continued rubbing, and a moment later the wolf had pulled him close and buried him in a deep, passionate kiss.

Volle curled his tongue around the slick, warm wolf tongue, keeping his paw busy. Streak was already mostly erect, and Volle's fingers concentrated on the warm shaft, feeling its smoothness and curling around its volume. His pawpads slid easily along the red flesh, and when they teased at the tip, the wolf gave a little yipping moan into Volle's muzzle. When his paws felt the knot at the base of Streak's shaft start to swell, he stopped, and broke the kiss.

"Mmm. It's so nice to be able to feel you," he said softly, and Streak looked back into his eyes.

"You feel wonderful," he whispered.

"Helfer has some stuff here," Volle said. "Don't move." He left Streak panting, red tongue and red shaft hanging out, and went to one of the chests. Inside, he found a small cup full of an oily substance, and removed it.

"Ever used this stuff?"

Streak sniffed it. "Something like it, I think, if it's what I think it is." He grinned. "This smells better, though."

"I think it is what you think it is." Volle grinned back. He took two fingertips and dipped them into the cup, then rubbed them up and down along the wolf's erection until it glistened. Streak moaned and squeezed his eyes shut, and then opened them again when Volle took his fingers away.

"And some for you, too?"

"Some for me." Volle lay down on his back, opened the robes, lifted his shirt, and reached into the cup again. He rubbed the oils under his tail, slowly, letting Streak watch as his fingers slipped slightly into himself and back out, smoothing the fur away from the pink opening under his tail. His erection was already visible, and as he lubricated himself, it grew fuller, resting against his newly-white belly fur. When he'd done with himself, he rested a paw on his erection, brushing the remaining oils up and down it, and spread his legs.

"Come on," he grinned up at the panting wolf. "You promised, all those weeks ago."

Streak laughed, and moved forward. He slid his paws under Volle's hips and lifted them to meet his own. Volle felt the tip of the wolf's thick shaft for an instant before it slid easily into him, filling him. He gasped; he'd gotten a bit tighter over the past six months.

"You okay?" Streak was shivering with tension and had moved his paws up to Volle's back, but there was concern in his look too.

"I'm okay." Volle smiled and wiggled his hips. "You're big. And I'm not as easy as I used to be. But I'm okay."

"You do feel tight." Streak nuzzled him gently.

"You feel wonderful." Volle reached up and pulled the wolf closer, pressing his hips forward until he felt the full thick length inside him. Streak gasped and returned his embrace, and for a moment they just lay like that. Then the wolf drew his hips back and pushed them forward, and Volle felt a wave of pleasure course through them both. He brought one paw down to his erection and started stroking himself in time with Streak's thrust. With the other paw, he traced a finger gently up and down the black streak of fur that ran the length of the wolf's supple white hip.

Streak's control didn't last for too long. Volle could feel his knot with every thrust, and as the thrusts got faster and harder, he tried to time his own paw's strokes. He shivered every time Streak's length slid past his tailhole, and he knew that the knot stretching him would just about send him over. It was hard to keep his paw from stroking faster; it wanted to. The desire in him was taking over, as it did at the best of times, and like the last time with Streak, he felt that the wolf was a part of it and not just the object of it.

There was a subtle difference in Streak, though. Volle thought he knew what it was. The wolf was thrusting with passion, and yes, love, but also with a touch of guilt. He was trying to restrain it, but as his control eroded and desire took over, the emotions became clearer in his muzzle and in his actions.

Volle observed this with a detached part of his mind and set it aside as he let his passion take him over as well. They moved together, each feeling his own arousal as well as the other's, and when the moment came at last and the wolf's thick knot stretched his tail hole and then popped inside, they both moaned with the same voice.

Volle's muscles squeezed the wolf's knot; Streak's knot stretched the fox's tail hole. The same motion drew them both upward, together, and their shared moans gathered intensity as their bodies gripped each other and shared a dazzling climax. Volle's shaft shivered in his paw and covered it with fluid, while inside him, Streak's erection spilled its own fluids. Both pressed close to each other, trembling in the grip of their passion, and their muzzles sought each other out, tongues meeting to hold the moment as long as possible.

Even the afterglow felt special to Volle. He wrapped his legs around Streak's hips and rested his head on a cushion. Streak lay gently atop him and nuzzled quietly, arms tight around him.

"I don't love you because the sex is so good," Volle said softly. "I think the sex is so good because I love you."

Streak nuzzled his ears and said softly, "I love you, too, Volle. I like knowing your name."

"And you think this is the last time we'll be together."

"What?" Streak jerked upright, pulling at Volle's tail hole.

"Ow!"

"Sorry!" He leaned over Volle again. "What do you mean? I'm not leaving you. Unless you want me to."

Volle brushed Streak's muzzle with his clean paw. "It's okay. You're a darling wolf, but you're not all that good at hiding your emotions. And there have been other signs, too. The rescue, the hiding here...it was all too easy."

"What do you mean?" But Streak was looking guilty, near tears now. "Don't you trust me?"

"Shh." Volle tried to lift his muzzle to kiss him, but the wolf didn't respond. "They told you that if you got me to give you the papers, then... what? You'd get promoted? You'd have me in your personal care? And you were so desperate that you had to try it, but in your heart you don't believe I'll betray my country, do you?"

"I...I didn't..."

"I don't blame you, Streak, my sweet young wolf. I know you did it out of love. Or at least compassion. Otherwise you wouldn't be so sad, thinking that at least we had this little time together before they take me back."

A tear dripped onto Volle's chest. "I do love you," Streak whispered. "I don't know how it happened or how they knew. They told me we could go away together, as long as they got the papers back."

"They used you," Volle said, reaching up to lick at Streak's muzzle. "They isolated you, kept you friendless, and told you to go do something against your nature. Then they made sure the only person you talked to would be me—a prisoner desperate for companionship and almost as isolated. We were all each other had for that time. And you're gorgeous, and I guess you saw something in me..."

Streak licked him back, another tear dripping down the other side of his muzzle. "How did they know?"

"The chimney hole, I would guess. Listening to everything we said and did."

"Quite astute." The sharp voice came from the doorway.

They both turned their heads to look. A slender rat was standing there, one paw twiddling his whiskers. He was dressed in a simple black outfit: sleeveless vest and pants, with a silver belt. His hairless tail swung idly against the doorframe.

"Dereath." Volle laid his ears back. "I wondered when I'd see you."

"You were supposed to wait outside!" Streak growled.

"Hardly any point to that now, is there?" Dereath smiled at them, a nasty smile that Volle remembered well. "It wasn't hard to figure out what you came in here to do, so when I heard you leave I thought I'd slip in and listen to the show. You perform quite well," he said to Streak. "I think we may have an opening for you. When you're done with that one, that is."

He leered at them, and Streak's growl deepened. "Minister or not, I'll break your muzzle for that."

"Oh, I don't think so, dear boy. Not for another five or ten minutes, at least." He smirked at their joined hips. "And in any case, I'm not stupid enough to come in here alone. Don't worry, the soldiers will stay in the parlor. This show is just for me."

"You said if you got the papers, we could leave together!"

Volle stared at Streak, realizing for the first time what the wolf had meant. He had put his whole career on the line. He'd been willing to give up his livelihood, the only life he knew. Even if he hated it, it was still a significant gesture.

"So I did. But now that he knows you're working for me, I think the

The Prisoner's Release

probability of that is very slim." Dereath looked at Volle. "Unless this wolf actually means something to you."

"He does," Volle said evenly. "Not that you'd know anything of meaning, you poor excuse for a person. So if I tell you where the papers are, you'll let us go?"

"Of course, Lord Vinton." The rat bowed mockingly. "There is a carriage already ready at the door."

"We've arranged for our own transportation in the street outside," Volle said. "If you don't mind."

"Ah." Dereath straightened, smiling his oily smile. "We would be deeply offended if you chose to forbear our hospitality."

Volle watched the glint in his eyes and hoped Streak could see it too. He had a feeling he knew where Dereath's carriage would be taking them. "Very well." Streak's arms tightened around him. He felt the wolf's knot slip out of him, and the wolf prepared to draw his hips back, but Volle tightened his legs warningly. Streak stopped moving, and Volle didn't think Dereath had noticed.

"Lord Yardley has the papers."

Dereath's expression turned from triumph to puzzlement. "There is no Lord Yardley any more."

"Of course not," Volle said. "Behind his painting in the east wing gallery, there is a small concealed space. That's where I hid the plans I stole."

The rat grimaced. "We'll soon see if you're telling the truth. Meanwhile, you can stay here."

He turned and disappeared from the curtain for a moment. They could hear him talking to someone in the parlor, and in that moment Volle let Streak's length slip out of him. He restrained a gasp, and whispered in the wolf's ear, "The wardrobe. First chance we get."

Streak's eyes widened, but he nodded. Volle pulled their hips together to conceal the fact that they were no longer tied, just as Dereath's muzzle reappeared in the curtain. "There are still three soldiers here, in case you're thinking of trying something," he said suspiciously.

"Could you have them fetch us something to eat, leaving you alone and unprotected?" Volle didn't want to take too much time, but he did want to let the rat lower his guard.

"Ha ha." Dereath sneered.

"Could we at least have some privacy to be made presentable before you force him to take me back to prison?"

"Oh, you've got nothing I haven't seen before. Or won't see again," he leered.

Volle shrugged. "Fine." He wiped his belly with his shirt, and motioned for Streak to get up. "I need to change my shirt, though." Deliberately, he held his shirt up, giving Dereath a good view of his sheath.

"Mm." The rat was looking at both him and Streak. "Sure, fine."

Volle had to work to keep his tail still as he walked to the wardrobe. At the door, he turned to Streak, who was pulling his pants up. "Wolf? Can you help me pick out one?"

Streak looked at Dereath, but crossed the room before the rat could say "Wait!" He slipped into the wardrobe, and Volle closed the door behind them both. He slid the bolt and walked to the back.

"Why does Helfer have a lock on his wardrobe? And what does this gain us?" Streak fastened his pants and followed Volle to the back of the wardrobe.

"I figure we have about five minutes," Volle said, fingers running over the stonework at the back of the wardrobe. "Ah, here it is." He pressed on a stone about seven feet off the ground. There was a sharp click, and a section of the wall swung inward, revealing a dark passageway. The air inside was chill and dank, and smelled of mildew and rot.

Volle stepped into the passage. He held out a paw to Streak. "Coming?"

The wolf's eyes lit up. He bounded into the passage, almost knocking Volle over, and swept him up in a tight hug.

"Hey!" Volle laughed softly. "Careful! We need to get that closed. See the handle there? Pull it closed with that."

Streak licked the fox's muzzle and set him down carefully. He pulled the door closed with a satisfying click. Volle thought it was one of the sweetest sounds he'd ever heard.

The passageway went only a short distance before ending in a ladder. They climbed down a long ways, and at the bottom, Volle's arms hurt again. Only then did he feel it was safe to talk.

"Helfer used this passage to get himself in and out. So he wouldn't have to bother with security when he wanted to bring uninvited guests back, usually. I only used it a handful of times."

"Pretty lucky that you knew about that," Streak said. Volle grinned back at him. The passage wasn't quite wide enough for two, but Streak was walking close behind him. The wolf seemed to have a bounce in his step again, and his tail was wagging.

"I'm sure there are several other ways into and out of the castle." Volle knew of two others for certain. "I'm lucky that I got to know Hef well enough that he trusted me with this one."

At the end of the passage, Volle listened at the wooden door, then opened it slowly. They emerged into a dark cellar full of barrels and crates. A line of light at the far end indicated where the stairs to the street were, and gave them enough light to see that the cellar was deserted. Volle closed the door, which seemed to merge with the paneling of the cellar. He followed Streak across the cellar toward the stairs.

"You took your sweet time." Seir hopped off a crate and walked toward them. She looked exactly as Volle remembered her: half his height, thin and wiry, with a nondescript tunic tied with a length of rope around her waist. He remembered the scar in her left ear that she wouldn't tell anyone the origin of. He remembered the swing of her tail. And he remembered the way her eyes could look soft and hard at the same time, as they did now.

Streak growled and bared his teeth, but Volle waved him off. "Seir's a friend of mine," he said. "You got the plans okay?"

"Safe and sound and on their way home. And so should we be." She stood a foot away from him, arms planted on her tiny hips. "We were so worried, Volle. When I got your note…"

He stepped forward and hugged her, and she threw her arms around him. "It's okay now," he said. "Long as you can get us home."

"Us, eh?" She eyed Streak warily, stepping back from Volle.

Volle took Streak's paw. "He saved my life."

"Uh-huh. And more than that. I can still smell, you know." Seir nodded curtly to Streak. "Sorry. This one has a tendency to think with his cock sometimes."

Volle's ears flattened in embarrassment, but Streak just smiled politely. "We found that we do think a lot alike."

Seir chuckled, and walked over to Streak, examining him up close. "All right. I like him. Well, we'll have a good long time to get to know each other. It's a week and a half to the border, and we won't dare show our muzzles outside the carriage most of the way."

"The border?" Streak's paw tightened around Volle's.

"You don't have to go if you don't want to." Volle squeezed back. "I won't ask you to do anything against your country."

Seir looked back and forth, and stepped back. "So, ah, let me go get the carriage. Back in five. Don't go anywhere." She climbed up the stairs and slipped out the door, letting a brief burst of evening air and light into the room.

"You already gave her the papers?" Streak said, not letting go of Volle's paw.

"Afraid so. I told the truth about the portrait, but I had a friend get the papers early this morning." He chuckled. "I fear Dereath is in for a number of disappointments."

Streak wasn't smiling. "So…you could've escaped any time today."

"I…well, I guess so."

"But you stayed. For me?" Streak's voice had dropped to a whisper.

"You didn't think I'd run off without you, did you? Not after all you did for me."

"You knew I was betraying you and you still stayed for me?" Streak was sniffing back tears now.

Volle stepped forward and pulled the big wolf into his arms. "Of course I did, you silly. Because I knew you were doing it out of love. And I thought I had a pretty good chance of getting you away from Dereath. I mean, his tail isn't nearly as nice as mine."

Streak's composure broke, and his body shook with half-laughs, half-sobs. "No, your tail is much, much nicer." Volle held on to him and nuzzled gently. He nuzzled back, and then they were sharing a kiss again, and that's how Seir found them.

"Break it up, you two." She grinned. "Plenty of time for that on the way back."

They sat together in the carriage, with the shades drawn until it was safely outside the town limits. Volle leaned against Streak, who put an arm around him, and Seir smiled from the opposite seat. For a while, none of them spoke. Streak rubbed Volle's chest through his shirt, and Volle rested a paw on the wolf's pants.

"What are you going to do when we get back?" Seir said as the carriage turned a corner. "They might want you to stay on as an advisor."

Volle's tail swung lazily back and forth, brushing Streak's leg and foot. "I just spent five or six months in prison. I don't think I feel much like doing anything at the moment. Maybe I could get a minor estate somewhere in the country. Though I don't really know anything about farming." He tilted his head back and smiled up at the wolf.

"Mmm," Streak said, brushing a paw gently over his muzzle. "I think I know someone who might be able to show you a few things."

"Really? What's his name?" Volle grinned.

The wolf leaned over and kissed his nose. "You can call him 'Streak.' He likes that just fine."

The Prisoner's Release

Taurin Fox '04

"You stayed. For me?"

HOME AGAIN

As Volle looked back at the land of Tephos, where he'd very nearly just lost his life, the feeling he couldn't shake out of his fur was a deep longing to return.

The ride over the mountains had been rough, but Seir thought it essential that they get out of Tephos as quickly as possible. With winter approaching, it made more sense for them to veer south, and so of course all the pursuit would be going there. That was small comfort as their carriage climbed snowy mountain slopes, crossed the border into Ferrenis, and skidded down the ice on the far side, but Seir assured Volle and Streak with chattering teeth that it was necessary.

Once over the mountain, the mouse relaxed. To be safe, they hired a new driver at the first opportunity and took the south road, coming to the capital city by a circuitous route that avoided any large towns. Volle protested that only Dereath Talison knew of his escape, and he wouldn't be able to commandeer enough troops for pursuit without explaining to his superior, the Minister of Defense, what he'd done. And if Volle knew the rat--and he did, much to his eternal regret--they would be well into Ferrenis before the Minister of Defense heard anything about that.

"Better safe than sorry," was Seir's only reply, and whether it was through her devious wanderings or not, they saw no pursuit all the way to Caril.

Volle was not as concerned about pursuit as he was about Streak, and himself. The white wolf who'd rescued him from death in the Tephossian prison had clearly not thought far beyond the rescue. He'd been whisked into the carriage as Seir came to get Volle, and in an hour they were outside the walls of Divalia, the capital of Tephos. He'd looked back quite a lot as they left Divalia, but after that he seemed to relax, chatting with Seir as the carriage slid through the snow and ice and then made its way across the Ferrenian grasslands. The mouse told him about Caril, and the young wolf asked incessant questions about Ferrenis. When they stopped at farms for the night, even though Seir had money to pay their board, he volunteered to help with farm chores, "because I can," he grinned when Volle asked him why.

So at night, while he worked, Volle and Seir talked quietly about what would happen back in Caril. Seir hadn't had any return communications from their superior, Duke Avery, since notifying him of Volle's escape. The most she could do for Volle was reassure him that he wouldn't go to a Ferrenian prison--probably.

"What do *you* want to do?" she'd ask, and each time he shook his head. The euphoria of his escape had long since deserted him, and now that he faced the reality of freedom, he found himself at a loss to know what to do with it. Teach in the Academy? Retire? He'd joked about living on a farm, but seeing the farms they stopped at, the life seemed dreary and confined compared to what he'd been used to in Divalia. Nothing appealed to him, because the only thing he really wanted was to go back to his life as a Lord and spy, which he could now never do.

And if he couldn't define his own future, how could he offer anything to Streak? He knew they cared for each other, that they'd come together in the loneliness of the prison, but did they have a life together? Whenever he thought about that, he thought of the others who'd tried to share a life with him: Ilyana, the noble vixen he'd married in order to continue his fictional lineage, Arrin, the shy romantic fox he'd courted back in the castle, and Xiller, the cougar soldier who had been as young, passionate, and naïve as Streak. His life had carried him away from Arrin and Xiller, while Ilyana was very likely in danger because of his capture; at the very least, her position as a Lady was in jeopardy. What if Tephossian agents came after Volle? He didn't want to put Streak in danger.

Tired from his imprisonment and the long journey, Volle was usually asleep before Streak returned from his work to climb into bed with him. One night, when they had some privacy, Volle stayed awake and welcomed the wolf back to bed with a kiss, which led to shedding their clothes, and then he was gently pushed down, made to lie back as Streak applied his muzzle to the fox's sheath. Volle grew hard quickly, but found it difficult to let his arousal crest into climax. In prison, he'd been forced into abstinence for weeks and months on end, and he'd almost come just at the wolf's touch. Now, free from his chains, fatigue and worry combined to keep him from finishing, something he'd rarely felt before.

Finally, the warm, patient tongue won out, bringing him the rush of release. He arched his back and moaned as he came into the warm muzzle. His climax exhausted him further, and when he tried to return the favor, Streak pushed him back down and kissed his nose, telling him to rest.

The other nights, he contented himself with waking in the morning with his back to the wolf, nestled in the strong white arms, feeling the press of the wolf's sheath against his tail, but not under it. A year ago, he would have had trouble sleeping with the sexual energy inside him racing at the close warmth, but six months in prison had taken their toll, and not until they approached Caril did he feel close to his former self.

They arrived at the perfect time, just before sunset, when the red cliffs to the east of the city glowed brightly over the white marble of the palace and the nobles' quarter. Volle shifted so Streak could sit near the window, catching the red highlights on his white fur. He smiled at the wolf's rapt expression and rested a paw on his tail, watching over his shoulder.

Once they'd entered the south gate, Volle slid over to his own window. Seir pointed out landmarks as they passed them, more excited than the fox even though she'd been back just two years ago and for Volle, it had been five. He remembered his first ride through Divalia, how the city had seemed familiar, yet different; now it was Caril that felt different to him.

They skirted the Academy, a neighborhood where he'd lived for six years, but even the sight of the large, austere building couldn't make him more than nostalgic. "Nice to see the old neighborhood," Seir said, but when she said "old neighborhood," Volle thought of the Jackal's Staff, the Lonely Cock, and the streets around the palace in Divalia. The fox who had frequented the Academy was someone he remembered being, but distantly, as if he'd been only assuming the identity of a spy-in-training before he left for his mission, and had discarded it once he'd left the city.

"Is that the Hungry Bull?" Streak asked, pointing to a swaying wooden sign painted with a wide-mouthed bull.

"That it is," Seir said. "Volle's second home, once upon a time." Volle glanced at the sign and nodded, remaining silent. "Well, fine. I thought you'd be happy to get home. Am I going to have to celebrate by myself?"

Streak put a paw on Volle's knee, and the fox covered the white one with his own. He felt adrift in the carriage, floating past familiar images without any connection to them at all. But Seir was real, and so was Streak. "I'll have a drink with you," Volle said to the mouse. "It's just a little...overwhelming, you know?"

She glanced at Streak, and her expression softened. "Yeah, okay. Sorry." She smiled. "I'm just relieved to be home. The past six months..."

He nodded. "I know. It's over now." But he knew that this wasn't only an ending. It was a beginning, too; what he didn't know was of what.

They pulled up outside a building that dwarfed the others on the block in size and elegance, with a large arched entryway and smaller arches over each of the sparkling glass windows. A pair of weasels chattered back and forth cheerfully as they cleaned the yellowish stone of the building's walls, one from the street and one walking across an upper story ledge. No dangling wooden sign hung over the arch; golden letters carved into the stone proclaimed the name of the building to be "The Feathered Friend."

Here, Volle did smile broadly. Seir grinned. "Ah, I thought you'd like that."

Streak looked out at the inn, and then back to Volle. "What's this place?"

Volle waved a paw at the elegant white arch, the gilded sculpture of the phoenix over the keystone, and the cupolas that rose over the rest of the neighborhood. "This is where visiting dignitaries stayed when they came to visit the King," he said. "If they weren't cougars, that is."

Streak cocked his head, looking back out. "Why not cougars?"

"Because cougars are all noble-born, and they stay in the palace. Other nobles are ambassadors from other lands, or else have titles bestowed on them. Only cougars are allowed to inherit land, though." As Volle said that, he thought about the land he'd falsely claimed, posing as the son of the long-dead Lord Vinton in Tephos.

"Oh." Streak flicked his ears and nodded.

"It's only for three nights," Seir said. "But Avery didn't even question the expense when I asked."

"Maybe he won't castrate me, then," Volle said, and laughed at Streak's alarmed expression. "It's okay, wolf, put your ears up. I'm pretty sure he was joking."

"Who's Avery?" Streak said, his ears coming up only partway.

Volle glanced at Seir. "Well...he's my superior." He'd told Streak that he was working for Ferrenis, but not many more details, and the white wolf hadn't pressed for any. Now he just nodded and looked back out the window.

"Will they have a water bath?" he asked.

"I'm sure they do." Volle grinned. "I could use one myself. It's been a dusty trip."

"You're free tonight," Seir said. "I'm staying with some friends down the street. I'll let the Duke know you're here and I or someone else will come by to collect you tomorrow."

"All right." Volle took her paws in his. "Thank you, Seir," he said. "For everything."

"I should be thanking you." She smiled. "You may have averted a war."

He remained silent as they disembarked and walked into the inn, at first thinking about what Seir had said, and then overwhelmed by the luxury inside the inn. His paws sunk into the finely plush carpeting woven in an intricate gold and green pattern, so thick that he could only tell that the floor was solid stone underneath because of the gleaming white showing around the edges of the carpet. Portraits adorned the smoothly finished walls, each one depicting a noble as elegantly dressed as the velvet-clad wolf behind the mahogany desk.

Seir approached him while Volle and Streak toured the portraits. Volle knew some of them, and could guess at others, but more than once he found himself saying the name of some Tephossian noble: Lord Creane at the picture of the aged raccoon; Lord Vanadi at the portrait of the young grey fox.

He was just getting frustrated at his ignorance when one of the inn's servants, a bear, came to take the bags to their room. Seir gave Volle some silver Royals for his food for the night and bid them good-night.

The bear led them up the curved marble stair to an immaculate room with a finely made bed, a low chest of drawers, and several silver candlesticks scattered about the room. After setting their bags carefully next to the chest, the bear lit their candles and then stood attentively before them. "Water baths are on the ground floor, my Lords, and are kept heated at all hours. The chamberpots are emptied in the morning; there is a necessary down the hall if you do not wish to use the pots in your room. Food is available beginning at sunrise. If you wish food brought to your room, summon one of our staff by means of the bell-pull located at the door, and we will be delighted to oblige. Is there any other way in which I can make your stay more pleasant?"

"Do you have powdered scents available?" Volle asked.

"Indeed, my Lord. I will bring a selection to your chambers immediately."

"Thank you." Volle turned to Streak. "Anything you want?" When the white wolf shook his head, Volle dismissed the bear.

"This is pretty nice, eh?" he said, fingering the silken bell-pull by the door.

"Beautiful," Streak said, sitting down on the bed. He grinned and patted the bed beside him.

Volle turned and padded over the soft wooden floor to sit beside the wolf. He looked at the white fur, candlelight flickering across it, but didn't say anything.

Streak turned to nuzzle him. "Are you sad I came with you?"

"No!" Volle leaned against him. "I'm sorry, I just don't know what I'm going to do now. I didn't think when I dragged you away that I didn't know what I was getting you into."

"It's okay." Streak smiled. "I had to decide to trust you. I'm sure whatever happens, it will be better than what I left behind."

Volle smiled. "Tonight will, for sure. You're going to be pampered. Want to take that water bath?"

The wolf nodded and rose to his feet. "Sounds wonderful."

It was. The tubs were stone with high walls, the water was heated and constantly refilled by from a walled balcony above, keeping the room reasonably private. Four different scented soaps lined the edge of the tub, and an otter around the corner attended a stack of fluffy towels. A wooden bench faced a small fireplace where a cheery blaze had been set, above which another lovely portrait hung.

Volle and Streak stripped and climbed into the bath together, easing into the steaming water carefully. Volle sighed as he felt it soak through his fur. He'd soaked in Helfer's bath after his release from the dungeon, but this felt better still. He was less exhausted now, and less worried that in cleaning himself, he would scrub away chunks of his fur. The dust and grime of their travel came away easily as he pushed his fingers through his fur.

When they'd soaked for a few minutes, Volle stood free of the water, reached lazily over to the nearest soap, and rubbed it between his paws to produce a lather. As he washed himself, Streak began to do the same. Volle watched the wolf's paws rub down his chest and stomach to his sheath, fondling there perhaps a little longer than was necessary. The wolf met his eyes and grinned, then moved on to soap the rest of his body.

Volle slid his paws over his own sheath, feeling the stirrings inside it as his eyes wandered over the rugged white landscape. On the white wolf's hip was the streak of black fur that had led Volle to give him his

He waved as the otter slipped out the door.

Home Again

nickname, and Volle still thought that the way it traced the outside curve of his lip was as sexy as anything he'd ever seen.

His sheath betrayed his thoughts as arousal pushed his pink member free from the tip. He slid a paw over it, catching Streak's eye deliberately as he stroked himself.

The wolf grinned, leaning back against the stone wall and watching. "Make sure to get that nice and clean," he said.

"I am," Volle replied, and just as he was about to say, "Come over and feel for yourself," the door to the bathroom opened and a small otter scurried in. The tub was high enough that he couldn't see anything below their chests, and he wasn't looking anyway. He ran directly to the fireplace and stoked the fire, then threw two more logs onto it and watched for a moment.

"Sorry, sirs," he said cheerfully. "Got 'er all good an' ready to dry your fur out when you're done."

"Thanks," Volle said, and removed the paw from his sheath to wave as the otter slipped out the door. When it closed, he put it briefly back, but the moment had passed, and Streak felt it too. They finished washing quietly, toweled themselves as dry as they could, and then sat together on the bench in front of the fire. Volle leaned into the wolf's side and slid an arm around his waist, Streak lifted an arm across the fox's shoulders and pulled him closer, and they stayed like that, talking quietly about matters of little consequence until the fire's heat had mostly dried their fur out, except for their rumps and the small patches where they'd pressed against each other.

The patterns of dancing light in the fire began to make Volle's eyelids droop, and when he saw Streak yawn widely for the second time in as many minutes, he mustered his strength and grinned. "Time for bed," he said.

"I think so too." Streak smiled as they got up and retrieved their clothes. "It was really nice, though."

"They certainly know how to treat nobility well here," Volle said.

The wolf nodded. "I guess you'd know."

"Yeah." Volle thought about the accommodations in the palace in Divalia, and sighed. "Best enjoy it while we can, I suppose." He cast a wistful glance back at the sluices that carried the heated water down into the tubs. "Maybe we'll take another bath tomorrow."

Streak laughed as they climbed the stairs to the second floor. "Two water baths in two days? I never had two in a month before."

"Neither did I before I went to Ferrenis."

"You're not a Lord? I thought since we were staying here..."

Volle laughed. "Canis, no." He paused. "I suppose I should get used to calling on Fox again."

"Fox?" Streak's ears flicked. "Oh, right. Seir said, the church here has twenty-two houses, not six. So we're not in the same House, here?"

Volle paused. They had reached the second floor hallway, and he turned to look up at the wolf. "I hadn't thought of that, but no. It doesn't matter, though. We don't separate the Houses at services here. They just all attend together. So we can still sit together."

"That's good. And Gaiaday is...in three days, right? Seir said the week is different here."

"Just think of it as the way the week would be when a Felid is on the throne, in Tephos. Because it's always cougars here."

Streak paused and thought about that. "Oh, yeah...that makes sense."

They disrobed and got into bed, and although Volle felt some stirrings of interest return as his damp rump pressed back into the wolf's sheath, Streak just curled an arm over the fox and rested his muzzle in the crook of his neck, breathing steadily. Volle was tired enough not to press the issue; much like the other nights, he fell easily asleep.

The sun woke him gradually, and the smooth sheets and white ceiling pulled him back to Divalia for a few groggy moments. He'd dreamed often enough of being back in his Lord's bed only to wake up naked in a cold stone prison, and that fear prickled his fur before he came fully enough awake to realize that the luxury was real.

The white wolf next to him was very real too, and still asleep. Volle ran a paw over the fluffy white chest and down the stomach, hesitating before moving back up. He kept pushing his fingers through the soft white chest fur until Streak blinked awake. He yawned and smiled. "Morning."

"Hi." Volle kissed his ears.

The wolf reached around to hug him. "You have to go to the palace today."

Volle slid a paw down the wolf's back, pressed against him. "Probably not for a little while."

Streak nuzzled him and smiled. "Hold that thought. I need to use the necessary. I'll be right back."

Volle watched as the wolf slid out of bed and into a pair of trousers, and disappeared out the door. He leaned back in bed and stared up at the ceiling.

"You need to be up in the palace at noon," Seir said from just inside the door, making Volle jump and almost fall out of bed.

"I what? When did you come in?" He sat up, holding the sheet to his chest.

"When your wolf left. What, you think I was here all night watching?"

He chuckled. "I know you weren't. Noon? Do I have anything to wear?"

She tossed a pouch onto the chest of drawers. It clinked as it landed.

"Go to the High Market and get yourself a nice outfit. You have about an hour and a half, then you'll have to come back here and dress and a carriage will be waiting to take you up there."

"An hour and a half?"

"There's a fox from the Academy downstairs who will take you to the clothing stalls. You should have plenty of time. The High Market's only ten minutes walk from here."

"All right. Thanks, Seir." She smiled at him and started to leave. "Hey. I guess if they want me to dress up nice, I'm not going to be tossed back in prison." The mouse rolled her eyes and walked out.

Volle chuckled, rolled out of bed, and pulled his clothes on. When Streak returned and tilted his muzzle at the fully dressed fox, he handed the wolf his shirt. "Come on," he said. "We're going shopping."

The grey fox in the lobby introduced himself as Kevar, brushing muzzles with both of them before hurrying them out of the inn and onto the street. "I'm led to understand that neither of you have been to the High Market?"

"Just once," Volle said, and Streak looked at him in surprise. He smiled. "I couldn't afford anything there, and I'm not a thief."

"Well," Kevar said, "the market is most crowded in the morning, but that can't be helped. Stay close to me. All the best clothing merchants in our price range are in the same area, so we will find you an outfit in no time." He strode briskly up the street.

Streak had no trouble keeping up with him, but Volle fell behind, his legs still rather weak. Walking up a slope was particularly taxing, and several times the others had to stop and wait for him. "Sorry," he apologized.

"Don't apologize," Streak growled, looking at Kevar. "You were chained to a wall for six months. You can't be expected to run up a hill."

"I didn't know," Kevar said, spreading his paws in apology and lowering his ears. "We can go slower. Let's cut along this street. It's level and it will take us parallel to the market. We'll come up closer to the clothing merchants."

"Let's stop here and rest," Streak said. He pointed across the street to a bakery. "How about some of those cakes in the window?"

"Honey cakes," Volle said. "With spice."

Kevar looked about to argue, and then just nodded. "All right. We've got time." He took the coin Volle was holding out, and walked over to the bakery.

Volle smiled up at the wolf as he leaned against the wall. "Thanks."

"Well, I mean...you can't walk that fast." Streak appeared to be struggling with what to say. "Especially without breakfast."

Volle took his paw and held it loosely. "You don't have to explain," he said. "You'll like these cakes. I don't remember having them anywhere in Divalia."

"We had honey cakes, but there's something different..." The white wolf lifted his nose as Kevar returned with the cakes.

"Cloves," Volle nodded. "I'll have to find a place that does spiced lamb pie before we leave. That's something I missed, too."

"I can show you my favorite place for lamb pie," Kevar said as he handed out the cakes. "Once we're done shopping."

Volle bit into the cake, felt it crumble in his mouth, and savored the sweetness and spice. "Show Streak while I'm at the palace, if you're able to stay that long," he said. He watched with a smile as the white wolf bit into a cake, his muzzle curving into a smile as he chewed. When the fox took another bite, he savored it as if it were the first time he'd had them, feeling Streak's enjoyment.

When they'd finished the cakes, they set off at a pace Volle could keep, walking along the street and turning up a gentler hill to the edge of the High Market. "The Low Market is down there," Volle said to Streak, pointing down the hill to where they could now see bustling merchants, tented stalls, and smell the aroma of meats and fruits. "Mostly food and cheaper products, simpler clothing. High Market is finer goods. Closer to the palace." His sentences were becoming clipped as he tried to save his breath; even on the gentler slope, he was winded again.

"Want to wait for a moment?" Kevar said, though he was shifting his weight back and forth and his tail tip was flicking.

"No. I'm okay." Volle nodded to Streak, who was looking sternly down at him. "Really. Let's go on. I'll rest by the stall."

Volle's only visit to the High Market had been years and years ago. He'd forgotten the press of people through the narrow passageways between the stalls, and the jumbled array of smells assaulting him from all sides: the people around him as well as the wares from the stalls. He smelled freshly polished wood, glazed clay, and one particularly rank stall where small lizards scurried around in cages. He watched as a wolf dressed in velvet and dyed buckskin handed one cage to his delighted son, but whether as a pet or snack Volle never learned; they were gone from his sight a moment later as he hurried to keep up with Kevar, dodging cubs who snaked between him and his companions with giddy ease on their own private errands.

The fox led them to a walkway that was entirely festooned with clothing. Shirts, trousers, belts, caps, scarves, and anything else Volle might have wanted, as well as several things he didn't, were hung from every available hook or line, a kaleidoscope of colors and smells, as each fabric carried its own natural scent and some had been pre-scented. The colors made him briefly dizzy until he steadied himself against Streak. The wolf grinned at him and said, "This is amazing!"

He almost had to shout to make himself heard over the rumble of customers haggling and merchants shouting their wares. Coins clinked from paw to paw in a light counterpoint, and under it all was the shuffle of paws across the stone of the plaza. Volle didn't even try to speak in response, just nodded and smiled. He'd never done his own shopping, even in Divalia, and he was sure that Divalia didn't have a market like this one.

Kevar, standing at one of the stalls, motioned them forward. "See anything you like?" Volle scanned the stall, looking over the shirts for something approximating his favorite outfit from Tephos. He spotted a nice yellow shirt and transferred the coins to his other paw so he could point it out to Kevar. A moment after the jingling pouch hit his fingers, a bobcat had appeared at the stall.

"Good morning, my Lord," he said solicitously. "Just back from a trip? I have just the thing for your coloration...such lovely red fur, really, it should be offset with a light brown. I happen to have just the thing back here. Brand new, you know, you'll be the only one wearing it. So distinctive..."

Kevar flicked his ears deliberately. "The Baron knows what he wants," he said. "Sir?"

Volle overcame his surprise at the mock title to indicate the shirt he had his eye on. "I think the yellow actually would suit me better."

"Oh, I do regret to inform you, sir, but that is not one of mine. I do have something in yellow, if you'll allow me just a moment." He disappeared, and Volle saw that the yellow shirt was indeed part of another display, smaller than the bobcat's. A grey fox stood below the shirt, engaged in conversation with a weasel.

"Sir, if you will..." Volle turned to see the bobcat holding up a yellow shirt, but he didn't like the lines on it. The one in the fox's stall had a brown diamond pattern trim and was a brighter yellow. He shook his head.

"Thank you, but I like that one a little better." He started to move away, and the bobcat reached for his arm.

"Sir, may I just point out the craftsmanship in this shirt? It is the finest in all of Ferrenis. Look at the stitching here. The material is provided by Diggin and Melchoit. The buttons are inlaid with mother-of-pearl..."

Kevar tugged Volle away. "The Baron does not have time for this," he told the bobcat, who looked momentarily annoyed before moving to another customer.

"Hope you don't mind me taking the liberty of giving you a title," Kevar said. "They'll take you more seriously, and you do carry yourself like a noble."

"I wish you could give me a real one," Volle said, smiling at the merchant as they approached his booth. "Could I see that one?" He pointed up at the yellow shirt.

"Lovely choice." The grey fox's voice rasped hoarsely. "One of my new designs. It suits you admirably." He took the shirt down and presented it.

Volle fingered the fabric, and offered it to Kevar. The student felt the material and nodded his approval. "Perfect," Volle said.

"Five silver, sir," the grey fox said, taking the shirt back and folding it carefully. "Can I provide anything else?"

"Trousers," Kevar said.

"And, I think, a scarf," Volle said.

"You'll want to visit Tamar for trousers. We coordinate, and he has a nice brown pair with yellow trim that will set off this shirt beautifully. I would recommend a light orange scarf."

"Thank you," Volle said, counting out coins to pay the fox.

"And if you're asked about the shirt," the fox said with a smile, "tell them you got it from Mikka in the High Market."

"I will," Volle said.

"Baron," the bobcat from the other stall called, "let my son take you. He knows where Tamar is." A little bobcat kit sprang up to them eagerly, whiskers twitching.

"Thank you," Kevar said, "but I'm familiar with the Market." Only then, glancing back at the booth, did Volle notice that Mikka's ears had laid back. They came up again at Kevar's words.

The kit grabbed Kevar's arm anyway and said, "This way, this way!"

The grey fox removed the kit's paw firmly and said, "We know the way, thank you."

"Come this way, come this way!" Now there was another kit, a skunk, joining the bobcat. Volle wasn't quite sure what to do, but fortunately, Kevar did.

"Just walk, and ignore them, they'll go away," the grey fox muttered, stepping behind Volle and Streak and putting a paw on each of their backs to push them in the right direction while keeping the kits back from them. "They'd take us to some other merchant that the bobcat has an agreement with, not Tamar."

Tamar was a large, friendly porcupine, surrounded by his family, and when they showed him the shirt, he knew instantly which trousers to get. "The merchants all know each other," Streak murmured as the porcupine's wife was fetching the trousers and Volle paid the merchant.

"Of course," Kevar said. "They work here side by side for years."

"Why not just sell from their stores?"

The fox shrugged. "And make the nobility walk all over the city? Here they can show off their best next to the best of their competition, and the nobles, or their servants, need only stroll through a small space to see what they can purchase."

Streak nodded, looking across the stalls, and his ears and whiskers perked up. "Oh, fox," he said. "There's a nice scarf over there. That would look good on you."

"I know where to find a scarf!" one of the chubby porcupine girls piped up, and this time Kevar let her guide them.

Home Again

Ten minutes later, Volle let Streak tie the scarf on him over his dusty travel clothes. Kevar raised an eyebrow, and said, "You should really not wear it with that tunic," but Volle grinned and shrugged, and left it on because of the smile the white wolf got when he said he liked it.

Streak thought they were done, but Kevar insisted on purchasing a doublet for Volle to wear over the shirt, and then a pair of dyed calfskin armbands to go with them. By the time they reached the jewelers, to pick out some wrought silver clasps for the new clothes, they had acquired a retinue of shouting cubs of various ages, all trying to pull them in different directions and running to bring things to show off to them. Streak laughed and looked at each thing they brought, and Volle tried to maintain his good humor, but he was exhausted and the shrieking was giving him a headache.

Kevar, somehow, managed to ignore them, except when one of them brought a shirt he liked. How he picked it out of the hodgepodge of items being thrust at him by grubby paws, Volle couldn't say, but once he'd gotten Volle's nod of approval, he nodded curtly to the mouse holding the shirt, and they were off to another stall, where he bought the second shirt from an old mouse who seemed to have an army of children scouring the market for potential customers. He haggled more with her than he had with the other merchants, and their banter made it obvious that they knew each other. When he handed Volle the shirt, Kevar was wearing a huge grin, the kind Volle was used to producing himself only when he was relaxing in the warm glow of a fading orgasm. The grey fox's dedication to shopping reminded Volle of Welcis, the skunk who had served him faithfully back in Tephos for five years.

Welcis would also have helped him dress, but for that he now had to rely on Streak. Once they'd made their way back to the inn, Kevar waited while Volle returned to his room and tried to dress in his new clothes, guiding Streak through the lacings as best he could. In the end, he thought, looking at himself in the mirror and adjusting a silver clasp with an amber gem to match his yellow shirt, it turned out rather well.

"You look very noble," Streak said. "I feel like I should kneel, or something."

"Not because I'm noble," Volle said, winking at the wolf. "But time for that later. I think I hear the carriage out front, and I don't want to be late. You'll be okay with Kevar?"

Streak nodded. "Of course."

"Find us a nice place for dinner. We can eat here if you want, but we don't have to."

"All right. You don't have a favorite place to go back to?"

Volle shook his head. "No. Not around here, and not really anywhere. The places I used to eat were..." Smoky taverns, with cheap food and available young males to spend an hour with. "...not that good."

Streak nodded. "Good luck at the palace."

"Thanks. I'll see you back here tonight." Volle stretched his neck up for a kiss, and when their muzzles parted, Streak was grinning widely. "What?"

"I never kissed a noble before," the wolf said, chuckling.

"These are for special occasions," Volle smiled, gesturing to the clothes. "Don't get used to it."

Waving to the white wolf as his carriage pulled away, he thought about those words and wondered again what fate awaited him at the palace. Given the choice, what did he want? Remain at the palace as an expert on Tephos? That was what Seir had guessed, but it sounded extremely dull and Volle wasn't sure whether he wanted that, to be constantly reminded of what he'd left behind. He wasn't even sure he'd be offered it, considering that no matter what Seir had said about him preventing a war, he'd failed in his mission: he'd been caught.

He didn't particularly want to go back to the Academy, either, though he could probably be a valuable asset to them. He'd been in constant conflict with the teachers there, and his best friend from those days had remained in Divalia, a valuable point of contact for future spies.

Of course, all the wondering he was doing was pointless; the decision would most likely not be his. The head of the Academy, and the person he would report to in the government, was the one who disliked him most in all of Ferrenis, and the more he thought about that meeting, the less certain he felt that he would even be allowed to remain in the country.

He tried to control the fear, knowing it was affecting his scent, but he was sure that everyone from the footservant who greeted him at the palace gates to the secretary who told him to sit and wait in the antechamber of the office could smell it. He forced himself to think about all he'd accomplished in the nearly six years since he'd sat in this office, and had managed to soothe himself into a reasonable facsimile of calm by the time the secretary said, "Duke Avery is free now."

The formidable wolf behind the desk was the most familiar sight Volle had yet seen in Caril. He could never have forgotten the broad physique, the shaggy cheek ruffs, the perfect claws, and the searing eyes. Just the scent of the office took him back to his days as a nervous young student. He'd steeled himself for the glare he received, but when the wolf rose and extended a paw, Volle found himself caught completely off guard. He stared blankly.

Avery grinned at him, another memory Volle would never lose, but this grin was not menacing. "Don't they shake paws in Tephos?" he said.

"Uh," Volle stammered, and stepped forward, extending his paw. Avery's tough pads closed around it and held it as the wolf leaned forward. Volle couldn't bring himself to touch muzzles, but he got close enough to exchange scents, and sat down heavily in the chair in front of the desk.

"Don't get me wrong; I still don't like you," Avery rumbled in his deep bass voice. "But there's no need for you to be afraid, any more. You've done a fine job and served your King well. So relax, Volle. You managed to outdo even Seir's inflated expectations."

"I'm sorry I got caught," was all he could think to say.

Avery sat down as well, and shrugged his massive shoulders. "It was in a good cause. Did they torture you?"

Volle nodded slowly. "Dereath was afraid to leave marks, I think, or he didn't want to..." The thought had occurred to him more than once that the rat's obsession with him might have saved him from disfigurement.

"What did they use?"

Volle swallowed. "The rack. Sticks. Needles." He held up his right paw. "Broken fingers."

The wolf's eyes narrowed. He leaned forward. "Healed well?"

"Yes. Thanks to your training."

Avery snorted. "Glad to see you absorbed some of it. Well, obviously you didn't give away any secrets. No one was compromised. So thank you, again. Now..." He unrolled a pair of documents onto his desk, and motioned for the fox to sit forward. Volle did, though he didn't need to be any closer to recognize the documents he'd taken from the Minister of Defense's office, six months and a lifetime ago. "What do you make of these?"

Volle shook his head. "There's not been a war. Have the troop movements matched what's recorded here?"

"Some of them." Avery indicated the numbers with a claw. "None for almost seven months. Which corresponds exactly to the time of your capture."

"That was the plan," Volle said. "The theft was supposed to make them think twice about launching the attack. Surprise was of the essence, and if the documents were gone, then so was the element of surprise. They would have to fear the worst, especially since Prewitt."

"They know that one was us," Avery said. "How are the two connected?"

"It established our ability to strike inside the palace despite their security." Volle had heard many conversations about this in the year after a noble had been assassinated by Ferrenian agents inside the palace.

Avery nodded. "How much do you know about their security?"

"Some," Volle said. "My last year there I was in line to be on the Defense council. I've told Seir everything I know."

The wolf stroked his chin thoughtfully as his eyes slid back to the parchment. "We have notes on all that, of course. But back to the war plans. The curious thing about them is the haste they call for. A campaign such as this is traditionally built up years in advance, especially with a bear on the throne. Weasel, even a wolf, might strike quickly to gain the element of surprise, but a bear?"

"The Minister of Defense is a wolf," Volle said.

"Quite," Avery said, studying the plans. "These are in his writing, unless I miss my guess."

"Yes," Volle said. "That's what I told Seir."

"So they could be legitimate."

Volle blinked. "You'd thought they weren't? "

Avery looked back up at him. "Since no action has been taken, we can't discount that possibility."

"Then why…?"

"A hypothetical exercise. The King might have asked the Minister to write out the steps necessary to perform an operation, for his inspection. Or he might have asked for the plans to be drawn up as a contingency if we moved against the Reysfields. That last is rather unlikely, since we did not move any troops into the area in the past year, but I can tell you for certain that our own King has made such requests of his own Minister of Defense." He grinned again.

"Oh."

"The other option is that it was deliberately set as a trap for you."

Volle's fur prickled. "For me?"

Avery nodded. "You had some trouble in your first year, and the assassination made them suspect that there was an agent inside the palace. This could have been bait."

"Bait? But my…" He had so effectively removed the name of his contact in the palace from his mind during his time in prison that even now, he couldn't recall it. "My contact didn't say anything about a trap."

"If it was a trap, then it would only have been revealed to those who absolutely needed to know. Your contact would not necessarily have been told. But that possibility is also remote. To go to the pains of moving these troops, all for the sake of a trap, seems excessive, especially years after the initial suspicion."

Volle stayed quiet. Avery might be right, even knowing about the Tephossians' obsession with security and Dereath's vendetta against him. But Volle was disturbed that the possibility hadn't occurred to him before.

"So, in your opinion, what action should we take in regards to these plans?"

"Me?"

Avery grinned again. "Yes, you. We have the opinion of your "contact," but I want your thoughts as well."

Volle had given advice before, but had never expected that it would be asked of him by Avery. He collected his thoughts. "Well…if they haven't moved yet, then either it wasn't real, or they've reconsidered because the plans were stolen. In either case, I see no need to precipitate a war. I would have our troops remain on alert for any more movement matching those plans, but otherwise…do nothing."

Home Again

The large wolf nodded. "That matches the other advice we've received. And my own thoughts. Good." He made a notation on another paper on his desk. "So. The next question is, what do you want to do now?"

Volle hadn't expected to be given the choice, but he was ready for it. "I just want to rest. I don't want to teach, or anything. If you need advice on Tephos, I'm happy to give it, but I don't want to sit here thinking about it all the time." Not when each moment would remind him of the palace, and when the people he would be asked to consider as elements of intelligence were real friends of fur and bone.

"All right. We can arrange that. In recognition of your services, the King has found some run-down farm in the country that he's chosen to bestow upon you."

"A farm?" He thought about the dreadful tedium of the farms they'd stopped at. Then he thought about Streak's enthusiasm in helping with the work, and his ears lifted.

"I know you're not a farmer, but you've been pretending to be one for years now. Think of it as a punishment befitting your crime." The wolf grinned. "I believe it's a County by the name of Farrian."

"So I'd be Count Farrian?"

"Count of Farrian. Surnames are taken only for inherited land, you know."

Volle thought again about the land of Vinton that he had ruled, false pretenses or no, for five years. He had a governor and had visited his lands three times, the last two times to see his wife and son. "Do you know anything about Ilyana? Has she been stripped of her title?"

He'd asked Seir, but she didn't know, and the question had worried at him not only throughout his imprisonment, but on the ride back as well. Avery shook his head. "According to what I've been told, she is still Lady Vinton. When news of your unfortunate circumstances finally leaked out, you were sought for trial, and of course they did not find you. She is in no immediate danger. However, once a replacement is found, she will lose her title, of course."

"Right." Volle sighed and rubbed his muzzle. "I wish I could do something for her, and Volyan. They shouldn't suffer because I was caught."

"There are risks in everything," Avery said.

"And Volyan won't have a future now," Volle said.

"If you want to visit him in Vinton, that can be arranged. You'll just have to be careful."

Volle shook his head. "I want to see him, but I don't want to put him in danger. Maybe he'd be better off without me."

"Your decision." Avery rolled up the paper. "So am I to understand that you want to go live in Farrian?" Volle nodded. "Then, if there's nothing else you have to tell me, you have an appointment with the Steward and some papers to sign, and I have many other things to do."

Volle rose from the chair, bowed, and extended his paw. The wolf half-stood and took Volle's paw, clasping it tightly before releasing it. "Thank you," Volle said, "for all your support."

A surprised grin crossed the wolf's muzzle. "I admit that I didn't think you would last five years. Nor that you would do anything of this magnitude. So enjoy your retirement. Are you taking that guard who rescued you?"

"If he'll come," Volle said. "I haven't really asked him."

"You can't let him go back to Tephos," Avery said, his eyebrows lowering.

"No. I guess I can't." Volle curled his tail around the legs of the chair. "Well, he'll come with me, then. Whether he wants to or not."

Some hours later, a sheaf of papers in one paw, Volle stepped down from the carriage in front of the Feathered Friend and trudged inside. The clerk acknowledged him with a nod as he climbed the stairs to his room. The day at the palace had proven every bit as fatiguing as a day of travel, and even though he was hungry, he wasn't sure he'd have the energy to go out for dinner.

Voices were murmuring behind the door of his room. He paused automatically to catch the scents inside and had identified Seir and Streak before he realized it probably didn't matter.

The white wolf bounded up from the bed and greeted Volle with a warm hug. "Hey, fox!" he said, tail wagging. "I found a great little place two streets over. They have the lamb pies you were talking about and some really nice honey mead that I tried a little of."

Volle kissed him and returned the hug. The wolf's energy was contagious; despite his fatigue, he found himself saying, "That sounds great!" He smiled at Seir, who was also getting up. "Are you joining us?"

"I'd love to," she said. "How did it go?"

Volle held up the papers. "I'm now the Count of Farrian."

Streak nosed his muzzle. "So you *are* a Lord!"

"I wasn't this morning." Volle laughed and nuzzled the wolf back. "And it's not that impressive. It's a farm with a little bit of land, that's all."

"Still," Seir said, "it's land, and the King doesn't hand that out lightly. Congratulations."

Volle stepped back from the wolf to give her a hug, too. "Thank you. I wouldn't have lasted a year without you."

"So are you ready to eat, or do you want to change?" Streak brushed a paw along the fox's doublet.

"I'm ready," Volle said with a smile. "I own land now. I should dress the part."

The little inn Streak led them to was managed by a large bear, who was impressed enough with Volle's wardrobe to give them a secluded window seat with a view of the river, albeit over several rooftops and down a hill. On the other side of the river, the nobles' quarter gleamed in the moon's light, and the palace shone white behind it all.

"So you're going to live on this farm?" Seir said.

Volle nodded, though he wasn't sure he'd ever be able to call a farm home. "I just want to get away from it all."

"Is it a good income?"

"Enough to live on. Not what I was getting, but…enough."

Streak was still taking large spoonfuls of the vegetable stew that was their first course. "What do they farm?" he asked.

"Um…I don't know, actually," Volle said. "I guess we'll find out when we get there."

The white wolf's ears perked up. "We?" He glanced at Seir. "Are you going too?"

She shook her head. "No, I have to stay in the city. I don't know what my next assignment will be. It's just you two."

Streak smiled at Volle, but the fox couldn't help but recall his words to Avery: *whether he wants to or not.* What if the wolf grew tired of him? Did he realize he was being trapped into this life? He might want it now, but what about later? He was younger than Volle and had his whole life ahead of him, and they barely knew each other. "Are you excited about going to a farm?"

"I do kind of miss it," Streak said. "Will you like it there?"

"If it's quiet, it'll be perfect," Volle said.

The bear brought their lamb pies himself, setting them down and wringing his paws nervously. "I hope you like them," he said. "Our cook grew up in the south and he says this is just how he remembers them. Are you from the south, sirs?"

Volle shook his head and smiled. "I remember these from Caril," he said.

"I hope they prove worthy of your memory," the innkeeper said. He produced another small bowl. "With my compliments. Some figs from the south. They go with the pies. That is, they can be eaten with the pies, if you like…"

"Thank you," Seir said. "The Count loves figs."

"Yes," Streak chimed in. "Particularly black figs. They're his favorite."

The bear beamed at Volle. "My compliments," he said again, and bowed, and backed away from the table.

Volle grinned across the table at the others. "You are enjoying this far too much," he said, mostly to Seir.

"I know what you went through," she said as Streak picked up a lamb pie, shifting it quickly from one paw to the other before cramming a bite into his muzzle. His eyes widened; he gulped quickly and reached for the cup of water.

Kyell Gold

"Hot!" he gasped, swallowing quickly.

"They're steaming, silly," Volle said, laughing. "Didn't you notice?"

The wolf's ears canted back. "I was hungry!"

"They'll still be there in a few minutes." Volle grinned. "How do you like them?"

"They're good! I think."

"You think?" Seir said, breaking apart her pie and sniffing the steam that arose from it.

"I can't really taste it any more. I think I burned my mouth."

Volle broke his own pie apart and held up a piece, sniffing. "You should always be careful before you just put something in your muzzle."

"I usually am," Streak said, looking pointedly at him, and Seir rolled her eyes.

"You two," she said.

Streak took another bite, blowing on it before biting down, and nodded. "Mmm. I like those spices. So when do we leave for the farm?"

Volle met the wolf's eyes, and felt the weight on him lighten somewhat. "Tomorrow. Maybe the next day. There's no reason for me to stay here, except the water baths at the Feathered Friend."

"How far from the city is it?" Seir asked.

"Not far. A day's ride."

"Good. I'll come visit."

Volle smiled at her. "You'd better."

She left them after dinner, returning to her friend's house for the night. Upstairs in their room at the inn, Streak locked the door and grinned at the fox. "Now," he said, "why don't I see if I'm better at getting you out of those clothes than getting you in?"

By way of answer, Volle spread his arms. The wolf's fingers picked at the knots and tugged at the fabric until the clothes fell away, leaving the fox standing naked in the center of the room.

"Now you," Volle said softly, raising his paws up to the wolf's tunic as Streak caressed slowly down his sides. He lifted the tunic off, then rubbed his muzzle against the broad, strong chest as his paws unfastened the wolf's trousers and slid them down the hips.

Streak's paws cupped his rump while Volle's black paw traced the black line across the wolf's hip and then rose up his back. Pressed together, they kissed, and as the wolf's tongue slid against his, Volle felt his sheath stir and harden, pressed against Streak's, which was also definitely fuller than it had been a moment ago. Fatigue fell away from him, and he arched his tail.

Streak slid his paw under it, teasing a claw at the fox's tail hole. "I've got a surprise for you," he whispered, his breath teasing the soft fur inside Volle's ear.

"Oh?" Volle sighed and pressed back into the finger. "What's that?"

Home Again

"Seir got us a little present."

"She's so nice," Volle murmured. "What did she get us?"

"I'll have to go get it. Promise you won't go anywhere?"

Volle kissed him. "You don't have to chain me up," he said with a smile.

"I wouldn't." Streak held him for another moment and then let go, backing away to the chest of drawers. From the top of it, he took a small jar that Volle didn't recognize, but he knew what it was when Streak dipped a finger into it.

"She thinks of everything," he chuckled.

"Well," Streak said, flicking his ears, "I did kind of ask."

Volle grinned, and turned around, keeping his tail up. When he didn't feel a slick finger under his tail, he turned his head. Streak was grinning bashfully back at him as he worked his finger under his own tail. Volle raised his eyebrows.

"If you wouldn't mind...since I've had you and all." Streak's tail wagged as he looked at the fox.

"I think that sounds just fine," Volle said, feeling his sheath harden further at the thought.

"Only fine?" Streak grinned and reached around the fox's hips, his paw closing around Volle's maleness. "Feels like you think it's a little more than fine."

"Really fine?" Volle closed his eyes and shivered as the gentle paw stroked, pulling him further out of his sheath. The wolf's pads slid up and down his member until he was fully erect and dripping. "How about wonderfully fine?" he panted, his tail flagging.

"That's better." Streak grinned.

Volle turned around and cupped his paw under Streak's sac. "How about you? Are you ready?"

The wolf looked down at his sheath, his pink member only partially protruding. "Maybe I need a little help."

Volle smiled and dropped to his knees, curling his tongue around the sac and dragging it slowly up the wolf's warm sheath. When he closed his eyes, he could let everything else go: the worries, the regrets, the lingering aches in his muscles. He curled his tongue around the tip of the hardening shaft, tasting wolf, and the taste awoke memories in him, reminding him of their meetings in prison, the wolf a ray of light in the hopeless darkness of his imprisonment. He closed his lips around Streak and explored his shape with a soft tongue, sucking softly and enjoying the feel of the wolf's arousal growing at his attentions. It had been so long since he'd been able to enjoy another's company in leisure. The last one had been...he couldn't remember. Then the months in prison, and several anxiety-filled encounters with Streak, and then freedom.

"Fox," Streak gasped, holding his shoulder, and he realized that the musky taste had grown stronger, that the wolf was probably close. He lifted his muzzle, caressed the hard wolfhood with a paw, and stood.

"Sorry," he said, grinning. "I got distracted."

"I don't mind," Streak said. "I just didn't want to finish before you do."

"You'd better get up on the bed, then," Volle said, groping below the wolf's tail and feeling his slickened passage. He took some slickness and some of his own saliva and rubbed it over his shaft while Streak clambered up onto the bed and got on all fours. He situated himself and lifted his tail, looking back at Volle with his tongue lolling out just enough to melt the fox's heart. "All right," he said, "I'm coming."

He knelt up behind Streak and positioned his shaft between the shapely curves of the wolf's rump. Pushing against the minimal resistance, he slid easily in, gasping in unison with Streak and placing his paws on the wolf's sides. He could feel the muscles ripple below the fur as Streak pressed back, taking more of his shaft until Volle's growing knot slid just inside the wolf.

He pulled it out again, feeling his blood quicken as he slid back and forth. Reaching under the wolf for Streak's dripping member, he closed his paw around it and stroked firmly as he moved his hips. He pushed his knot into the wolf again and pulled it out, with some difficulty as his arousal mounted. His body shuddered with desire, the scent of Streak's musk mingling with his own as they rocked back and forth together. Beneath him, Streak panted and whined softly, and as Volle felt the warmth in his sheath grow along with his knot, he squeezed the wolf's shaft and pumped it harder, pressing to force his knot through the tight tail hole.

With the slick oil helping, he pushed abruptly into the wolf. The pressure on his knot made him yelp, made him thrust as much as he could into Streak now that he could no longer pull back out, and made him pant and moan and clutch the muscular body below him tightly as his nerves sparkled with his release, and he felt the seed rush out of him into his lover.

Streak's rear clenched around him, holding him and pulling him forward as the wolf's body tightened with his own climax. Warm seed spurted over Volle's paw as it pumped, slickening his grip on the long, hard member. He kept stroking until the rush of seed slowed to a trickle, bringing his other paw down to squeeze the large knot at the base of the shaft.

Streak yelped and wriggled at the teasing, and looked back with such a desperate, pained expression that Volle had to giggle and release him. The wolf gave him a sloppy lick and then collapsed to the bed, his trapped tail wagging between them as Volle lay atop him. "You feel really good inside me," he murmured.

"You feel really good under me," Volle replied. The heaviness he'd felt in worrying about the wolf and his future had remained at bay, and as he nuzzled Streak's ears and gave them a soft lick, he started to wonder if he'd been worried for nothing. "Do you really want to come to the farm with me?"

Streak laughed. "You picked now to ask me that?"

Volle relaxed further, laughing along with him. "I wanted there to be no chance you'd say no."

"Did you think there was?"

"I didn't give you much of a choice."

"Silly fox." Streak turned his head, looking at Volle out of his left eye. "I made my choice. There's nothing I miss back home, except the things that are already gone."

"But you barely know me."

"I know you, fox. As well as you know me. You're a good person, you're loyal, and," he wriggled his rump, tugging at Volle's shaft, "you're gorgeous."

"*I'm* gorgeous?" He hugged the wolf. "I'm skinny, I'm..."

"Hush. I love you, fox."

Volle kissed the white ear. "I love you too."

He realized as he said it that that was what he'd been overlooking in his worry about the future. There would be no danger for Streak, not like there had been for Ilyana. The only danger would be old age, or boredom, and those would not be so bad. Streak had grown up on a farm, and he was used to it. Volle would just have to get used to a slower pace of life, to living without looking over his shoulder or worrying about every action he took. That, he could do. With Streak by his side and no need to worry about him, he could face life with his muzzle held high. Even on a farm. Even with his old memories tugging at him, his friends back in Divalia. He couldn't go back, so he would have to put them out of his mind.

Streak was saying something. "What?"

"I said, do you think you can be happy with a plain farm wolf? I know I don't know much about how to act around a Count."

Volle grinned and pushed himself in further before working his knot out. He rocked back on his knees, and let the wolf turn over on his back. Streak smiled up at him as he climbed over the wolf on all fours and dropped onto him. "Tonight's a good start," he said.

Streak laughed and kissed him, and Volle felt his worries melt away again. "Really?" the wolf said.

He sighed and let himself relax, wrapping his arms around the strong white chest. "Really," he said, resting his muzzle against Streak's as the wolf hugged him back. The white-furred arms around him were warm and strong. They felt safe. They felt like home.

FOR LOVE OR FAMILY

Chapter 1

I was in the Jackal's Staff because I wanted to be, plain and simple. I knew what it was, and I knew that Kigi and Rashi had gone on their fifteenth birthdays, because they'd told me so. After I'd been there for about ten minutes, looking around at the all-male clientele and the lone female in the room crooning up on a low dais, I felt like an explorer in a foreign land. I was excited, and if I hadn't known my brothers were playing a joke on me, I wouldn't have even considered leaving.

They had been here, but probably not on their fifteenth birthdays; they'd sat at a table, had some free wine, and then slipped out. And they thought it'd be funny to send in their youngest brother, who'd kissed exactly one non-relative in his fifteen years. It was the latest in a sporadic series of jokes at my expense, which I bore with the patience of a brother. They were waiting outside for me, no doubt snickering, and it had taken me all of three minutes to figure out that they had lied about their experiences here. Oh, they'd described them well enough, and I can't say how I knew, but I just felt it in my gut.

Okay, I can say how I knew: because I knew how I was feeling, and I knew neither of my brothers felt that way. Not about males, anyway. Kigi had grown into a young lupine heartthrob, so that everywhere he went outside the palace, a gaggle of young bitches stood nearby and giggled. Inside the palace, he usually had one on his arm—Canis knows where he found them. Maybe they lived in the walls with the rats and only came out when he lured them with his masculine musk.

Rashi, a year younger, was scrawnier but taller, and I remember wondering a few years back whether Kigi had pulled his head away from his shoulders one day when I wasn't looking; that's how quickly he sprouted. The girls didn't tag after him as they did around Kigi, but he pursued them relentlessly, and as he was usually around Kigi, he never had any trouble finding one.

And what's more, they talked about girls constantly. And I mean, *constantly*. My sister Kira and I shared one room of our quarters while they shared the other. When they came of age, they wasted no time bringing girls back to it. Most nights, one or the other of them sprawled out on the floor between Kira and me while the other went at it with some young bitch. And come first light, they were back in their room talking loudly enough that Kira and I could hear, comparing notes and ranking their experiences.

And whenever I could, I joined in their talk, adding my observations about whether the one with the dark eyes liked Rashi or Kigi, or whether this other one was chewing skerroot to make her fur lighter. But my contributions were crafted for my brothers, for things I knew they cared about, and they were never things that I cared about.

The things that I cared about were why I always wanted Rashi to pick burrs out of my fur after a romp in the garden, but wanted Kigi to be the one to carry me inside. Why I could sit and look at Kigi with his harem for hours on end and never get tired of the way his muscles moved under his short fur, or the glow of his blue eyes, but my favorite nights were the ones when Rashi lay on his back on our bedroom floor and told me and Kira about how he and Kigi had snuck into the kitchens after hours and gorged themselves on cake, or had found a difficult way to get up on the roof of one wing of the palace, from which you could see the walls of the city, or had seen an actual southlander in the local pub.

I knew that by their thirteenth year, both of them had been interested in bitches, because I knew their histories by heart. But at my thirteenth year, I had no interest in any of the things they did. I thought it was just because I was a trailer (I heard that enough from my trainers—"Cef is just a trailer; he'll catch the rest of the pack eventually"—though never from my tutors, and the trainers all told me Rashi was a trailer too), but then I realized that I was interested in bitches, just not the same way my brothers were. I was interested in how my brothers acted around them.

And two months into my fourteenth birthday, I convinced one of my friends, a bobcat named Wix, to show me how his privates were changing, in return for which I showed him mine. We progressed from looking and touching to sniffing and licking, and then he got nervous and claimed he'd forgotten that he told his parents he'd be back early, and he practically leaped into his clothes and ran off. And the next day, he acted as though none of it had happened, so of course I followed suit and didn't tell him about stroking myself until my body snapped inside, nor about the sticky, musky mess on my paws afterwards. But it didn't take me long to connect it to the noises Rashi and Kigi made in their room, and to their inexplicable new use of the word "come."

Growing up with three brothers and a sister in a small apartment left me little time for self-exploration, but once I had a reason to, I got time alone to myself. I found that I didn't need Wix to get a tongue on my sheath, that the white stuff tasted salty, and much better fresh than licked off my paws, and that in all the times I was doing this, I rarely thought of a girl there with me. I didn't picture my brothers, of course—that would be gross—but I had a few favorites among the guards, and when they failed, heroes from childhood stories like the great wolf Granzer, who had single-pawedly held off the jaguar king Criven and his army at Vista Pass, or even the famous vulpine archer who'd freed the poor farmers from the tyrannical reign of the cougar king, back before the Bishop Mikan installed King Carod on the throne and began the Circle (here, at least; the cougars still ruled over in Ferrenis).

And I knew that when my brothers had stepped into the Jackal's Staff, it was mostly out of curiosity, not about the muzzles and paws of non-lupine species, but about whether gay males acted any differently from straight males. They hadn't felt shivers at the thought of buying a service there, probably hadn't even brought enough money to pay for one.

I had. I felt in my purse and rubbed the silver coins against each other, the metal cool against the soft pad of my paw. When they'd told me about this place, how it was so cool to be with another species and I had to try it, it had all sounded so plausible. Or else I'd ignored the lie in their voices because I wanted so badly to be with another male, of whatever species. Of course, the females they'd been with had only been wolves, but Kigi said he'd had a blow job from a raccoon (he didn't have to explain to me what that was, not after some of their conversations), and Rashi said he'd been inside a fox, actually mounted him. I wanted to ask him how that worked, how it felt, but I didn't dare let on how interested I was. I just shrugged and said, "Sounds cool. I'll do it."

Again I fought the urge to go back outside. It was what they wanted, so I wanted to make them wait as long as possible. If I lingered, though, they would know I'd bought a service here, and that might potentially be more damaging to my reputation. A gay cub, even with three older brothers, was not ideal for a landless peerage, and my father did not own land, but had been given the title of Lord Fardew along with his commission as Minister of Defense and Intelligence. We would remain a noble family, but after my father's commission was ended, our best chance of regaining a title would be to marry into it. And a noble bitch was unlikely to take a gay husband if she had another choice.

I think Kira knew, but she didn't tell. Maybe she hoped I'd grow out of it, or she was too busy attending social events with young noble male wolves. None of the others knew, of course. But they might if I stayed too long.

It didn't seem like I'd have a choice. I was already half out of my sheath from the musky scents in the air and from my own anticipation, and the madam was coming across the floor to me. No, wait; the white cougar was male. I caught his scent, which belied the pink-dyed muzzle and feminine dress and gait. He was smiling and purring as he stopped in front of me.

"Evening, sweets. I'm Tally."

"Cef." I met his extended muzzle with mine.

He brushed my whiskers. "Welcome to the Jackal's Staff, Cef. First time?"

"No," I said stoutly.

"All right then," and he grinned as if he could see right through the lie. "What would you like?"

"A cup of wine," I said, stalling.

"One of our servers can get that for you," he said. "Are you here to meet up or to hire one of our experts?"

Experts. "Hiring," I said. "The wolf or the fox, whichever's free. I mean, available."

"We don't have a fox on staff," Tally said. "Richy's available in about half an hour."

I'd just assumed they would have one of every species. "Well, who's available now?"

He grinned. "Alicar, a bobcat; and Terry, a bear."

Neither of those sounded particularly appealing. "I'll wait," I said. "I'm not quite ready yet anyway."

"Richy is five silver," Tally said.

"Oh. Of course." I took the silver out of my purse and dropped it casually into his paw.

He smiled. "Thanks, sweets. I'll tell you when he's ready. Have a seat."

I padded to an empty table, surveying the room one more time as I sat down. Plenty of the customers were looking back at me, too. I affected not to notice, arranging myself in the chair and trying to look bored.

It wasn't five minutes before someone was dropping a note on my table. I looked up at a slender squirrel. "Some wine, sir?"

"Please. What's this?" I picked up the note.

"From the rabbit." He indicated a portly rabbit sitting a few tables away, smoothing his ears down. "I'll be right back with your wine."

The note read: "I'll pay for the room and buy you a nice dinner afterwards, cutie." I almost laughed—did he not know I lived in the palace? I could get a better dinner than most people in the city just by sneaking down to the kitchens and rooting through the leavings. When I looked back up at him, he was smiling in what I suppose he thought was an alluring manner. I ignored him.

The squirrel returned with a pewter goblet full of wine. I handed him the note back and said, "Tell the rabbit I can find my own dinner." Well, it wasn't the cleverest thing, but it would do for the moment.

I sipped the wine and scanned the rest of the room. It certainly seemed like half the customers were looking at me, so I sat up a little straighter and let my tail swing back and forth behind the chair.

The squirrel was back five minutes later. "The weasel by the podium, sir. Should I bother bringing any more notes, or are you waiting for someone?"

The note read, "How about it?" I handed it back to him with a chuckle. "I'm waiting for one of your staff, but you can keep bringing the notes."

He didn't say anything, just walked away. Rather rude, but I was too keyed up to care. This must be how Kigi feels all the time, I thought, glancing around the room at the eyes on me.

Nobody else sent a note, sadly enough. Maybe they were intimidated by me now. In any case, when Tally came back to lead me to a room, I sprang out of my chair and nearly knocked it over.

For Love Or Family

"Careful, hon," he said. "Don't want to spend all your energy before you even get there."

A few of the nearby patrons snickered. "Don't worry about that," I said, and their snickers changed tone slightly: with me now.

"Ah, to be young again," one of them murmured as I passed. I held my tail a little higher and wagged it as I followed Tally into the back.

He led me through one of the back doors, down a corridor of rooms where the smell of sex grew much sharper and more immediate, making my tail twitch and my paws clench, and then to a door marked only with a number "3."

"Enjoy yourself," he said. "And if you want to leave any extra money for Richy afterwards, give it to me on your way out."

"All right." He padded away quietly and I stared at the number, sniffing the air as I did customarily to get a sense of what lay beyond. I smelled wolf, and again the thick scent of sex. I felt almost as though I'd drunk five or six glasses of wine; my head was spinning and the number seemed to blur the more I tried to focus on it. I closed my eyes and pressed the latch down.

"Hi." His voice was smooth and sultry. My eyes fluttered open.

His pink silk robe hung open to show off a firmly defined chest, a fluffy white stomach, and a nice pair of legs with brownish-grey fur darkening from mid-thigh down to his dark brown feet. Of course, I saw most of this later, because the first thing I saw was his white sheath, the inch of pink protruding above it, and the soft white sac lying casually on one thigh.

"Going to come in?"

It took me a second to realize that I was standing in the open doorway with my muzzle partly open. I stepped in, closed the door, and looked into a pair of sparkling green eyes.

"Hi, cutie." He patted the bed next to him. "Wanna come sit down?"

He had the most gorgeous muzzle, slender and white. Most of the rest of his face was grey, but as he flicked his ears, I saw their black tips. None of my family had black-tipped ears, and I thought they were the handsomest thing I'd seen. If he hadn't had his sheath out, I could happily have stared at his muzzle for hours.

"Yeah." I licked my lips and padded over to sit next to him. I thought my heart would jump out of its chest. He didn't know I was a noble, didn't even know my name, and he was about to reach over and...

His paw was warm on my shoulder. "What's your name?"

"Cef." I squeaked out my nickname, then cleared my throat. "Cefalo. But everyone calls me Cef."

"Pleased to meet you, Cef. I'm Richy." He smiled, not showing too many teeth, and oh, at that moment I'd have done anything he asked just to see that smile again.

"I...I know."

"First time here?" The lie didn't even enter my mind. I nodded. "Okay, do you have anything in mind or want me to give you some suggestions?"

I didn't say anything, but my eyes flicked downward to his sheath. For Canis's sake! I hadn't felt this tongue-tied since I was eleven and my father took us to meet the king.

Richy smiled. "You can touch me if you want. Do you want to?" He drew his robe back a little more, showing off the clean white fur of his thighs and the grey outside on his hips. There was a little more pink now, and I couldn't seem to look away from it.

I nodded again, croaked out a "yes," and reached a paw towards him. He slid his arm around my waist and smiled at me as my fingers touched the soft fur on his sac, then his sheath. I hesitated, and then brushed my pads across his pink skin.

It was amazing. It was strange. I'd seen my brothers naked, but never erect, and I'd only ever touched myself. It was like touching myself, but all the sensation was coming through my fingers. I loved it.

I explored him, tried some of the strokes I liked and found that positioning my paw was a little trickier from this angle. I glanced at him for approval and got that warm smile back, and after a couple times, I stopped glancing.

His breath tickled my ear. "You want me to touch you too, Cef?"

"Yes…" I was so hard it was painful. His fingers figured out my trousers without difficulty and freed me from their prison. And then it was a strange duality: I was stroking with one paw and feeling strokes between my legs, but the sensations were separate. I closed my eyes as his paw traced my knot, already full and swollen. Then he gripped me, I squeezed him back, and I felt a surge inside and I couldn't hold back a small yelp.

"Oh." I looked down at myself, at his paw covered in my come, and my ears folded down.

Richy tightened the arm around my waist. "Nothing to worry about, Cef." He held my member up, examined it from each side, and then brought his paw to my muzzle. "Want to clean me off?"

I lapped at his paw, but after a few licks I said, "I…like it better fresh."

"All right." He gave me another smile and his eyes danced, and he reached behind him for a towel. "I just want to make sure you get your money's worth."

"Can I…" I swallowed. "Taste you?" I didn't know how to say it. I was beyond worrying about him seeing me as a kid now; after spurting all over his paw, there wasn't anything I could do to appear mature.

He cocked his ears, and then leaned forward to kiss my nose. "Of course, Cef. Just mind the teeth."

"Uh." Now he'd said that, I was nervous. I imagined my clumsy muzzle gouging him with my teeth, even though I'd never even gotten close to hurting myself. Maybe I'd just start with licking.

I lowered my head along his chest and stomach, getting just a hint of his musk. "Tell me if I hurt you?"

He stroked me between the ears. "Just don't bite down." His tail wagged, and seeing him want my touch gave me back my confidence. I leaned over again, and he swung his legs up so he was lying on the bed. I hardly noticed.

I loved his musk, and the feel of him in my muzzle. Once I felt my teeth graze him, and stopped, but he didn't say anything, so I kept going, just more carefully. For a while, he made happy moans and yelps, but when my jaw started to hurt and he still wasn't any closer to coming, I let him slip out.

"Getting tired?"

I nodded. "Does it usually…take this long?"

He rubbed my ears again, and tried to lift them up. "It depends," he said.

"I'll keep going, as long as it takes…" I bent back down, but his paw stopped me, holding me under the chin, drawing my eyes up to meet his.

For several heartbeats, he didn't say anything. Then he leaned forward and took my paw, and wrapped it around his length. "Slide up and down while you're sucking," he said, and laid back.

That worked a lot better. I felt him respond after only a couple minutes, his knot swelling and body tensing, and after a few more strokes, he shuddered and arched his back, and I got a muzzle full.

I kept licking as he moaned, and forgot about my teeth for a second, but I don't think I hurt him. I tried to swallow, gagged, tried again and succeeded, but in the process I'd let a good bit dribble back onto his fur.

"Oh, I'm…" I reached for the towel and wiped off what I could.

He laughed, sat up, and hugged me. "That was just fine, Cef. You must've been practicing on yourself."

"Kind of. Doesn't everyone? I can't get myself that far in, though." I could still taste him in my muzzle. I licked my lips, getting more of the taste.

His tail thumped the bed. "Well, you did a nice job. You have a little more time…are you ready to go again?"

I was. "I don't have to…I mean, you don't have to…"

He put a finger to my muzzle. "It's my job." He winked. "And my pleasure."

Oh, Canis. He took me into his muzzle and I don't know how I didn't come again right there. I could tell right away that I hadn't been half this good, because he hadn't been thrashing around on the bed like he had whitemouth. I'd never felt anything like it, even when I had myself in my muzzle. I think I kicked him once, and I know I was making all kinds of incoherent squeaky noises, until finally I thrust up against him as hard as I could and came for the second time in an hour.

"Oh." I panted over and over again, lying back. "I definitely need to practice."

He brushed a paw along my stomach. "I hope this was a night to remember."

"I'll never forget it," I panted. "I wish I didn't have to go so soon."

Richy slid up beside me and kept the paw on my stomach. I wanted him to keep it there forever. "Why's that? You think you could do three times?"

"No. I just like…I like being here with you."

"Oh." He paused, so that I turned to look at his eyes. They brightened when he saw me look, and he kissed my nose. "You can stay a bit longer if you want. We've only been about forty minutes, and you paid for an hour."

My tail wagged against the bed. "Could you…this might sound weird."

He laughed. "I've heard weirder things than you can imagine, Cef dear. Go ahead."

"Could you just…hold me for a bit?"

By way of answer, his arm slid around me. I hugged back and edged my body towards his, and rested my head against his chest. He stroked me down the ears and neck, and flipped his tail over my hip, and I was in heaven.

"What nights do you work?" I murmured.

"I'm here every night but Gaiaday night."

"Can I come back and see you?"

"Of course you can, Cef."

I rubbed my muzzle against his shoulder, drinking in the texture and scent of his fur. The underlying sexual attraction never really went away, but it was faded now, and I could focus on his scent, his muscles, the way he held me, the rumble of his voice in his throat when he talked, and it was all wonderful.

"How long have you been here?" I wanted to hear his voice more than I wanted to know the answer.

His claws dragged through my fur. "A couple hours. My shift starts at sundown."

"No, I mean…how long have you been working here."

"Mm." He was quiet for a moment. "A long time."

"It's my birthday," I said. "I'm fifteen."

"O ho," he said, and kissed my ear. "Your friends take you here?"

"Brothers," I mumbled.

"Nice family."

"Sometimes."

"Where do you live?"

"Palace." I tried to muffle the response in his fur, but he heard anyway and exhaled.

"Oh. So I really might see you again."

I lifted my head to look into those warm green eyes. "You will."

Out in the main room, my head had cleared and I paused for another cup of wine before meeting my brothers outside. Let them wait longer, if they were still waiting. I wanted to relax and savor the moment, and mask the scents on my muzzle with the deep richness of wine.

Technically, I suppose, I hadn't been a cub since a couple months ago, when one of Kigi's former conquests took me out into the gardens and showed me where everything went. That had been enjoyable enough, and had given me plenty of material to talk to my brothers about, but it had been nothing like tonight. Tonight I felt like a grown-up wolf for the first time.

And I couldn't stop thinking about Richy. I could smell him, hear him, feel him, taste him. Even though I'd just about exhausted myself and had only one silver left, I had to fight the urge to run back in there.

"Hi, Cef. Had fun?" Tally pulled up a chair and sat at the table with me. "Mm, I can see you did."

I blinked at him, and only realized as I spoke that my muzzle was relaxing out of a huge grin. "He's great. I'll definitely come back."

"That's what I like to hear."

I remembered why he was there, finally, reached into my purse, and slid my last silver across the table. "I'll have more next time."

He pocketed it smoothly and flashed me a smile. "Stay as long as you want. There's another singer coming on in ten minutes or so."

"Can I reserve Richy?" The words just seemed to burst out.

"Of course, dear. Tomorrow night?"

"Yes!"

He smiled. "Same time?"

"Sure." All my newfound maturity had vanished. My tail was wagging and I believe I might even have been drooling. Just a bit.

"Consider him yours. See you then." He patted me on the shoulder and walked off to another table.

It took a few minutes for what I'd just said to sink in. I was going to come back tomorrow, which meant I needed to get another five silvers. More if I wanted to leave a tip. My allowance was only one a week, and the six I'd brought tonight were a quarter of my savings. Really, though, the only reason I didn't have more money was that I'd never needed it. I drank the rest of my wine and walked out, already looking forward to the rest of the week.

Chapter 2

I gave a raccoon couple a cheerful wave as I passed them, feeling well-disposed to everyone at the moment. The sun was just setting, the warmth of the day was still in the air, and the thieves and scoundrels were still lurking in their dens waiting for true darkness. I thought the street had never looked so beautiful. I wondered if Richy worked evenings, if he ever got to see a sunset.

The giggle of girls as I approached the tavern down the street from the Jackal's Staff told me that Kigi and Rashi had waited for me. I pushed the door open and braced myself to meet them.

The Cup and Crown was a large pub, with two front windows and an entrance over which the owner had painted "Serving the palace for seventy years." Inside, the first thing that always hit me was the smell from the pine shavings, scattered on the floor to reduce the smells of the customers and soak up spilled alcohol. Tonight, the giggling came from the benches and chairs arrayed around the crackling fire, the social area. To the left, fifteen to twenty lamp-lit tables of various sizes accommodated those customers who wanted to eat or drink in peace. The host, a large bear, was at one of those tables talking to an important-looking couple, but besides him, the only employees in the room were two barmaids. The bartender worked in the back room. I'd never met him.

This was where Kigi and Rashi had taken me to get me drunk on ale for the first time, about a year ago. At the times we were allowed to go, it was usually not very busy. I'd been there late twice, but it was hard to find a place to sit when we went that late, and the crowd was loud and smelly. We preferred to go early and have the place to ourselves.

If I'd had to guess from the noise, I would've said there were at least five giggling girls, but there were only two hovering by my brothers: one of the barmaids and her sister. There weren't many other customers, which was good, because as far as the barmaid was concerned, Kigi was the only one there.

He was in one of his usual poses, shirtless with his chest thrust out, arm flung casually over the back of his chair. The firelight cast flattering shadows on his chest fur—not that there was a light that didn't flatter him. Usually that made me wish he weren't my brother, but this evening I just wished he were a little thinner, and that his eyes were green.

They lit up when they saw me. "Hey, there's our li'l brother. Wow, Cef, you were there a long time. Fall in love?"

The giggling took on a different tone. They must've told the girls where they'd sent me. I flopped down into a chair and grinned my most casual grin. "Don't worry, Kigi, I wouldn't piss on your rock."

"What's that mean?" He hadn't quite lost the amusement, but he did sit up and look at me.

I held out my paws, mocking placation. "Hey, hey, settle down. I didn't ask for your favorite muzzle, what's-his-name, the raccoon."

I'd intended to pay him back by getting rid of the girls, but for some reason they were eyeing him with more interest than before, if that's possible. Maybe they hadn't understood. Rashi definitely had; he was giving me a warning look, no doubt remembering what *he'd* claimed to have done in the Staff.

Kigi growled, "I don't know what you're talking about, Cef."

I affected innocence. "Sure you do. You told me how that raccoon's muzzle felt so good, better than any bitch you'd had…"

He looked for a minute as though he was going to lunge across the table at me. Then he remembered the girls; I saw his eyes flick back to them. "We'll talk about that later," he said.

"Okay." I shrugged. I probably shouldn't have kept smiling, but I was still warm with the glow of my evening and I couldn't really help it. I'd deflected the questions and that was all I wanted to do.

When we left, I stayed a bit behind the others. Kigi had chosen the smaller and cuter of the girls, keeping her arm locked through his as they strolled along the sidewalk. She wouldn't be able to come into the palace, but that didn't mean this time was wasted; Kigi would come down for an afternoon sometime and a quick tumble in the back room of the pub, or maybe he'd just take her in some alley somewhere. He'd only done that once, but he talked about it every time Rashi or I brought up our much more limited experience.

As a matter of course, the rejected bitch would console herself with Rashi's company, usually not letting him touch her, but walking next to him. This night, however, she dropped back to walk alongside me.

"Caf? Is that your name?"

"Cef." I saw Rashi look back at me and gave him a grin. After all, he'd been in on this too.

"I'm Dasha. Nice to meet you."

"Pleasure." I didn't really know what to say, but watching Rashi's ears fold back was incentive enough to keep going.

"Did you really…you know…in there?"

Now I *really* didn't know what to say. I settled for ambiguity. "I just want to be like my brothers."

"Your brothers said they played a joke on you."

"Maybe they were playing a joke on you."

She looked ahead at Kigi and the girl on his arm. "I don't think so. They don't smell like it. I can't tell about you, though."

"You can smell it? What's it like?"

"I don't know, it's just something you notice." She nudged me. "What about you? Did you really?"

"Can't you smell it?"

She flicked her ears. "I told you, I can't tell from you. Look, if you don't want to talk about it…"

I didn't, but I happened to glance at Rashi, whose ears had come up again. "No, no, it's just that I don't really know what to say."

"Well, did you or didn't you?"

We were almost to the palace gate. "No," I said. "Should I have?"

"I was just curious, you know, what it was like. Two boys together…" She grinned and nuzzled my ear. "Come see me if you ever try it and want to compare."

Surprised, I looked up at her smile and returned it. "All right. I will."

Kigi and his bitch were sharing a long kiss while Rashi was glaring at me, ears still back. I saw Dasha look at Kigi and then at Rashi, and so, impulsively, I brushed my nose against hers and kissed the side of her muzzle.

She focused back on me and cupped her ears forward. I tried to look charming, and I got a kiss back—nothing like Kigi was getting, where it looked like she was trying to crawl down his throat, but I could definitely taste her. I imagined she was Richy and dreamed about what he might taste like, if he kissed me.

"Come on," Rashi said. "We're gonna be late."

Kigi disentangled himself from his bitch and touched noses with her. "See you later, gorgeous," he said, and then walked to the gate without even looking at me or Rashi.

"Bye!" I waved quickly to Dasha, and hurried after Rashi. Kigi was already showing his papers to the guards. They knew us, but they had to follow procedure, so by the time Rashi and I were done, Kigi was halfway through the gardens.

He couldn't hold a grudge, though, especially as he had a different bitch on his arm the next day. Rashi, on the other paw, collected grudges like fleas. He and I took History instruction together, a lesson I occasionally found interesting, but which paled next to my own recent history. I suppose Rashi must have misinterpreted my silly grin throughout the lesson, because he cornered me as we left our tutor's chambers.

"Hey, runt," he said, "You better not get any ideas about taking my girls."

"She came up with the idea, not me." I shrugged his paw off of my shoulder.

"We're going out tonight and you're not invited." His finger stabbed me in the chest.

"Fine. Whatever."

My indifference confused him enough to let me escape to lunch. Truthfully, I was glad he'd spared me having to feign illness or something to keep from tagging along with them. It was funny that he felt so threatened by me. Maybe he was worried I'd replace him at Kigi's side.

No fear of that. There was only one wolf whose side I wanted to attend.

To do that, I needed more money. My father was in his office that afternoon. I asked the secretary to announce me, and she came out accompanied by Dereath, the rat who was my father's top assistant. He gave me a smile that didn't reach up to his eyes, and told me to go on in.

My father pushed aside a stack of paper and perked his ears up as I walked in. "Hi, Cef. Aren't you supposed to be at your rapier lesson right now?"

I shrugged. "I wanted to ask you something. Torry won't mind if I'm late."

"You should always be punctual," he said, but smiled. "What did you want to ask?"

"Well, I'm fifteen now, and I have…" That wasn't feeling right. "There are some things…" No, then I'd have to explain what. Best just to get to the point. "I was wondering if I can have a raise in my allowance."

He chuckled. "I should have known. Kigi and Rashi have been flaunting their money, haven't they?" I nodded, though in truth they bought me drinks or sweets as often as they lorded their wealth over me. "I suppose that's reasonable. We can give you two silvers a week."

I smiled. "I was hoping for something like five."

"Five? What could you possibly want that much for? You always seemed content with your allowance."

"I was. But I met this girl last night, and…" I had prepared my rationale, down to letting him imagine why I wanted the money. He would be overjoyed at the prospect of having his youngest son courting, and he would grant what I asked for.

"Is she from a noble family?"

Here's where it started to break down. A lie would be exposed quickly. "Nooo…"

"Cef, you know that I have some very nice prospects for you. Even Kigi won't get to keep the girl he wants."

"But…"

"And he certainly doesn't spend five silver a week on all his girls. We'll make it three, and you come see me if you need more for special occasions. Okay?"

When he said "okay" like that, there was little point in arguing. Three should've made me happy, too, because Kigi and Rashi only got two a week. All I could think, though, was that it meant I'd only see Richy every other week. "I wouldn't have asked you if I didn't need it."

"For what, Cef?"

I was silent at first, but he waited me out. A white lie about meeting a girl instead of a boy was one thing. To justify five silver, I'd have to make up something more elaborate than a getting-out-of-trouble lie. I couldn't begin to think of how to go about it, not even with Richy as incentive. "I dunno," I mumbled finally.

Dereath was hovering by the door.

For Love Or Family

"If you can't tell me, I don't like thinking about what that might be. So why don't you go have your rapier lesson before your allowance goes back down to one."

I knew that warning tone well, though I'd only ever heard it directed at my siblings. "Fine." I turned and marched out of the office.

Dereath was hovering by the door as I walked through it. He followed me out into the corridor, and put a spindly paw on my arm. "Cef, I couldn't help overhearing…"

"What?"

He smiled, and suddenly I felt his paw press a coin into mine. "I know what it's like to be young," he said. "What good is being a child of privilege if you can't enjoy the rewards, eh?" With that, he inclined his head and slipped back into the office.

We'd never talked much before, he and I. I knew he'd screwed up badly, recently, but my father hadn't told us any details. I had assumed that Dereath would be let go, but he had endured somehow, almost as if whatever it was had never happened. He can't have much money, I thought, but it was a nice gesture to give me a silver.

Then I looked at the coin he'd given me, and held it up to the torchlight so I could be sure the gold gleam wasn't just my imagination. It wasn't—he'd given me a gold Royal, worth over three weeks of my new allowance, and two visits to Richy.

Chapter 3

"Cef? Cef?"

"Urrr…"

Richy's laugh echoed softly in my ears. "I guess you liked it."

"Rrrrrrf." I nuzzled his neck and kissed it over and over again, unable to form words. My arms were tight around his chest and my hips pressed right up against his, my cock buried in him and locked in there by the biggest knot I'd ever gotten, it felt like. I was still seeing stars from that climax.

He turned to lick my muzzle. "You'd never tied before?"

"Uh-uh." I pushed my nose into his fur. His scent was freedom: chilly winter air and a pine forest, better than any wine.

He shifted his weight. One paw covered mine. "You feel good."

"Rrr. Did you…?" I slid the other paw beneath him. He was hard and wet, but I couldn't tell if the wetness was before-wet or after-wet.

"Mm-hmm." He nuzzled me again. "Couldn't help it."

"Mmmm." I licked his ear. "How does it feel?"

He wiggled around me and smiled. "Good. Do you want to try it tomorrow?"

I was quiet, resting my muzzle on his shoulder. Finally I said, "I can't come tomorrow."

"Oh."

"We have this family dinner."

"Okay."

I sighed, exhaling through his fur. "And besides, they'll start to wonder where I am every night."

"You don't tell them?"

"No. We—my brothers and sister and I—all need to marry into noble houses."

"But you live in the palace…oh. Are you a servant's family?"

"No! My father is the Minister of Defense. But we don't hold land."

"Oh." I felt his tail twitch against my stomach.

"Do you have a family?"

His ears flicked. "Just the one here."

I nudged his ear, because he sounded sad, and he let out a sigh. "They're good people, but I miss some of the ones who've been here over the years. The only ones left from when I started here are Pike and Tally."

"What happened to the others?"

He shook his head and smiled at me. "I don't want to talk about them today, Cef."

Through that smile, he could've asked me to walk out onto the street naked, and I would've done it. I settled for kissing him. It was nothing like Dasha; the taste in my muzzle was fire that I inhaled greedily, fire that fed the heat in my loins. My knot had been loosening, but the kiss brought a surge back into it.

Richy wiggled his hips, grinned up at me, and put a paw on my shoulder. "Hold on." He lay on his side, rotating around my knot with a motion that made me squirm and yelp. He hooked his leg around my waist and lay on his back, looking up at me.

I looked down at his chest as I leaned over, resting my paws on either side of him. He touched his nose to mine. "Go ahead if you're ready again. I don't mind."

"I think if I do, I won't be ready when my hour's up." But I wanted to, so badly that my hips were pressing in again despite my words.

He reached around, pulled my rear against him, and gave me a kiss. "I said I don't mind."

That was all the encouragement I needed. If you think it's tough to get all the way to climax when you're already tied, then you've never been young and in love. I wanted to be a part of him so desperately that just being around him, I was halfway to orgasm, and a kiss and a smile brought me most of the rest of the way. He slid his arms around me and held me as I let his wonderful scent and beautiful body sweep me upward until I was shaking against him and emptying myself into him again.

I collapsed on top of him and just lay there while he stroked my back. His muzzle brushed my ear, and as I floated through a warm haze, I heard his voice.

"What would you like to be doing in ten years, Cef?"

"This," I murmured.

He laughed. "Silly. I mean, will you be working? Maybe for your father?"

"Maybe. I don't know, I'll probably be a lord of some province. That's what Rashi says he'll be doing."

"I thought your family didn't own land."

"Well, it would be my wife's land."

"Wife? You want to get married?"

"I have to. I told you about my family."

"It sounds like you have enough brothers, though."

"If they all find noble wives, then I might not have to, but there's no guarantee of that. Kigi will probably end up married to some barmaid." I grinned. "He doesn't know what he's missing." I rubbed my stomach over Richy's sheath.

He smiled and nuzzled me. "What do you want to be doing? If all your brothers marry noble bitches and your father says you're free to do what you want, what would you do?"

"I don't know. I've always liked geography. I could be an explorer."

"I know someone who went to Ferrenis." He rested his muzzle between my ears. "Pike says he's doing well."

"I wouldn't want to go there. It's all explored already, and anyway they're all nasty."

"Not all of them."

"Well, anyway. I'd rather go north to the icy wastes. I heard there are white wolves there ten feet tall, and fields of snow that hurt your eyes. Or down the river to the south, where they say there's a plain of water and a mountain of sand."

"A plain of water?"

"A huge expanse, like a valley that's flooded, but it's so deep that you could swim straight down for a month and never get to the bottom. Can you imagine?"

"Mmm. It sounds strange." He nuzzled me. "But fascinating. Tell me more."

"An explorer who went south said they've built huge boats, bigger than the ones we use on the river here. He said you can be floating across the water for days until you can't see land any more."

"I've thought about going down the river, sometimes. You should go, and come back and tell me what you see."

"What's down the river?" I trailed a paw through his stomach's fur.

He smiled. "I don't know. But I've also thought about going to Ferrenis, or just quitting. I never will, though."

"Why not?"

"This is where I belong. I've been here…a long time. I don't know where else I would go." His paw brushed mine. "And I like working here, too. I get to make you make that cute face and those funny noises."

I looked away and curled my ears back, but I couldn't stop grinning. "I like that too."

He squeezed me, and I felt myself slide out of him. "Awww." He thrust out his lower lip in a mock pout.

"I've been here too long anyway." I sat back, then slid off the bed, letting my eyes travel up and down his body.

Our reverie was broken by a knock at the door. "Just a minute," I called, hurrying to get my pants on, but there was no answer.

"That was Tally," Richy said, sitting up. "Time is up."

"Sorry." I slid into my tunic. "I'll be out of here in a second."

"Don't worry about it." He smiled and helped me lace up my pants. "I said it was okay."

"Are you going to be in trouble?"

"No more than usual." He straightened the wrinkles from my shirt and patted my shoulders. "Go on now."

I leaned forward to kiss him. He hesitated and then met my muzzle briefly. When we parted, his green eyes were sparkling and a smile was forming on his muzzle. "Go!" he said, and patted my rump.

For Love Or Family

I wandered back through the main room in what was fast becoming a familiar daze. It was crowded tonight, so I had a choice between leaving without a drink and sharing a table. I compromised, gulping a cup of wine while standing and then heading for the door, dizzier than ever.

The cool evening air helped some, but I was still feeling unsteady as I got back to the gate. The guards didn't say anything as I showed my papers, and fortunately I knew the palace well enough that I could have found my quarters with my eyes closed. Which I almost had to do.

I was lost in a happy fantasy that I don't think I need to detail here when Kira walked back in. Half-dreaming, I barely noticed her until she sat down on the edge of my bed.

"Hey, squirt."

I struggled back to full consciousness. Even in the darkness, Kira was a beautiful, imposing wolf bitch, an inch taller than our oldest brother and almost as stocky as Kigi. Her eyes fixed me with a green shine, and I could see the ghostly image of her teeth when she talked.

"Hi, Kira."

"So tell me what's going on."

"Huh?" I tried to rub sleep from my eyes.

"You've disappeared almost every night this week. I saw Rashi and Kigi go out and thought I'd ask you to come for a walk in the garden, but you weren't here again tonight. You come home smelling of wine…" She hesitated there. "Not very good wine, either."

"Sorry," I mumbled. "I'll try to drink better."

She put her paw on my shoulder. "Is it that barmaid, the one Rashi was complaining you tried to steal from him?"

"Uh?" Barmaid? Oh. "Dasha?"

"Is that her name?" I saw her teeth flash in a grin. "You're sweet on her and you're worried about Father finding out because he wants you to meet Jelila tomorrow."

"Yeah." I stuck my nose into my bed. "Can I sleep now?"

"Sure." She got up. "Your secret's safe with me." Out of the corner of my eye, I saw her tail wag as she crossed the room to her bed.

The dinner was worse than I'd suspected it would be. Jelila was a year younger than I was and cute, but apparently had spent so much time grooming her fur that she'd forgotten to develop any personality. All of her responses to any questions we asked were delivered in one soft syllable. Even when she introduced herself, the last part of her name seemed to drop to the floor unheard.

Her parents were at the dinner as well, and though they weren't palace residents, her father was apparently a cousin to Lord Rhychel and had been here before. They told us that Jelila was a beautiful singer, and came of healthy stock. Kira told me later that that meant that she wouldn't die in childbirth, like our mother had when delivering Sheni, my sister who'd died six months later.

The awful part of the dinner was that my father kept telling Jelila's parents about *me*. I thought she was going to be the topic of conversation, but every time Father opened his muzzle, it was "Cef is doing *so* well in his studies" or "Cef is learning three different weapons at the same time," leaving out that they were all three swords, and I was doing poorly in all of them. And Kira was worse. "Cef gets around the palace all the time and knows half the lords by name."

That one led to "Have you met Lord Rhychel?"

I had, but I hadn't been paying much attention at the time, so I had to maneuver through the questions after that without giving offense. Like, instead of "he sounded really pompous and used lots of big words," I said, "He seemed really smart." Instead of, "He ignored me and didn't say a word to me the whole time I was there," I said, "He's really involved in a lot of important affairs." And rather than say, "He smelled kind of like old cheese," I said, well, nothing.

After dinner, we sat around and talked further, and Kira got to leave for that part. As the center of attention, I couldn't, though believe me, I tried. It took two agonizing hours to escape, and the worst part was that I couldn't escape to Richy's embrace afterwards. It was too late, and I hadn't come up with a way to get enough money to visit him again.

Rashi and Kigi were gone, too. I stomped into my bedroom and sat on the bed.

"How was the talk?"

Kira was lying on her bed, brushing her tail out. I growled. "Agonizing."

"Well, the family want to be sure they're getting their money's worth."

"Why not put Rashi up there, or Kigi?"

Kira grinned at me. "You think those two haven't been through that?"

"Where are they now, anyway?"

"I don't know. Back at that tavern, I suspect. Kigi said he was going to get that barmaid tonight." She rolled her eyes. "That was the meat of what he said, anyway. He went on for quite a bit longer."

I imagined Kigi describing exactly what he was going to do, and that at least made me grin. "I could use an ale. I'll go join them."

"Of course you will." She winked at me, and it took me a moment to remember what I'd told her the other night. It was an odd feeling, the disconnect between what she thought I was going to do and what I was actually thinking of doing. I dug my last silver piece out of my savings, dropped it in my purse, and winked back at her as I walked out the door.

To my surprise, Dasha cornered me almost as soon as I walked in. We talked, and talk led to a back room, and that led to her trying to convince me that she was as good as Richy. At least she enjoyed herself in the process, and while we were tied afterwards she pressed me about Richy, and I finally broke down and told her what I felt. I had to tell *someone*. We weren't a family used to keeping secrets.

It felt good to take her into my confidence, initially. Then she kept harping on about Richy being "just" a prostitute and that I was paying him to be whatever I wanted, and I should be careful. It ended up souring the mood, and I left wishing I hadn't said anything at all.

Chapter 4

Two days later, on Ursiday, I got my allowance, and scurried straight down to the Jackal's Staff that night to spend it. The clouds had come in over the afternoon, dripping a fine mist that soaked into your fur so you didn't realize you were wet until you stepped into a dry space. I stepped under the sign and through the door, shook myself off in the entryway, and stopped dead.

The room itself had gained a certain familiarity, but the people in it were always changing. So every time I walked in, I looked more at the muzzles than at the room itself. There was a young wolf with his back to me who looked more familiar than the room, as if I'd caught my own scent in a place I'd never been. It took me only a second to recognize Rashi.

He'd figured out my secret and was waiting for me. I couldn't convince my paws to take me back out the door, and a moment later it was too late. The host that night, a raccoon I'd seen once, was coming towards me and Rashi, alerted by the motion and the breeze, glanced back to look. When he saw me, his muzzle curved into a smirk.

"Good evening, sir," the raccoon said. "You've got the appointment with Richy? He'll be free in just a minute."

"Yes," I said automatically. "I'll wait over there."

I'd gestured vaguely, still not sure if I wanted to ignore Rashi or confront him. He made the issue easier by walking towards me. I braced myself for the crowing I would have to endure, and mentally wondered if I could live in the Cup and Crown in a spare room until I came of age next year.

"You see, squirt, you're not so smart." Rashi sneered down at me. "I don't know how you figured this out, but I caught on fast."

I stared at him helplessly. He barked a short laugh. "You might've gotten one night with Dasha, but you're not going to get any more."

"No," I shook my head. If that were his price, I'd pay it gladly.

"Once she sees me coming out of here," he went on, "she'll forget all about you."

I blinked. "She will?"

"She's all over that gay thing. That's the only reason she liked you, because she thought you were doin' it with other males. I'll walk out in a couple minutes and head over there and then we'll see who she likes better."

He didn't know. He'd been too far to hear the raccoon mention my appointment, or hadn't been listening. I almost panted with relief, and I had to stop my tail from wagging. He thought...I wanted to laugh. To buy time while I processed this, I said, "She likes me better."

He waved a paw. "She was only interested in you because we tricked you into coming here. Don't kid yourself."

She had been pretty interested in my experiences here, but she'd also said I was cuter than Rashi. "Well," I said, "you're probably right. She really wanted to hear what it was like, and I don't think I was very convincing. I'm not a very good liar." I'm a *great* liar.

The raccoon was signaling to me; I nodded to let him know I'd be right there. I had to wait until Rashi was either out the door, or until he'd taken my bait. Right then, looking at his narrowed eyes, I thought it was about even chances on either. He said, "She did?"

"Yeah. I tried to pretend but she saw right through me. Said she'd talked to guys who'd done it with other guys and she could tell right away when someone was lying."

Now he definitely looked worried. "She won't be able to tell when I am."

I nodded. "Oh, I'm sure you're probably right. You're a much better liar than I am."

He started for the door, then stopped. "Go ahead," I said. "I'm going to find out what it's really like." And with that, I walked towards the host and into the back without looking back.

Richy was waiting for me in a blue silk robe that highlighted his eyes. I almost tore my clothes off before he could get up.

"You're grinning," he said after he'd pulled my naked body against his soft robe and kissed me.

"I think I just tricked my brother into getting a blow job here."

He shook his head. "I shouldn't ask about your family, right?"

I laughed and moved my paws inside his robe, feeling the curve of his side where it angled slightly outward into his hips. "Probably not."

We kissed again. He nuzzled me when we finally pulled apart, and breathed softly, "I've missed you."

I held him tighter. "Oh, I've missed you too."

"Mm." I couldn't get enough of my paws in his fur, or his paws in mine. He pressed right above the base of my tail, making it arch, and kissed my cheek ruff. "You want your first time tonight?"

"You think I'm ready?" The thought scared me. I'd tried pushing a finger up under my tail, knowing that eventually I wanted to do this with Richy. It felt nice, but I didn't think I could fit much more than that. When I was inside him, though, he seemed to enjoy me so much. I wanted to feel that too, and I wanted to feel it with him.

He pulled back and touched his nose to mine. "I don't think you'll ever get more ready." His paw brushed my ears. "It will probably hurt, but I'll be gentle and we won't tie tonight."

"You're the expert." I couldn't keep a quaver out of my voice.

He held me. "If it hurts too much, we'll stop."

"I know." I was cross with myself for being afraid, and for making him worry by showing it. "I'll tell you."

"Promise?"

"Promise."

He had me lie on my back at the edge of the bed, and worked his fingers into me first. It wasn't as bad as I'd thought it would be, just uncomfortable. It helped that he was stroking me out of my sheath the whole time, too. "Try to relax," he urged, and I wasn't quite sure how, but I tried my best.

Then the fingers slipped out (relief!) and he put one paw on my hip. "I'm ready," I said with more bravery than I felt.

He kept his eyes on mine and nodded. "All right. Remember, tell me if it hurts."

I nodded and watched his hips move forward. I felt the pressure first, and then...whoa.

"Are you okay?"

I gulped and nodded. He pushed a little more. "Wait!"

He stopped instantly. "Hurts?"

"Yes. No. Could you..."

He slipped out of me, and the relief went flooding through me. I lay my head back, disappointed. After all that, I was too tight, too virgin to enjoy him that way, inside me. As I lamented my inconvenient anatomy, the soreness started to fade, almost as though my body were listening to me. Strangely enough, my body missed him. I wanted him back in.

"It's okay." He was starting to move away, but I gestured him back.

"Try again. I want..." He looked at me, and I smiled. "Just try again. I'll tell you if it hurts."

"All right." He put some more oil on his cock, and I felt that pressure again. This time, though, when he moved into me, it wasn't as uncomfortable, and as he stretched a certain part in time with a paw on my shaft, I felt a thrill.

"Oh. Wow. That's..."

"Okay?" He smiled down at me and I got lost in those eyes.

"Yeah."

"Uncomfortable?"

I nodded. Like I said...hard to lie when you're making love. "But there's good feelings too..." Canis help me, I was babbling.

He kissed my nose. "Good. The discomfort goes away with practice."

"Oh." I panted as he slid further in. "I want...a lot of practice."

He just smiled and started moving back and forth. And with his paw moving and his cock moving, I was squirming and yelping and moaning and spurting before I knew it. Oh, Canis, it was great. Until I started to come down off the climax. Then the big hard thing stuffed up my rear was much less comfortable.

Richy seemed to know it, though; he slid out as soon as he saw me relaxing, and that little thrill of relief gave me another spurt. I just lay there, panting, staring up at him and past him and making little moaning noises as I came down.

He lay next to me and rubbed his paw through my chest fur while I recovered. "You've still got forty-five minutes," he said when I turned to look him in the eye again.

I smiled. "And you've still got a date with my muzzle."

And after that was concluded to our mutual satisfaction, we lay on the bed and held each other and talked about our days. He never said much about his work, just that he'd gone out shopping with some friends and gotten a new shirt, or that he'd taken a walk down to the park, or that he'd had a really good stew at the pub for lunch. I told him about the palace, about Dasha (he didn't seem upset that we'd made love), and about seeing my brother outside. If we wanted to be quiet, we would just brush each other's fur, but we never ran out of things to say.

I hated leaving, but I had to. I told him I'd be back as soon as I could, and we kissed and held each other before I walked out.

This time I lingered long enough to drink two cups of wine. Rashi was nowhere in the main room, and I was sure he'd be over at the Cup and Crown by now. Besides, my butt was kind of sore, and I was hoping it would go away if I sat long enough.

It didn't. Finally I had to start heading back to the palace. I walked out the door and had barely gone three steps when I heard a familiar voice.

"Well, well."

I turned to see Dereath behind me. Hadn't even seen him when I left. He was looking very pleased with himself, with a thick oiled coat wrapped around his thin frame. "Uh...listen, I just went in to look..."

"For an hour and a half?" He sounded amused as he sauntered closer.

"The wine's pretty good."

"Better than the free wine and the serving bitch over there?" I couldn't think of a reply, and he laughed. "Don't worry, cub. I won't tell your father. I heartily approve of your new hobby."

His paw appeared from a pocket, flipped something towards me, and disappeared into the same pocket. I caught the flying object reflexively and looked at it in the fading light. Another gold Royal.

He strolled past me. "See you back at the palace."

I watched him go, holding the coin in the rain. I'd been planning to stop by the Cup and Crown, but I found I no longer really wanted to.

My father was just about to turn in when I got back to the rooms. I was going to go right on to bed too, in case there were some scents still on me, but something occurred to me. "Dad? What happened with Dereath?"

I could tell he hadn't expected that. "What do you mean, Cef?"

I studied the grey of his muzzle. Despite that sign of age, his brown eyes were bright and his ears were perked up. He was as stocky as Kigi, if no longer as muscular, but I was sure he could still hold his own. "I remember you said something about him screwing up a few months ago. What happened?"

Now he smiled, just a little, like he always did when we asked him about work. "If I wouldn't tell you then, why do you think I'll tell you now?"

I shrugged. "I thought maybe it wasn't as secret any more."

"You haven't been talking to him, have you?"

I avoided his gaze. "No. Not much."

"It'd be better for you to stay clear of him."

I nodded. "Okay, Dad." But my paw closed around the gold Royal in my pocket.

Over the next month or so, I did try to steer clear of Dereath, but he always managed to track me down, and every time he saw me, he tossed me another gold Royal. "Spend it well," he said, and by the time the summer was rolling around and the rains coming more frequently, I started to seek him out. Every gold Royal meant two more visits to Richy, and those were worth more to me than anything.

I started to fidget early in the afternoon of days I could visit him. Sometimes I drifted off in a lesson and found my sheath full and straining at my pants as I blinked away thoughts of him and tried to get back to the lesson. Dinner always seemed to take forever, especially if there were some noble family and their of-age bitch for me to be polite to. And then I was off, free of the palace and free to see him.

There I got all the practice and instruction I could ask for. He was right; I took him inside me several more times, and each time it was more comfortable and more pleasurable. One night, near the end of the month, he pushed his knot all the way in and came inside me, and we lay there locked together. It felt beautiful. I couldn't stop touching him, that gorgeous wolf, part of me.

"Is that okay?" he said, and I kissed him to stop him asking silly questions.

I told him about the other noble bitches my parents had lined up for me—two since Jelila, who'd been back with her family for another look. It felt good to list their shortcomings, because nobody else would listen to me, not even Kira. Richy not only listened, he laughed, but his ears weren't quite as perky as usual. I asked him why.

He traced a finger down my chest. "I'm just sad. I know one day you'll stop being able to afford me, and you'll marry one of those lucky nobles."

"If I can't afford to see you, I'll sneak in the back."

"You'd get in trouble."

"Don't care." I kissed him again and pressed myself to him. "As long as I get this."

He held me, and didn't say a word.

I was especially dreamy that evening as I drank a cup of wine at the Cup and Crown. Dasha was keeping me company, Rashi's strategy having fallen flat. At least, it had with Dasha; I'd heard him bragging to Kigi that girls were finally getting interested in him, but I didn't know which unlucky bitch he'd fooled. Kigi had finished with Alisha, so he only came to the Cup and Crown on nights when she wasn't working. With both my brothers away, I felt more comfortable talking to Dasha in the common room.

"Did you come twice again?" she asked me with a grin.

I shook my head. "Just once, but he locked inside me."

"Nice, isn't it? Well, I've never done it from that end, but it's nice from the front."

I grinned. "It takes a little practice. But it's nice, yeah."

She took a drink and gave me a curious look. "You know, there's a wolf my brother knows who's gay. He's a couple years older than me, but I don't think he's seeing anyone. If you wanted..."

I shook my head. She sighed. "Why, Cef? You're a cute guy. You could get yourself a mate..."

"I don't want a mate."

"I just hate to see you get all hung up on this prostitute. You think when you run out of money, he's going to give you freebies?"

"It doesn't matter. I'm going to be married off to some bitch before too long. Kigi's already engaged, did you hear?"

She shook her head. "Noble?"

I snickered. "No. She thought he was noble and had him over while she was in heat. He says he tried to resist."

She laughed along with me. "So she's carrying now."

I nodded. "Dad was angry, but not too angry. I think we all pretty much expected it to happen."

She took another drink. "So does he feel the same about you?"

I knew she meant Richy again. "I think so. I mean, he acts all..." I trailed off, knowing what she would say next.

She said it, of course. "That's because you're paying him to. Have you ever seen him outside the house there?"

"No. But that doesn't matter. I know how he feels. You've never even met him."

She bristled. "I don't have to. I hear stories from there. I know what whores do."

I pushed my chair back abruptly. She leaned across the table and flicked her ears back. "I'm sorry, Cef. Listen, why don't we go upstairs..."

"Not tonight." I stood up and dropped a couple coppers onto the table. "Maybe some other time."

Kyell Gold

I sat on a crate across the alley and waited.

For Love Or Family

She didn't say anything as I walked out. I breathed in, letting the cool night air dispel the sour taste in my muzzle. What did it matter if Richy really felt for me the way I did for him? I was happy. Wasn't that all that mattered?

Except that I'd had the same thoughts and always quelled them. Whenever I thought of him with other clients, or ached to see him, or woke up from a dream thinking he was with me, I wanted to make him mine and mine alone. In more lucid moments. I realized how silly that was, but that didn't stop my heart from wanting.

I would ask him, I decided. I would stop him on the way home from work and just talk to him, just ask him if he really felt anything for me or if it was just an act. And then I would know. If he was acting, then so be it. If not...

I told myself that this was a stupid idea, one of the worst I'd ever had, but I was already crossing the street. Dasha had brought the uncertainty in me to the boiling point, and now I needed to know.

The Jackal's Staff was a huge building, much larger than I would have suspected. I finally found the alley that ran behind it and a door that I suspected to be the back exit. At least, it smelled of recent traffic, and I thought I could catch the faint smell of sex beyond it. I sat on a crate across the alley, back in a shadow, and waited.

While I sat there, getting colder, my mind ran through the choices. He didn't feel the same. He did. He didn't, but it didn't matter. He did, but it didn't matter. For each scenario, I constructed elaborate dramas and tearful partings, tearful commitments, or tearful confessions.

I heard the door open, but it was just a mouse leaving. He didn't see me. I drew my clothes closer around myself and waited, and at some point my imagination drifted into dreams.

The sky had just a tinge of light to it when a rough paw shook my shoulder. I blinked up into a black-masked muzzle.

"What in Gaia's name are you doing out here? Are you lost?"

I rubbed my eyes, wondering why this raccoon was in my room and why my room was so cold. It took me a minute to wake up. "Um. I need to see Richy."

The raccoon's muzzle furrowed. "He's asleep. Didn't you just see him?"

I nodded. "I have to ask him something."

"Well, come back again and ask him then."

"I can't. I need to...I need to ask him when I'm not paying him."

At that, he stepped back from me and folded his arms. "No. No meeting with clients outside work."

"But..."

He shook his head. "No. Go home."

My paws clenched into fists, but there was nothing I could do. I glared at him stubbornly and folded my own arms.

"Don't make me call the guard, cub."

His black eyes glittered. I knew he would do it. And then Dad would know.

I got up, wincing at the stiffness in my leg and shaking it to bring it back to life. "Fine."

"Maybe you should take a week or so off before coming back," he said as I limped down the alley. I snorted at the advice. As easily say I should go a week without water.

I paused within sight of the palace gates. Richy had talked about a pub he frequented. I could go wait there; it was a public place. If I went back to the palace now, there would be explanations demanded, endless fountains of guilt, and there would be no more leaving for at least the rest of the day, and probably not until tomorrow. Better just to stay out. If Richy didn't show up at the pub, then I would go home and think of some other idea.

The Cup and Crown was closed by now, or I would've gone to apologize to Dasha. I felt far less sure of myself walking stiffly around the city in the cold pre-morning than I had the previous night at the pub. I walked on past the closed doors and further away from the palace.

The crowd in the streets at this time of morning was interesting, mostly mice and weasels and other smaller people. I saw two raccoons (one a guard) and a fox, but nobody else my height until the sun was peeking above the horizon.

By that time, I'd found the Dirty Dog, Richy's favorite pub. It catered to the daytime crowd, which was, I think, why he went so often; nothing else was even thinking of opening this early. Even here, it wasn't until the entire sun was above the horizon and I was beginning to think I'd never feel my ear or tail tips again that a portly weasel wandered up to the door and opened it.

"You waiting for me, sahr?"

I nodded.

"Come in, come in! Mustela and Gaia, I never have people lined up before. You must be cold!"

"Been out all night," I managed through chattering teeth.

"What kept you out?" He gestured me inside, where it was not appreciably warmer but at least there was less wind.

"Waiting for someone."

"Ah, broken tryst?" He clucked and started preparing a fire, then looked at me. "Say, if you can set a fire, I can start in back."

"Sure." I knelt by the fireplace and took over the job from him. I didn't have much practice, but I'd at least gotten the wood shavings to light by the time he returned.

"Very nice! Warm here in no time. So tell me what brings you here, what sad story you have." He kept his ears perked towards me as he bustled about the room, setting out cups.

"It's not exactly a tryst," I said. "I was hoping to run into someone here."

"You wait all night for this place to open? Bed is more comfortable!"

"No, I...I waited somewhere else but he didn't come there. I know he comes here a lot."

"Oh? Does he have a name?"

I hesitated, but there didn't seem to be any way or reason not to tell him. "Richy."

"Oh, the adorable wolf. Yes, I know him." He shot me a sidelong glance. "You are liking him?"

I nodded. "But I don't know if he feels the same. When I'm not paying him, I mean." That slipped out before I realized he might not know Richy's profession. My ears burned, folding back.

"So." He nodded, paws moving quickly around the tables. "You listen to a little of Cori's advice?"

"Who's Cori?" I asked stupidly.

He grinned. "I am Cori. I have owned this tavern for eleven years and I have seen many stories. And you are?"

"Rashi," I said, taking my brother's name as a feeble attempt at disguise. I didn't even think about it.

"Then Rashi, I will give you some advice." He had come over to my table, and he patted my paw. "Ay! Stay here and get warm. That is first advice. Next advice is this: go home. Forget about adorable wolf and find yourself a nice boy wolf your age and do all things young wolves do. Be happy." He squeezed my paw. "Richy is very nice wolf. But stories of romance, with his profession, they are not having happy endings."

On top of a night when I'd argued this with myself over and over, sitting in the cold and not getting nearly enough sleep, this truth seemed devastating to me. I pictured Richy's muzzle, his beautiful eyes and ears. Then I saw him turning away from me. My throat got tight and my face got hot and I knew I would start bawling if I tried to say anything. I also knew that I had to say something, because Cori was looking expectantly at me to see if his advice had sunk in.

"I...can't. It's not that...simple..."

His ears flicked. He came around the table and put his arms around me. "Ah, cub," he said softly. "It hurts, yes. But better small hurt now than big hurt later."

"This doesn't...feel small," I managed.

"Shh," he said, patting my back softly. I had to lean over to rest on his shoulder even though I was sitting down and he was standing, but his embrace comforted me. I cried for a little while and then sat back, wiping my eyes.

"I'm sorry," I started, but he waved my apology away.

"Don't be sorry. Hurt brings tears." He gave me a kindly smile. "You go home now?"

I nodded. "I think so." I wanted to wait, but I was tired, and I was scared of what I might see. At least if I left now, maybe there would be another solution to my problem.

"Good boy." Cori smiled and patted my paw. "You come back here some evening. Cori look for nice boy for you."

"Okay." I smiled at him and got to my feet, shakily. "Thanks."

The day was getting brighter. My stomach growled, reminding me that my family would probably be at their morning meal and wondering where I was . The streets were bustling now, so it took me nearly an hour to press my way back to the palace. Twice I turned around and started to head back to the pub; both times I only took a few steps before remembering Cori's words. What I was most scared of was losing Richy. At least if I didn't do anything to change the situation, I could keep seeing him a couple times a week. Touching him a couple times a week, that is. I saw him every time I closed my eyes.

They were closed a lot as I passed the gate, showing my papers to the guards automatically, entered the castle, and stumbled back to my chambers, where my nose told me my family was back. I braced myself and walked in.

My father was talking to Kira about something. They both turned around when they saw me.

To my surprise, my father was smiling. Not a happy smile, but a knowing one. He patted me on the shoulder.

"Cef, I don't mind if you play around out there, but if you're going to be out all night, let us know, okay?"

"Huh?"

"I was worried even when Kira told us where you were."

I stared at Kira. "How did she know?"

"It wasn't hard to figure out, squirt," she said, putting a gentle paw on my shoulder. "I mean, you've been out with this bar girl so often lately…"

"Oh, right." I nodded as sheepishly as my fatigue would allow.

"She's not in heat, is she?" My father's tone got sharper.

"No."

He relaxed. "All right. Don't get too attached." That was his last bit of advice before leaving.

"I'm going to the kitchen," I told Kira.

"You've got training in ten."

"I'll eat fast."

She followed me down the steps. "You know what's going on, right?"

"No, and neither do you. Dad never tells us."

"You think he's got another thing going on?"

"Course he does. He was all distracted like he was last year when there was that big military thing. Remember?"

For Love Or Family

"Oh, yeah. But that's not what I mean. You know what's going on with you?"

"I'm getting breakfast?"

She hissed impatiently. "After Kigi got himself stuck, they started really pressing to get you and Rashi married off. Nobody's biting on Rashi, what with the rumors, but they've got two families interested in you."

"What families? What rumors?" We were rounding the corridors that led to the kitchens and my nose was occupying most of my brain.

"You've just been upwind of everything, haven't you? The rumors about Rashi. How he hasn't found a mate yet, and he was apparently seen in some gay brothel..."

I froze, a wave of nausea temporarily overcoming my hunger. "Gay brothel?"

"Some place near the palace. I don't believe it, but you know how people love to talk."

"Yeah." I started walking again, slower.

"And Jelila's family is interested in you, and one other is too. I forget the name of the bitch. They haven't brought her over yet."

"What about you?" Hunger and anxiety made me snappy. "How's your search for a noble mate going?"

Her ears flipped back and then her muzzle smoothed into a smile. "That depends on you and Rashi. Mom and Dad might be able to afford to marry me to Lord Deverin."

I snorted. "The cheater?"

She shrugged. "He's got land."

By this time, I was cramming half-warm meat into my muzzle, so I didn't answer. I only got a couple pawfuls in before Kira reminded me that I would be late for training, so off I went.

That was the start of a horrible week. It wasn't so much that I was too tired to train properly and ended up sore from strained muscles and bruises, or that I had to endure two more dinners being picked over like a riding mount. It was the mornings I woke up convinced Richy was beside me, reached out, and found nothing. It was sitting in the palace in the evening with nothing to do and slowly realizing that the rest of my life was going to follow that path. I would be married to a wife I would not love, have enough sex to have cubs, and in exchange I would retain the privilege of living in the palace, or near it, and being well enough off to support my family as they grew older.

I loved my family, but I didn't want to sacrifice my life for theirs.

Chapter 5

These maudlin thoughts, or some like them, were in my head when Dereath approached me, nearly a week after my ill-fated nighttime adventure. I had just gone through another training session and was finally beginning to work some of the soreness from my muscles. He cornered me in the hallway upstairs from my chambers. Sneaky, too; the first inkling I had of his presence was a black shadow and a faint waft of cinnamon in the air. Then he appeared in front of me, dressed in his typical black tunic and silver belt. I wondered if he owned any other clothes.

"It's been a lonely week," he said.

I shrugged. "Sorry. I've been busy."

"So you have. All inside the palace, too. No nighttime excursions. I feel terrible about that."

"Not your fault." I kept walking, heading for the stairs, but he headed me off.

"Why don't you talk to me for a bit?"

I flicked my ears. "I kind of want to relax."

"You don't find me relaxing?"

"I never really thought about it." I sniffed the air, and realized for the first time that he was gay too. That made me wonder anew why he was so interested in me. "I've got to change for dinner."

"Another lovely ball and chain?"

"What?"

"It's a shame," he purred softly, "that such a passionate, lovely cub should be tied down for family reasons. Where's the justice? Where's your freedom?"

"Well..." He was articulating all of my own adolescent cries, and I had to take the part of my family. "It's my duty..."

"What about Kigi and his duty?" I shook my head. "And so the burden falls to you. After all, your poor brother Rashi...is not as discreet as you are."

"Well, there's nothing I can do about it now."

"But there is." He leaned closer.

"What can I possibly do?" He was making me a little uncomfortable, but I was intrigued.

He chuckled. "That's what I want to talk to you about. What I mean is that once you're married, of course your visits to the brothel will be curtailed. But what if you could bring him to the palace to be your personal servant?"

"We can't afford a servant."

"Ah, but your new wife will be able to."

I shook my head. "It'd never work."

"My boy, do you have any idea how many of the personal servants in this palace, male and female, serve part of their function in their lord or lady's bed?"

"N-no."

"I can assure you the number is significant."

"But he works at the brothel."

"So you buy him. It would only take maybe forty gold."

"Ha." I snorted, more depressed than before. "Where would I get forty gold?"

"I could get you the money," he said softly.

Now I looked right into his shiny black eyes. "For what?" Would I sleep with him for forty gold? In a heartbeat.

He laughed, and it had a harsh tone I didn't like. "Not for that, cub. Lovely as you are. No, I just need some help."

"All right...with what?"

He looked around and continued in almost a whisper. "I'll come find you in a couple days and talk to you about it then. Best to discuss it in my rooms."

"Oh. It's not…"

He put a paw to my lips. It smelled of cinnamon and of his neatly groomed fur. "Later." He gave me a smile, turned, and walked away.

Two more days passed before he came to fetch me. In that time I had, at a rough count, five hundred different fantasies about life with Richy. Every personal servant I saw became him, beckoning me into an empty room, or even an intimate nook of the hallway, pressing his muzzle to mine, holding me in his arms. I ran my paws down his sides a thousand times in my dreams, held him against me, felt him inside me or around me, and sometimes the dreams were so real that I dropped out of them into cold reality with a physical shock. One night, they were so real that I woke with a start, shuddering in pleasure that bridged the dream and reality, my paw holding my hard cock as I came all over my stomach.

Kira smelled it the next morning, of course, and clucked at me with a grin. "You need to go see your barmaid, *squirt*."

I snorted, my ears flicking. "It was just a dream."

"Must have been a good one."

"Mmm." We didn't talk much about sexual matters, leaving that to Rashi and Kigi, but she had caught me playing with myself once or twice. I had asked her if she ever did, being curious how girls would even do it, and she'd just smiled mysteriously.

"I'll cover for you if you want to slip out tonight."

"Thanks, but no." Dereath hadn't given me any more gold, and I didn't have enough of my allowance left to visit Richy. The prospect of spending the evening with Dasha wasn't enticing enough to keep me away from the palace. If Dereath came by to tell me how I could be with Richy forever, I wanted to be here to hear it.

"Suit yourself." She wrinkled her nose. "Try to keep your dreaming under control, though."

"Yeah, yeah." I had balled up the dirty sheet and now I threw it at her.

"Ew, Cef!" She batted it away and stalked out.

I grinned, picked it up, and took it down to the laundry, dreaming on the way down that Richy walked behind me playing with my tail.

Dereath found me that afternoon just before dinner. When he appeared after my history lesson, I jumped after him, and he put his paws up with a grin. "Settle down, cub. Just come along this way." Tail wagging, I followed him up the stairs as eagerly as if Richy waited at the head. And in a way, I suppose I thought he did.

I'd never been in his rooms. My first impression when I walked in was that I was in a high noble's chamber. I had to turn my head to take in the tapestries on the walls, the finely carved chairs and small tables, the elaborate writing desk, and the bureau next to it. The floor was carpeted too, soft under my paws. I glanced down at the beautiful designs as I walked over to a chair and sat down, sliding my tail between the seat and the back.

I wagged it as I leaned forwards towards the chair he was sitting in. "So how can I get the money?"

He leaned back. "I really hope you'll be able to help me. You might have heard about a bit of unpleasantness I was involved in a few months ago." I nodded. "I doubt you've heard what it was about. No? To be brief, I unwisely brought a lover into the palace who turned out to be an agent of a foreign government. I know, I know, but you should have seen him, Cef. He was so slender and beautiful, and he wrote me the most lovely letters while we were apart."

I closed my eyes and saw Richy. The admonition, "you still should've known better" died on my tongue.

"After he escaped, your father took all the letters he'd written me and locked them up in a chest in his office. I just want to get them back."

My eyes flew open. "I can't do that."

"Of course you can. Listen..."

"You don't understand. He always locks that chest when he leaves the office. There's secret things in there that only the King has seen. He keeps the key around his neck and only takes it off at...night." He was watching me with those black eyes and what he wanted clicked in my head. "Oh, no. I can't. He'd kill me."

"He doesn't have to know."

"But he will! That's his job!"

"Listen. You give me the key outside your chambers. I run down, get

For Love Or Family

my letters, run back up, give you the key. It takes five minutes. Ten at most."

"He'll miss them. He'll know one of us took the key."

"First of all, he doesn't need them any more. He's just keeping them for records. It might be a year 'til he misses them. By then, he won't know when they were stolen. Trust me."

I chewed my lip. Dereath was my father's closest assistant. He knew my father's habits better than I did. On the other paw... "I can't steal from him."

"I'm not asking you to. I'm just asking you to help me get back something that's mine. Those letters...they're all I have left, Cef." His eyes were pleading now. If that seemed uncharacteristic to me, I paid it no mind. "Think if your wolf had written you letters and then gone away or died, and you had nothing left, nothing else to remember him by, and those letters were being locked away for no reason."

I swallowed. "Well..."

"Just think of the nights you'll have with your darling, while your wife takes care of your noble-born cubs and your happy father lives in the next chambers." He sighed. "And at least I'll have my love's letters to grow old with."

"You promise I won't get in trouble?" I was trying to stop from getting hard at the images he was calling to my mind.

"I promise."

I looked away, down at the carpet. The patterns danced through the fabric, and for a moment I traced them with my eyes, trying to find my answer in them. It wasn't there; it was between my legs, and beating in my chest. "All right."

He reached across and clasped my paws. "Thank you, Cef. You've made me—and you—very happy."

I nodded, wishing I could take back my words. Only for a moment, though. The next moment I was dreaming about walking into the Jackal's Staff with my forty gold and walking out with my wolf. If I could keep paying him for the rest of my life, it wouldn't matter if he really loved me. We could be happy together.

"I don't need to tell you not to tell anyone else about this, do I?"

"No. What do you think I am?"

"A very generous and lucky cub," he said.

"Lucky?"

"Of course. Few people meet the love of their life, much less get the chance to spend it with him." He looked me up and down, and the gleam in his eye didn't fit with his mood of a moment ago. Maybe he was just happy that I was going to help him.

"Hey, Cef," he said as I got up.

"What?"

"I'll give you five more gold to let me mount you right now."

I searched his eyes, trying to figure out if he was kidding. "Five gold right now?" In the back of my mind, I was thinking I could see Richy tonight.

"No. When the job's done."

"Why not now?"

He grinned, stepping closer. "Because I don't want you running out there tonight. I want you to be focused. With five gold in your pocket, you might get cold paws and back out on me."

"I won't." Already, though, I was losing any inclination I had had to accept his offer.

"Besides, wouldn't it be sweet if the next time you saw him, the next time you held him, he was yours?"

I thought about that, and I had to admit, he had a point. "Then no."

He chuckled. "Never hurts to ask."

"When do I have to do this?"

"Probably tomorrow night. Maybe the night after. I'll wear a white shirt to dinner on the night I want you to do it."

"Okay. What time that night?"

"Whenever you can safely do it. I'll be watching your chambers. Just walk outside with the key. I'll come find you."

"All right. Anything else?"

He shook his head. "Thanks again, Cef. I really do appreciate this."

"You're welcome," I said, but something in his smile made me uneasy, and I got out of there before I could have any more second thoughts.

Outside the opulence of his rooms, walking through the spare stone walls of the corridor felt like waking from a dream. I am making my dream into reality, I told myself firmly, but I couldn't stop misgivings from gnawing at my stomach all the way back to my chambers.

At dinner, I avoided my father's eye, because every time I looked at him I felt I was betraying him. When dinner was over, he stopped me with a heavy paw on my shoulder, and I thought he was going to hear the loud, fast beating of my heart.

"Cef, I have been talking to the Darishu family."

"That's Jelila, right?"

He looked about to lecture me on remembering names, but just nodded. "They regard you as an excellent prospect. They have a good dowry for her as she's their only daughter, and they come from a good line. Morrif of Darishu is Lord Rhychel's cousin..."

I rolled my eyes. "I *know*."

"...and he holds fifty acres in Rhychel. It would be a good match."

I found I was able to look him in the eye without feeling so much guilt. "So?"

"So. Jelila will be in heat in two months. That's a little early, but if they don't insist on throwing her a cotillion, we could finalize the arrangements by then."

For Love Or Family

"Two months?"

"*If* they don't want a cotillion. Morrif doesn't care, but Sharia wants her to have one. If they do throw one, then you'll have to wait for her next heat."

I folded my arms. "What if I don't like her?"

He looked genuinely puzzled. "Why wouldn't you like her? She's a nice bitch. You'll love your cubs, and you'll be living with us."

"Don't you want me to be happy?"

"What is all this about?"

"Nothing." I slumped back against the wall. "Nothing. Just tell me what I have to do."

"Cef..." He stepped closer to me, pine and strong male wolf, the scents I'd known all my life and associated with comfort, safety, and security. "We don't have the privilege of freedom. I've worked hard to get to where we are. I want you and my grand-cubs to have all the things we didn't have..."

"Please don't tell me about your brothers starving to death again."

He recoiled. I relished the hurt in his eyes, and hated myself for it. "All right. But this is a good match for you."

"No. It's a good match for you. You don't know anything about me."

"One day, Cef, you'll look back and realize that this is the right thing." He released my shoulder and his tone grew sharper. "Until that day, you'll do as I tell you. And that includes a formal dinner the day after tomorrow, and whatever else is expected of you."

I composed and swallowed a bitter retort, and just nodded. He studied me for a heartbeat and then walked away.

Chapter 6

I'd lain in bed for what I thought must have been hours. I hadn't heard a sound in at least twenty minutes, other than Kira's steady breathing on the other side of the room. The last voice I'd heard had been Rashi wishing Dad good night. Slowly, I crept out of bed, as quietly as I could.

I tried to keep my toes up, but my claws still clicked lightly on the stone floor. Ears perked for any sound, I eased the door of our room open. The chamber was still. I padded to the door of my parents' room. Only their breathing sounded inside. I put a paw on the handle, then hesitated. What if they weren't quite asleep? I waited, put my paw on the handle again, waited, and stood there with my paw on the handle for probably ten minutes, heart beating faster and faster, until finally I convinced myself to push the handle down.

It clicked, as loud to my perked ears as if I'd slammed it. I held my breath and waited. My father grunted, but no other sound came from the room. Slowly, I pushed the door open.

My heart was still racing. I discovered that if I looked at my parents, I felt a wave of paralyzing guilt. I stepped quietly into the room and fixed my eyes on the small nightstand where my father kept his purse, and where I knew I would find the key.

The problem was, there were three keys on the stand.

Two were linked together with a leather thong. In the dim light, it took me a moment to recognize the key to our chamber door, which was usually only locked at night. I had a key just like it. So the smaller one, the one not attached to the others, must be the chest key. I picked it up, careful to hold it gently so my scent wouldn't get onto it. I should have brought a handkerchief, I realized belatedly.

Too late now; I'd touched it already. I carried it gingerly out into the main room and eased the door shut, but not all the way. I was terrified of hearing that click again.

If I'd thought that was bad, the sound as I slammed into our door, forgetting it was locked, was a hundred times worse. If I'd knocked a stone loose from the ceiling, it couldn't have made more noise. I froze, waiting for someone to come out and ask me what I was doing.

Canis was watching over me that night—or perhaps he wasn't. In either case, nobody woke up. I panted to relieve some tension, and unlocked the door as quietly as I could manage, then slipped out into the hall.

Away from the familiar scent of my family chambers, the danger of what I was doing was less palpable. I set the key on the floor carefully, not wanting to hold it any longer than I had to. I looked from it up and down the corridor, pacing as my relaxation slid back into worry. Where was Dereath? Wasn't he supposed to be watching? Why was it taking so long?

I was close to picking up the key and going back inside when a rabbit came strolling down the corridor, as though it wasn't the middle of the night. His plain tunic marked him as a servant of some sort. I didn't recognize him, and his scent was so faint it didn't register until he was very close. I slid one of my feet over the key to hide it, trying to be casual.

"Dereath sent me for the key," he said softly when he was within sniffing distance.

My ears folded back. "What key?"

He pointed to my foot.

"Where's Dereath?"

He shrugged. "I'm supposed to take the key."

"To him? He was supposed to come and get it." I was starting to panic.

"Plans change."

"How do you know about this, anyway?"

"He sent me to get the key."

I shook my head. He looked up at me without any expression I could discern, and for some reason I found myself thinking of Richy. If I took the key and went back inside, I wouldn't get the forty gold. Dereath might be upset and drop the whole scheme. I considered the rabbit. How could he have known about the key unless Dereath had sent him? Slowly, I moved my foot.

"That's a good cub," he said, bending to pick it up. "I'll be right back."

He moved back into the shadows. I thought it was creepy the way he moved, without scent or sound. To distract myself, I leaned against the wall and closed my eyes, and imagined Richy next to me. It had been over a week since I'd seen him, but I could smell him and see him clearly, and thinking about him still relaxed me and brought a smile to my muzzle.

I was still alert to every sound and noise, and twice I was sure my father was just about to come through the door and ask me what was going on. I kept my eyes closed and thought about Richy, and when I opened them again, the rabbit was standing there, smirking at me.

"Here," he said, and dropped the key in front of me.

My fur stood on end. I grabbed at it and barely stopped it from slipping through my paws to the hard stone floor. "Hey!" I hissed, but the rabbit was already halfway down the corridor, and in another moment he was gone.

I crouched there, and slowly stood. Opened the door slowly, slipped through into the quiet, safe chambers, closed the door behind me. Took a breath. Pressed slowly on the door to my parents' room and slid inside.

Both of them were still sleeping, breathing rhythmically, unaware of my presence. I set the key softly on the nightstand and slid out.

That easily, it was over. My feet hurt from trying not to let my claws click on the floor. Inside my room, I closed the door and sank down on my bed, letting my toes relax.

Chapter 7

For the first half of the next day, I was on edge. I kept expecting my father to grab me and demand to know what I'd done, or Dereath to appear and ask me where the hell I'd gone, that he hadn't sent any rabbit, or Kira or Rashi to tell me they'd seen me leave the rooms. None of that happened. I didn't even see my father all day. Finally, I relaxed and started looking forward to getting my paws on my gold and my love.

I didn't see Dereath at dinner, but I couldn't stop thinking about my gold. I hurried through the meal, ignoring the looks my siblings gave me, and when we'd finished, I padded through the palace to the rat's chambers and knocked on his door.

I couldn't smell the rat, so I was surprised when the door opened. I looked down at a long pair of ears and the rabbit's neutral expression. "Where's Dereath?" I blurted out.

"Master Talison is away. But he did leave something for you." He turned and walked back into the room, and though I itched to follow him, I waited politely by the door, tail wagging back and forth.

The rabbit was gone for a while. My ears caught the clink of what might have been gold coins. I shifted my weight and looked up and down the corridor. A lord I didn't know passed and glanced my way, then walked on. I studied the gilt reliefs on the door, not really seeing them, just trying to occupy myself so that I wouldn't pull my fur out from excitement.

Finally—finally!—the rabbit came back holding a large purse with both paws. He held it out to me and I snatched it from him, opening it and peering inside.

"That's yours," he said. "Did you need anything else?"

I didn't hear him at first, captivated by the shine of gold as I had been with the first Royal the rat had pressed into my paw. There was enough money here to...well, I knew what I wanted it for. It was heavy enough that I got tired holding it in one paw while the other plunged into it, feeling the weight of the coins all around.

"Is that all?" he repeated, and this time I looked up and nodded. I must have looked like a foolish cub, with a broad grin, ears all perked forward listening to the clink of gold, but I didn't care.

He shut the door, and I wandered some ways down the corridor before I heard the click of claws on the stone and realized I shouldn't be caught wandering around the palace with forty Royals in my paws. I started to walk back to my room to hide it, but then I started to worry. What if Kira found it? What if someone saw me walk in and asked what it was? What if, what if, what if. There wasn't any safe place for it here.

I could take it to the Cup and Crown. Dasha would...no.

I fretted, pacing back and forth, and then the perfect solution occurred to me. I would go buy Richy right now. I wanted so badly to see him, and then I wouldn't have to worry about forty gold being stolen or discovered by my family.

I nearly skipped down the corridors and through the gardens, so excited the closer I got to the Jackal's Staff that my tail couldn't wag fast enough. The guards gave me a strange look as I walked quickly past them, hunched over the purse, but I didn't have time for them. I shoved through knots of people on the street, barely registering any of them, focused on my destination.

When I got there, I just stood inside the door, looking around. The usual array of muzzles turned towards me, and turned away again. Many of them knew me already. Tally spotted me a moment later and tilted his broad muzzle curiously at my posture. His expression cleared, becoming more professional as he approached me.

"I hear you had a little trouble the other night, dear. What do you have there?"

"I'm sorry about the other night," I said quickly, "but I've got it."

"Got what?"

"Here." I shoved the purse at him.

He took it and staggered at the weight. "Cef, dear, what..." He looked inside. "Oh my."

"It's for Richy." I couldn't stop my tail from wagging.

Tally looked at me. "Why don't you come back to my office?"

"Okay." I followed him, head held high as I walked past all the other poor slobs who could only rent their love for a night. He led me to one of the doors I'd only seen him or the raccoon come out of, and held it for me.

Inside, he made straight for another door. I barely had time to look around the small room and see a board on the wall that held several tags with names on them, one of them Richy's.

He closed the second door behind me and motioned me to one of the chairs behind the broad desk that he dumped the purse on. He sat himself on the edge of the desk, fingers playing with the purse strings as he talked to me.

"You want to buy Richy?"

"Yes." Tail wagging. Grinning. Unable to believe this was happening.

"Are you sure, cub?"

"Yeah."

"How much is in here?"

"Forty."

"Hmm."

I leaned forward, the wag going out of my tail. "Is that enough?"

For Love Or Family

"Oh, it's enough." He smiled. "Let me go get Richy."

All the while he was gone, I tapped my paws on the floor, drummed the edge of the desk, and wagged my tail. I glanced at the purse once or twice, and I know forty gold is a lot of money, but it never occurred to me to do anything else with it than what I was doing. My heart (and sheath) felt like they were about to burst.

I caught his scent before I saw him, and it perked me up right away. When I turned my head, there he was, looking down at me with a smile. I sprang up and hugged him, and he held me, and I wanted to cry, it felt so good.

Tally shut the door and sat himself back on the edge of the desk. He politely waited until we'd disengaged to talk.

"I hate to see a good employee go," he began, "but Cef has enough money here to cover your contract, Richy. I've decided to accept his offer."

Richy nodded and touched his nose to mine, still smiling. "All right."

"Go ahead and get ready. I need to talk to Cef for a couple minutes."

"Are we leaving right away?"

They both looked at me. My throat was dry. "Yes," I croaked.

Richy nodded and left. I watched the door after he'd walked through it until Tally said my name.

"I want you to understand what's going on here. He's not a slave. When his father brought him here, I paid for that first seven-year contract. When it ran out, he was free to do whatever he wanted. He chose to stay here, and we signed a new contract whereby I provide a place for him to live and work for him to do, and I pay him for that work. In return, he agrees to work for the length of the contract unless he comes up with the gold necessary to buy the contract from me. Are you following this?"

I nodded, though I was barely hearing every other word.

"You're still obligated to pay him, whether in money or room and board is up to you and him to work out. And after another five years, you'll have to renegotiate a new contract. Though by then most likely you won't want to."

That caught my attention. "Oh, no," I said. "I want him around forever."

Tally smiled. "That's very sweet." He didn't go on, but rummaged through the purse and sorted the coins into four gleaming piles on his desk. He handed three of the coins back to me. "The price of the contract is thirty-five gold. I'll take two extra for the inconvenience."

I nodded. I would've agreed if he'd kept all forty.

"So you understand the terms of the contract you're buying?"

"Yes."

Richy had come back. I could smell him waiting on the other side of the door. I started shifting my weight, wagging my tail, and fidgeting with my paws. Tally grinned at me. "All right. But don't get any thoughts about setting up any competition for me."

Shocked, I shook my head. "Oh, no no no!"

"Go on then." He waved to the door. "Richy will show you out the back."

I followed the wolf, my wolf, out the back in a sort of dream-like state. The door of the brothel closed behind us, and for the first time I saw him in real light. The sun was setting just behind him, outlining his ears in gold and making it hard to look at him, but I didn't want to look away. He had put on a plain tunic with a nice leather belt, and he held a bundle under one arm wrapped in a worn cloth. He shifted it to the other arm and tilted his muzzle at my gaze.

"What's the matter?"

"I just can't believe I did it." Forgotten were all my worries about how he felt, what we'd do, anything outside of the immediate moment. He could do that for me.

"You're adorable," he said, and smiled. "Do we have somewhere to celebrate? I presume we're not going back to your parents' rooms."

"No, I thought we'd go to the Cup and Crown. I have friends there. Or we could go to your bar. Does he rent rooms? Oh, but he told me not to..." I trailed off.

"You went to the Dirty Dog?" He cocked his ears. "Why?"

That night was so far away now. It was as if another Cef had been crouched out in the alley where we were standing now, had plodded miserably across several blocks, and had gone home in a daze that morning. "Looking for you," I mumbled.

"Aww." He touched my cheekruff and I leaned into the paw. "I'm not allowed to play outside work, you know that."

"I know. I just wanted to ask you something."

"What's that?"

"Oh, it, uh, doesn't matter now." I tried to pull my ears up. I knew they were flat, but I couldn't help it.

He lifted my muzzle gently. "I'd like to know."

"I wanted to ask how you felt. You know. About me." I swear by Canis that I hadn't meant to say anything, but the truth just spilled out when I looked at him.

He smiled. "Come here a moment." The alley was much the same as I remembered it, except that it had been dark last time I'd been here. In the light, it didn't feel as sinister, just empty. Though of course, with Richy there, it couldn't be more full. He sat me down on the crate, set his bundle next to me, and took my paws. "I know how you feel about me, you know."

This didn't sound good. I nodded, ears still down.

"You know, I've fallen in love. Sometimes three or four times a night. It works the other way, too. A lot of people have fallen in love with me

For Love Or Family

over the years. I knew there was something special about you, though. I always looked forward to your visits." He knelt, so I could look down into his green eyes, tinged with gold from the sunset. "You know something else? Tally doesn't just sell contracts to anyone who walks in with thirty or forty gold. He asked me if I wanted to be sold to you."

I blinked at him, processing that information. "You said yes, right?" He gave me the most beautiful grin and a quick nod.

With a whoop that didn't come close to expressing what I was feeling, I jumped off the crate to hug him, and we tumbled to the ground, tangled in each other's arms. I was trying to kiss him and he was giggling, nuzzling back and saying, "Hold on, hold on." Finally, I settled down, though my tail was still wagging, splatting against the wet ground. I looked up with ears perked for what he had to say.

"Shouldn't we go to a room somewhere?"

"Oh. Right." I kissed his nose, scrambled to my feet, and belatedly remembered to reach a paw down to help him up.

He took it, then retrieved his bundle from the crate. "The Dirty Dog, then?"

On the way there, I reached for his paw and he grasped mine in return. My wet tail sprayed drops back and forth in my enthusiasm.

Richy knew the bartender on duty, who was not Cori the weasel. I paid a gold piece for two weeks in a small upstairs room, and when we were finally alone there and Richy had set his bundle on the narrow bed, he gave me a grin and set his paws on my shoulders. "So. What now?"

I slipped a paw down and held the bulge of his sheath. "You can't guess?" Our muzzles met in a kiss, and the night just got better from there.

Chapter 8

I woke up next to him on a blanket on the floor, with the sun streaming into the room. When I reached out to touch him, he was really there. His scent was all around and I just wanted to bury my nose in his fur. He was sleeping so peacefully that I just propped myself up on one elbow and watched.

When he opened his eyes and saw me, he smiled. "Hi."

"Hi."

"This is weird." He reached over and touched my chest. "Not waking up in the Staff. First time in…five years."

"I thought you'd been there longer than that."

"I have." He grinned at me, his tail wagging slowly. "Would you believe I spent a night in the palace once?"

"I'd believe anything."

"It was a long time ago…" Richy sighed. "Hard to believe that's all over."

"Tell me about it sometime."

"I will." He rubbed my fur and looked up. "Are you going to stay all day?"

"I can't. I'm already late. Last time I stayed out all night they worried. I want to, though."

"It's okay. I can wait."

I nodded, and kissed him. "Probably not too long. Once I get married, we'll work something out."

He rolled onto his back and put his paws behind his head. "I'll go downstairs and talk to Cori. And I'll be here when you get back."

I grinned. "Better be ready for more of the same."

His green eyes sparkled in the light. "I don't have anyone else to distract me now."

My tail, matted and sticky from the night before, thumped the floor.

I wanted to wash before I went home, but I was already missing a lesson and I could imagine how upset my father would be. That led me to thoughts about the previous night. Strolling by the bright light of the sun, I felt a warm glow inside burn away any lingering unease. Dereath had gotten his letters back. I'd gotten my love. Everything was going to be fine.

I kept that feeling all through the lecture from my father, the tedious morning lessons, and the reminder of the formal dinner with Jelila for which I would be excused from my afternoon lessons to have my fur groomed. I enjoyed that, though I admit I was more looking forward to showing off for Richy later.

When I got back to my chambers, Kira was the only one there. "My, don't you look fancy! Jelila sure is lucky."

I snorted at her. "Where is everyone? We're supposed to go down to dinner in half an hour."

"Dinner's canceled. Dad said he had something important come up."

"Canis above. What could be more important than shackling his son to a soulless husk of a bitch?"

"Jelila's nice," Kira said. "Have you ever talked to her?"

"No, and I don't care to."

"Just because she isn't as crude as that bar girl..."

I stuck my tongue out at her. "So I'm free for dinner? No family dinner even?"

"I don't know where Mom and Dad are. I was going to go down in a bit, if you want to wait."

I gave her a toothy smile. "I don't feel like wasting a rare night of freedom."

She sighed. "Just don't stay out all night again. You'll be confined to the palace or something and then I'll have to listen to you whine all night for a month."

"Don't worry, big sister. I'll be back before we lock up."

"Oh, that reminds me. Did you go out night before last?"

All my good cheer turned to ice. "No. Why?"

"Dad said the door wasn't locked in the morning."

My fur prickled. I'd forgotten. "He didn't say anything to me about it."

"He asked me and Rashi."

"Well, I didn't go out."

"Okay, okay. Rashi and I didn't. Maybe one of us was sleepwalking."

"Maybe Kigi came back."

She shrugged. "Nothing's missing. Not that anyone could get into the palace to steal anything anyway."

I nodded. "Okay. I'm leaving now. I'll be back tonight, I promise."

"You'd better be."

I considered staying out all night again, just to annoy her, but with the whole unlocked door problem, it wouldn't be a good idea. I hurried out and past the guards, and through the streets of the city. If I got to the Dirty Dog before it was too late, I could have dinner with Richy.

The bartender from the previous night, a weasel like Cori (probably a relative), recognized me and waved me upstairs. I waved back and bounded up the stairs two at a time.

Richy was in our room (our room!) and greeted me with a hug and a kiss. I licked him sloppily back and ran my paws down his sides. "Guess what?" He was smiling.

"What?"

"Cori says I can help out serving below when they get busy. He'll pay me some."

"That's good."

I guess I wasn't quite enthusiastic enough. He lowered his ears and said, "I thought I'd work for a while. Just to keep busy. You know, I can only exercise for so long."

"I know. I'm sorry! I just thought...I mean, I didn't think of what you'd be doing all day. I'm sorry about that. I never even..."

"Shh, it's okay." He smiled. "I'm just not used to having all this time. But it's not bad."

"Okay. Just tell me if you want anything."

"Dinner, right now. I presume you've already eaten?"

I shook my head. "Dinner was canceled. What would you like to eat?"

"Let's just go downstairs."

So we left the room, locking it, and went down the hallway. From the top of the stairs, we couldn't see the main room below, but when we turned on the landing, we got a nice view of the bar and about two-thirds of the tables. I was talking to Richy, but when I started down the second flight of stairs, I glanced down and slowed. There was a large wolf talking to the weasel at the bar, a wolf with a brightly patterned orange tunic and red velvet vest on. I knew that vest.

"What's the..." Richy followed my gaze.

"That's my father," I whispered.

As I said that, the weasel at the bar saw us. I saw him start to point, and scrambled backwards on the steps. Richy followed me as I hurried down the hall, muttering to myself, "Don't panic, don't panic, don't panic." But he had to take the key from me because my paws were shaking too much to fit it into the lock. Footsteps sounded on the stairs as we ducked into our room and closed the door.

I collapsed on the bed. "He knows. What am I going to do?"

"Won't it be in his interest to keep this secret?" Richy sat next to me and put an arm around my shoulders. "Maybe it'll be a good thing."

"No, no, not that. I..." I swallowed. At this moment, he cared about me, he loved me, maybe—somewhere in the back of my mind I realized he'd never said that—and he wanted to be with me. If I told him how I'd gotten the gold, would all of that change? Instead of Cef the romantic, lovable wolf cub, I would be Cef the thief. I hadn't stolen the papers myself, but I'd helped. When I'd talked myself into it, I'd told myself that it wasn't stealing and that I wasn't the one actually doing it, but now those arguments buckled and broke under the pressure of discovery.

I took a breath. If I hid this from him, if I didn't come clean, then I would be Cef the liar. Whatever else I was, I could never be that to him.

Head down, tail wrapped around my hips, I talked quickly, anticipating a knock at the door any moment. "I stole—I helped steal some papers from him. Someone who works with him got in trouble with a lover—I mean, his lover got in trouble, and my father was keeping his love letters. He gave me forty gold to help him get them back."

He didn't answer. His arm didn't move. "I didn't think it was wrong. I mean, I knew it was wrong, but it wasn't as wrong as stealing the money would have been. I was so afraid."

"Afraid? Of what?"

"That I'd have to get married and I couldn't come see you."

He nudged me gently with his muzzle. "I have lots of married clients. Who put that idea in your head?"

"I couldn't afford…" I was starting to get confused now. It had all seemed so clear earlier.

"Once a week?" He nuzzled me again. "I'm not that expensive."

Now I had to look at him. "I'm so happy when I'm with you," I said, aware that everything might have changed forever and the present tense might no longer be valid. "I wanted that for always."

That, of course, was the exact moment that the knock came.

I looked at the window. "We could jump."

Richy shook his head. "Did you tell me everything about what happened?" I nodded. He gave me an encouraging smile. "Maybe this is about something else. Better to face it than to run and never know. Go ahead and open the door."

I looked into his eyes for a long time, and then kissed him. "Okay." Shakily, I got up and walked to the door, and opened it.

My father's grey eyes looked down at me. They flicked to Richy, whom I heard stand up, and then back. His ears were perked, but there was no smile on his muzzle. "May I come in?" he asked evenly.

I stepped aside and closed the door behind him. He gave Richy a longer look then. "So this is your accomplice?"

"No. He had nothing to do with it."

He was sniffing the air. His eyes widened. "Not just an accomplice."

"Not an accomplice at all!"

"You and Rashi both. How strange." He stroked his muzzle.

"What? Oh, Dad. Rashi's not gay."

He looked at me. "He was seen in that brothel. He bought a service there."

"He was only doing that to impress the bitch in the bar."

"The one you were dating?"

"I wasn't dating her."

"So you lied to me." He waved a paw. "Obviously, I know very little about the romantic lives of my children. But that's not why I'm here. I want to know what you plan to do with the forty Royals you stole from my office. And to ask you why I shouldn't turn you over to the guard."

Richy stared at me, and I gaped at my father. "I didn't steal anything!"

"Cef, I was holding fifty Royals for an operation in my secure trunk in the office. Two nights ago, our chamber door was unlocked and forty of those Royals were taken."

"Someone could have broken in and gotten the key," I said. Both Richy and my father were looking at me, neither seeming particularly inclined to believe me.

My father produced the key from his pocket and held it to his nose. "Your scent and mine are the only ones on this key."

"What?" I yelped. "What about the rabbit?"

He dropped the key back into his pouch. "What rabbit?"

The one with no scent, I almost said. I realized that would sound crazy, but nothing else came to mind. He folded his arms. "Well?"

I remembered the other person who had handled the key that night. "What about Dereath?"

"Stop changing the subject. I want to know why you stole that gold."

"I'm not. And I didn't. I...Dereath said you had some papers of his that he wanted back, and he would give me forty gold if I got the key for him. He promised he wouldn't take anything else. His scent should be on that key too!"

He closed his eyes and pressed his paw to his forehead. "Just tell me you were going to run away with your lover. Don't make up stories."

"I'm not!"

"Cef, Dereath watched me lock the money in the chest two days ago. I had the key on my person from that time until the time I put him in a coach after dinner and sent him to Saraffin to check on troop movements. He won't be back for two weeks. He never touches this key."

"That's not possible." Of course it was. Dereath had removed himself from the scene very neatly, leaving his scentless rabbit to do his work, and me to take the blame. "He...wanted his letters. Love letters."

"Love letters?"

What had sounded so plausible through the filter of my hope now sounded ridiculous. "He said you'd kept them because they were evidence in some case."

"Do you expect me to believe that?"

"I don't know!" I was shouting, near tears. "It's the truth!"

"Don't lie to me! I know you heard some rumors about him, but don't try to pin this on him. He's in trouble, yes, but he's not a thief."

"Sir." Richy spoke quietly. He was holding out a piece of paper. "This is a receipt for about thirty-five in gold. I think we have two more in coins. If we give that to you, will you let us go?"

My father paused, then walked over and examined the paper. He looked up at Richy. "You keep your money in a brothel?"

"I have friends there," Richy said. "It's safer than a bank."

"How do I know this is any good? My son's a liar and a thief, what's to say you're any better?"

"Hey!" I snarled. "He's not lying!"

My father turned and fixed me with a stare that had always intimidated me in the past. This time, I didn't back down. "If he says it's worth that, then it is." I tossed my purse to him. "Here, that's everything we have."

He caught the purse and held it and the paper, looking back and forth between us. Richy said, gently, "You don't want your son to be imprisoned, do you?"

"I don't know." He looked at the paper again. "I'm going to go claim this. If it's good…"

"It's good." My hackles were still up, ears still back.

"Calm down, Cef," Richy said. "Sir, I should go with you. It is made out in my name."

"I think you both should come with me."

"Fine." My hackles were lowering and some of my fear was coming back. Richy walked over to stand with me, and grasped my paw. My father saw that, and turned toward the door without a word.

The walk to the Jackal's Staff took forever. My father kept us in front of him, as though we were going to make a break for it—with no money and no belongings—and I was so worried about how the situation would end that I tripped over cobblestones several times. Richy kept hold of my paw and squeezed it several times. He didn't seem worried at all, and that more than anything else kept me from descending into all-out panic.

The raccoon was working as host at the Jackal's Staff that night. His eyes widened when he saw the three of us. "Richy?"

"Hi, Pike. Is Tally around at all?"

Pike shook his head. "What do you need?"

"Can you get some money I have on deposit?" Pike eyed my father as Richy said that, and my love managed a small laugh. "I'm not being coerced. It's okay."

"Sure. Do you have your receipt?"

My father handed it to him. The raccoon looked at it, up at my father, and then at Richy. "You sure about this?"

"Very."

"All right. Come on back."

He led us through the tables, to a couple comments of "Nice wolf pack!" and "Need a fourth?" back into the back room I'd visited just the day before.

"Wait here," he said, and went into the office himself.

We stood around the room silently. I noticed that Richy's tag was still hanging at the bottom of the board, so I unhooked it and slipped it into my purse. Richy saw me and smiled. My father looked stonily at the door and said nothing.

Pike came out again with a large bag that clinked. "Here." He handed it to Richy. "Are you sure you're okay?"

"I'm fine, Pike." He handed the bag to my father. "There it is."

My father glanced into it, shook the coins around, then closed the bag. "All right. You are honest, it seems. Maybe you can be a good influence on my son. I don't expect to see either of you again."

"Dad…"

"You may have given back most of the money, but you still stole it." His ears, flat as his gaze, told me that he was still angry, no matter how calm he was. "If I see you again, I'll turn you over to the guards."

I shrank back against the wall. My father turned to Pike. "Is there a back way out of this place? I would prefer not to leave through the front."

"Of course. Let me show you. Richy, you know the way out?"

"Wait a moment." Richy glared at my father. "That's all? You're turning your back on your own son?"

I loved him for saying it even though I knew it was futile. The set of my father's ears and the coldness in his eyes told me his answer before he uttered a word. "You know nothing of our family. I'll thank you to keep your mouth shut."

"I know your son," Richy said. "Maybe better than you do."

"Aye," my father said. "Then you're welcome to him."

"Listen," Richy started. My father took a step toward him and growled, his ears even flatter.

"No. You listen." He stabbed the air in my direction. "He knows what he's done. He knows that trust and honesty are how he was raised. He has lied to me and betrayed my trust, and he was destroyed the last hope of his family to maintain everything I have worked so hard for twenty years to build."

Richy, Canis bless him, leaned back but did not step back. "Nobody needs to know," he said. "We can go back to the palace. I can be…I can work in the kitchens, or as a servant somewhere. You have the gold back. Cef can be married just as you planned."

My father's eyes shifted to me. I saw the attraction to the plan flicker and die. "And how would I ever trust him again? What would happen when his wife finds out about him and you?"

Richy glanced at me, less sure now. "Would that matter?"

My father straightened, looking down at both of us. "Apparently not to him, or you. But it matters to me." He held my eyes for a moment and then turned away. The last time I saw my father, he was following Pike out the door. He didn't look back at me, not once.

Richy took my paw. "Come on, Cef. There's another way out."

I followed him, tail between my legs, ears flat. We wound our way through the corridors and ended up at a small door. Richy reached into a small hole in the wall and pulled out a key. "This is our emergency door," he explained, holding it open for me. He locked it from the outside and then pushed the key into a hole on the other side of the wall. I heard it drop and clatter.

We'd emerged into a different alley than the one we'd sat in the night before. This one was narrower and smelled worse. The walls were filthy, but I leaned against one anyway. "What are we going to do?"

"I'd imagine we should leave Divalia," Richy said. "As long as your father is convinced you're a thief, it won't be safe here."

I looked into those green eyes that meant the world to me. "You believe me, don't you?"

He just smiled. "You have to ask?"

"You gave away all that money."

"All I had."

"For what?"

He took both my paws. "You bought me. I bought you. Now we're even."

"Oh..." I leaned against him, pressing my head into his shoulder, and he wrapped his arms around me.

"Come on," he said gently. "The light's going. We should get back to the Dirty Dog tonight."

I sniffed. "But my father..."

Richy kissed my ear. "He said if he sees you. I don't think he'll come looking."

That wasn't what I had been about to say, but I let it go. "Okay. Then what?"

"Well..." He nuzzled me, holding me tight. "I've always wanted to see the ocean."

I couldn't believe how stupid I'd been, or how lucky.

For Love Or Family

Chapter 9

I collapsed onto the straw mattress and slumped against the wall. There was barely room to sit up under the other bunk, but I wedged myself in. Across the tiny room were two more bunks, luxurious accommodations for half of the eight-man crew of the barge *Moving Paw*. Richy and I had been allowed to move our mattresses together on the floor, while the two badgers who shared the room with us occupied the upper bunks.

Richy came in a few minutes later with a steaming bowl that smelled of meat and some floury sauce. He sat down next to me and set the bowl down on the floor near the mattress. "They told me you came back here."

"I'm so tired," I whimpered.

"I know. Let me see your paws." I held them up, and he inspected them, then licked them gently. "They look better today."

"You're lying. You know what they call me? They call me 'softpaws.'"

"You don't want to know what they call me."

I growled. "Who? Was it Annis?"

"Shh." He shook his head and kept grooming.

I relaxed, and my mind drifted back to the day, our third on the boat. "I saw a pack of wild dogs, and stopped to look at them. The big one, the bear, what's his name…Mirrak…told me to get back to work. When I tried to explain about how the wild animals fit into Families just like people, he told me to shut up."

Richy lowered my paws and smiled. "I think he was just uncomfortable with anyone who knows more words than he does. That's everyone."

"And this mattress has bugs in it, and we don't have any privacy…"

"Annis and Jare said they'd give us time when we wanted it."

I sighed. "The worst part is that you have to go through all this too. Just because of me."

"Hush." He touched his nose to mine. "This is an adventure. It's another part of my life. It won't be forever. But it's exciting and different, and one of the most different things about it for me is that I get to share it with you."

"I know…"

"Do you still love me?"

I jerked my head up and hit it on the upper bunk. "Ow! Of course I do!"

"I'm sorry!" He reached up to where I was rubbing my head.

"It's okay, I'm fine. Why would you think I wouldn't? I'm the one who screwed all this up, I should worry about you loving me."

He held my paw, and it hurt, but it felt good too. "It was scary for me, leaving the Staff, but it was time. I really did like it there, but…" He looked away. "I had a friend there, years ago, who hated it. He liked the work, but he hated all the restrictions and he was convinced there was something better. I didn't really know what he meant until I met you.

"You didn't know anything about me except what I let you see. But I know you. You're proud and passionate, young still, and impatient, and I think you're adorable. I just didn't know if you'd get tired of me when we weren't just having sex."

"Oh." My voice sounded very small. Looking back, I couldn't believe how stupid I'd been, or how lucky. Even sitting in the squalid hold of a flea-infested ship, still slightly ill from the motion, I felt lucky. "I'm not tired of you. I'm glad you're here. I just wish 'here' was someplace nicer."

"Things will get better, Cef. We'll look back on this time and laugh, or shake our heads. When we get to the port city, um…"

"Tiria." I gave him a small smile. "You know everyone's name on the boat in a day, but you can't remember the name of the one city we're heading for."

"People names I remember." He nuzzled me. "When we get to Tiria, maybe we'll stay with the boat. Maybe we'll stay in Tiria. Maybe we won't even make it there before we find someplace better. But I'll stay with you, and you'll stay with me, and that's enough for me. I hope it can be enough for you too."

I nodded, because my throat didn't seem to work too well, and then I leaned close to him, because that's where I wanted to be. Plain and simple.

For Love Or Family

About the Author

Kyell Gold writes anthropomorphic erotica from an undisclosed location rumored to be in California. His works appear regularly in Sofawolf Press's *Heat*, Bad Dog Books' *FANG* (www.baddogbooks.com), and his own LiveJournal (kyellgold. livejournal.com). He is currently working on a set of stories set outside of Argaea, though he's sure to return there soon. He lives with his very patient partner and their dog.

About the Artists

Cover. **Sara "Caribou" Palmer** spends most of her time in a 100+ year old house chasing her Egyptian Mau cats and her young daughter, and managing to find time to draw as well. Her comic and illustration work has been featured in several publications, and she was the Guest of Honor at Anthrocon 2000. Her work can be found on the web at www.caribouink.com and in various Convention art shows around the country.

Inside the Cage. **Vince Suzukawa** is a long time comic artist whose current projects include i.s.o. (http://community.livejournal.com/isocomic/profile) and John Nunnemacher's Buffalo Wings (http://buffalowings.griffinparkstudio.com/). He also once upon a time worked on the retired webcomic The Class Menagerie (www.theclassm.com).

The Prisoner's Release. **Taurin Fox**'s art can be seen at http://www.taurinfox.com.

Home Again. **Adam Wan** has been displaying his art online since 2001. He has previously been published in *Heat*.

For Love or Family. **Leo Magna** is the creator of the beloved online comic *Fur-Piled* (also available in print form from Sofawolf Press). His comic and other art can be seen at http://www.liondogworks.com/.